# ONE KISS TURNS FRIENDSHIP TO LOVE . . .

"You're very beautiful," Marco told her, leaning forward to set a tender kiss on her lips.

Hazel knew it was going to happen, could sense his intention. She heard it in his voice when he spoke. As his face came closer, she found herself wondering why it always took her by surprise to see that his eyes were a deep shade of blue. Then she felt his mouth on hers and felt his thumb slide slowly across her brow. Then her eyes fluttered shut, and all reasonable thought fled.

It was as if she were in a spell, caught in the splendor that was Venice. The touch of his lips became part of the atmosphere enveloping her, filling her senses and thrilling her soul. When his cheek rolled against hers, glowing skin against skin, the shock spread all through her body. She felt dazzlingly alive, her breath coming faster, her heart beating hard. . . .

*Berkley Books by Laura Simon*

A TASTE OF HEAVEN
DREAMS OF PARADISE

# DREAMS OF PARADISE

## LAURA SIMON

BERKLEY BOOKS, NEW YORK

DREAMS OF PARADISE

A Berkley Book/published by arrangement
with the author

PRINTING HISTORY
Berkley edition / March 1991

ISBN: 0-425-12677-3

A BERKLEY BOOK ® TM 757,375
Berkley Books are published by The Berkley Publishing Group,
200 Madison Avenue, New York, New York 10016.
The name "Berkley" and the "B" logo
are trademarks belonging to Berkley Publishing Corporation.

PRINTED IN THE UNITED STATES OF AMERICA

10   9   8   7   6   5   4   3   2   1

*For Jimmy*

I would like to thank the following people for graciously and generously sharing their expertise with me as I gathered information for this book:

Roly Fraser, Sarah Jane Fraser, Perth, Scotland; John Ross, Inchnadamph, Scotland; Mr. Scott, British Wool Marketing Board, Evanton, Scotland; Andy Oates, Nantucket Looms, Nantucket, MA; Linda Darbey, Nantucket, MA; Jessica Randolph and Patricia Marky, Museum of American Textile History, N. Andover, MA; Walter Oleszek, Washington, D.C.; Miro Silvera, Milan, Italy.

# PROLOGUE

## July 1892

"Exceptional," the voice behind her said.

Startled, Hazel Merriwether spun around, her pencil arrested in midstroke. An extraordinary-looking gentleman stood several yards away in the hot *piazza*, his hands clasped behind his back.

"I beg your pardon?" Hazel asked.

"Exceptional," he repeated, coming a step closer. "Your drawing of the Duomo is quite exceptional." He nodded his head toward the mammoth cathedral of Milan, squatting in Gothic splendor across the square. His voice was musical and tinged with humor, despite a very correct English accent.

"Thank you, sir," Hazel replied. "It's very kind of you to say so." She turned back to her sketching, her long slender fingers wielding the pencil with authority. Nothing in her even tone suggested that the striking stranger had sent a ripple down her spine. Nor did her unruffled attention to her work suggest that it was he she was seeing, rather than the massive church. After only a moment's glance his image was clear in her mind.

A big man, on the verge of thirty, he carried himself with the assurance of one who knew his appearance was also quite exceptional. Although his size was imposing and his dark curly hair was worn a trifle longer than was generally considered appropriate (and without any of the pomades, brilliantines, or aromatic oils that most men favored), it was his face that was so dramatic. A large regal nose with a bump at the bridge, a generous mouth, and high, rosy cheeks gave the impression of tremendous vitality,

1

even power, like the paintings of Renaissance nobles Hazel had been viewing on her tour of Italy.

"Is there anything wrong?" another voice asked, interrupting her again.

When Hazel looked up this time, she saw four people gathered in a semicircle in front of her, their glossy blond hair and delft-blue eyes identifying them as members of a single family. But this time she smiled as she answered the speaker. "Nothing at all, Frederick," she said. "I'm perfectly fine."

"I was expressing my admiration of this excellent drawing," came the voice behind her. Four pairs of blue eyes stared with ill-disguised interest at the unknown man. Hazel turned to look at him, too. Hands still clasped casually behind him, he seemed unfazed by their scrutiny.

"I've watched legions of aspiring artists positioned in every conceivable spot in this square," he commented. "While some have succeeded in rendering the intricate details of the Duomo's facade with faithful, even painstaking accuracy, very few have captured the spirit of the architecture so effortlessly." He addressed himself, quite properly, to Frederick, the only male and obvious head of this little band of Americans abroad.

"Such a talent requires more than a clever hand and a quick eye," he added. "It's a gift that comes from the soul."

"Yes. Well," Frederick responded, caught between his natural suspicion of such unreserved praise and the awe that praise inspired. He snuck a glance at the sketch on Hazel's pad.

"A most gallant observation," Hazel said smoothly. "But I'm certain that if my drawing can, in any way, be considered a success, it's owing more to the grandeur of the Duomo than to my small ability." With a slight dip of her head she turned back to her sketching again. And again, nothing in her unhurried motion or polite response gave a hint of the excitement his compliment caused.

Tall and graceful, Hazel Merriwether was a study of poise. Her large gray eyes were steady and calm in a lovely oval-shaped face whose perfectly cast features and lustrously clear skin might have belonged to one of the classical statues described in the Baedeker guide that was tucked under her arm. Masses of thick, dark hair were swept off her forehead and twisted into a fashionably loose knot on top of her head. Its silkiness couldn't be hidden by an understated straw hat, anchored in place by a deceptively simple jet pin. Except for a tiny beauty mark above the left-hand corner of her mouth (giving her an unexpectedly sultry sparkle), Hazel presented an aura of unmarred elegance.

As she continued to sketch, outwardly tranquil, her friends arranged themselves around her. They stood in the sunbaked Piazza del Duomo, trying, as good manners required, both to ignore the intriguing stranger behind them and to take an interest in the important cathedral in front of them. Despite their impeccable breeding and their best intentions, though, their collective attention began to wander.

Pretty Lucy Whitaker, closest in age to Hazel's twenty-three years, absently fanned her flushed face with a postcard she'd bought a week ago in Florence and hadn't yet written. Her twelve-year-old sister, Charlotte, shifted from foot to foot, hunching and unhunching her shoulders, making her blond braids bob up and down. And although Mrs. Whitaker, an older, plumper, more faded version of her daughters, kept her face firmly forward, her eyes looked beyond the square, across the wide avenue, to the magnificent glass-domed Galleria Vittorio Emanuele with its cool and luxurious shops.

Only Frederick Whitaker, older brother to Lucy and Charlotte, appeared genuinely engrossed. He followed every stroke of Hazel's pencil, his eyes alert, his handsome face rapt. Even his posture bespoke concentration. His long legs were braced and his athletic body slightly bent. It must be said, however, that as someone more at home on a yacht or a tennis lawn than confronted by Art, it was the artist who captivated him rather than her subject.

Nearly finished with her drawing, Hazel suddenly glanced up. Her pulse was still thumping and she felt oddly agitated, a state that was uncommon for her. Instinctively she sought reassurance from the familiarity of her friends. Her quick glance became more anxious, though, as she saw how distracted they were. Her eyes flicked from one Whitaker to the next with increasing distress until they came to Frederick. He smiled. Admiration and approval were apparent on his fine, fair face.

Hazel returned the smile. Dear Frederick, she thought. He's been so devoted to me on this trip. Her agitation washed away, her serenity was restored. She dropped her eyes to her sketchpad again.

"May I be so forward as to make a suggestion?"

They whirled around eagerly, released. "Sir?" Frederick asked, that single syllable quivering with curiosity.

"I would highly recommend that you visit the roof," the stranger said. He spoke with almost deliberate blandness, as if to counteract the boldness of his looks. "It's a tedious climb, but well worth the effort. The view is incomparable." He gave an assessing look skyward, then added, "The air is clear enough today so that Switzerland should be visible. But on any day the real reward is the roof itself." A shrug of his ample shoulders dismissed the panorama.

"Over two thousand statues have been set in place since construction on the Duomo began in 1386," he told them. "And hundreds more are expected to be installed before its completion sometime in the next century. It's a fantasy world in marble. Besides"—he nodded aloft at the profusion of spires and turrets rising from the roof—"with the sky for ceiling, one senses the true splendor of the cathedral up there."

"Oh. I see," Frederick said, his voice going flat with disinterest. "Most kind of you, sir. We'll keep that in mind."

The matter would have died right there had not Hazel, prompted by an unusual impulse, revived it by saying, "Baedeker also advises a tour of the roof." She pulled the leather-bound volume from under her arm and held it out as proof. "Mont Blanc and Monte Rosa are said to appear with remarkable clarity from that height."

"But it *does* look quite a climb," Lucy objected. She was clearly disappointed, having expected a more provocative suggestion from this man. After looking at churches and views for the better part of three weeks, she had no wish to trudge up an endless number of stairs to see more of each. "It must be twenty stories to the top," she said, not even bothering to raise her eyes.

Hazel consulted the guidebook she was holding. "The tower is 345 feet above the ground," she admitted. "But I don't believe it's necessary to go all the way up the tower. We should be able to see the sights perfectly well from the main roof." She scanned the page further. "There's a statue of Rebecca by Canova that shouldn't be missed." Her voice held a note of pleasurable anticipation.

"As well as a superb Adam and Eve," the stranger added, taking several steps forward. He extracted a visiting card from an exquisite leather case and handed it to Frederick. "If you'll permit me," he said, "I'll gladly accompany you. I've been up on the roof many times in my life. Perhaps if I were to point out some of the more notable sights, it might enhance your enjoyment."

Frederick fingered the card a moment before replying. "It's quite a generous offer, Mr., uh, Signore, uh . . . " He paused, not sure if the man was English or Italian, and peered at the card. MARCO MACGREGOR, it read. The name did nothing to clear up Frederick's confusion. "It's quite a generous offer, Mr. MacGregor," he repeated, having decided that, after all, they were speaking in English. "But I'm sure it's too much of an imposition."

"Not a bit," Mr. MacGregor said, with improbable mildness. "It gives me great pride to show off the treasures of my country. Especially to so appreciative an audience." His smile included all of them, but his eyes rested longest on Hazel. Another ripple ran down her spine.

"Oh, yes, Frederick, do accept," Lucy put in quickly, her delicate features more animated than they'd been in days. His offer to guide them gave the proposed tour a totally different complexion. "Think how fortunate we are to have the opportunity to see these great works with someone so knowledgeable," she coaxed.

"Yes, Frederick, do," Charlotte agreed, eyeing first Mr. MacGregor, then the wedding-cake top of the Duomo, and sensing an adventure.

Frederick frowned in indecision. Certainly there was nothing about Mr. MacGregor to suggest he was anything less than a gentleman. He had neither the shabby attire nor the wheedling manner of the boys and men who continually approached them selling postcards and souvenirs and carriage rides. His suit was impeccably tailored, and the linen, though copious, was of excellent quality. His behavior was correct, his speech well educated, and his visiting card was engraved on heavy cloth bond rather than printed on pulp paper.

Yet one simply did not go about accepting invitations from foreigners to whom one had not been properly introduced. Frederick looked at Hazel. Head down, she was studying the guidebook intently. Looking back to Mr. MacGregor, he was about to regretfully decline when his mother spoke.

"I wonder if it's cooler on the roof?" she asked no one in particular.

"The temperature is much the same, madam," Mr. MacGregor answered, his hands behind his back again. "Though there's usually a refreshing breeze."

"Is there?" Mrs. Whitaker seemed to gather strength from that statement. She looked expectantly at her son.

Pursing his lips slightly, as if to signify the matter were out of his hands, Frederick said, "We would be most grateful for your company, Mr. MacGregor."

One hundred and eighty-two marble steps later the last of Frederick's misgivings evaporated. The roof was everything Mr. MacGregor had promised it would be, and more. It was like walking through a fairyland, or an ice palace, with spires and finials and intricate crockets carved from gleaming white marble. Life-size marble statues stood atop each of the one hundred and thirty-six spires and large marble flagstones were laid beneath the feet. All around were marble arches and marble gargoyles and marble busts in marble niches. Set so high in the air, halfway to heaven, it was, indeed, a world in itself.

Hazel was thrilled. "How perfect," she said, more to herself than to her friends. Seeing the almost reverent light on her lovely face, Marco MacGregor smiled, satisfied.

For the next hour he led them through the magical marble landscape. He showed them the relatively recent statue of Napoleon and the very old bust of Caesar. He pointed out the majestic Alps to the north and the gentler Apennines to the south. He waited patiently, and appreciatively, while Hazel made quick, sure sketches on her thick pad. He posed unselfconsciously while Frederick captured them all with his Kodak.

When they wound their way down to the hot *piazza* again, he said, "You must allow me to offer you some refreshments. I have a theory that it's unwise to nurture the soul without also nourishing the physical body." As he gestured toward an unknown destination, his glowing skin and well-fed frame seemed an indisputable testimony to his philosophy.

"I know of a place not a five-minute walk from here," he said conclusively, taking Mrs. Whitaker's arm and leading the way. "It's a tiny garden where they serve the best *gelato* in all of Milan. Possibly it's the best in all of Italy. Although," he added more thoughtfully, "there's a small restaurant in Genoa that can't be ignored." He pondered the merits of each for a moment before giving another expansive wave of his hand. "No matter," he reassured Mrs. Whitaker, who was not the least bit worried about which was superior so long as she could sit down for a while. "This *piccolo giardino* will not disappoint you."

No one disputed him. Nor resisted his lead. Not Charlotte, who had learned early in their sojourn that *gelato* in English was ice cream. Not Lucy, who was more diverted by this live Italian man than by any of the saints or apostles in the interminable age-darkened paintings she had seen. Not even Frederick, who had forgotten his initial uncertainty and welcomed the male companionship of their self-appointed host.

Only Hazel was uneasy, though she followed her friends without protest. Partly because protest was not one of her habits. But also because even she, who found inexpressible pleasure in gazing on rare and wonderful objects and art, was not immune to heat and fatigue.

What made her hesitate, if only in the privacy of her mind, was the unusual effect Mr. MacGregor continued to have on her. Not only did he cause unaccustomed sensations to shoot through her body, but she was astonished to find herself thinking of him as rare and wonderful, as well. As she walked next to Frederick, she shook her head, trying to dispel the unsettling, and unsolicited, notion.

Ten minutes later, however, when she sat in front of a frosted goblet in which a snowball of coconut ice cream was strewn with shavings of dark, nearly black chocolate, she had to agree that this had been an outstanding idea after all. The first cold spoonful of *gelato* slid down her throat, a shocking combination of smooth, bitter, and sweet. A shiver of sheer delight brought goose bumps to her skin.

"Is it to your satisfaction, Miss Merriwether?"

Startled from her reverie, Hazel looked across the table at Marco. She flushed with embarrassment when she realized, from his wide smile, that he'd been watching her closely and had seen her ecstatic expression, all because of a bowl of ice cream. "Yes, thank you, Mr. MacGregor," she answered with her usual composure, though her cheeks remained somewhat warmer than normal. "It's very nice." She picked delicately at the melting confection with her spoon and wondered why she hadn't noticed before that his eyes were deep blue and, like his voice, filled with humor. Then she immediately wondered why it should matter to her.

As she carried a bit of coconut *gelato* to her mouth, suddenly unconscious of the taste, she saw him shake his head in exasperation. Her flush deepened, although she understood neither what he found in her polite response that was so vexing nor, once again, what difference it should make to her. Instead, she turned to Frederick and said, "It's a pity that the opera season is over at La Scala. Most likely we'll still be able to have a peek inside, but even the grandest theater has a melancholy cast when its seats are empty and its stage is dark. Wouldn't you say so?"

"Quite right," Frederick answered vaguely. Culture was not his strong point, though he thought its pursuit an admirable female occupation. "A keen observation."

They spoke then of Leonardo da Vinci's painting of *The Last Supper* and the church of Sant'Ambrogio and the museum at Brera and other sights of interest. At the end of an hour Mr. MacGregor escorted them back to the Piazza del Duomo, shook Frederick's hand, wished them well for the remainder of their journey, and sauntered off. They resumed their tour of the cathedral, inspecting the interior, and chatting lightly about the charming hospitality of foreigners. Though Hazel joined in, she felt oddly saddened.

The following Tuesday found the American tourists in the antique city of Mantua. Guided only by Hazel's mapless Baedeker, they were wandering through the sprawling Palazzo Ducale. "This was the seat of the Gonzaga family who ruled Mantua from 1328 until 1708," Hazel explained. "They were famous for their patronage of the arts, especially during the reign of Francesco Gonzaga and his wife, Isabella d'Este." There was a note of uncertainty in her voice as she glanced around. Most chambers were badly in need of attention and restoration, though no amount of neglect could disguise the beauty of the stuccoed ceilings or the marble friezes of putti.

"Isabella was well known for her taste and education," Hazel continued, still peering around. "Under her sponsorship, artists such as Andrea Mantegna and Lorenzo Costa thrived. Da Vinci painted her portrait." Despite being confused by the maze of rooms, Hazel's admiration for the sixteenth-century marchioness was obvious.

"She was also reputed to be a strong-minded woman who showed no compunction about badgering Mantegna—hardly a weak-kneed sycophant, himself—into selling her antiques he had bought for his own collection." The interruption was startling in this empty old *palazzo* in this forgotten old town. Especially since Hazel recognized the voice even before turning around. Her pulse started pounding and her own voice was choked.

"This is impossible!" Lucy cried, hands clasped to her pretty pink cheeks in astonishment. "It defies belief!"

"Remarkable," Frederick agreed, striding forward, his hand outthrust. "A truly remarkable coincidence that our paths should cross *here*, Mr. MacGregor. I didn't have the impression you were also on tour."

"An accurate assessment, Mr. Whitaker," Marco assured him. "In fact, I'm in Mantua visiting a cousin. I'd just finished taking a coffee with him in Piazza Sordello when I saw you enter the *palazzo*. I called out, but apparently you didn't hear me, and by the time I crossed the square and bought my admission ticket, you'd disappeared from view. It took me some time to locate you in this labyrinth.

"Are you enjoying it?" he asked. "Does it delight you? From what I overheard, Miss Merriwether has been providing you with her usual thorough insight. I'm beginning to think she rivals Isabella d'Este, herself, in her appreciation of the arts." Though his tone was light and humorous, his words were sincere. And his gaze was deep and direct. Hazel swallowed.

"I'm sure Isabella knew her way around much better than I," she replied, willing her voice to work. She adopted his lightness of tone, but chose to ignore both his undercurrent compliment and the message in his eyes. Her heart was beating too hard. "She would have gone sleepless and hungry if she'd been as lost as I."

"I'll concede you only that point," Marco returned, unperturbed. "Though it's a minor matter and easily overcome. I've been through the *palazzo,* and its connecting castello and galleries, many times. It's one of my favorite places in Italy. For me, the most beautiful sight I've ever looked upon is the Camera degli Sposi. Come. I'll show you."

With that, he wound Hazel's arm around his own and started down the hall. The move was executed with such flourish and decision it was impossible to think him forward. Only Lucy looked a little bit put out as all the Whitakers stepped readily in behind him. After their rooftop tour of the Duomo and their *gelato* break in the Milanese garden, they hadn't the slightest doubt that any time spent in Mr. MacGregor's company would be highly entertaining.

Given such circumstances, Hazel could hardly object, even if she'd been able to speak. Her heart had leaped to her throat the instant Marco had taken hold of her arm, leaving her mute, but in no way numb. She was acutely aware of being close to Marco, of being joined to his large body by their linked arms. Though his touch was neither insolent nor rude, it couldn't be considered impersonal. Nothing about him was reserved, Hazel realized. Nothing was inhibited or dull. Even the bland tone and nice manners he assumed couldn't mask the fact that he was a man who lived with all his senses. His huge appetite for life practically burned through his skin.

The realization increased Hazel's unaccustomed state of turmoil. She'd never encountered anyone like Marco in her proper circle of society, nor had she been led to believe that anyone like he could exist. In the back of her mind lurked the uneasy conviction that his unbound spirit was probably impermissible. Certainly her own agitated reaction to him had to be.

But for the moment that thought remained in the back of her mind, while the front of it was thrilled with what was happening. Marco led her, and the Whitakers, with unerring direction, through the ducal complex. It was an exhilarating experience to sail through chamber after majestic chamber on the arm of a man who seemed sprung from the very frescoes on the walls.

Marco recited the names of the rooms they passed through: Galleria degli Specchi, Sala dello Zodiaco, Galleria della Mostra, Salone degli Arcieri. In his rich Italian accent, they sounded like arias in an opera. He pointed out special works by special artists and spoke of them so familiarly and so affectionately, Hazel could sense their presence in the *palazzo*. She felt swept back through the centuries by the man who was twined to her arm. The sensation was intoxicating.

Then they turned a corner and breezed through a door, coming to a stop in the middle of the floor. "Oh, my," Hazel murmured, looking around the Camera degli Sposi. Even Lucy was silent in awe. Marco smiled.

It wasn't one of the *palazzo*'s bigger rooms, but its impact was immense. Every inch of its walls was covered in frescoes of Lodovico Gonzaga and his family and court, along with couriers and dogs and magical cities on mounts, painted by Andrea Mantegna at the peak of his brilliance. Wonderfully stuccoed cornices and wreaths circled the ceiling, framing its centerpiece:

an illusive painting of an opening to the sky. Clouds puffed by, and pretty girls and fat cherubs and a Turk and a peacock peered over the edge.

"Didn't I tell you so?" Marco asked triumphantly.

"Yes, you did," Hazel admitted, not taking her eyes from the frescoes. She answered naturally, somehow knowing he was addressing her, knowing he wanted to hear her response. For a fraction of a moment, mesmerized by the magnificent paintings, she forgot there was anyone else in the room. Then the Whitakers chimed in, talking all at once.

"You were absolutely right!" Lucy exclaimed. "It's so pretty."

"Too true," Frederick applauded. "What a clever idea, that ceiling."

"Did they have peacocks then?" Charlotte asked.

Reminded of their presence, Hazel let her own reply lapse, but didn't allow their chatter to disrupt the spell that enveloped her. She let her arm slide free of Marco's and wandered around the room by herself, walking slowly, reveling in the colors, in the composition, in Mantegna's singular style. When she came to the door, however, she halted. There, above the marble header, holding aloft a tablet, were seven frescoed angels with wings like brilliant butterflies. Hazel looked from the chubby cherubs to Marco, then back to the angels. His face was the same. The same full, glowing cheeks, the same sensuous mouth, the same head of undisciplined curls.

Hazel snuck another comparative peek at Marco. He was staring directly at her with a smile on his face that said he knew what she was seeing. Blushing, Hazel turned quickly, taking refuge in her scrutiny of the wall. Then her embarrassment turned to mortification. The cherubs were naked. Those sturdy little cherubs, who looked just like Marco, hadn't so much as a leaf to cover them as they floated, unconcerned, through the air. Her own cheeks were red hot as Hazel rapidly shifted her gaze to a fuzzy-haired dog crouched behind Lodovico Gonzaga's legs, her mood instantly broken, her enjoyment drastically curtailed. Reality, and propriety, returned. Deflated, she trailed along as they wound their way out of the palace.

When they were standing again, a bit dazed, in the vast, sun-scorched Piazza Sordello, Marco said, "It's an affront to the spirit to step from the world of the Gonzaga into the nineteenth century so precipitously. We'd be well advised to cushion the jolt with some refreshment. I have in mind a small *trattoria* . . . "

"Let me guess," Lucy teased. "It's the very best *trattoria* in all of Mantua. Possibly in all of Italy."

"Now, Lucy . . . " Frederick admonished his sister's sauciness.

"No, no," Marco protested, waving both hands to intercept Frederick. "She's quite right. At least in intent." Smiling, he offered a very willing Lucy his arm and started across the cobbled square. "While I can think of one or two other local places where it might be better to take a meal, I happen to know that the Trattoria Bonacolsi has just received a basket of freshly picked *fragoli dei boschi*—the tiny wild strawberries whose fragrance and flavor are unparalleled. Moreover, we can sit in the shade of an ancient grape arbor while we eat bowls full of the berries with, perhaps, a slight sprinkle of sugar." With his free hand he demonstrated the delicate shake necessary to sweeten the fruit, just that much.

"I'm convinced that you know the best places to eat in every village in Italy," Lucy said, laughing gaily. "And the best food, too."

"You're too generous," Marco responded with mock humility. "I haven't been to half the villages in Italy, never mind having discovered their specialties. Not even a quarter of the towns. However," he added, his eyes widening in relish, "I must try to correct this deficit. Such a goal is truly noble."

Though Lucy laughed again, her mother, puffing along, took Marco's words more seriously. "Spare yourself, please, Mr. MacGregor," she implored. "Surely such a task is hopeless."

"Not hopeless, Mrs. Whitaker," Marco replied, turning his head toward her. "Herculean, perhaps. Even unobtainable. But never hopeless. On the contrary, the pursuit of the exquisite, whether it be the wild strawberries that thrill the palate for only a few moments a year, or the frescoes of Mantegna that thrill the soul for centuries, this quest is the very epitome of hope."

He paused to let his eyes rest a moment on Hazel, walking at Mrs. Whitaker's side. On her clear profile, on her graceful carriage, on the enticing beauty mark above her mouth. "Would you agree, Miss Merriwether?" he asked.

She lifted her large gray eyes and looked at him. "Very nicely expressed, Mr. MacGregor," she said.

When annoyance flashed across his face, Hazel wondered, as she had in Milan, what he had found in her unexceptional reply to cause irritation. This time, though, she didn't follow up the thought by wondering why Marco's opinion should matter. Chastened by the recent soaring and subsequent crash of her spirits, both caused by this extraordinary man, she didn't want to think about him at all.

Turning away, she said to Frederick, "We musn't neglect to visit the Palazzo del Tè. It's a bit distant from the center, but it contains an unrivaled display of Giulio Romano's frescoes and grotesques."

Even as she spoke, she was aware that her words sounded dry and lifeless, without Marco's sense of magic, but chivalrous Frederick seemed not to care. "We'll make an excursion first thing in the morning," he promised. "How fortunate we are to have you with us, Hazel. We wouldn't know which foot to put forward without your direction."

Hazel gave him a golden smile of gratitude, the tightness within her loosening. Dear Frederick, she thought, not for the first time. Still feeling Marco's stare, though, she made no further response.

"Ruskin considered this to be one of the most interesting mythic pictures in Venice," Hazel told the Whitakers as they stood in front of a fresco by Tintoretto. It was their second morning in Venice and they were making their way through the vast, and very august, Doges' Palace.

"Ruskin?" Charlotte asked incredulously, her attention suddenly engaged. "Mr. Ruskin who sells bouquets of roses on Boyleston Street? Has he been to Italy?"

"Oh, no, silly goose," Lucy scoffed, though she offered her sister no further explanation.

"Not *our* Mr. Ruskin, Charlotte," Hazel said, smiling at the thought of the rheumy-eyed Boston street vendor squinting at the *Deposition of Christ*. "*John* Ruskin is a well-regarded art critic who has written what many people believe to be the definitive books on Venetian art and architecture." As she spoke, she glanced over her shoulder, half expecting to see Marco posed dramatically behind her, ready to add some cogent remark. Instead, she saw only another dozen or two tourists, drifting in pairs and small groups from one masterful painting to the next.

Refusing to acknowledge the stab of disappointment she felt, she continued talking. "Ruskin also praised Tintoretto's *Venice as Queen of the Sea*. He called its conception 'daring.' " She looked at the ornately framed fresco in the center of the Senate Hall's ceiling, and the others followed her lead.

"Oh," Charlotte said. Her attention wandered again and so did she.

"Ummm," Lucy commented, looking down and rubbing a crick in her slim neck before meandering off to gaze at the throne from which the reigning doge had presided.

"Inspiring," Frederick murmured. "Truly inspiring." Which is what he had murmured at the other frescoes and sculptures they'd seen. Then the zodiacal clock caught his eye, and he moved away to study it. Mrs. Whitaker said nothing but went to look wistfully at the carved rows of senators' seats, barred from nineteenth-century sitting by a velvet rope.

Head tilted back, alone in the middle of the floor, Hazel continued to stare at the ceiling. She tried to generate the appropriate awe, but her effort was of little avail. She couldn't help but compare the earnest figures populating Tintoretto's heaven to the interesting faces that had peered down from Mantegna's sky in Mantua. In fact, nothing had measured up since that afternoon in the Gonzaga's city. Even her breakfast strawberries at the Hotel Royal Danieli had fallen far short of the intensely flavorful wild ones at the Trattoria Bonacolsi.

Lowering her head, Hazel gave up on her futile scrutiny of the fresco, but refused to speculate on the cause of her sudden ennui. Instead, she looked around for another Important Work to study. As before, though, she had to admit defeat. All looked equally important, with their yards of heavy gilt framing scenes of God and glory. And all failed equally to capture her interest.

With a sigh she turned to rejoin her friends, but could no longer see them in the huge hall. There were several English couples, one French family, and a band of Germans dutifully following their minister's lead. The Whitakers, apparently, had continued on to another room.

Unalarmed, Hazel strolled through a door and into the vestibule of the Doges' private chapel. The room was small and contained no art of significance. Not surprisingly, it contained no Whitakers either. She went on to the Chiesetta. Although Titian's only known fresco, of S. Cristoforo, graced one wall of the chapel, her friends weren't there to admire it. After a quick glance at the impressive figure, Hazel completed the circle to the Senate Hall.

Still no Whitakers. She made a hurried loop of the Collegio, the Anticollegio, and the Hall of Four Doors. Back in the Senate, an English headmaster was reedily expounding on the Venetian form of government, which had worked efficiently for half a millennium. Apart from a group of bored schoolboys, there was no one there to listen. When the teacher paused in his lecture to give Hazel a suspicious look, she retreated through the door.

Puzzled, but not panicked, Hazel descended the Scala d'Oro. They probably expect to rejoin me by the entrance, below, she decided. They're probably waiting there now.

But no familiar faces greeted her at the bottom of the Golden Staircase. A handful of Italians and an Irish priest were standing in line at the ticket booth. In the courtyard an intense-looking art student was hunched over his easel. Completely mystified, Hazel stepped just beyond the main gate and into San Marco Square.

The *piazza* was immense and filled with tourists and pigeons. Hovering near the palace, she scanned the crowd.

"*Mi da un soldo, signorina. Una palanca, per favore.*"

Hazel turned to see a ragged boy before her, his grimy palm outstretched. Pushing up next to him were several other boys, not one more than ten years old, but all wearing the hard expressions of old, uncaring men. Their clothes were stained and torn, their hair was crudely cut and greasy. The littlest one had lost his front teeth in a childhood passage, the biggest one had broken his in a fight.

"No," Hazel said, responding as Frederick had instructed her. "I have no money to give you." When they failed to go away, only thrust their dirty hands closer, Hazel moved away instead. They followed her.

She tried to ignore them, to pretend interest in the Byzantine Basilica of San Marco, glittering and glorious at the head of the square, but their incessant begging made it impossible. "*Un soldo, signorina. Gelt. Un sou.* Money."

"No," Hazel said more firmly, picking up her pace. "No money. *Niente.*" Walking purposefully, she kept her head raised, as if studying the bronze Moors striking the bell atop the Clock Tower. Actually, she was trying to look over the urchins' heads. They waved their hands higher. "*Un soldo, signorina.*"

This time she only shook her head and passed through the arch of the Clock Tower, putting Piazza San Marco, and the Doges' Palace, out of sight. Although perturbed by the situation, Hazel wasn't seriously worried. She was on the Merceria, the widest, most elegant shopping street in Venice. Obviously she was safe.

Larga San Marco also looked busy. Hazel waited until she had almost walked past the street, then quickly turned right and took a running step. "*Un soldo. Un soldo. Un soldo,*" the beggars demanded close at her back. Chagrined, she realized she hadn't lost them yet.

She tried the same tactic a hundred yards later, this time darting left into a narrower *calle* where there was still ample activity and enough people to reassure her. Two gossiping ladies and a porter balancing an enormous basket of cheeses on his back filled most of the skinny street. With less delicacy than was her wont, Hazel pushed around them, finally putting some space between herself and her pursuers.

Pleased with her success, and therefore encouraged to repeat the maneuver, Hazel turned right at her first opportunity. Her heart plunged. She was on one of the myriad narrow, crooked *calles* that thread through Venice. Ahead of her was a lane no wider than a hall. A similar one was off to her right. "*Un soldo, signorina,*" came the children's clamor. She couldn't go back. She blindly turned left.

For the first time Hazel felt genuine fear. She was in a malodorous little courtyard, blocked from the sun by sinister buildings looming up around it. The only exit was a low tunnel at the far end. With her heart pounding wildly, Hazel stumbled across the broken bricks and ducked through the passage. She felt a hand graze her arm and heard the voices grow more insistent.

Thoroughly lost and frightened, Hazel fled across a small square, over a canal on a footbridge, and down an alley. Gray laundry was strung overhead. From out of nowhere, a cat leaped across her path screeching and climbed straight up a stucco wall. Her heart leaped, then froze.

She nearly wept in relief when they burst onto a busier street and when she saw a big church standing in an even bigger square. But when she flew over the intervening footbridge and aimed for the door, she realized the pack was herding her into an isolated corner. Unable to run anymore, almost out of breath, Hazel tried to assemble her unraveled nerves and to make a stand.

"No," she said in a quavery voice, flicking through her Italian dictionary with shaking hands. "You must stop. Uh . . . *Fermo*. Do you hear me. *Fermo*." The book was snatched from her hands, and the boy with the broken teeth grinned at her, so close she could smell his foul breath.

"Give that back," she said, without much conviction.

Rather than return the dictionary, the unsavory boy reached for her leather-bound journal. Suddenly half a dozen hands were grabbing at her guidebooks, pulling away her purse, even clawing at the cameo brooch on her blouse. "No!" Hazel cried, terror choking her throat as she batted helplessly at the tearing hands.

"*Bastardi!*" a voice roared. "*Figli di puttane! Basta!*" And as suddenly as the assault had started, it ceased. The ragged boys were ripped away from her and flung to the ground, one on top of the other. Each yowling like the cat in the alley, they let go their booty, scrambled up, and ran.

"*Via!*" her rescuer shouted at their backs. "*Andate al diavolo!*" Then he turned around to help her. It was Marco MacGregor.

What little breath Hazel had left seemed instantly restricted.

"You!" she gasped, shrinking against the wall. This was too much to absorb. She had been separated from her friends in a foreign land, chased through a maze of menacing streets, and finally been cornered and attacked by a band of evil-smelling beggars, as deeply afraid as she'd been in her life. But to be rescued by the one man in Italy whose mere presence made her pulse race and her customary composure crumple was too much to rationally take.

"You've been following me," she accused him, pointing a trembling finger. "Don't try to pretend otherwise. I know you have. You've probably been following me all over Venice. All the way from Mantua. No doubt, even from Milan."

Marco dropped the arm he had extended, but lifted his eyebrows instead. "Actually," he said, stooping to retrieve her books and purse, "I suspect that the reverse is true. I think that *you* have been following *me*." He carefully straightened the pages that had gotten bent in the scuffle, his face deadpan earnest. "I daresay it's suspiciously odd that you turn up wherever I am. It's *my* country, after all. *My* city, in fact."

"You can't be serious!" Hazel exclaimed. Though her tone was incredulous, her voice was steadier. His absurd counteraccusation had shocked her out of her near hysteria.

"Of course I'm not serious," he answered, breaking into a grin. "I was just teasing you. Which is a habit my mother deplores. She feels it demonstrates an essentially humorless character, but I think it's simply the result of being educated in England. It's impossible to survive Eton without learning to tease and be teased by one's friends. It's practically an academic requirement.

"But speaking of friends," he said, holding out her possessions, "what have you done with yours?"

"I haven't *done* anything with them," Hazel answered, ignoring the proffered books and edging away. Her mind was whirling in confusion. "We just lost one another in the Doges' Palace. I was looking up at the ceiling in the Senate Hall, and when I looked down, they were gone." Then she remembered that it hadn't been Tintoretto's fresco that had distracted her attention, but thoughts of Mantua and Marco. She shut her eyes in increasing distress.

"So you were wandering around San Marco, hoping to sight them," he surmised, tucking the rejected books under his arm. "And at the very moment that those rascals attached themselves to you, I was crossing the *piazza* from the Caffè Florian and was able to see your predicament and chase after you." He nodded in satisfaction at having pieced together the plot.

"It's remarkable to contemplate," he added, musing, "that if I hadn't run into my cousin Umberto this morning and he hadn't insisted that we have a coffee, this scenario would have been completely different. Fate is an awe-inspiring force, wouldn't you say, Miss Merriwether?"

Hazel's eyes flew open again, her suspicion rearoused. Her jumbled thoughts suddenly found a focus. "Fate?" she scoffed. "More like flimflammery. Do you honestly expect me to believe in the existence of another cousin and another coffee at yet another conveniently placed café? Really, Mr. MacGregor. Your story may have fooled us in Mantua, but a second telling reveals it for the fiction that it is. Your cousins are pure fabrication."

Far from reacting with either outrage or embarrassment, Marco didn't even have the grace to look guilty. "If that's the case," he said, treating this outburst of distrust as earnestly as the last, "Umberto will be disappointed to hear that he doesn't exist. As will my cousin Eduardo in Mantua. And it follows that his brothers Giorgio, Silvestro, and Leopoldo will as well. Not to mention his sisters Margarita and Ortensia.

"Most probably, my cousins Alessandro, Maddalena, and Rosa, who live in Padua, will also be distressed to learn of this change in their status from real to fictional, but Aunt Portia, who is my mother's oldest sister and is quite excitable, will be impossible. She'll write immediately to my cousins Dante and Isabella in Verona, who, I'm sure, will be surprised, too." Here Marco paused a minute and rubbed his chin meditatively. Finally he threw his hand out in a gesture of dismissal. "My Maretti cousins are also in Verona," he confided, "but they are, all seven, so dull I don't think they'd notice if they disappeared. Certainly no one else would.

"The Bellati, now, *they* are amusing," Marco continued, brightening. "There's Manfredi, who makes beautiful photographs, and his very fashionable English wife, Nally. They're in Milan and are almost the sole reason I visit that city. He's actually my mother's brother's nephew by marriage, though their delightful son Bartolomeo calls me uncle. . . ."

Hazel collapsed on the ledge carved along the church's exterior, close to tears. It was difficult enough to try to sort her residual terror from the disturbing excitement Marco always aroused, but to be subjected to this recitation of his relatives and their respective cities was too overwhelming. Nothing in her life had prepared her for as bizarre a moment as this.

Nor was his solace any more conventional. Rather than soothe her with stilted phrases and references to her feminine frailty, Marco sat his large body on the ledge next to her, resting her books and purse on his knee. "How fortunate we are to find ourselves in the Campo Santa Maria Formosa," he remarked, as if, for all the world, they had ambled there while sightseeing. "In the square, behind the church, is a wonderful little *osteria* with an excellent wine cellar. I promise you, their Prosecco is so perfect that I've tried begging and bribing to obtain the source, all in vain. Come now, Miss Merriwether, we'll go get us a glass."

When Hazel didn't respond, only sat struggling to regain her reason, Marco frowned. Slightly more seriously, and more insistently, he said, "It's well past noon, and I'm willing to wager that you've been trekking around the Doges' Palace for hours. No doubt your fright is compounded by hunger and thirst. A plate of fresh, grilled sardines will set you to rights. Come now, Miss Merriwether," he repeated, putting his hand under her elbow and hoisting her up.

Hazel let herself be led. As she'd discovered once before, Marco's tone might seem bland, his comments might seem frivolous or strange, but there was no mistaking the power and force in his touch. They were almost turning the corner by the side of the church when a single thought finally found its way through the upheaval in Hazel's mind.

"Oh, no," she said, abruptly pulling free from his grip. "I must go back and find the Whitakers. I'm sure they'll be frantic with worry. How can I possibly think of my own comfort when they are scouring the city looking for me?"

"Nonsense," Marco said, retaking her arm. "If you hurry back to San Marco now, I'll tell you exactly how it will go. While you are rushing from room to room in the Doges' Palace, they'll be racing around the Basilica. And when you climb to the top of the Campanile, they'll be searching below in the Loggia. It will be hours before you all join up again at your hotel, thoroughly worn out by fatigue and famine. Moreover, the memory that you carry back to America of Venice's most famous treasures will be an exhausted blur. That would be a pity. Especially, Miss Merriwether, for someone of your fine sensibility."

The unexpected compliment was as unsettling as the warm, strong feel of his fingers around her arm. His argument sounded logical, but it couldn't possibly be proper. Could it? In the end Hazel didn't so much decide as succumb. "Perhaps you're right, Mr. MacGregor," she conceded. "Perhaps a cup of tea and a small cake would be restorative."

"Of course I'm right," Marco responded, guiding her around the corner and into a vast square. Surrounded by three-story stucco houses with striped awnings above the windows and small shops offering everything from cured hams to hairpins, it looked like a bricked-in village green. "But don't expect to find tea and crumpets here."

When she saw the *osteria,* Hazel revised her requirements, feeling an involuntary twinge of anticipation. A vivid green vine climbed up the facade to frame a window in which a tableau of splendid vegetables and beautiful breads was arranged. Through the open door drifted tempting smells. She had seen tiny restaurants like this one on the back streets of Florence and Milan, but she and the Whitakers had always eaten safely in their hotels.

Marco settled her on a plain wooden chair at a plain wooden table laid with a sheet of butcher paper. The walls were stark white without any decorations, but the ceiling was painted ocher and the trim around the window and door was rich red. A copper-topped counter stretched half the length of the room, and on it stood jars of brined olives and hard almond biscuits and crockery jars filled with bouquets of basil. It was a far cry from the grand columns and the silken tassels of the Hotel Royal Danieli.

"I think I'm feeling better already," Hazel decided. Marco nodded his approval.

She felt better still after the promised plate of grilled sardines, and even better than that after the spider crab dressed in olive oil and the tender cuttle fish that followed. By the time she had finished a dish of spaghetti with sweet baby clams, and had washed it all down with the dry, sparkling Prosecco, she was enjoying herself immensely.

"Shall we have dessert first or go directly on our tour?" Marco asked.

Hazel hesitated, her napkin halfway to her mouth. Then she patted her lips and returned her napkin to her lap. "Our tour?" she asked, her customary calm restored.

"Yes," Marco said casually. "I thought to show you Venice as you'll never find it in a guidebook." He laid his arms on the table and leaned forward to forestall the protest that was already forming. "You needn't worry that I'll make you tramp across bridges and through alleys," he assured her, knowing full well that wasn't her concern. "We'll do the whole tour in the comfort of a gondola.

"Mind you, I haven't had time to prepare a tour as sumptuous as Henry III's," he said, his tone still light, but tantalizing. "These days it's practically impossible to find four hundred Slavs to row a galley on a moment's notice. Or to fill a barge with glassmakers blowing fanciful objects for your amusement. And I'm afraid there'll be no welcoming banquet with twelve hundred courses and three thousand guests. No triumphal arches designed by Palladio, no paintings commissioned from Titian and Bellini. I'm afraid I won't be able to wrap you in cloths of gold or to lay rare carpets from Persia under your feet."

He leaned back in his chair, locked his hands across his chest, and regarded her intently for a moment. His voice grew softer as he continued. "Venice may no longer be 'The Bride of the Adriatic' or 'The Eye of Italy.' She may no longer be a treasure box of jewels and silks from the East or the mighty power that conquered a quarter of the known world. But she is still 'La Serenissima,' Miss Merriwether, still the most gorgeous city in the world, and I can show her to you better than any Baedeker."

There was silence when Marco finished speaking while Hazel sat with her hands folded in her lap. In her mind she saw the opulent excesses of art and beauty, the paintings, the tapestries, the ropes of pearls. And she remembered how exhilarated she'd felt in Mantua, being swept through history on Marco's arm.

Finally she spoke. "I think I'd better have dessert first," she answered him. With a smile Marco signaled, and a bowl of lemon sorbet sprinkled with fresh currants in syrup appeared.

Later, lulled by the good food and wine, Hazel leaned back in the gondola and watched Venice glide by. With occasional directions from Marco, the gondolier poled them beneath beautiful bridges and past magnificent palaces, lit by the mellow gleam of late afternoon summer sun. They went down the Grand Canal, a watery boulevard, and wound along rios scarcely wider than their slender boat.

It was a continuous exhibition. Borrowing from the Romans and the Greeks and the scintillating Byzantines, the Venetians had built their city. It was a monument to their love of grandeur and pageantry. They had sculpted and stuccoed and carved and decorated. They had used marbles and mosaics, arches and capitals, windows from *A Thousand and One Nights*. Even the plainest building had some striking detail: a bas-relief of prancing horses or happy putti, a pot of purple heliotrope balanced between the glistening white columns of a balcony, a pair of huge flame-shaped hinges on a canal-level door.

Her fright and confusion were long forgotten. In fact, Hazel felt as if she herself were floating. At first she attributed it to the wine, but she was hardly in a stupor. Quite the opposite, all her senses were heightened. She was acutely aware of shapes, sounds, and colors. Of the carillons coming from antique bell towers and of the pinks, the yellows, and the faded blues washed on centuries-old plaster walls. She was aware of the unique mark Venice had made on the world, of the extravagance and power she had displayed.

Most of all, though, she was aware of the man at her side. He was so close to her on the gondola cushion, she could smell the faint scent of sandalwood soap that clung to his rosy skin. When he flung a hand out to indicate a particularly outstanding sight, she sensed his enormous size. Not only of his physical being, but also of his limitless horizons and spirit. And when he turned toward her, his marvelous face lit up, rejoicing in her own appreciation and enjoyment, she felt positively euphoric. Marco and Venice were intertwined, each dramatic to behold, each irresistibly appealing.

"You're right to be so proud of your city," Hazel said, letting her head fall back against her seat. "Venice is spectacular."

Marco beamed.

"And yet," she added more pensively, rolling her head to look at him, "I detect a certain detachment in your tone, a distance, perhaps. It's rather as if you're an uninvolved witness, the narrator of some great and entertaining epic rather than one of the participants." As soon as she made it, Hazel was astounded by her remark. And by her languid posture. The one was impolite, the other improper. Both were entirely inappropriate. She sat up a little straighter.

Marco, however, took offense at neither. In fact, his easy nod seemed to express approval of her observation as well as agreement with it. "Partly it's Venice," he explained, tossing his head at the beauty all around them. "Sad to say, she's only a shell of what she was. She's a memory or an entertainment, as you suggest. A museum whose citizens have become curators."

He gave another glance at the resplendent *palazzi* before turning to look at her. "But partly," he went on with an elaborate shrug, "this tone you detect can also be blamed on my education. The English are masters of detachment. I'm quite convinced it's the cornerstone of the national character. Like teasing, it's an academic requirement."

A decidedly schoolboy grin broke across his face. "It's not unlike the biology laboratory," he said. "Only instead of dissecting the legs from dead frogs, the lads practice detaching emotion from fact." His hand cut through the air in demonstration. "They slice the passion from their souls."

Although Hazel swallowed hard at the analogy, something inside compelled her, against every standard of modesty and manners, to say, "You seem to imply that this is undesirable." Back home in Boston all talk of emotion and passion were left to poets and actors. And young girls. "You leave the impression that you hold a different opinion."

"Quite different, Miss Merriwether," Marco replied, twisting not only his face, but his whole body toward her. The gondola gave a sharp rock. "I believe that genuine emotion is the essence of life, its single most gratifying gift. To ignore it—or worse, to deny it—is terribly wasteful, even sinful. It strips life of its fullness and steals away its wonder. It reduces life to mere existence."

"That's rather an extreme view, Mr. MacGregor," Hazel murmured, not sure whether her heart was pounding because of the quick tip of the boat, because of the daring topic they were discussing, or because of Marco's steadying hand on her arm.

"Extreme?" Marco asked, both eyebrows raising. Then he gave another shrug, his hand sliding away. "I don't consider it extreme," he told her. "On the contrary, I consider it the only rational view one can possess. Just think, Miss Merriwether, what this world would be like without passion. No, wait," he said, erasing his words with his hands. "Let's take a more obvious example. Think what this city, this Venice, would be like without passion." His waving hands flew wide to encompass everything around them, an arabesque-windowed building, a wild cat sitting on a mosaic quay, a marble Madonna in a flower-filled niche.

"Without emotion it would still be mud flats," he said, his voice almost ringing with feeling. "Mud flats and marsh grass and, perhaps, a few drab huts. Because without passion the forces that shaped Venice would be too weak and worthless to create anything like this." Again his hand flew out, and, following its sweep, Hazel saw the lowering sun set fire to the distant spire and golden dome of San Giorgio Maggiore.

"Tintoretto, Bellini, the Doge Enrico Dandolo, who conquered Constantinople at the age of eighty-eight, all these great men were motivated by great emotions. By love and by hate and by greed, if you will, but not by cold, calculated facts." Marco thrust his hand forward and started to count off on his fingers. "Without passion," he enumerated, "beauty is dull. Power is impotent. Imagination is dry. Courage, valor, ambition"—he ran out of fingers and threw the hand in the air—"without passion they're hollow."

"I see," Hazel said, stunned.

Her quiet words cooled him down, and he reassumed his wry manner. "Do you, Miss Merriwether?" he asked, smiling. "Will you tell me, as you did in Mantua, that my speech was 'well expressed'?"

Hazel felt her own cheeks turn rosy remembering how he'd looked at her that afternoon when he'd eloquently equated exquisiteness to hope. "I shall if you wish it, Mr. MacGregor," she replied, "but I suspect that you're teasing me again. It's another trait, like detachment, you pretend to decry, yet you admit to owning, all the same."

"The teasing, yes," Marco agreed, still seeming amused. "A regrettable habit. I'll do my best to expunge it. The detachment, however," he continued, shaking his curly head, "that's a mere inflection. A tone I acquired with the language. But I can assure you, Miss Merriwether," he added, his voice suddenly softer, "it's only a tone."

"I see," Hazel repeated, more slowly this time. Then looked abruptly down, her thoughts spinning.

"Do you, Miss Merriwether?" Marco asked, also repeating, as he lifted her chin with his fingers. He smoothed a strand of shiny hair away from her face and touched the tiny dot above her mouth. "You're very beautiful," he told her, leaning forward to set a tender kiss on her lips.

Hazel knew it was going to happen, could sense his intention. She heard it in his voice when he spoke. As his face came closer, she found herself wondering why it always took her by surprise to see that his eyes were a deep shade of blue. Then she felt his mouth on hers and felt his thumb slide slowly across her brow. Then her eyes fluttered shut, and all reasonable thought fled.

It was as if she were in a spell, caught in the splendor that was Venice. The touch of his lips became part of the atmosphere enveloping her, filling her senses and thrilling her soul. When his cheek rolled against hers, glowing skin against skin, the shock spread all through her body. She felt dazzlingly alive, her breath coming faster, her heart beating hard.

Then the gondola bumped gently against a mooring post, jarring her only infinitesimally. It was enough. The spell burst apart. "Oh," Hazel gasped, pulling away. She pressed a shaky hand against her forehead and struggled for control. Venice was rapidly receding, becoming just a beautiful backdrop, as the decorous parlors of Boston reclaimed their hold on her mind.

"Really, Mr. MacGregor," she said, fanning herself with her hand and refusing to look at him. "I'd supposed you to be a gentleman, but I see now that I was wrong. My trust was sadly misplaced. You must take me home at once." Huddling against the railing, she added, "And don't come near me."

But Marco was already standing, and as far away from her as the confines of the gondola permitted. "Please accept my apologies, Miss Merriwether," he said, obviously annoyed by her response. "Apparently my impressions were wrong, too. I thought you were a beautiful frog who could leap away from her cage if released. But it appears to be too late. They've already done their work on you in the laboratory. What a pity. What a waste."

Hazel cringed at his harsh tone, but still couldn't meet his eyes. "If you have any chivalry at all, Mr. MacGregor," she said, "you'll take me home immediately." Her voice was tight. Inside she was churning. "I don't wish to discuss this any further."

"You *are* home, Miss Merriwether," Marco said curtly. "Observe that we're tied to the pier by the Royal Danieli. You are restored to the bosom of your friends, and, unless I am again mistaken, here comes Mrs. Whitaker to rescue you."

When Hazel looked up and saw it was true, she got swiftly to her feet. Too swiftly. The gondola dipped and so did she. "Steady, Miss Merriwether," Marco breathed in her ear as his arm caught her around the waist. A shiver ran through her, and for an instant she fell against him before regaining her balance.

"Hazel, my dear!" Mrs. Whitaker cried as she approached them. "And Mr. MacGregor. Where have you been? We've been tormented with worry. Positively stricken ill. We've crisscrossed St. Mark's Square a hundred times, and Frederick has gone back, again, for another search. What happened? Mr. MacGregor, did you spirit her off? Really, you ought to have left a message."

"You mustn't blame Mr. MacGregor," Hazel said before Marco could speak. She disengaged herself from his grip and stepped ashore. Still not looking at him, she took Mrs. Whitaker's arm and steered her toward the hotel. "I was waylaid by a pack of beggars in the *piazza*," she explained, as briefly as possible. Her head was starting to throb and her throat felt dry. "They chased me to a remote street and would have succeeded in robbing me if Mr. MacGregor hadn't serendipitously intervened."

"Too dreadful!" Mrs. Whitaker exclaimed, placing her hand over her heart in a gesture of horror. "Poor, dear Hazel," she sympathized, never questioning why this uncomplicated act of villainy took five hours. "What a trial you've had to endure. And without your parasol, too." She brushed her hand against the lovely skin on Hazel's cheek, still flushed with feeling. "I can see that the sun has reddened your face," she said. "I hope it doesn't freckle."

Then remembering Hazel's savior, she turned back to Marco. "How grateful we are to you, Mr. MacGregor," she said, extending her hand. "In the past your hospitality has been more than generous, but now you can't know what a noble service you've performed."

Marco's eyebrows raised and he shot a glance at Hazel. When she studied the spiral stripes on the mooring post, he gave one of his shrugs. Taking Mrs. Whitaker's hand, he said, "I'm relieved to know that Miss Merriwether is back where she belongs."

Hazel spent the rest of their Venetian stay in her room at the Royal Danieli. Ostensibly she was recovering from the fright of her encounter with the street urchins, but in reality she was avoiding the chance of another encounter with Marco. She passed her days seated by the window, sketching the changing views below. Trying to come to terms with that extraordinary afternoon, she went over and over every detail in her mind. Even, and especially, the luxurious feel of Marco's large body when she fell into him on the boat. Finally, on the train to Switzerland, surrounded by refreshing Alpine scenery, she decided that it was merely one of the unusual experiences that happens when one travels in a foreign land. It was a very Italianesque incident. Beautiful and overblown.

# CHAPTER

## 1

"Mr. and Miss Whitaker are here to see you, Miss Hazel," the maid announced from the doorway.

At the sound of her voice the paintbrush in Hazel's hand jumped, washing leaf green where petal pink was meant to go. Giving the ruined watercolor only a brief glance, she set the brush in a pot of water, saying, "Thank you, Annie. Please ask them to come up."

"No need," Lucy said, breezing into the Rose Parlor. "We're already here." She plopped onto the sofa, still swathed in her cashmere cloak, its dark mink collar making a pretty contrast to her blond curls. "Honestly, Hazel," she chided, "I think it's extremely unkind of you to have your studio on the third floor. You might have done it downstairs."

"Climbing stairs is very good exercise," Frederick said, unwinding his silk muffler as he entered the room. He handed it along with his top hat and overcoat to Annie. "It strengthens the legs and the lungs and it stirs the blood. It's the ideal way to train for tennis competition." Walking over to where Hazel sat, he seemed an exemplary endorsement of his theory, tall and trim with an athlete's natural grace.

Hazel rose to greet her guests, holding out her hand to Frederick and smiling. "I assure you, it wasn't my intention either to distress you or to establish a gymnasium, but only to put Mama's room to good use after she died. When the drapes are open, there's a wonderful light for painting and needlework." She returned

28

Frederick's gentle squeeze and met his gaze. He looked so fine and handsome, his blue eyes lit with devotion. "But had I known you'd be visiting, I would have waited in the parlor below," she added.

Lucy waved a delicate hand as she pulled off her mink-cuffed glove. "Of course you couldn't have known," she said. "I scarcely knew myself until Frederick pulled me up your front steps." She laughed delightedly as Frederick frowned in embarrassment and even Hazel's cheeks turned faintly pink.

"We were out shopping for a Christmas gift for Mother," Lucy explained. "And on the way home, Frederick insisted we stop in. I was sure this was your afternoon for that sewing circle where you stitch aprons and baby clothes for the poor, but Frederick said no, that you've all taken a Christmas sabbatical. I think he knows every move you make, Hazel," she declared, laughing again.

Hazel felt her cheeks flush pinker and her heart beat a little faster, but maintaining her customary poise, she slipped her hand free of Frederick's and crossed the room to give the bellpull a tug. "I'll make your heroic exertions worthwhile," she promised. "Mrs. Harrigan baked the most delicious currant cakes this morning. She swears that they're Prince Albert's favorite sweet and that she has the recipe from her niece who works in the kitchen at Buckingham Palace. A plate of cakes and a pot of tea should help revive you, Lucy."

Nodding in agreement, Lucy threw her cloak open on the back of the sofa. "It has been an exhausting afternoon," she willingly admitted. "The stores are teeming with people and the clerks are rude. Everyone is pushing and grabbing. You can't believe how common they are." Her small nose wrinkled.

"I'm sure it was very trying," Hazel commiserated, settling into one of the rose velvet armchairs for which the parlor was named. She patted the button-dimpled seat of its twin, inviting Frederick to sit.

"I don't see any packages to show for your expedition, though," she said as Frederick sank down next to her. "Or did you leave them in the foyer? What did you buy for your mother?"

"Nothing," Lucy moaned. "It was dreadful. We simply couldn't decide. We looked at music boxes and opera gloves and finally thought to get a pretty bed jacket. You know how Mother likes to lie in every morning with a cup of hot chocolate and a novel. But then Frederick wanted the pale yellow quilted silk, which I thought was ordinary. And he objected to the white sarcenet with ribbon rosebuds that drew my attention." She lifted her hands helplessly. "You decide, Hazel. You tell us which one we should get."

"I'm sure that they're both lovely," Hazel answered smoothly. "And I'm equally sure that your mother will be very pleased with whichever one you choose. She'll be touched by your thoughtfulness."

"No, no," Lucy said, shaking her head vehemently. "You can't slide away from it that easily, dear friend. I want a genuine response. I trust your taste implicitly. In all the years I've known you, I don't think I've ever once seen you looking less than enchanting." She wagged her finger at Hazel. "So don't think you can get away with a mush-mouthed reply about how pleased Mother will be by our thoughtfulness. She'll be considerably more pleased with a beautiful gift." With a final wag of her finger, she asked, "Which one is it to be, Hazel?"

"Now, Lucy," Frederick admonished. "It's unfair of you to press Hazel so."

"Nonsense," Lucy refuted, tossing her head.

Hazel laughed. "Since you're so determined to have my opinion," she said, enjoying both Lucy's extravagant praise and Frederick's stalwart protection, "I'll tell you, for what it's worth, that I often find yellow to be unflattering for someone of your mother's fair complexion. And could the sarcenet be just a trifle too young for her?"

"You see?" Lucy cried. "I knew you'd know best."

"It's true," Frederick agreed. "You do seem to have an instinct for aesthetic matters. We ought to have stopped to fetch you on our way *to* Washington Street, rather than on our return. It would have made the afternoon more agreeable on many counts." He leaned over to place a hand on Hazel's arm and to look at her intently. "We'll have to extract a promise from you that you'll accompany us on our next shopping foray."

"Gladly," Hazel said, laughing again. This time, though, it was to hide the excitement Frederick's touch created. It was thrilling to be the center of his attention, to command the admiration of so splendid a man. Not only was his appearance highly appealing, he was highly regarded by society, as well.

She knew he was considered extremely affable by the members of the Algonquin Club, where he dined several nights a week. Exceptionally able by the members of the Eastern Yacht Club.

And very charming by the wives and sisters of both. She also knew that her father was impressed by Frederick's family, by the wealth and respectability that went back for generations. All in all, it made her pulse race to see his delft-blue eyes fixed on her face and to feel his strong hand resting on her arm. Frederick was the perfect representative of the life she had been born and raised to lead.

When the tea tray arrived, Hazel poured out, her graceful motions and shining expression indicating the pleasure she found in this refined ritual. In fact, as she sat in her pretty parlor, munching Prince Albert's currant cakes with her friends, Hazel felt profoundly content. Italy, with its strange, stirring effects on her senses, seemed an eternity removed from here, an aberration. Even the euphoria of her afternoon in Venice seemed faded and distant. Her cosseted life in Boston was more immediate and real.

"Hello, dolly," her father said, poking his head into the parlor. "Lucy. Frederick." He nodded his greeting. Frederick rose instantly to shake the older man's hand.

"Hello, Papa," Hazel responded, her face brightening that much more. "I hope it's Christmas spirit and not some unpleasant occurrence that brings you home so early."

Edgar Merriwether was the foundation of Hazel's gilded existance. A portly man, with a neatly trimmed mustache and cool gray eyes behind gold-rimmed spectacles, he was unquestionably the king of his castle. His obvious fondness for Hazel was the only softness about him. To the rest of the world he presented the calculation and confidence of a self-made man.

"It's your irresponsible brother that brings me home," Edgar answered, a note of irritation creeping into his voice. "Cornelius has been sent off for Christmas recess with a warning from the dean. He's been truant from classes again." He shook his head disgustedly. "And after all the trouble I went through to enroll him at Harvard."

His irritation increased as he continued, "He never has cared a whit for school, but he refuses to come into the wool broker-age, either. That boy needs to do some growing up. Well," he concluded, shrugging off his outburst, "if you see him send him straight down to the library. Don't let me disturb your tea any further." With a brief wave of his hand, he withdrew.

"Oh, dear." Hazel sighed, her good spirits deflating.

"Problems?" Lucy asked, casually prying.

It was Hazel's turn to shake her head, though in regret. "They just can't seem to get along," she said. "Papa and Cornelius. Neither wants to see the other's point of view. And I'm caught in the middle. I find it so distressing."

"Of course you do," Frederick soothed. "After all, you've practically raised Cornelius since your mother died. It's only natural that you should sympathize with him. Still," he added more practically, "your father is right. Cornelius needs to grow up. All he ever talks about is baseball. He has no interest in anything else."

"I know," Hazel admitted, sighing again. "His only ambition seems to be to play on the Boston team. What do people call them? The Beaneaters? The very idea makes Papa choke with rage. And to make matters worse, as Papa said, Cornelius is completely disinterested in his business." She looked up at Frederick, her large gray eyes pleading. "Is baseball really so very bad?" she asked.

Frederick hesitated before replying. "It isn't *our* type of sport, Hazel," he said carefully, focusing his eyes on the needlepointed fireback that stood in front of the hearth. "It attracts rather a low class, both as participants and as spectators. It isn't like yachting, you know." His gaze returned to her face and he leaned forward earnestly.

"I've tried to interest Cornelius in sailing during summers at Marblehead," he said. "That's a sport for gentlemen. Why, look at the men involved in the America's Cup." He held out a hand in illustration, as if there were a group of yachtsmen standing right here in the Rose Parlor, looking natty in their navy blue blazers. "I heard only yesterday that Archibald Rogers of New York is commissioning a boat from the Herreshoff yard with the intention of competing this year. And it's an English lord who owns the *Valkyrie,* the challenger.

"Henry Bryant and General Paine are said to be in league to build a Boston contender," he continued. "You can't find more decent men than those two. Say, wouldn't it be tremendous if they produced a winner and the Cup could spend the next two years in our trophy cabinet?" Involved in *his* favorite topic, Frederick started to go off on a tangent, but caught himself in time and returned to the matter at hand.

"My efforts have been to no avail, however." His tone was slightly offended. "Cornelius just doesn't seem to take to boats. Tennis doesn't interest him much, either."

"I know," Hazel repeated worriedly, taking a cake off the plate and giving it an absentminded nibble. "How I wish he'd listen to Papa," she said. "I'm sure Papa must know what's best."

"Is there any more tea?" Lucy asked, stretching out her cup and saucer. Her initial curiosity had given way to boredom when the talk produced no gossip, only another discussion of sporting events. She wanted to return to more amusing subjects.

"How about more cakes? They look first rate."

All three turned sharply toward the source of the interruption. A young man, not quite out of his teens, came striding through the open door, his free-swinging arm narrowly missing a pair of photographs in silver filigree frames that stood on a lace-draped stand. He seemed unconcerned about their fate as he made a bee-line for the tea table. While his face still retained traces of the innocence of boyhood, his dark hair, gray eyes, and classical good looks easily identified him as Hazel's brother.

"Cornelius," Frederick said, rising again and extending his hand. "How nice to see you." His voice had the heartiness of one who has been caught in the act of discussing the other. "Say, what do you think of the goings-on in the Hasty Pudding Club? Quite a scandal, isn't it?"

Cornelius reluctantly removed his attention from the Prince Albert cakes and turned it to Frederick, coming over to shake his hand. "The Hasty Pudding Club?" he asked hazily. "Oh, yes. You mean Professor Peabody." He shrugged. "It doesn't matter to me." He released Frederick's hand and reached for a cake.

He took half of it in one bite while Frederick was forced to finish single-handedly the conversation he had started. Cornelius paid no heed as Frederick explained that Professor Peabody, formerly a member of the Hasty Pudding Club and now the professor of Christian Morals at Harvard, had secretly removed from the club's records a poem he had written during his exuberant student days. Some members of the club were calling for his resignation, a request with which Frederick was inclined to agree, as such behavior "set the wrong example for our youth."

While Frederick delivered his monologue, Cornelius wandered over to where Hazel sat and settled his long, lean body on the arm of her chair. He placed an affectionate kiss (and a few cake crumbs) on the top of her hair. When Frederick paused for breath, he said, "Hello, Sis. Why so solemn?"

Hazel smiled warmly at Frederick to show she had been listening to his speech, then turned to her brother, her smile disappearing. "Papa wants to see you in the library immediately," she told him. Cornelius sighed, his wiry frame tensing in anticipation of the imminent scold. "Oh, Cornelius," Hazel said, clutching her slender hands in her lap. "Why must you do this? You know how it frustrates Papa. Then he becomes angry with you and you both are miserable. Why haven't you been attending classes?"

"Because they're boring," Cornelius answered candidly, his chin rising in momentary defiance. He stuffed the rest of the cake in his mouth. "And because I've found a few fellows who like to hit baseballs," he added, his head dropping a bit as he mumbled around currants and crust.

"In this weather?" Hazel's eyes opened wide in astonishment. "I thought baseball was a summer game. You're always so dejected in September when the season's over. How can you play baseball in the winter?"

Cornelius reached for the last cake as much to evade the issue as to satisfy his hunger. When Hazel continued to wait for an answer, though, he said, "It isn't really winter yet, you know. We still have one day to go."

"Cornelius," Hazel said patiently.

"Well, we aren't *playing* baseball," Cornelius responded. "It's more like batting practice. I fire 'em in and the other fellows hit 'em out. Just to keep in shape for next spring. Once we get warmed up, we don't really notice the temperature." He took a polite bite of the cake this time, then added, "I'm getting quite sharp, you know."

"Are you?" Hazel was genuinely pleased with his achievement even though she wasn't exactly sure what it was. "Perhaps you should tell Papa that," she said, quietly reminding Cornelius of his appointment. "He's always admiring of success."

Cornelius's hand stopped halfway to his mouth at the mention of Edgar. "What kind of a mood is he in?" he asked.

Hazel considered a moment. "He was, um, a little vexed," she finally answered, patting her brother's hand in sympathy. "But on the whole, I think he's approachable."

"He always is to you," Cornelius said gloomily. "He saves up all his black thunder for me." He lifted the half-eaten cake, partly in resignation, partly as a farewell salute. He stood up and headed for the door, a good deal less jaunty than when he had entered.

"Oh, dear," Hazel said again when he'd gone. "Poor Cornelius."

It was Frederick's turn to pat Hazel's hand. "You mustn't put yourself in a fret pitying Cornelius," he said, not unkindly. "Your brother has brought this on himself. He's old enough to know that he can't play games whenever he pleases."

This time Hazel seemed immune to Frederick's touch as she struggled to find a solution for the problem that created the one discordant note in her contented life. "Baseball is a professional sport," she said hopefully. "If Cornelius were to be paid for playing, it wouldn't be like a child's game. Given his enthusiasm for it, perhaps it would be the wisest course for him to pursue."

"Baseball is a poor man's sport," Frederick explained indulgently, echoing the argument that Edgar had made a hundred times before. "Cornelius would earn barely enough to buy a clean collar once a week. Besides, it's a young man's sport. His career would be over before half his life had passed. Then where would he be? It's a foolish idea." He shook his head. "I can excuse you for suggesting it in a flurry of feminine sentimentality, but Cornelius needs to be more sensible."

Her slender neck arched gracefully and her dark eyelashes made a beautiful fringe against the pale, silky skin of her cheeks as Hazel looked down at her hands, again clutched together in her lap. After a moment she unclasped her hands to smooth an imaginary wrinkle from her skirt. Finally she looked up. "I'm sure you're right, Frederick," she said softly.

"Of course I am," Frederick said, smiling his approval of her conclusion.

"If you two are going to continue talking about baseball, I'm going home," Lucy said with a pout. Her annoyance was only partially pretend. She stood up and reached behind her for her cloak, then made a great show of adjusting it around the big, mutton-leg sleeves of her silk blouse.

"No, please don't go," Hazel begged, jumping up and going over to her friend. She took both of Lucy's hands in hers and pulled her back down on the brocade divan. "We'll change the topic instantly," she promised, more than willing to do so for her own sake as much as for Lucy's. She had felt strangely uneasy on the rose velvet chair, a tickle of doubt disturbing her usual serenity. She was glad to have the opportunity to remove herself physically and mentally from the uncomfortable position.

"Tell me how plans are progressing for your Christmas party," she said, her equanimity returning already. Mollified, Lucy launched into a description of the pine-bough sprays and boxwood garlands that would decorate the Whitakers' mansion around the corner on Commonwealth Avenue.

The huge house looked every bit as festive as Lucy had prophesized when Hazel entered on her father's arm on Friday evening. An immense wreath, laden with bunches of fruit and nuts and tied with tartan bows, hung on the wide front door. Swags of red velvet ribbons and holly branches festooned the foyer, where a flock of maids waited to take their wraps. Down the staircase drifted the sound of an orchestra playing Strauss's *Blue Danube* waltz. And everywhere the daily glow of gaslight had been replaced by candles. Hundreds of them, burning from silver candelabras and crystal chandeliers.

"It looks wonderful," Hazel told Lucy as soon as she spotted her at the bottom of the staircase, greeting guests. "You and your mother have done a spendid job."

"It does look lovely, doesn't it?" Lucy said happily, looking very lovely herself in a blue moire gown the color of her eyes.

"Merry Christmas, Mr. Merriwether," Mrs. Whitaker said, coming up beside Lucy. She smiled and held out her hand. "How nice to have you here."

"I'm honored to be here, Mrs. Whitaker," Edgar replied, taking her hand and bowing slightly.

"It's so seldom we see you," Mrs. Whitaker continued. "Dear Hazel is like one of our family, you know. Sometimes I worry that you'll think ill of us for stealing her from you so frequently."

Edgar gave a deprecating shrug and struck a pose with his hands behind the back of his black evening jacket. "Not at all," he said. "I'm satisfied that she's in the best of company."

"Edgar. Merry Christmas," Mr. Whitaker boomed, joining them with his hand extended. He scarcely gave Edgar a chance to graze it with his own before he moved on to Hazel. "How are you tonight, dear girl?" he asked. John Whitaker was as tall as Frederick, and as imposing, though not nearly as trim. His features, once as finely cut as his son's, were now lost in the puffiness that comes from too much sherry before dinner and too much brandy after it. "You look even more enchanting than usual."

"Indeed you do," came Frederick's voice behind them.

Hazel turned, smiling in pleasure at the admiration in his tone. Her gown of claret-colored peau de soie was extremely elegant, swooping low to reveal the luscious skin of her breast, then swirling from her slim waist with simple grace. It was the excitement of the evening, though, the happy spirit of Christmas, that brought an extraordinary light to her eyes and an almost beatific radiance to her expression.

"Merry Christmas, Frederick," she said, that radiance reflecting in her voice. "I must say that you look especially dashing this evening, too." They made an exceptionally attractive pair. Frederick's blond hair and snow-white shirt accented Hazel's dark hair and gown.

"You two can't loiter in the foyer ogling each other forever," Lucy said saucily, giving Hazel a little push. "Go up and enjoy the party. I promise I'll send Frederick along as soon as everyone has arrived."

"Lucy, you're very naughty," her mother reprimanded mildly. "But, yes, you must go on." She shooed the Merriwethers toward the stairs with the peacock feather fan she wore suspended from her wrist.

"Save some space on your dance card for me," Frederick called after Hazel, just catching her arm with the tips of his fingers.

A shiver shot through Hazel at the touch of his warm hand on her bare skin. "Of course," she said, turning around on the first step, her slow smile telling him he could claim as many dances as he wished. Then Edgar gave a gentle tug on her arm, and she turned forward again to sweep up the stairs and to enter the ballroom with an exclamation of delight.

"How clever of Lucy and Mrs. Whitaker to use candles, don't you think, Papa?" she said, feasting her eyes on the gay sight before her. "The light has such texture. Quick! Look at Elizabeth Baldwin," she said, discreetly gesturing at the waltzing figure of her friend. "Don't her diamond earrings seem like sparkling stars?"

Looking around the room, she almost wished she had brought her sketch pad. "Wouldn't it be wonderful to capture this scene forever?" she murmured, momentarily lost in thought. "It's like a painting come to life."

Edgar stared at the swirl of dancers, his forehead furrowed, but he saw only a party. A very sumptuous party with very grand guests, but only a party nonetheless. "Pretty," he commented matter-of-factly. "But not so pretty as you, dolly," he added with decided pride. "Did you see? They all agreed. There isn't a lady here tonight who is your match, with or without diamond earrings." He gave the curt nod he habitually gave in business to signal his offer wasn't open to negotiation.

Hazel quickly returned to the present, laughing gladly and hugging the arm she was holding. She felt as if her heart were dancing, even if her feet hadn't yet started. It was a glorious world, resplendent in Christmas finery, and tonight, for two very important men, she was in the middle of it.

Her happiness only increased as the evening went on. As they drank eggnog toasts rich with Caribbean rum. As a hundred voices joined to sing joyous carols. As they went down to a supper of Cotuit oysters, Maine lobsters, and champagne ice. Mostly, though, as she sailed around the dance floor clasped in Frederick's arms.

"This has been the most marvelous evening I've ever spent," she told him when the evening had long passed into night and was heading toward morning. They were floating around the nearly empty ballroom as the orchestra wrung out its last few weary notes. She was tired, but in a languid, delicious sort of way. For one brief instant as the music stopped, she leaned against Frederick's hand, splayed in the middle of her back. It felt so strong, so sure, as if he could hold her secure forever. She let her eyes flutter shut, sealing the pleasure of the moment.

"The evening isn't over yet," he told her softly, close to her ear. Her eyes flew open and her fatigue vanished. He was so near, she could feel his breath on her skin. Her heart was pounding wildly as she looked into his eyes, blue and intense. "I still have to give you your Christmas gift," he said in a voice so low she had to lean over closer to hear him.

"My Christmas gift?" she echoed, barely able to breathe. "But it isn't Christmas until Sunday." Her own voice sounded faint, her words silly. She couldn't collect her thoughts.

"I can't wait until Sunday," Frederick said, the corners of his eyes crinkling in a slight smile. He reached into the pocket of his jacket and drew out a tiny velvet box. His smile deepening, he placed it in her palm, then folded her hand over it. "Merry Christmas, Hazel darling," he said, lifting her hand and laying a kiss across the curled fingers.

For a moment Hazel couldn't move. She stood paralyzed in

the center of the vast room, conscious only of the smell of candles guttering out. And of the box in her hand, its velvet surface crushed against her palm. She stared at it.

"Open it, darling," Frederick prompted.

Hazel raised her eyes and saw Frederick looking at her, his face mellow in the light of the candles. Beyond him, around the fringes of the dance floor, she saw her father, his arms folded expectantly over his starched white shirt, and Mr. and Mrs. Whitaker, and Lucy, hovering in excitement. In her mind she saw the lavish ballroom as it had been when she'd entered, awhirl with beautiful silk gowns and scented of perfume. She looked again at Frederick and saw a strong, handsome man, perfectly part of this scene. Suddenly her racing pulse slowed and a sense of peace filled her.

She opened the box. A ring sat inside. A ring with an enormous cabochon sapphire surrounded by dozens of glittering diamonds. "It's magnificent, Frederick," she said, her voice calm and sure.

Frederick plucked the ring from the box and slid it onto her finger. He again held her hand to his lips. "Darling Hazel," he said solemnly, "would you do me the extraordinary honor of becoming my wife?"

Hazel looked directly at him and smiled. "Yes, Frederick," she said. "I will."

"My dearest one," he said fervently, clutching her hand in both of his. The orchestra began to play the "Spring Concerto" from *The Four Seasons* by Vivaldi, a forgotten work by a forgotten composer, but one of Hazel's favorites. "It shall be my undeviating goal to make you happy," he promised her.

Hazel smiled again and lifted her face to him for a kiss. "I'm sure you shall, Frederick," she said. "I'm sure I'll always be very happy." The chaste touch of his lips on her cheek made her feel warm and happy already.

"My blessings, dolly," Edgar said, appearing at her side. "I wish you both a good life. I know that Frederick will take care of you."

"Thank you, Papa," Hazel said, gently extracting herself from Frederick's grip and leaning into her father's stiff embrace. She knew that Edgar approved of the match, that, in fact, he'd always hoped for it. No doubt he'd quickly given Frederick his permission for the marriage.

"Congratulations, dear girl," John Whitaker boomed.

"I'm so pleased to have you for a daughter," said his wife.

"And I'm pleased to have you for a sister because now you'll have no choice but to loan me your hats and shawls when I ask," said Lucy, giving Hazel an affectionate hug.

Laughing, Hazel returned the hug. "Not the ones I bought in Paris," she warned.

Then she stood next to Frederick, and they accepted the good wishes of the friends who crowded around. Hazel's smile grew wider and her pleasure deeper with every compliment. "You know you've made the catch of all times, don't you?" Elizabeth Baldwin whispered.

"You're just what Freddy needs," Frank Bigelow told her. "You'll show him there's something else in the world besides that sloop of his."

"Or the tennis lawn," Horace Parker seconded.

"You're the perfect match," Marian Chapman decided. "Like the characters in one of Laura Jean Libby's novels."

"Happy endings, eh?" Edgar said to John Whitaker as they stood on the edge of the group. "I couldn't be more pleased to have our families joined."

"Mmmm," John responded noncommittally. "Hazel's a jewel," he added more enthusiastically. "We all adore her."

"Yes, she's a pearl," Edgar agreed. "I'll miss her. But I know she'll be in fine hands. Frederick's a good lad."

"Indeed," John said dryly, disliking to have his son's character assessed by Edgar. Although he wholeheartedly approved of Hazel, finding her not only beautiful but also unquestionably refined, he was less expansive about the other Merriwethers. He thought that Cornelius was a churlish youth and that Edgar displayed the tasteless traits of the newly rich.

"Quite interesting, too, don't you think, that both families should be involved in wool?" Edgar continued. "Different aspects, of course, but interdependent, eh?" He was referring to the fact that while his business was brokering raw wool, the Whitakers owned mills that turned those fleeces into yard goods. They had two mills in Lawrence, the reputed "worsted capital of the world," twenty-five miles north of Boston, one in Maine, and one in Providence.

"Quite interesting," John agreed politely, looking around for a plausible escape.

Edgar seemed unaware of John's discomfort. "You might say it was prophetic that I bought some shares in your Great Stone

Dam Mill in Hazel's name," he went on. "At the time, of course, I bought them as a tribute to her friendship with Lucy, but look how things have turned out." He gave a nearly humorless chuckle. "Full circle, eh?"

John Whitaker gave him a weak smile. He had found Edgar's purchase slightly ostentatious when it had occurred. He found Edgar's mention of it now definitely déclassé. "Ah, here's an opening in the crowd," he said. "I think I'll take this opportunity to offer Frederick my felicitations." He gave Edgar a light slap on the shoulder. "Nice chatting with you," he said, moving away.

Except for Cornelius's stoic reception of her engagement, Hazel's happiness remained untouched throughout Christmas and the week before the New Year. There was a dinner or a dance almost every night, which she attended with Frederick. Always a favorite guest in the past, now Hazel found herself the focus of each gathering. The attention was exhilarating. What a wonderful life we'll have together, she thought.

Until the party at Elizabeth Baldwin's, celebrating the first day of 1893. In deference to it falling on a Sunday, Elizabeth had invited only a few friends for a quiet afternoon by the fire. Roasting chestnuts and drinking mulled cider, they reminisced about the past year and made resolutions for the new one.

"Do you remember the bet Harry Russell made with Lester Howland last summer in Marblehead?" Frank Bigelow asked, pulling the pan from the fire and shaking the roasted chestnuts into a bowl.

"Those two are forever wagering over something," Hazel said, curled up on a fringed hassock by Frederick's chair. She reached for a chestnut when Frank passed the bowl. It was burning hot. She quickly juggled it from one hand to the other until it was cool enough to peel. Then smiling, she looked up at Frederick and offered him the fragrant treat. Beaming back, Frederick took it and popped it in his mouth.

"Do you mean the raw egg bet?" Marian said, grimacing. "That was disgusting."

"What's this?" Frederick asked, curiosity distracting him from his contemplation of Hazel.

"You can't tell me you've forgotten already," Frank said incredulously. "It was the high point of the summer."

"The low point, you mean," Marian amended.

"We weren't in Marblehead last summer," Frederick reminded them. "You'll have to enlighten us."

"Oh, right," Frank said, slapping his forehead. "You were abroad. Well, the way it went—"

"Simply put," Marian interrupted, not anxious to have the story drag on, "Harry bet Les that he couldn't swallow two dozen raw eggs. Which Les did and then was vilely ill."

"How awful," Hazel said in distress, while the others laughed. "Whatever possessed them to make such a bet?"

"As I started to explain," Frank said, giving Marian a quelling glare, "Harry's mother had this peculiar old opera singer for a houseguest. A Spaniard, I think."

"He was Italian," Marian corrected, undaunted. "Signore Cavatelli. He *was* a bit queer," she added. "He used to wear his bedroom slippers to the beach." This time Hazel laughed with everyone else.

"Anyway," Frank continued, raising his voice above the laughter, "Signore Cavatelli had the habit of taking a raw egg with whiskey every morning. He claimed it was good for his throat. He made quite a ceremony of it. It finally became too broad a target for that pair of clowns to miss. One evening when they'd had a trifle too much champagne at Charlie Gardener's regatta party, they got into a debate over the merits of an egg toddy. Les took the position that it was a sound idea, and Harry, typically, disagreed. The next thing we all knew, the bet was on. And the rest . . . well, Marian's told you the rest."

"They're so passionate about their food, those Italians," Frederick remarked when the roar of laughter subsided this time. "Do you remember that odd fellow we met in Italy, Hazel? The one whose name was half English and half Italian?"

Frederick's question was merely rhetorical and asked with only a quick glance at Hazel. Without waiting for a reply, he continued telling his story to the eager group. "He was well behaved enough. One didn't mistrust him, but what a funny character. He kept appearing in the cities we were visiting. In Milan and Verona and Venice. With that almost childlike sense of hospitality they have, he would insist on showing us around the main cathedral, or what have you, then he would take us for refreshments." Frederick laughed and shook his head.

"What a to-do," he said. "He would offer us some flavored

ices or a bowl of strawberries as if they were the crown jewels. He was so proud of them."

While the others laughed again, Hazel pressed the back of her hand against her forehead. It was fortunate that Frederick hadn't expected an answer because she'd been unable to respond to his question. Or to correct his mistaken geography. His mention of Marco had had an instantaneous effect on her, choking off her breath and sending hot and cold flashes shooting through her. She certainly did remember him. She remembered him all too well.

She remembered his Renaissance face with its high rosy cheeks and the air of tremendous health and vitality that he exuded. She remembered his large, dramatic build, his deep blue eyes, and the scent of sandalwood soap that always clung to him. Mostly, though, she remembered him saying, as they drifted down a Venetian canal in the late afternoon, lulled by delicious food and exquisite wine, "Genuine emotion is the essence of life."

"Hazel?"

She looked up, dazed, to see Frederick's worried expression. "Are you all right, darling? You look so flushed. Is the fire too hot? Shall we move the fireback?"

"No, no," she said quickly, jumping up. "I am a bit warm, but I'll just move my seat." Before Frederick could protest, Hazel dragged the hassock a few feet away. She felt the same inexplicable need to distance herself from him as she had felt the afternoon he and Lucy had dropped in for tea a few weeks ago. She had no idea why, but the excitement had suddenly gone out of the afternoon—indeed, out of the whole holiday season. It had even disappeared from the prospect of her marriage.

She shook her head. It can't be true, she thought in alarm. I'm just annoyed at Frederick's patronizing description of Marco. Then, in greater alarm, she wondered how that thought had entered her mind. It seemed disloyal to Frederick. I'm just overtired, she thought, forcing her attention back to the party. Marco means nothing to me. I'll never see him again.

Later, when she and Frederick were walking home through the early winter twilight, he suddenly halted, turned her around toward him, and took both her hands in his. "I must tell you, darling, that you look especially beautiful tonight."

Hazel's heart started beating rapidly as she sensed what was going to come next. Strangely, though, it was anxiety and not anticipation that caused her agitation. Still, her voice remained calm as she said, "Thank you, Frederick. It's very gallant of you to say so."

She gave a tentative tug on her hands to see if she could free them. Frederick's grip was firm. Her heart beat harder. "I've always been fond of the cerulean-blue color of this dress," she said, a tiny touch of desperation tingeing her tone.

Frederick drew her closer to him. "It's very nice," he said, his voice low. "Very nice." He leaned forward and crushed his mouth against hers.

Fighting back the panic that jolted her entire being, Hazel told herself that Frederick had every right to expect a kiss. After all, he's going to be my husband, she thought. Her lips felt dry and bruised beneath the pressure of his mouth. We shall have a perfect marriage, she told herself resolutely. We were made for each other. Everyone agrees.

But when his hands released her and rubbed against the cashmere bodice of her coat, she leapt back, her heart pounding in her throat.

"Forgive me, darling," Frederick said instantly, although his contrite words were at odds with the desire making his voice hoarse. He reached out a hand to steady her, but Hazel reflexively flinched away.

"I'm so sorry," Frederick said, withdrawing his hand, his voice returning to normal. "I was overcome. I apologize. It was unconscionable of me not to be more considerate. Please say you'll forgive me."

"Yes, of course," Hazel said, somewhat shakily. "You took me by surprise is all. It was merely a moment's fright. I'm afraid I'm unaccustomed to the force of masculine, uh, ardor."

Even as she said the words, though, the memory of another kiss intruded. A warm, languorous kiss full of the splendor of Venice and the joy of life. She had known that one was coming, too, but she had waited for it serenely. She had welcomed it, and she had lost herself in it. Unconsciously, her hand came up and wiped across her lips, but as she took a deep breath and rethreaded her arm through Frederick's, she wasn't sure which kiss she was removing.

# CHAPTER

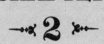

Beethoven's Fifth Symphony was still reverberating in Hazel's head as she turned on the top step to wave good night to the Chapmans, waiting in their carriage at the curb. Then she let herself into the house. It was late and she didn't want to disturb the servants.

They had just come from the Saunders Theater, across the Charles River in Cambridge, where they'd heard not only Beethoven's Fifth, but also Bach's Suite in D Minor. Knowing that Frederick would be away overnight, Marian had invited Hazel to the concert. What a dear friend she is, Hazel thought fondly. How fortunate I am.

Her contentment with her life had returned. As winter had slid into spring, she had managed to suppress the memories that had caused her such consternation on New Year's Day. She had regained her equilibrium. And her enjoyment of being engaged to Frederick. She liked attending costume balls at the Hotel Vendomme or after-opera suppers at the Ritz on his arm. It also gave her great pleasure to pick out delicate dishes and fine linens for her future home. However, each time Frederick asked her to set a date for the wedding, something inside her froze.

"It's such an important decision," she would tell him, and herself, too. "I must have more time to think about it."

She wasn't thinking about it tonight, though. As she unfastened her evening cloak and shook off the raindrops clinging to it, she was thinking only that she was glad she hadn't accompanied

Frederick to New York as he'd suggested. It was raw for the end of April, no weather to be outside watching the international naval pageant he had gone to see. She had no doubt it was magnificent, with the finest ships from ten nations parading about in New York Harbor, firing off salutes to the review of President Cleveland, himself, but she preferred the more subtle splendors of the Boston Symphony Orchestra.

With her cloak draped over her arm, Hazel walked quietly up the stairs, pausing in surprise in the second-floor hall. There was a light coming from the library at the front of the house. In the moment that she stood debating whether to go in or go on up to bed, Edgar came bursting through the doorway in pajamas and paisley silk dressing gown. Behind his spectacles, his eyes were as cold and grim as the night. His mustache was quivering with rage.

"Papa," Hazel said, reaching out a hand in concern.

"Past time for you to be in bed, young lady," Edgar snapped as he brushed by her on the way up to his own room.

Shocked, Hazel jumped back, nearly falling down the stairs. Her father never spoke to her like that. She moved quickly to obey. Halfway up the second flight of stairs, it occurred to her that the light had still been on in the library when Edgar had left. That wasn't like him, either. Her feet slowed, then stopped. She hesitated. Her father's harsh words had replaced the Beethoven ringing in her ears, but curiosity finally won out. Tiptoeing, she retraced her steps and peered around the half-open door into the library.

"Hello, sis," Cornelius said. Hands stuffed deep in his pockets, long legs stretched straight out in front of him, he was the picture of dejection as he slumped in a green velvet chair.

"Whatever has happened?" Hazel asked, coming swiftly into the room and closing the door behind her. "What are you doing home on a Thursday night? And at this hour? You've missed your curfew. Is that why Papa is so angry?"

She perched on the very edge of a chair opposite her brother, her evening cloak still over her arm. "He was practically apoplectic, Cornelius," she said, leaning forward. "I'm afraid it's dangerous for his health. What could you possibly have done or said to put him in such a state?"

Cornelius shrugged and lolled his head back against the carved flowers and crests on the top of the chair. "I'd tell you," he said, "but you'd only take his side. You usually do, and I've already had an earful of that opinion tonight. I'm not up to another lecture on my foolishness."

Dread and remorse filled Hazel in equal parts. She sat back on her chair. "I'm sorry if I seem to appear unsympathetic," she said, choosing her words carefully. "I can only hope you realize that it isn't my intention—that it's never been my intention—to hurt or belittle you in any way. I want, more than anything, for you to be content with your life."

Abruptly leaning forward again, she stretched an anxious hand over to her brother's knee. "You've joined the Boston baseball team, haven't you?" It was more of a statement than a question.

A wide smile split Cornelius's face for the first time that evening. He had an endearing grin, full of white teeth and bracketed by double dimples. It made his gray eyes squint. Hazel had been unable to resist his grin ever since he was a baby and she was a little girl in braids.

"I wish I had, sis," he said, pulling his hands out of his pockets and locking them together behind his head. "If it were as easy as going over to the grounds and signing up, I probably would have done it long ago. But the fact is that they pick me more than I pick them."

Hazel sat up straight. "Well, if baseball isn't the problem," she said, truly puzzled, "what is?"

"I didn't say baseball wasn't the problem," Cornelius answered, studying the stucco patterns on the ceiling. "I just said that I hadn't joined the Beaneaters." He peeked at her out of the corner of his eye. She was sitting quietly, no sign of wrath or condemnation on her face. "I took the train to New York today to see the opening ball game of the season," he blurted out, quickly reverting his gaze.

"Oh, dear." Hazel sighed, her shoulders sagging. "So Papa's angry because you were truant from your classes today."

"No, not exactly."

"No?"

"Well, yes, Papa's angry, but no, I wasn't exactly truant from my classes today."

"Cornelius," Hazel said firmly, laying her cloak across her lap and folding her hands on top of it. "Please stop inspecting the plaster work and tell me exactly what *did* happen."

Reluctantly Cornelius shifted in his chair, crossing his arms high on his chest and peering over them at his sister. "I was thrown out of Harvard last week," he mumbled into the lapels of his coat. Hazel stiffened but didn't say a word. "The dean called it 'profound intellectual apathy.'"

A ghost of his grin returned as Cornelius hitched himself up in his chair. "I guess he meant I was failing all my subjects," he said. After a moment's reflection he added, "Unless he was referring to the fact that I rarely showed up for lectures."

"Oh, Cornelius," Hazel said with another deep, worried sigh.

"Stop." Cornelius held up his hand. "I can guess by your expression that you're going to tell me it's time for me to grow up, that I'm ruining my life, wasting golden opportunities, throwing away my future, and so on and so on and so on." Defiance made him sit up a little straighter. "Well, you needn't bother to expend the breath. I've had that speech twice already tonight, and I certainly don't need to hear it a third time."

"Twice?" Hazel asked, more surprised by that fact than by her brother's outburst. She *had* been about to make precisely that same speech, though she couldn't really blame him for being upset at the thought of it. He knew it as well as she did, they both having learned it from Edgar.

"Yes, twice." Cornelius slouched back down in his chair. "First from your fiancé, and then from Papa."

"My fiancé?" This time Hazel was incredulous. "Frederick?"

"Frederick," he confirmed bitterly. "I had the misfortune to come head to head with him on the train coming home from New York."

For a moment Hazel's worry moved from Cornelius to Frederick. "What on earth was Frederick doing on the train?" she asked. "He wasn't meant to come home until tomorrow, after a gala reception at the New York Yacht Club. He was very much looking forward to it."

Cornelius shrugged, as indifferent to Frederick's frustration as Frederick was to his. "He said something about a problem in one of their mills in Lawrence that required his attention first thing in the morning."

"I hope it isn't serious. Did he say?" Concern furrowed her brow. "It had to be fairly grave if it caused him to miss the reception," she reasoned out loud.

Cornelius shrugged again and stuffed his hands back in his pockets. "I doubt it," he said. "He couldn't have been too preoccupied or he wouldn't have been able to preach to me the usual sermon *and* escort me home *and* bang the knocker on the door until Papa woke up."

"Frederick did that?" Hazel asked. Her brow unfurrowed as an increasingly familiar sense of disquiet filled her.

Cornelius nodded sullenly.

"Well," she said quickly to distract herself from the unwelcome feeling, "I'm sure he was only thinking of your best interest." Reaching up, she busied herself with unpinning her hat and patting her hair. "I'm sure he only wants to see you change your ways for your own good."

"Maybe I don't want to change my ways!" Cornelius shouted, jumping up with a fist clenched. "Why doesn't anyone ever think of that?" He shook the fist at Hazel. "You see? I knew you'd side against me. I knew you'd take Papa's view." He stalked over to the fireplace and leaned against the mantel, his jaw jutting angrily.

Guilt squeezed Hazel's stomach and made her ears burn. He was right, she thought. She wasn't being fair. She looked down at the pile of clothes in her lap, absently curling the ostrich feather on her hat around her index finger. It was the same situation: She felt twisted and torn between what made Cornelius happy and what their father said was right.

She looked up at Cornelius. "Papa can't be completely mistaken, can he?" she asked. "See what a good life he's provided for us. He started out poor. You know that he was conscripted into the army during the war. He was a private, as low ranking as there was. But he worked hard and he seized opportunities . . . "

"And he got a contract to sell woolen blankets to the Union Army," Cornelius interrupted. "I've heard the story, too. A dozen times. How he used his profits to start his brokerage and how he's built it up. I know. I know." He banged his fist on the mantel. "But it's *his* business," he said. "It's not mine."

"It will be yours someday," she reminded him.

"I know," Cornelius repeated, but in a more defeated tone. He ran his hand through his hair, then, eyes closed, he rested his forehead against its palm. "I have to start work at the warehouse tomorrow," he said in a barely audible voice. "The first day of my life-long career."

There was such obvious pain in his voice, Hazel's heart wrenched. She stood up, putting her cloak and hat on the chair behind her, and walked over to where he stood. "I'm sorry," she said softly. Taking his free hand in hers, she lightly rubbed each individual finger, as she used to when he was little and needed comforting.

Cornelius opened his eyes and looked at her. "He's forbid me to go to the ball grounds, sis," he said miserably.

"Oh, no," Hazel said, dismayed. She hugged the hand she was holding.

"I've half a mind to go off and play ball anyway and hang the consequences," Cornelius muttered, but without a lot of conviction. "Maybe I'm not good enough to pitch for Boston, but there's bound to be a team in some town, somewhere, that would pay me a few dollars to play."

"Oh, no," Hazel said again, more alarmed. "You mustn't."

"Why not?" Cornelius asked sharply, pulling his hand away from her. "Are you going to tell me one more time what a mistake I'll be making?"

"No," Hazel responded simply. "I'm going to tell you how terribly much I'll miss you if you go."

"Oh." For a minute there was silence, then he said gruffly, "I guess I'd miss you, too."

"Cornelius," Hazel said coaxingly, taking his hand again, "if you stay and start working in Papa's warehouse, I promise I'll try to talk him into letting you go to a ball game now and then. Sometimes he listens to me."

"He always listens to you," Cornelius corrected, as he squeezed her hand in affection.

"Well?"

"All right," he consented.

"Good." She smiled up at him, the tranquillity restored to her face.

He smiled back, then said, "I guess I'd better hit the hay if I'm going to start work early tomorrow morning." Throwing an arm around Hazel's shoulders, he walked with her out of the room, turning off the light as they left.

"How was the game?" Hazel asked. "I hope it was worth all this fuss."

Cornelius gave an ironic hoot of laughter. "It was rained out," he responded.

Almost two weeks went by before Hazel saw an opportunity to keep her end of the baseball bargain. Over the years she had

learned to gauge her father's moods and to present him with her
requests accordingly. She had only a vague idea of what precipitated his spurts of good humor, guessing that it must be some sort
of business triumph, but she had no trouble recognizing them or
taking advantage of them. Just as she knew better than to approach
him with a problem, either personal or household, when he was
tense or distracted.

Cornelius, however, was ruled more by impatience than perception. "When are you going to talk to Papa?" he asked, barging
into the Rose Parlor on his way upstairs after work. "The home
opener is next Monday and I'd give anything to go. Kid Nichols
will be pitching. He had a bang-up season last year—thirty-five
and sixteen with an E.R.A. of two point eight three. And it seems
like he's primed to do even better this season. He beat Washington
yesterday, nine to three. I've just got to go."

"That certainly sounds impressive," Hazel commented, resting
her sketch pad in her lap and regarding her brother calmly.
"Although I'll have to take your word that it signifies an exceptional performance."

Grinning a bit sheepishly, Cornelius dropped into the chair next
to Hazel. "It does," he said, pulling the sketch pad out of her hands
and turning it around to have a look. "He's the best wheelman that
Boston's got. Say, where's this?" He cocked his head as he tried
to place the palaces and canals in the drawing.

"In Italy," Hazel answered evenly, retrieving the book and
placing it facedown on the table on the other side of her. "Perhaps
I'll talk to Papa after dinner," she said. "He was in a very anxious
state at the beginning of the week, but he seemed nearly normal last
evening. And when he came home a little while ago, he appeared
quite amiable. Yes, tonight," she decided. "Make an excuse to
leave the parlor early, Cornelius."

The excuse Cornelius made was plausible enough, but a touch
overdone on the delivery. "Hooo, hum," he yawned, stretching
his long arms miles over his head. "It's been an exhausting week in
the warehouse. I think I'll try to get a few extra hours of sleep."

Only a slight twitch of the tiny dot above the corner of Hazel's
mouth revealed her amusement. "That seems like a wise idea,"
she said, looking up from her petit point without missing a stitch.
"I'm sure you'll feel more refreshed in the morning. Good night,
Cornelius."

"Good night. Good night, Papa."

Edgar regarded him over the top of the *Boston Evening Globe* for a moment before nodding and saying, "Good night." He lifted the newspaper again and continued his reading.

After Cornelius had gone, the only sound in the room was the ticking of the ormolu clock over the mantel and the occasional turning of pages. Finally Hazel set down her needlework and said, "Papa?"

From behind the paper Edgar answered, "Yes, dolly?"

Hazel waited patiently until her father had finished what he was reading and looked over at her. "Papa," she said again. "Cornelius has been working awfully hard lately. Shouldn't he have some time off?"

Edgar's eyebrows raised, but he confined himself to saying, "He has his Sundays off."

"Yes," Hazel conceded, looking at the strand of petit point yarn she was running between her fingers. "But I was thinking it might be a treat for him to have a few hours on Monday afternoon as well. The Bostons will be playing their first baseball game of the year at the South End Grounds, and you know how much pleasure Cornelius gets from attending."

Edgar lowered the paper to his lap with a loud crumple. "So that's what that little theatrical was all about," he said. "He's put you up to this, hasn't he?"

Looking directly at her father now, Hazel shook her head. "I offered to speak to you," she said quietly. "It seems a small enough reward for his labors."

"Labors?" Edgar snorted. "Your brother is a hale and hearty youth of nineteen who's been counting bales of wool for scarcely two weeks. That's not what I call labor." Warming up, he wagged a finger at Hazel. "When I was nineteen, I marched all over Georgia with a fifty-pound pack on my back, sleeping in the mud and eating weevily biscuits. There was no thought of playing games, nor of any rewards, either. And there certainly wasn't any thought of taking time off."

Hazel let her gaze drop again. She felt the twinge of frustration that usually accompanied her efforts to bridge the differences between her father and her brother. "I'm sure it was very difficult for you," she said in a low voice.

"Of course it was difficult," Edgar replied, almost irritably. "It was a war."

He looked at her bent head, then added in a kinder tone, "Don't get me wrong, dolly. I don't wish a war on Cornelius." His voice grew harder again as he continued. "But your brother has got to learn what it means to work. He's got to learn the skills of doing business. He can't afford to go about with his head in the clouds, daydreaming about playing baseball. It was an unpromising ambition when he was ten years old. Now it's completely unacceptable.

"There are shaky times afoot," Edgar said, thrusting a handful of newspaper forward as if to show her the stories. "The economy is unstable and that damned Sherman Silver Purchase Act is going to bankrupt the Treasury. Every day there's another bank that's gone under. This is no time to be thinking about games. It's a time to get a solid grasp on business. The only way Cornelius is going to accomplish that is to set his nose to the grindstone and his mind to the task."

With another annoyed rattle of his paper, Edgar added, "He has a golden opportunity at the brokerage. I'm willing to teach him everything I know and to pass the company on to him someday. There are hundreds of bright young men who'd give their eyeteeth to be in Cornelius's position right now. And if I'm not mistaken, there'll be thousands more before the year is out."

"I had no idea things were in such a serious state," Hazel said, considerably startled. There hadn't been any hint that their pleasant life wasn't as comfortable and secure as it had always been.

"There's no reason you should have," Edgar said, his tone instantly moderating. "It was thoughtless of me to frighten you. I apologize. Don't think twice about it. Whatever happens is not going to affect us one bit. I'll see to that." He shook out his newspaper and resumed his reading.

Her moment's alarm relieved, Hazel picked up her needlework again. Papa's right, she thought. As usual. I'll just have to tell Cornelius what he said.

Her quick stitches slowed as she imagined her brother's reaction. He'll be horribly disappointed, Hazel thought. He'll be disinterested in Papa's dire predictions and unconcerned that thousands of young men might be eager for his job. He'd be just as happy to let one of them take his place. Poor Cornelius. It really doesn't matter to him if he inherits Papa's brokerage one day or not. I doubt he even cares whether he lives in a lovely house on Marlborough Street or in a tent. The only thing he truly wants is to play baseball.

"Papa?" she said, setting aside her needlework and sitting up on the edge of her seat. "As a special favor to me, Papa, would you let Cornelius go to the baseball game on Monday?"

Edgar let the newspaper drop into his lap again. He studied his daughter with a mixture of exasperation and affection. "That isn't a favor for you, dolly," he said. "It's a favor for Cornelius."

"But it would please me very much," she said softly.

Sighing in resignation, Edgar said, "You've got a good heart, Hazel. You're always asking favors for someone else. For your brother or some arts society or the coal man's sick child. All right, dolly. You know I can't refuse you. I'll let Cornelius off for a few hours on Monday, but I want you to promise me something."

"Anything, Papa," Hazel said, a delighted smile illuminating her face.

"Promise me you'll think of a favor I can do for *you*."

Hazel laughed, her heart light again. "I promise," she said.

"They won!" Cornelius announced at dinner Monday evening, his cheeks sunburned and his spirits completely restored. "It was a top-notch game, and they beat the New Yorks eight to six. Kid Nichols had those Giants swinging at shadows with his fastball. It's really something to see him on the mound."

"I understand the governor was in attendance," Hazel gently interrupted as she helped herself to a salmon crumpet and sliced cucumbers from the platter that Annie was holding. She could see a frown developing on her father's face and was anxious to make the discussion more palatable to him.

"Who, old Russell?" Cornelius asked, momentarily checked. "Yes, he was there, puffing on his fat Havana." Cornelius dismissed him with a shrug. "The grounds were packed. Someone told me there were ten thousand people in attendance. Did I tell you that Germany Long homered in the first inning?" He switched back to the more interesting topic. "What a surprise to see that horsehide sail over the fence. Long's just a little guy. He's the shortstop, you know, and he hit only six home runs all last season."

Edgar's interruption was more definite than Hazel's had been. "As a general rule," he stated, "I dislike discussing business at the dinner table, but I'm going to make an exception this evening." He waited in the surprised silence that ensued until Annie had set the platter on the sideboard and had gone back down to the kitchen.

To heighten the expectation, he sliced off a bite of the steaming croquette and slowly chewed it before continuing.

"I've booked passage for England on the twenty-sixth of this month," he announced.

Hazel's fish knife clattered to her plate. "What?" she exclaimed. "But that's next week. You can't just go abroad on a moment's notice."

"I don't see why not," Edgar replied, enjoying the shock—and the attention—his news created. Even Cornelius was staring at him, his baseball game forgotten. Edgar took another leisurely bite of salmon crumpet.

"I have some business to do in London," he explained. "Some of my best wool sources in the American Southwest have become unreliable because of the constant conflicts with cattlemen. As it is, American sheep can't begin to supply the quantity, or the quality, of fleeces that our mills require. I've been importing from England, Australia, and the Argentine right along, but I feel it's time to develop my English contacts."

"Remarkable," Hazel murmured, not only giving her father polite encouragement, but also expressing her amazement. In the last three minutes she had learned more about the affairs of Merriwether, Inc., than she had in her entire twenty-four years.

Edgar's nod acknowledged her remark at face value. "Mind you, English wool is two to three times the price of American stock, by the time the tariff's been paid, but the quality and variety is superb. And the English are too sensible to engage in these foolish sheep and cattle wars. They're more interested in making a profit."

He paused to push the last of his crumpet onto his fork. "There was a time when England wasn't so ready to do business with us, you know," he said, jabbing the laden fork through the air for emphasis. "Back in our colonial days, she actually prohibited the export of raw wool to us for fear we'd start weaving our own yard goods and lose our dependence on her. Of course, those times are long over."

He stuffed the salmon morsel into his mouth and followed it with the last wilted round of cucumber. "That was long before automation," he added. "There were no mills back then. Just individual weavers at their hand looms."

"I see," Hazel said, although she wasn't too sure of what he was saying. "How long will you be gone?"

"Not much more than a month, dolly," Edgar answered, just as Annie reentered with a platter of roast chicken and parslied new potatoes that had trundled up from the kitchen in the dumb-waiter. "I thought I'd take you with me, Cornelius," he said casually.

This time Hazel managed not to drop the silver serving pieces she had poised above a potato, though she looked up sharply as Cornelius gave a yelp. "Me?" he asked, dismayed.

"You," Edgar said more sternly. "This trip will give you a far more interesting view of the wool business than you're getting in the warehouse. It occurred to me that it's just what's needed to stir your enthusiasm for the brokerage." What he didn't add, but what everyone, including Annie, understood immediately was that this trip would also take Cornelius away from the temptation of the Boston diamonds. Not only did they have more sheep in England, they didn't have baseball.

"Maybe," Cornelius said glumly, spearing a drumstick as Annie held out the platter.

Once she got over her initial surprise, though, Hazel found that she agreed with her father. A month of travel had to be more stimulating than the daily grind of the warehouse. She wasn't sure what her brother did there all day, but he always came home looking pale and discouraged. "The sea voyage should be extremely pleasant at this time of year," she told him. "And London has some magnificent sights, not to mention an impressive portion of the Gonzaga art collection."

When Cornelius failed to look moved by this last information, she hastily added, "I know it isn't of much interest to you, but I'm very anxious to see it. There are some Mantegnas that are meant to be breathtaking. It was Vincenzo II, the seventh duke of Mantua, who sold the collection."

Cornelius poked his potatoes.

"I'm sure it's very lovely, dolly," Edgar said. "And I've no doubt that you'll see it one day. But I know you'll also enjoy staying with Lucy while we're gone."

"With Lucy?" It was Hazel's turn to feel a stab of dismay. In thinking of her brother's situation she had neglected to consider her own. She didn't know why, but the thought of being left with the Whitakers made her distinctly uneasy. "Surely it's improper," she said, casting around out loud for a logical reason. "Because of my relationship with Frederick, that is to say," she elaborated.

"Frederick can stay at his club while you are in residence on Commonwealth Avenue." Edgar waved his fork to indicate it was all arranged. "It's perfectly comfortable for him and perfectly respectable for you."

The uneasiness persisted. "Why can't I stay right here?" she asked. "There are seven servants in residence to safeguard me, and this way no one need be displaced. Doesn't it make more sense?"

"You know better than that, dolly," Edgar said between mouthfuls of chicken. He seemed to be the only one with an appetite. "I can't leave you here alone. It's unthinkable."

"Then let me come along," Hazel suggested. It was a last desperate attempt to avoid being sent to the Whitakers, but as soon as she said it, she liked the idea on its own.

· "This is a business trip, Hazel," Edgar said reproachfully. "Not a grand tour."

In any other situation Hazel would have tranquilly accepted her father's edict, but today she felt compelled, by an undefined and completely uncharacteristic urge, to press her case. "You can't possibly be doing business every moment of the day and evening," she cajoled. "Especially not on the crossings over and back. Think how pleasant it would be to have the whole family together in those instances. And during the time that your affairs occupy you, I can amuse myself in the galleries and art museums. It would be ideal for all of us."

"I think it's a first-rate scheme," Cornelius chimed in, looking animated for the first time since Edgar proposed his plan. If he had to go to England with his father, there was no question in his mind that the trip would be more agreeable if Hazel came along, too.

Although Edgar didn't give his consent, he didn't find the idea unappealing, either. There was something rather splendid about the notion of taking his daughter to England to indulge her desire to see some Italian paintings. "And what of Frederick?" he reminded her. "You can't just go off and leave your fiancé like that."

"It won't be for *very* long," Hazel hedged. "The month will go by swiftly for both of us. Besides," she added lightly, "you know the old saying, 'Absence makes the heart grow fonder.' "

"They'll have all summer in Marblehead to be together," Cornelius interjected persuasively.

When Edgar remained unconvinced, Hazel played her last card. "Papa," she said, putting her unused fork back on the table and folding her hands in her lap. "Remember when you made me promise to think of a favor you could do just for me?" She leaned toward him, her large eyes intent. "I've thought of it," she said. "Papa, will you please take me to England with you?"

"Well, dolly." Edgar patted his lips with his napkin while he digested this latest entreaty. "Well," he said again, spreading the napkin back across his chest. "Since you seem so determined, I suppose you might come along. But you'll have to set it right with Frederick," he warned.

Hazel sat back beaming, relief making her feel nearly dizzy. "I will," she said, taking up her fork again, her appetite returned. "He's very considerate. I'm sure he'll understand."


"What a piffle-brained idea," Frederick said in annoyance. "You can't just go traipsing off to England on a whim."

"It isn't precisely a whim, Frederick," Hazel answered calmly, though an icy knot had suddenly formed in her stomach. They were strolling under the willows in the Public Garden, watching the Swan Boats peddle by in the pond. Perfectly groomed patches of spring-green lawn rolled and dipped between the winding paths. "Papa has business to do in London, and he wants Cornelius to go with him. That would leave me in Boston alone."

"You'd hardly be alone, darling," Frederick said, the term of endearment at odds with his increasingly irritated tone. "You would stay in Commonwealth Avenue with Lucy and Charlotte for companionship and with Mother and Father for chaperons. It's a far more sensible idea. After all, it's time to set a date for our wedding and to start making plans. What could be more convenient than to have all you females under one roof to select the flowers and bows."

Although it was a beautiful May afternoon, Hazel was barely aware of the blue sky and balmy breeze. Flicking aside a feathery willow branch, she fought down a tiny wave of panic. "We can think about those details this summer," she said, her voice still calm. "We'll be more relaxed at the seaside, and plans will just fall into place. Besides, Frederick," she added, stopping and looking up at him, "this may be my last opportunity to be with my father and brother as a family."

Frederick looked down, his irritation diminishing at the sight of her lovely face. He took hold of her hand, resting lightly on his arm. "You ought to have consulted me before you made your travel arrangements," he admonished more gently. "While I certainly sympathize with your sentiments for making this trip, I feel you should balance them with your new responsibilities to me."

Hazel gave the hand holding hers a slight squeeze. "Of course you're right to be cross, dear Frederick," she said. "I haven't been fair to you, have I?" She tucked her hand more snugly into the crook of his elbow and recommended their leisurely stroll along the path. "I just thought that as it's only a little more than a month, you'd hardly notice I was gone."

Mollified by her show of contrition, Frederick was more expansive. "Not notice you were gone?" he asked in astonishment. "My darling, I miss you every moment that you aren't by my side."

"It's very dear of you to say so," Hazel told him with a smile. "Although I suspect that you're exaggerating."

"Not a bit," Frederick replied staunchly, returning her smile and dipping his head so his lips just brushed her hair. "You sustain me."

Hazel's smile broadened. "I doubt that as well," she said fondly. "I'm sure that someone as fit and vigorous as you requires more solid sustenance. For example, that wonderful apricot cake they make at the Ritz."

Frederick tossed back his head in a laugh. "I believe I detect a hint under that compliment. Very well. Shall we find our way out of the gardens and adjourn across the street for tea?"

With a matching laugh Hazel hugged his arm. "You are a dear," she said. "And I shall miss you, too, while I'm gone."

"While you're gone?" Frederick repeated, missing a step. He sounded distracted, as if he were trying to remember how and when that conclusion had been reached.

Although there was no break in either her smile or her even gait, Hazel found herself holding her breath.

"Well, yes, I suppose so," Frederick finally decided. "I'll be away a good deal myself next month. I promised John Paine I would help with the America's Cup trials. The Boston syndicate has come up with a challenger, you know. The *Jubilee*. She's a pretty boat, but I'm not sure she has the lines of a Cup holder. Her chine is a bit soft, in my opinion."

While Frederick expounded on the charms and flaws of the *Jubilee*, Hazel expelled her breath in relief.

# CHAPTER

—◦✦ **3** ✦◦—

A mound of fat, red strawberries, awash in double cream, sat in a glass bowl atop a frilly doily on a Spode plate on a heavy damask cloth. It looked elegant and delectable, but as Hazel stared, all she could see was a different dish of strawberries. Those had been tiny and wild and had been piled into a plain pottery bowl that had been set on a bare wooden table beneath an ancient grape arbor. Marco had sat next to her. She shook her head to rid it of the unwelcome image.

"I'm sorry, Papa. What did you say?" she asked, suddenly aware that her father was waiting for her to speak.

"Are your berries all right?" Edgar repeated from the other side of the hotel tea table. "You're glaring at them as if they had the blight. Shall I have the waiter bring you a fresh bowl?" He raised his hand to summon the stone-faced man in a black cutaway coat, standing at a discreet distance.

"No, no," Hazel said quickly, picking up the silver spoon laid by the plate. "The strawberries look wonderful. My mind was just wandering for a moment." Without elaborating, she scooped up the plumpest berry and took a bite. It was sweet and juicy. And tame. It tasted like neat English gardens rather than the Italian woods. "Delicious," she pronounced, smiling brightly. "I believe I'll have a lemon wafer as well." She reached for a cookie and took a nibble.

Cornelius was a lot less delicate, and a lot hungrier. He swabbed a crumpet with clotted cream, stuffed it in his mouth, chewed twice, and swallowed. "We had strawberries today at lunch," he told his sister as he contemplated the possibilities for the other crumpet on his plate. "And smoked trout and rack of lamb and fresh peas and potatoes with mint. We ran into this fellow at the Wool Exchange this morning, and he took us to lunch at his club. Wait till you meet him. I know you'll think he's first rate. And guess what, sis?"

"I can't imagine," Hazel replied, wondering how Cornelius could have any appetite at all after such an enormous lunch, let alone appear half starved.

Cornelius decided on gooseberry preserves. "He's heard about baseball," he said happily, slathering the jam on his crumpet.

"Has he?" Hazel asked idly, selecting another strawberry and remembering how Marco had insisted she have seconds.

His mouth full, Cornelius nodded. "Can you imagine an Englishman knowing about baseball?" he said after another gargantuan gulp. "He's even heard of Kid Nichols and that the Kid is having a record year. We had a bully talk about the Bostons."

"He's also the son of Lord Strathdorna," Edgar interrupted, looking considerably less enchanted than Cornelius by the baseball conversation. "The baron has one of the largest sheep holdings in the Scottish Highlands," he explained, taking a sip of tea. Evidently he'd been satisfied by the large lunch because he only toyed with a slice of date cake. "Although it seems to be his son Andrew, this 'fellow,' as Cornelius calls him, who runs the show. I did a bit of checking on him this afternoon," he said. "You see, Andrew invited us to be his guests at Strathdorna for several weeks. I accepted."

Hazel's spoon, rising out of the bowl bearing another perfect berry, fell back abruptly. "His guests?" she echoed. Edgar had her undivided attention now. "In Scotland?"

"Yes, dolly," Edgar said. He reached across the table to pat her hand. "I know it sounds a bit sudden, but Andrew was off to Scotland tonight and needed an answer before he left. I felt I couldn't pass it up. It's an excellent connection to have made and could lead to a very profitable business association. And," he added, lowering his voice, "he's a baron." Although it wasn't in Edgar's nature to be in awe of anyone, he was, like many self-made men, inexplicably impressed by titles. "All in all, I'd say it was a stroke of rare good luck." He sat back, well pleased.

"Yes, Papa, I'm sure it is," Hazel struggled to say. The idea of being a houseguest at a baronial manor wasn't completely unappealing, but she couldn't go barging in on someone she'd never met. "It's just that we know nothing about him. I don't even know what he looks like," she added, to illustrate the absurdity of the situation.

Edgar took her literally. "He's, um, tall." His hand waved over the top of his head as he sought to describe their new acquaintance. After a moment he gave up the task. "You'll see for yourself," he concluded, letting his hand fall back to his teacup. "He has a very nice manner."

"He wants me to teach him to play baseball," Cornelius said, eyeing his sister's almost untouched bowl of berries. The cream was turning pink. "When I told him we needed nine men to a side, he said we could get up two teams from among the crofters. That's what the Scots call the tenants on their land. Say, Hazel, are you going to eat your fruit?"

"A tall, nice, baseball enthusiast with sheep," Hazel murmured, pushing the plate toward Cornelius.

"We know a good deal more about him than that," Edgar said. He gave Cornelius a look that eloquently expressed his irritation with the incessant reference to baseball. "As I was saying," he continued, turning back to Hazel, "I made a few inquiries this afternoon and gathered quite a bit of information about Strathdorna's background."

"Yes?" Hazel sat forward to listen. She hoped the result of her father's investigation would make Scotland, and the Strathdornas, sound more enticing.

Edgar set his empty cup and saucer aside and folded his arms on the table. "I've learned that the present baron inherited the land from his father," he began, "who had inherited from *his* father, who came into possession of it back at the beginning of the century. There was some unrest at that time." Here he waved a hand in dismissal of that time.

"The Highland Clearances, Andrew called them," Cornelius interrupted, his voice surprisingly sober and focused. "It was a terrible period when tens of thousands of Scots were thrown off their farms so the landowners could graze English sheep instead."

"That will do, Cornelius," Edgar said warningly. Cornelius resumed his attack on the bowl of strawberries, though he seemed to lack some of his former appetite. Hazel again regarded her brother in wonder, her amazement this time caused by his outburst of indignation and compassion. It was the first time he'd ever shown an interest in something besides baseball.

Edgar cleared his throat pointedly. Hazel hastily returned her gaze to him. "Yes, Papa," she said. "The baron came into the land in the early part of the century. . . . "

"Correct," Edgar approved, continuing his lecture. "Now this first Strathdorna, I believe his name was Dougal, made a go of it. He got the sheep to turn a good profit. His son Hugh was equally ambitious and shrewd. He acquired adjacent holdings and increased the size of their flocks. Hugh reputedly knew more about sheep than any man in the Highlands. Some even claimed he was part sheep himself.

"It's the present baron, Malcolm, who seems to be uninvolved." Edgar paused, his brow wrinkling as he tried to understand this attitude. "There's a manager—factors, they call them here—but as I told you before, it appears to be Andrew who's taken charge." Edgar shrugged, not comprehending such an abdication of power, readjusted his spectacles, and went on.

"They say Malcolm only goes to Scotland for the shooting and the fishing in the summer and the fall. He spends the rest of his time here in town, either at his club or in the House of Lords. He's established *his* reputation as a speechmaker, although when I asked, no one could remember what his speeches were about."

"I see," Hazel said faintly. These Strathdornas were sounding more and more improbable. "And Lady Strathdorna?" she asked hesitantly, almost afraid to find out.

"Well," Edgar answered, suddenly hesitating, too. For the first time it occurred to him to view this trip from his daughter's perspective. Apart from the impressive title, it didn't have a lot to recommend it. "There doesn't seem to be a Lady Strathdorna," he said, his voice a little gruff, which was as close as he came to an apology. "There's no mention of her since Andrew was born. My guess is she died in childbirth."

When he saw the look of alarm on Hazel's face, he added encouragingly, "There's Malcolm's sister, Flora. She stays in Scotland all year long. Oversees the household, I suppose. She never married."

From the silence that followed, it became apparent that Edgar had finished, that he had given her all the information he had gathered. Taking a deep breath, Hazel drew herself up. "I'm sure it will be a very interesting trip," she started. Then stopped. She couldn't thing of anything else to add.

"I know this has come out of nowhere, dolly," Edgar said, still gruff. "It will delay our return by several weeks. I know how much you want to get back to Frederick so you can make your wedding plans. But this is a golden opportunity."

A guilty shock swept through Hazel when her father mentioned Frederick. She hadn't given him a single thought during this entire discussion. She'd been more concerned with the unknown Scottish lords than she'd been with her fiancé. Now that Edgar brought up the wedding, an increasingly familiar sense of uneasiness cut off her breath. While she could think of Frederick with perfect equanimity, actually with heartwarming fondness, when she imagined marriage, panic seized her.

It's just prenuptial flutters, she told herself. I'm sure that every future bride feels as nervous. Even so, the trip to Scotland suddenly had a lot more appeal.

"It'll be an adventure," she decided. "We'll probably go home with dozens of stories to tell."

At the conclusion of Edgar's business five days later, they boarded the *Royal Scotsman* and settled into their rooms in the sleeping car. Although Hazel frequently traveled by train, indeed, had toured the Continent by rail, she had never yet spent the night on a narrow berth, racheting through a foreign countryside. She felt scarcely rested at six the next morning, when they pulled into Glasgow Central.

After a hurried breakfast of scalding tea and wedge-shaped girdle scones, they piled their luggage into a hack and wove through the morning traffic to Queen Street Station to catch the train that would take them north. Stiff and sleepy and surrounded by satchels, Hazel saw very little of the city, although she could hear its voices. The rolling speech, with its burrs and lilt, hardly sounded like English.

The train that wound its way into the Highlands was a lot less luxurious than the one that had steamed up from London. Still, Hazel was grateful to be able to sink into a seat, no matter how shabby, and lean her head back. All morning she dozed and woke and gazed out the window at the changing scenes. It was green and lush at first, with fat cows grazing in stone-walled fields.

After Stirling and Perth, the Grampian Mountains rose up and with them rose majestic stands of pines.

At Inverness, Edgar dashed off the train and bought some oatcakes and boiled eggs from a vendor. As modest as it was, the lunch revived them and they sat up straighter. An hour later they stopped at Garve.

It was a station like many others, just a little bit of shelter, a picket fence, and a bench. Across the tracks was an inn with a pub on its side, a few stables, a stone wall, and some sheep.

"There's Andrew," Cornelius announced, peering out the window. He waved his hand enthusiastically. "He sees us. Here he comes."

"Pick up your sister's bag," Edgar instructed impatiently. "Hurry up. They don't stop long. We'll see Andrew in a minute."

Despite the tiring journey and her growing trepidations, Hazel felt a twinge of excitement. She tried to peek over Cornelius's shoulder to get a glimpse of Andrew, future Lord Strathdorna, but saw only a carriage and a muscular team. Even if Edgar hadn't been hustling them along, it wasn't appropriate to crane her neck. She demurely followed her father down the aisle.

Edgar descended first and strode forward to shake Andrew's hand. Then Cornelius jumped off and turned to offer Hazel his help. Eyes on the steep steps of the railroad car, Hazel carefully picked her way down from the train. Safe on the ground, she looked up. Her heart stopped.

"Miss Merriwether," the Scottish noble greeted her. "We meet again." It was Marco MacGregor.

For a fraction of an instant Hazel was unable to speak. She felt completely numb. Then her pulse started racing, her heart started pounding, and something inside her burst. The gracious manners that seemed an indelible part of her disposition all but disappeared. "You!" she exploded, swatting away the hand he held out. "You liar! You villainous, deceitful cheat!"

"Hazel!" Edgar cried, his face white with shock. Cornelius's mouth fell open.

Marco threw back his massive head and roared with laughter.

"Don't you dare laugh," Hazel commanded, stamping her foot on the grass. "You planned this whole charade. You deliberately withheld your identity. Don't try to deny it."

"I wouldn't dream of denying it," Marco said after he was able to speak. "When I realized you were Edgar's daughter, how could

I resist? Although I do think it's a bit unfair to accuse me of being a liar. After all, I didn't lie to you about my habit of teasing, did I?"

"Unfair?" Hazel echoed, her cheeks not white but fiery pink. "What could you possibly know about fairness, let alone truth, Mr. MacGregor? Or whoever you are today. You would have had me believe that you're an Italian who, when we last met, was visiting your mother in Venice and scores of cousins scattered throughout the Veneto. You're nothing but an unprincipled fraud." Her voice quavered.

"Unprincipled perhaps, Miss Merriwether," Marco conceded with another chuckle, "but certainly not a fraud. Your impressions were correct. I *am* an Italian and I *was* in Venice to visit my mother. However, it is, as Gilbert and Sullivan would say, 'a most unusual paradox' that I am also Scottish and that I spend a fair amount of my time here on my father's holdings."

"There you are, Hazel," Edgar interrupted heartily. Although he had little idea of what was going on, only vaguely surmising that Hazel had met their host on her trip abroad last summer, he was appalled by her explosion and was anxious to stem her flow of insults. "It's a perfectly satisfactory explanation."

Hazel recognized her father's rebuke for what it was, but she was still so overwrought she couldn't help muttering, "A likely story," as she shifted from foot to foot.

When Edgar seemed ready to deliver a stronger reprimand, Marco literally stepped forward. "She has every right to be upset and incredulous, Edgar," he said easily. "If I hadn't lived it all my life, I wouldn't believe my story, either. But come, Miss Merriwether," he said, taking hold of her arm and wrapping it around his. "Let's go across to the inn. We've a long trip ahead of us, I'm afraid, and we'll never manage it without a bracing cup of tea. And perhaps a slice or two of gingercake. They make a superb one here. I'll save my memoirs to amuse us on the drive home." He started over the dusty road to the inn, pulling a reluctant Hazel along.

The hot shock that had instantly shot the length of her body the moment his hand touched her arm had just as instantly unveiled something else. The force behind her unprecedented outburst, Hazel realized, was not a sense of betrayal, or suspicion, or even outrage at his actions. Rather, it was relief. Tremendous, soul-stirring, bone-deep relief that Marco, or Andrew, or however he was called, hadn't vanished irretrievably from her life. The discovery dismayed her.

Over refreshments at the inn Marco explained to Edgar and the dumbfounded Cornelius how he and Hazel had chanced to meet. Every possible hint of intimacy was omitted. Although he made liberal references to the artists and paintings that they had seen, he neglected to mention their Venetian excursion. Still trying to digest the stunning revelation she had made, Hazel didn't object.

On the long drive to Strathdorna Manor, Marco regaled them with a more colorful account. "When my father was a young man," he told his very interested audience, "he made his Grand Tour of Europe, as all well-educated young men must. He stopped the longest in Venice, where he was introduced to a lively and striking young woman named Serafina.

"They fell in love and were determined to be married, despite the politely expressed cautions of those who knew them best. Malcolm, having lived all his life in either the austere confines of school or up here"—he flung his arm wide to indicate the uninhabited hills they were driving through—"was dazzled by the splendor of Venice and by Serafina, whose ancestors included a poet, several painters, and an architect of some note. For her part, Serafina interpreted Malcolm's reserve as heroic stoicism and imagined life in a castle in Scotland, magically shrouded in heather-scented mists."

"How typical," Edgar clucked. "Young girls will fill their heads with romantic notions."

Marco raised his eyebrows, but only said mildly, "So it would seem in this instance." He gave Hazel a thoughtful glance, but she fixed her eyes on the horizon and not on him.

"In any event," he continued, "it didn't take Serafina long to draw the same conclusion. Strathdorna Manor, though old and imposing, is also miserably damp in the winter. And once removed from Venice and returned to his familiar environment, Malcolm also returned to his familiar habits. He passed his days stalking the heath with his rifle and his evenings drinking unblended whiskey with his friends."

Edgar looked uncomfortable and Cornelius even more dumbfounded, but neither made a comment. Hazel continued to study the undulating line where the gray-green hills met the gray-blue sky. "I suppose you might say I was the straw that broke the camel's back," Marco went on. "The day I was born, and for several days after, my father was knee-deep in a rushing stream some distance from here. You see, the salmon were running." He paused, but his audience remained silent.

"Irritated beyond endurance, my mother packed me up and left for Italy as soon as we both could travel. She's never again come to Scotland and my father has never again set foot in Italy, but I go back and forth between the two countries like the shuttlecock in a badminton game."

Hazel finally tore her eyes away from the view. "That still doesn't explain how you've come to possess two sets of names," she said tartly. The impact of his sudden reappearance in her life was still making her tone short and her manners even shorter. Besides, there was something about him that almost invited indiscreet questions. Maybe it was the way he seemed to offer his thoughts up for examination. "I may not be fluent in Italian, but I've enough knowledge to know that Marco isn't a translation of Andrew and that MacGregor has no connection to Strathdorna in any language."

"Hazel," her father cautioned again. Not only was Edgar aghast at his daughter's unusual rudeness, he was increasingly disconcerted by this conversation. It was far too personal. Although he considered it not merely acceptable, but essential, to "make inquiries" into an associate's background, he found it embarrassing to have the subject of his search divulge the information himself.

Sensing Edgar's disapproval, Marco made no effort to smooth his feathers as he had before. He simply ignored him and addressed himself to Hazel instead. "It's quite easy to clarify the last name," he told her. "Strathdorna is more on the order of a titular description, while MacGregor is our actual family surname. Hence, Malcolm MacGregor, Baron Strathdorna."

"Oh," Hazel said, turning away again. She suddenly felt foolish for having made such a fuss when the explanation was so obvious.

Marco saw the foolishness flush the anger from her face and change the accusation in her eyes to confusion. He felt his heart swell. He'd been drawn to her since the moment he'd spotted her while crossing the Piazza del Duomo last July. Always attracted by great beauty, her classical looks naturally appealed to him, but other of her qualities captivated him even more. He found her aura of tranquillity oddly soothing, an oasis of constancy in the world of opposites he inhabited. Yet there were plenty of placid women who would gladly give him their eternal loyalty, and he found them not enticing but dull.

He was intrigued by the sense of profound appreciation he saw beneath Hazel's composure, by the passion belied by her elegant poise. He had seen it first in her pencil sketch that day in Milan and then in her radiant face in Mantua. She had enjoyed the Mantegna frescoes in the Palazzo Ducale with a delight that had come from deep within. And however she rationalized it, she had allowed herself to be lured on his gondola tour of Venice by the promise of aesthetic adventure. An ordinary miss would have fled back to her hotel even before the sardines and the *seppie*.

Hazel was definitely different, Marco decided as he watched pink color creep across the lustrous skin of her cheeks. The problem was, he also realized, she didn't know it.

"When it comes to my seemingly unrelated first names, however, you are quite right in feeling deceived, Miss Merriwether," he went on, wondering how he was going to draw her out. "In fact, the two names *are* an act of deceit, though my parents', not mine, and they meant to taunt each other, not you."

When he saw her look carefully toward him again, he continued his explanation. "My father wanted to call me Andrew after the patron saint of Scotland. But my mother, seeking an expression of her fury with Malcolm, entered 'Marco' in the registry, naming me, instead, after the patron saint of Venice."

"For heaven's sake!" Edgar exclaimed, startled enough by this strange method of revenge to make a comment.

Marco nodded in acknowledgment of Edgar's remark, but kept his eyes on Hazel. He was rewarded for his vigilance by seeing sympathy flash across her face. "To this day, my father insists on referring to me as Andrew," he concluded. "And he further insists that *I* use that name when conducting estate business."

For a moment when he finished there was silence. Then Hazel calmly said, "A most unusual story, Mr. MacGregor." Marco sighed in frustration. Polite manners had closed her face as they had repeatedly in the past.

The silence was more enduring now. They drove steadily north and west. For a while Hazel was so immersed in thoughts and fatigue, she hardly noticed the subtlety changing scene. It just seemed empty. And then it began to affect her, to draw her in. It went from seeming barren and desolate to seeming beautiful and clean.

The hills weren't smooth and rolling, as they had been in the south, but were rough and crumpled, studded and strewn with rocks. They were split by deep ravines, veined with racing streams, and swathed in heather and moss. Overhead hung the sky, immense and commanding, almost Biblical in feeling as swirling gray clouds were shot through with shafts of sun.

Every few miles a stone house was nestled in a glen. Maybe even a pair of houses. Once there was a village of three. Otherwise there was nothing to interrupt the eyes on either side or in back or straight out in front. While Cornelius squirmed restlessly and Edgar napped, Hazel rested her chin on her hands and stared out the side of the carriage, more and more entranced by the scene. By the muted colors and the space and the celestial light.

Suddenly she sat straight up and rubbed her eyes. "Those rocks are moving," she said, pointing at the boulders high on the side of the hill. She turned back into the carriage to see who else had noticed.

"Where?" Cornelius demanded, craning to see what she had seen.

Marco smiled. "Those aren't rocks," he said. "Those are sheep. Sheep are everywhere in the Highlands. They outnumber people by hundreds to one."

"But up there?" Hazel asked, incredulous. "It's so steep. Surely they'll slip or fall."

"They walk sideways across the hills," Marco said. "Not up and down. Do you see those stripes?" He pointed, too. "The ones that make the hill look wrinkled?" When Hazel and Cornelius nodded, he told them, "Those are sheep trails."

They were quiet again until they came over a rise and found themselves alongside a noisy river running the length of a lush green glen. Hazel was surprised when they turned off the road and onto a wooden bridge, passing between two stone columns with *Strathdorna* carved in their capitals. She had been so mesmerized by the journey, she'd forgotten there was a destination.

The same could not be said for Cornelius. "Are we there?" he asked, half standing to get a better look.

"We are," Marco acknowledged with a gracious dip of his head. "Welcome to Strathdorna."

They clattered across the wood planks of the bridge and down an arrow-straight lane lined with maple trees. On either side of them were vast green meadows divided by miles of stone walls and spotted with sheep. In front and in back of them stern hills rose.

Edgar woke, cleared his throat, and pulled the watch from his vest. "Eight twenty-seven," he announced, then glanced doubtfully at the sky. It showed no sign of impending night.

"It won't be dark until after midnight," Marco explained. "And then it'll be dawn shortly afterward. We're quite far north."

At the end of the long lane Strathdorna Manor suddenly loomed up. It was huge. And imposing. Built from the rugged stone that the glaciers had left behind, it showed more attention to dimension than to design. There were only some peaks of slate roof, a turret or two, and a few windows imbedded in the walls to soften its severity. It was awe-inspiring. An impenetrable fortress hunkered against a stark hill. Impressed though she was by the grand scale of the manor, Hazel immediately understood Serafina's objections.

Theirs was not a casual arrival, as became apparent on their approach. A bagpiper in kilt and flowing plaid struck up a bleating tune of welcome even before they came to a halt by the entrance. A line of servants stood respectfully at the bottom of the steps while Malcolm and his sister Flora waited by the massive front door. A handsome black collie with a snow-white chest came tearing across the lawn and ran happy circles around the carriage, his tail streaming out behind him.

"Ho, Roger," Marco greeted him as he helped Hazel descend. "Come and meet the Merriwethers."

Although Roger couldn't be persuaded to stop, Marco's father and aunt came down the steps to shake hands. Hazel had a sinking feeling as she made introductory murmurs. Both MacGregors were tall and striking with thick gray hair and deep blue eyes, but the light in Malcolm's eyes was inflexible and the light in Flora's was vague. This was going to be a difficult visit.

Going inside did nothing to dispel that notion. The interior of Strathdorna Manor was even more intimidating than the exterior. The enormous entry hall was twenty-five feet high and hewn from the same unyielding rock as the outside walls. It was decorated, if that term could be used, with banners of the MacGregor tartan and with a formidable collection of guns, swords, and stags' heads.

"Don't worry," Marco said, seeing the alarm Hazel couldn't keep from her face. "None of the guns is loaded. You're perfectly safe."

Hazel gave him a quick glance to see if he was indulging in another bit of teasing. When she saw he was sincere, she looked away again. "I have no doubt," she replied politely. But she did. She had very serious doubts about her safety in this isolated stronghold of MacGregors. Not that she feared for her life, or even imagined any physical injury. Rather she was afraid of the disturbing effect that Marco had on her.

No matter how tired and shaky-legged she was from endless hours of traveling, no matter how distracted by the scenery, her incredible reaction to seeing him standing at the station was never far from her mind. She'd been relieved. *Relieved.*

How could I be? she thought, hoisting herself onto the huge, high bed in the cavernous chamber she'd been led to. How could I be glad to see him again when all he ever does is send chills down my spine and confuse my thoughts and make me uncertain about what I positively know to be true? Granted, he has very fine taste, she grudgingly conceded to herself. Granted, his bizarre ideas are usually exciting, she added even more grudgingly. Oh, all right. And he looks quite wonderful, too. But he says and does the most shocking things, she countered more vigorously. And he makes me behave outrageously as well.

Hazel punched one of the pillows at the head of the bed. It was as hard as the rest of Strathdorna Manor. Nonetheless, she let herself topple over on it. She refused to think about the outrageous ways he had made her behave. Like taking a ride with him through sunny Venetian canals. Like discussing such subjects as emotion and passion. Like returning his stunning kiss.

"It's only for two weeks," she announced to the room at large, though as she lay on her side her voice had a quaver. "For two weeks I can manage to keep my distance from him. If I don't give him the opportunity, he can't play any more tricks on me."

It wasn't as difficult to maintain her vow as she had thought. Most of the first week Edgar monopolized all of Marco's time, talking about and inspecting fleeces and sheep. Cornelius trailed behind them, the promised baseball game continually postponed. Even Malcolm had no success in diverting his guest's attention from wool. His offer to take the Merriwether men stalking for pheasant and ptarmigan was met with a polite but firm refusal. Edgar's favorite sport was business.

As a result, Hazel was relegated to the company of timid Aunt Flora. Despite her height, and her high, rosy MacGregor cheeks, Aunt Flora was a mousy person. She was overwhelmed by her brother and her nephew. And by sheep and wind and the Scottish sky. Consequently, she passed most of her life indoors. She moved, with the times of day, from the morning room to the afternoon room to the upstairs parlor. Hazel moved with her. Outside, it was sometimes sunny, sometimes stormy, sometimes both within a matter of minutes. Inside, it was always gloomy and chilly.

Hazel was forced to borrow a shawl, as the summer clothes she had brought from home weren't nearly enough to keep her warm. The dampness penetrated even the heavy linen of her skirts and the tight lace necks of her blouses. Wrapped in a plaid, a length of woolen cloth in the traditional tartan of the MacGregor clan, she needlepointed and embroidered and beaded a purse and worked hard to draw fluttery phrases of conversation out of Aunt Flora.

It was uncomfortable and boring, Hazel kept telling herself, but at least it was safe. Only at mealtimes did she see Marco, and then he was usually a few yards down the mammoth mahogany table. There were enough other people present to keep him from making personal contact. As soon as she was able every evening, she made her excuses and went off to bed. It wasn't dark outside, but it was dim enough in her room for her to fall into a restless sleep.

"Andrew has piqued my interest in the tweed-making they do in the Hebrides," Edgar told Hazel at dinner on the sixth night of their stay. "The island of Harris is particularly noted for its woolens. It seems that Lady Dinmore, the wife of the owner, got it all organized about forty years ago as a way to provide employment for the islanders. I've half a mind to go out there and have a look."

"You ought to, Edgar," Marco put in before Hazel could reply. "You'll be hard pressed to find yourself any closer than you are right now. We're only an hour or so from Ullapool, and once there you can get the regular steamer. You're always welcome at Strathdorna, of course, but who knows when you'll be able to come back again?"

Hazel looked suspiciously at Marco over a spoonful of cock-a-leekie soup, but got no satisfaction from either one. Marco's expression was innocent, and the chicken and leek soup, like everything else in the stone manor, was cold.

"Yes, I think you've convinced me," Edgar decided. "We'll go first thing in the morning."

"So quickly?" Hazel asked, setting down her spoon in surprise. She was getting used to packing up and traveling on a few days' notice, but this was really sudden.

"No time like the present," Malcolm stated. Aunt Flora's head bobbed in agreement.

"We'll only be gone for three or four days," Edgar said. "Maybe five, depending, I suppose, on the weather. But don't you worry, dolly," he added. "You needn't budge from where you are. I don't expect you to come tramping around from one weaver to the next. You'll be snug here with your needlework and Miss MacGregor for company."

Hazel was even more startled by the thought of being left here alone. She couldn't imagine sitting at this huge table with just Malcolm and Aunt Flora and the platters of congealing game. But she didn't protest. "I'm sure you're right, Papa," she said. "I'd only be in your way if I came along." She picked unenthusiastically at the poached salmon that had been laid on her plate.

"It's all set, then," Marco said. "I'll drive you to Ullapool myself in the morning. And after dinner we'll go into the library so I can draft a letter of introduction to some people I know. They'll treat you well."

Hazel's head shot up. She had assumed Marco would be accompanying her father and brother on this trip to the Hebrides. Now she realized he would be staying behind. It wouldn't be three for dinner after all. Her eyes narrowed. Marco's eyebrows raised.

# CHAPTER

## 4

The next day was clear and sunny. The only clouds to be seen were white. When Aunt Flora fell asleep in her chair after lunch, Hazel raced to her room for her sketch pad then escaped outside into the light. Several hundred yards from the manor she finally stopped running and took a deep breath. The air smelled of peat smoke and fresh grass. The sun felt warm. She sank to the ground where she stood.

For the first time in days she felt calm and content. Malcolm had ridden off on his chestnut stallion, Marco hadn't returned from Ullapool, and Aunt Flora was still napping. There was no one to bother her. Never moving from where she had landed, she drew a view of the manor and then of a thistle in bristling bloom. She was staring at the hills and wondering how to capture their grandeur on a single sheet of paper when she heard horse's hooves behind her. Her pulse leaped even before she looked. She knew it was Marco.

Turning, the cool comment she had composed dissolved in a reluctant laugh. He was overflowing a small two-seater cart drawn by a tiny pony. Roger was perched in the back, the long strands of hair on his ears drifting insouciantly in the breeze. "You look like the clown act in a circus," she informed him when Marco came to a halt next to her. "Surely you're too big for that poor little beast to pull. Look. He's exhausted." She pointed her pencil at the pony, who seemed to have fallen asleep under his nearly knee-length mane.

"Nonsense," Marco replied, completely unoffended. "He's just dreaming about his next bucket of oats. Do you see how fat he is? He can pull us both and never even feel it. So come along and let me show you something of the Highlands more inspiring than the inside of Strathdorna Manor." He held out his hand to hoist her into the cart.

"I think not," Hazel said, not moving. "I'm quite happy here."

Marco let his hand drop, but gave no sign of giving up. "Be sensible," he said. "You've been here almost a week and all you've done is sit in that pile of stones and stitch. It's a wonder you haven't taken sick. You'll go back to America thinking Scotland is a dungeon." He held out his hand again.

Hazel shook her head. "As I remember, you used a similar argument in Venice to persuade me to go to that restaurant and then on your tour. But you had ulterior motives then, and I'm convinced you do now. I suspect you even encouraged Papa to go to the Hebrides so you could lure me off alone."

"I admit it," Marco confessed cheerfully. "I enjoy your company. You're intelligent and discerning as well as being perfectly marvelous to look at. I'd be a fool if I didn't want to take you out driving."

Flabbergasted by his shameless response, Hazel could only stare. She couldn't help but feel thrilled by his compliment, even while she was upset by his boldness.

"Really, Miss Merriwether," Marco said, breaking the silence. "Do you intend to stay angry at me forever?"

Hazel considered that question carefully. "Perhaps," she finally decided.

Marco chuckled. "That may be the wise course," he agreed, "but it's certainly not the most amusing one. Come, now. Let's not be childish. We'll start over and this time I shall be the model of propriety. I won't lay a hand on you. I promise." He cocked his head in invitation. "It's all right," he added. "Roger will be the chaperon."

At the mention of his name, Roger looked from Marco to Hazel, his tail wagging amiably. As before, she couldn't help but smile. "I don't know how you can speak of not being childish," she said, "when you're riding around in a circus wagon."

"Don't quibble. Come." With a distinctly Italian flair, he waved her aboard.

Against her better judgment, Hazel got off the ground and

climbed into the cart. It *is* the only civilized solution, she argued
to herself. I can't very well ignore his existence when we're in
the middle of his estate. Yet as she crushed next to him on the
small seat, she had to admit that she enjoyed his company, too.
And he was also perfectly marvelous to look at.

The brisk Scottish air had whipped extra vigor into his rosy
cheeks and had tousled his dark curly hair. A comfortably worn
tweed jacket hung open over a corduroy waistcoat and a linen
shirt. His baggy breeches ended just below the knee and were met
by heavy socks and a pair of scuffed brogues. He was as perfectly
suited to these empty hills as he had been to the sophisticated
*piazzas* of Italy.

Marco clicked his tongue against his cheek. The little pony
woke up and started across the field. "I applaud your decision,"
Marco said, sitting with exaggerated stiffness and keeping his
hands resolutely on the reins.

"Thank you," Hazel responded, also sitting primly. She felt
something on her shoulder and, turning, saw Roger's paw. She
gave his head a rub and turned forward again.

"I also feel compelled to tell you that the MacGregor tartan
is exceedingly becoming to you," Marco said, referring to the
plaid that lay loosely around her shoulders. The bright red color
of the design made a pleasing contrast to her dark hair and clear
white skin.

Unconsciously, Hazel pulled the shawl a little closer across the
tucked front of her blouse. "Thank you," she said again. Feeling
more pressure on her shoulder, she turned again and saw that Roger had set both front paws on it. She gave his hanging head another
rub, but this time it wasn't enough. He eased himself over the seat
and nestled into her lap, doing his best to appear no larger than a
West Highland Terrier. Hazel had never had a fifty-pound dog sit
on her before and she looked helplessly at Marco.

"Don't stop stroking him," he advised. "Roger has an insatiable
need for affection."

For a moment Hazel felt he was teasing again, but then Roger
stuck his cold nose in her neck and leaned his silky head on her
breast. She suddenly laughed, relaxed, and gave him a hug. "Far
from having memories of Scotland as a dungeon, I shall always
think of it as an animal show," she said. "See what I mean? There
are some cows. And aren't those sheep?" She kept one hand on
Roger while she pointed beyond a stone wall with the other.

Marco gave her a sideways glance, but merely said, "Yes. That's part of our Black Face flock."

"Umm," Hazel said, running her hand down Roger's back. He sighed ecstatically.

"Mostly, however, we run North Country Cheviots. In this part of the Highlands, it's the only breed that does consistently well."

"I see," Hazel murmured. She gave Roger another long, slow rub. His eyes closed.

"Miss Merriwether!"

Hazel sat up abruptly and looked at Marco. She was astonished to see his face so intent.

"Do you have any idea at all what I'm talking about?" he asked.

"Well," she answered uncertainly, holding on to Roger. "Sheep?"

"Is that a question or an answer?"

"It's an answer," she decided after a moment. "I'm sure you must be talking about sheep."

"As it happens," Marco said, "you're correct. It would be hard to miss with that response anywhere in Scotland, though I have the distinct feeling that you're guessing."

"I don't know much about sheep," she confessed. "Until last week I'd never seen a live one before. No, that's not true, either," she amended. "There were sheep in the Christmas pageant one year."

"How is that possible?" Marco demanded, his indignation twisting him toward her on the seat. "How can you know nothing about sheep? This is how your father has made his fortune. It's these animals and their fleeces that provide you with your comfortable life. With your bonnets and your paint boxes and your leisurely tours of Europe.

"Wool is the currency of your life, Miss Merriwether," he pronounced, his voice ringing. "If for no other reason, it's your *responsibility* to inform yourself on the subject."

Stunned by the force of his criticism, Hazel was silent. Not only had no one ever chastised her so roundly, no one had ever suggested that her ignorance of sheep was inappropriate. Just the reverse, any sign of interest on her part had always been instantly diverted. She wasn't expected to be informed about sheep or wool. And she certainly wasn't expected to know about the source of Edgar's income. It wasn't ladylike. On the other hand, an unknown voice inside of her whispered that what Marco said made sense.

"I'm sure that Papa is only trying to protect me," she finally id. "Whenever I've asked him about his business, he's told me ot to worry."

Marco snorted, the nostrils of his regal nose flaring mightily. ven though he knew very well that this attitude was the accepted andard for genteel women, he couldn't accept it for Hazel. "I onsider it practically criminal to discourage the pursuit of knowl- dge," he said, his irritation getting the better of his manners. would suffocate if my curiosity were stifled. Knowledge is as nportant for the mind as art is for the soul. It enlightens, it enter- ins."

"I'm sure Papa is only thinking of my well-being," Hazel sisted somewhat desperately. "He would never deprive me of nything I need. It's just that he knows how squeamish I am, and ʒ's probably seeking to spare me any discomfort."

That effectively stopped Marco's tirade, his rage evaporating ; quickly as it had come. "Squeamish?" he repeated, puzzled. Why should that prohibit you from learning about wool?"

"Well, you know," Hazel answered, wrapping her arms around oger. "The fleeces?"

"The fleeces?"

"Yes. The poor sheep who have to die in order to get their eeces."

Marco turned to stare at her again. "Miss Merriwether, are you iying that you think a sheep has to be slaughtered and skinned order to get its wool?"

She nodded, hugging Roger closer.

Marco gave a low whistle. "You weren't exaggerating," he aid. "You really don't know anything about sheep, do you?"

Her cheek pressed against Roger's whiskers, Hazel shook her ead.

"We have four days until your father and brother come back om Harris. If we start immediately, we should be able to put a onsiderable dent in your ignorance." When Hazel turned to look him, a skeptical expression on her face, he told her, "Don't orry. I'm extremely qualified to teach you. You see, wool is ie currency of my existence, too.

"It's the commodity that pays for *my* rambles around the world. hat allows me to satisfy my particular appetites and to indulge in y predilection for collecting pretty things. I'm very well aware at if it weren't for our sheep, I couldn't afford to be driving about with a bonny lass in the middle of the day. In exchange f this privilege, I've made it my business to become well acquaint with all twenty thousand of them. Now let's get started."

"Perhaps I could just read something about it in the encycl pedia," Hazel offered, still divided between the way things ha been done all her life and Marco's peculiarly persuasive arg ments.

"Rubbish," he scoffed. "There's no book written that has much information as you'll find right here around you. You mig even call the Highlands the University of Sheep. Let's begin wi this matter of the fleeces," he went on, considering the issue se tled.

"Sheep have their fleeces *shorn* off every spring," he told he "And they grow a new one by fall. Far from being a brutal ac it's really a benevolent one. If the sheep weren't clipped in Jun by September its coat would be so long that when it rained th poor creature would be too waterlogged to stand up. Do you unde stand, Miss Merriwether?" he asked, searching her face for con prehension. "Are you now convinced there is no gore involved?

Hazel's nod acknowledged not only what Marco had said, b also the inevitability of her ovine education.

"Good. In a little while we'll drive by the fank. Murdo Matheso is shearing today."

"The fank," Hazel repeated like an attentive schoolgirl.

Marco smiled at her tone. At least she's listening this time, h thought. Out loud he explained, "We call the holding pens th 'fank.' The sheep are confined there while they wait their turn be shorn or dipped or sent to auction. But since that flock of Blac Face is so close by, let's give you a close-up look at a sheep onc and for all." He stuck a tweed elbow into Roger's flank. "Wak up," he ordered. "Time to go to work." Roger fluttered his lip but his eyes stayed shut.

"Lazy beast," Marco complained. "Every collie in the High lands would rather work sheep than breathe. Not this one." H gave Roger another nudge. "Up you go," he ordered more sterr ly. Roger finally opened his eyes and gave Marco a long-sufferir look.

"I know," Hazel sympathized, scratching behind Roger's ears "But he's quite keen on showing us these sheep."

Marco grinned and stopped the pony, who promptly fell aslee Roger lurched off Hazel's lap. Once on the ground he yawned an

stretched, then, tail waving, looked to Marco for a signal. Marco
gave a whistle and Roger took off, making a wide loop of the
group of sheep.

The sheep cast nervous eyes at Roger and edged in the direction of the cart. Roger moved a little closer. Weaving back and
forth, always keeping his distance and never barking, he gradually
herded the flock in for inspection. Marco whistled again and Roger
dropped where he was, panting and obviously pleased.

"That's marvelous!" Hazel cried. "He genuinely knows what
he's doing."

"Of course he does," Marco agreed. "These collies are very
smart dogs. But Roger is just an amateur compared with the cham-
pion herders. See how worried the sheep are? He was a bit too
anxious."

"But he did very well," Hazel maintained.

"Yes, yes. Now look at the sheep."

Obediently Hazel studied the animals milling in front of her.
"They're quite comical," she said, reaching for her sketchbook.
"How lanky their coats are." With a few deft strokes she captured
the sheep on her pad. They had long shaggy coats and long black
faces, occasionally relieved by white blazes or spots. Some had
horns that grew down and around like bony spit curls next to their
cheeks. Some had black patches on their knees.

Marco watched her for a moment to make sure she was drawing
them right. Satisfied, he nodded and took up the lesson. "That
lanky coat is extremely versatile wool," he told her. "All wool
is classified according to type. Coarse or fine or long or strong,
according to the breed of sheep. Black Face wool is unusual in that
it spans a number of types and has a number of uses, depending on
the staple."

Hazel looked up from her sketch. "What do you mean by staple?" she asked. "Is that the sheep's food?"

"No," Marco said, although he was glad to see this sign of her
attention. "What the sheep eats can affect the quality of the staple,
as can weather and health and a few other factors, but the staple
is actually any clump or tuft of hair that's pulled from the fleece.
It's a unit of wool measure, so to speak."

It was Hazel's turn to nod to show that she understood. She
resumed her sketching, adding some grass and Roger sitting in
the background while Marco resumed his lecture.

"The staple varies not only from breed to breed and flock to flock, but also on the individual fleece itself," he said, pointing at the nearest sheep. "There can be a dozen grades on each one."

"Who decides the grades and types?" Hazel asked, shading in a lamb trotting after its mother.

"There are professional graders, men with years of experience in handling fleeces," he answered. "Your father probably has some employed in his warehouse, and his buyers, no doubt, have graders of their own. To be scientific," he explained, "the softness of the wool is determined by the number of 'crimps' or crinkles in each single fiber. The more crimps the finer the wool. The graders, though, know just by sight and touch. They have highly educated hands."

When Hazel smiled at that depiction, he added, "They also have amazingly soft and smooth hands. The grease in the wool contains lanolin, one of the best hand lotions that exist."

The last of the flock drifted away, much to Roger's obvious disgust. Hazel set down her pad and turned to Marco. "And what are these many uses for Black Face wool that you mentioned?" she asked, surprised to realize she was curious. He was right again. It was enjoyable to learn something new. Although she never would have imagined that she would be interested in these creatures with the silly expressions on their faces, it felt good to fill her mind with information.

This time Marco answered her question with another question. "What would you guess their wool would be used for?"

Hazel eyed the sheep as they scattered. "Mops," she finally decided. "They look like big dust mops with legs."

"Carpets," Marco countered, laughing. "The medium grades are used for carpets while the strong or coarse grades make the best mattress filler imaginable. The very finest grade is reserved for tweeds."

Grabbing a handful of his jacket, he said, "You see, Black Face wool contains a lot of 'kemp,' which is dead hair, and kemp doesn't accept a dye. For some goods this is a detriment, but in tweed it's actually desirable." He let go of the lapel and rubbed his sleeve instead, inviting Hazel's inspection. As it was only inches from her nose, she could hardly avoid noticing it. "See all the white hairs shooting up?"

Nodding perfunctorily, Hazel was suddenly aware of how close they were, all alone, in the middle of nowhere. "Perhaps I ought to get back," she said, looking as far from him as she could. The scent of his sandalwood soap mingled with the smell of tweed, and his large body was pressed against hers on the little seat. The sensation was exhilarating. And unwelcome. "Your aunt will have woken up from her nap and be waiting tea for me."

"Aunt Flora can have tea by herself," Marco replied. He whistled for Roger, who leapt into the back of the cart, then clucked the somnolent pony into motion. "We still have to stop by the fank."

As they drove through the sweet green meadow, following and fording streams and brooks, Marco told her more about sheep and wool. He told her that sheep were either ewes or rams, except for the gelded rams, which were "wethers." That there was one human shepherd, two or three dogs, and six or seven hundred sheep for every eight thousand acres of graze. And that last year Great Britain had produced one hundred and fifty million pounds of wool.

He told her that some breeds, like Merinos and Suffolks, were called "down" sheep and had a very "close" staple that made a fine quality cloth. That the sheep indigenous to the Shetland Islands, way to the north, had a wool as soft as cashmere.

"Yes, I like cashmere," Hazel said, seizing on a term that was finally familiar. "Do you have any of those sheep?"

Sighing, Marco shook his head. "Cashmere comes from goats," he said. "It's not shorn, either, but combed free of the coat."

"Oh." She looked disappointed.

They rounded a grove of black birch trees, threaded onto a dirt road, and emerged in the middle of a fair-sized commotion. A stone-walled cottage sat next to a maze of stone-walled pens, where four men in knee boots were shearing several hundred reluctant sheep. Two women and a boy were piling the fleeces into burlap bags. Clumps of wool covered the ground and clung to the walls like snow.

"Oh, my," Hazel breathed, while Marco stopped the pony and climbed out. The cart gave a lurch.

He came around to her side and held out his hand. "Come down," he said. "Come have a closer look." She took his hand and descended.

The rocky pens, backed against a rocky hill, were a long way from tea at the Ritz, but Hazel instantly found them fascinating. She willingly allowed herself to be led through a wooden gate and into a shearing pen. Of course, it helped that Marco seemed so at home. He was on a first-name basis with everyone present, as they obviously were with him, though the older men automatically touched their caps to the son of the "laird."

"I've brought Miss Merriwether to see a sheep being shorn," Marco said. His announcement was greeted with murmurs and chuckles and stares.

Hazel accepted them easily. She liked the atmosphere in the pen. Liked the rough-hewn textures of the walls and the oak work benches. Liked the vigor of the Highland-bred people. She liked the crisp June air and the immense Scottish sky. She even liked the sheep.

"These are the North Country Cheviots," Marco told her.

They were completely white, where they weren't dirty, that is, and looked even more panic-stricken than their Black Face cousins. The fleeces were thick and dense and cracked apart when their owners moved. "I've left my sketch pad in the cart," Hazel said, turning to retrieve it.

"I'll get it," Marco said, laying a restraining hand on her arm. "You stay here and watch Murdo clip that ewe he's got by the ears. I'll wager he's done by the time I've fetched it. He's the fastest shearer in Strathdorna."

Hazel turned back gladly, though she was sure Marco had exaggerated about Murdo's speed. She was astonished, a minute later, to find out he hadn't. The bandy-legged Scot handled the ewe with lightning agility, flipping her backward so she was sitting on her rump, all four legs sticking out in front of her.

"She canna move in that position," a tall man with bristling eyebrows volunteered. Hazel nodded but didn't take her eyes from the sheep for fear of missing something.

In his right hand Murdo held a pair of steel shears. With his left he held the sheep's skin taut. Starting at her belly, he began the clip. Around, over, and up her neck, her fleece fell away in a foamy sheet. Murdo straightened. The ewe scrambled away, baa-ing piteously and looking . . . well, looking like a shorn sheep.

Hazel turned around to find Marco. He was just coming through the gate with her sketch pad and pencil. "Did you see that?" she asked excitedly. "It was over in an instant."

A smile spread across Marco's face. As much as he was drawn to Hazel's sense of peace and tranquillity, this show of animation attracted him even more. It made her gray eyes look huge and bright and gave a tantalizing glow to her clear skin. Mostly, though, it hinted at the deep passion for life he was sure lay hidden within her. She looked so lovely he was hard-pressed not to break his promise.

"I told you he was fast," Marco said, thrusting his hands out of temptation's way and wrapping them around the pad. "Now come over here and feel the wool."

Without hesitation Hazel knelt down next to the fallen fleece. Plunging her hand into it, she felt the springy fibers exuding grease. "It's hard to believe this will ever end up in my wardrobe," she said.

"It probably won't," Marco replied. "Although I've never seen you dressed for winter, it would be my guess that your clothes come courtesy of Merinos or other down breeds. Cheviot wool is more apt to be used for serviceable woolens. But we'll see the next step tomorrow."

Hazel spent most of that night lying in her massive bed resolving that there would be no tomorrow. At least, not a tomorrow that she passed squeezed against Marco on the seat of the little cart. It caused too many thrills in her body and too much confusion in her mind. She had no business finding his dramatic features and imposing size so appealing, she told herself. And she certainly had no business letting herself get caught up in his exuberant embrace of life. Hers was a more sedate existence. Which suits me very nicely, she thought.

She ought to have spent the night sleeping instead of worrying how to decline any further lessons on wool, because Marco didn't listen to her demurral. Shortly after lunch she found herself back on the cart seat and trotting down the dirt road past the sheep fank.

"I'm taking you to Gordy Fergueson's croft," Marco explained, raising his hand in a greeting to Murdo as they went by. "Gordy was crippled when a hay wagon spilled over on top of him, so he doesn't work with the sheep anymore. Instead, he and his family work at home with the wool. He usually does the scouring and picking while his wife and daughters do the rest."

"I see," Hazel murmured, her hands folded neatly in her lap. Today's activities didn't even have the intriguing ring of yesterday's. Why had she allowed herself to be bullied and coaxed into coming?

Marco noted her polite tone and her stiff posture, but paid attention to neither. Once she saw what was being done, he knew that interest would illuminate her again. "For commercial purposes, the fleeces go in a fairly unbroken line from the sheep to agents like your father," he said, beginning his explanation where'd he'd left off yesterday. "But for the home industry, wool is graded and then processed here. The first thing that has to be done is remove some of the grease. A freshly shorn fleece is almost fifty percent grease. And dirt and burrs."

This time Hazel didn't even bother to answer. She just nodded.

"There are some people who prefer to 'pick' it first," he went on, still ignoring her apathy. "That is, to take out all those bits of heather and twigs. They claim the wool is easier to spin when it's greasy, but the majority follow the big mills in 'scouring' before working it any further. Scouring is a fairly simple procedure. It's just some baths in warm water and soap."

"Umm," Hazel said. "Where's Roger?"

"He's home. He doesn't get on with Gordy's dogs. Are you listening to me?"

"Yes, of course," Hazel said hastily. "The wool has to be washed in warm water and soap. . . . "

"Correct," he approved. "Next the soapy solution is rinsed out, and the wool is hung on racks to dry in the wind. After it's picked clean, it's turned over to Jean and her girls. You'll like that part."

Hazel nodded more vigorously so he wouldn't question her attention but privately doubted his judgment. It was one thing to watch live sheep with their amusing expressions, quite another to watch their wool in a tub. As it turned out, though, Marco was right again.

Sarah Ferguson, a stocky fifteen-year-old with long red braids and a shy smile, had the job of carding. She sat on a boulder by the front of their stone cottage with a bulging burlap bag on either side of her and one of the dogs Roger didn't get along with curled up at her feet. In either freckled hand was a carding comb, a small wooden board studded with bent wire bristles. Sarah took a clump of scoured wool, set it on one of the combs, and drew the other one through it. The clump elongated slightly and lodged itself in the opposite card. She pulled the first one across again. And back and forth until the mass of wool had been combed into soft, ropy threads. Picking them out of the card, she smiled up at Hazel.

"Those strands are called slivers," Marco explained, looking over Hazel's shoulder. "Although in America I believe you call them rolag or roving."

Hazel smiled back at Sarah. This was interesting after all.

"Now come see what Annie is doing," Marco said, giving a nod of vindication. The rigid set of Hazel's slender body had disappeared, leaving her relaxed and graceful.

Sarah's sister, Annie, sat at a spinning wheel just inside the door of their house, positioned so she could soak up some sun when it pierced through the turbulent clouds. Her foot moved steadily up and down on a pedal, turning the big wooden wheel that made the spindle rotate. As it did, Annie fed it slivers. When one ran out, she simply added on another one. The spindle twisted them into a single, strong strand.

"The spinner can regulate the thickness of the yarn by varying how tautly she holds the sliver," Marco told her. "To make a thinner yarn she pulls it out more. To make a thicker yarn she eases up."

"Doesn't it also depend on the fleece, though?" Hazel asked, testing the knowledge she'd acquired yesterday. "That is, on the breed of the sheep and the grade of the wool?"

"Good for you," Marco answered, extremely pleased. "Yes, it certainly does. Finer wool makes a finer yarn."

"Oh, look!" Hazel exclaimed, suddenly noticing the cone-shaped spools of yarn stacked against every empty wall in the small house. They weren't the neutral hue of the yarn that Annie was spinning, but beautiful colors. Purples, yellows, oranges, greens, rich and real tones, reminiscent of flowers and plants and autumn days. "How lovely."

"I knew you'd like that." He sounded almost triumphant. "I knew you'd enjoy the colors. Jean Fergueson is the best dyer in the Highlands. She knows just what leaves and berries to pick or which roots to choose to make every color imaginable. I promise you, she can extract a rainbow from a stone."

"Och, Master Andrew, she canna," Annie protested, finally looking up from her wheel. "A stone canna give up color."

Marco smiled. "Perhaps I stretched the truth a wee bit, Annie," he conceded. "But it's no lie to say that your mother can make a dye from the lichen that grows on the stone."

"Aye." Annie went back to her spinning, satisfied. "The crottle make bonny colors. Besides which, they can be dried and kept for a season when there's naught else in either meadow or brae."

"And most of them dinna need a mordant," added another voice. As Hazel and Marco turned, a sturdy woman with apple cheeks and a broken-toothed grin said, "I thought I heard your voice, Andrew. Have you come for tea? Annie, put the kettle on."

"No, no, Jean," Marco said, holding up both hands to halt her. "It's not tea we need but a lesson in the magic you make. May I introduce Miss Merriwether from America?"

"I'm very pleased to meet you, Mrs. Fergueson," Hazel said, immediately finding this woman as warm and rich as her wools. "I've been admiring the wonderful colors that you've dyed your yarns. Annie said you make them from crottle, which I think I've decided is lichen, but what do you mean by mordant?"

Laughing, Jean clapped Hazel on the shoulder. Her hands were thick and strong and stained. "It's a different language we speak in Scotland," she said. "Though I believe the Sassenachs also say mordant, do they nae, Andrew?"

"They do, Jean, although you've only confused Miss Merriwether further. Sassenachs are Englishmen," he told Hazel.

"Aye," Jean agreed. "And mordant is what you use to fix the dye in the wool so it doesn't rub off or wear away. When I was a lass, my mother used to simmer the wool in old horse urine before she'd put it in a dye bath." When Hazel looked shaken by that statement, Jean laughed again.

"Dinna worry," she assured her. "Nowadays we mordant the wool with powders we buy from the apothecary and dilute in water. Come down to the shed and I'll show you."

She led the way to a low stone building that seemed almost carved from the side of the hill. Inside, though, freshly dyed loops and hanks and skeins of wool hung from the oak beams in the ceiling, filling the room with life. Across one wall were rows of wooden shelves, solidly lined with bottles, jars, and battered tins.

"These are Jean's potions," Marco said. "She brews them in those big kettles." He pointed to an assortment of caldrons standing on a hearth on the far side of the building.

"Dinna be making me out a sorceress, Andrew MacGregor," Jean warned good-naturedly. "They're only my mordants and dyes. You see, Miss Merriwether," she said, steering Hazel over to the shelf, "the type of mordant I use depends on the dye. The most common is alum, but some dyes need chrome or copper or iron or tin. Sometimes they need more than one."

"My goodness!" Hazel exclaimed. "How do you keep it all

straight?" She'd thought she understood colors from her painting, but this was a whole different dimension.

"I started as a wee lass at my mother's knee," Jean admitted. "But here. I'll give you a simple example." She reached up to the beam and pulled down a hank of yarn the color of sun-gilded hay. "I did this one yesterday with nettles and mordanted it in alum and cream of tartar."

Hazel was surprised. "But nettles are green," she protested.

"Aye, they are when they're growing in the earth, but not when they're used as a dye."

The idea delighted Hazel. She'd heard of dipping bits of cloth in tea to obtain a brownish tone, but this was far more exciting. "What about pink?" she demanded. "What if you wanted the wool to be pink? Or red?"

"Pink." Jean stroked her broad chin as she perused her shelf, finally pulling down a big shortcake tin. "This crottle gives a bonny pink when mordanted with chrome." She yanked off the lid and held the tin out for inspection. Hazel peered over. An uninspiring mass of dried lichen lay within. She shook her head in amazement.

"Bramble berries are also good for pink," Jean mused. "But you have to make a hot salt-water rinse. Red now. That's a wee bit more difficult. I can make a lovely red from a fermented crottle called cudbear, if I add vinegar. Mostly, though, we use madder these days." She pointed to a jar on the top shelf. "I get it from Glasgow," she confessed.

At Hazel's prompting, Jean told her how water lily roots or poplar bark made a black dye, bog myrtle or onion skins made an orange one, cow parsley made green, peat soot made brown, and various heathers produced hues from purple to yellow.

"I never realized where colors came from," Hazel said, ashamed of her ignorance.

"For the past few years most commercial dyes have come from coal tar," Marco said. "The tones they make are stronger and more reliable, and, of course, the dyes are less expensive. But I think the colors lack a certain depth."

Jean nodded her emphatic agreement. "Spiritless," she scoffed. "Next thing you know they'll be making the wool from coal tar, too."

"What a tragedy that would be," Hazel said. "Look at all this gorgeous yarn. I can just imagine how beautiful it must be when it's made into fabric."

"Och, dinna weary your brain imagining it," Jean said, shoving them toward the door. "Andrew, take this lass to see Donald MacDonald."

Hazel looked from Jean to Marco. "I will," he promised. "Tomorrow."

That night Hazel didn't waste time composing polite excuses for not going on the next day's excursion. Rather, she slept soundly and dreamed of wool growing like wildflowers in a field. She woke up refreshed and was ready and willing when Marco brought the carriage to the door. There was no use denying it. She was enjoying her wool tour.

Even the chilly rain didn't dampen her enthusiasm. The sheep had been comical and the scene at the fank a fascinating tableau, but the sight of the richly colored wool hanging from the beams in Jean Fergueson's dye shed had really captured her imagination. She wanted to do and see more.

Today at the fank they veered left instead of right, which eventually brought them to a stone cottage even smaller than the others. Peat smoke drifted out from the single pot on its chimney. Marco knocked on the heavy wooden door and, at a call from within, held it open for Hazel to enter. Roger brushed past and bounded in first, racing up to a silver gray-cat. The cat, never rising from the peat-blackened hearth, gave Roger a considered stare and a halfhearted bat with his paw. Ritual greeting over, Roger sank to the slate floor and both animals went to sleep.

One foot over the doorsill and frozen with dread, Hazel let out a sigh of relief. From across the room came a chuckle. "They're the best of friends, are Roger and Lev," an old man's voice said.

Quickly turning, Hazel saw Donald MacDonald sitting on a wooden bench in front of a loom that filled most of the little room. He was a small, wiry man whose thick shaggy hair was almost completely white. His face was lined and weathered by the Highland winds and by seventy-four years of living, but his expression was remarkably gentle. "Come in, lass, come in," he said, waving her into the room. "Is that Andrew MacGregor standing out in the rain?"

"It is," Marco answered, giving Hazel a nudge so he could step in behind her and shut the door. "Hello, Donald. I've brought you a basket of tattie scones and a visitor. Miss Merriwether has come to watch you weave."

"Both are very welcome here," Donald said. "Set the basket on the hearth, Andrew, and bring over that chair for the lass."

Marco did as he was instructed, and in no more than three minutes from their arrival, Hazel was seated and comfortable next to the loom. In no more than four minutes weaving had captivated her forever. She got lost in the movements, in the steady rhythm of man and machine, bending forward and back, leaning side to side. She loved the look of the threads, a neat, well-ordered web, as they stretched across the worn wood of the frame.

"You've the look of a weaver about you," Donald commented after a long while of silence.

Startled from her thrall by the sound of his voice, Hazel stammered her reply. "Oh, no. I've never woven before. That is, I've never even seen a loom until today."

"That does nae matter," Donald said with a shrug. "You still have the look of a weaver about you. We all started for the first time, once."

For some reason his remark went straight to her heart. Hazel had been included in many groups and societies before, but never had she felt so honored as she was to belong with this one. It pleased her no end to think she was part of Donald MacDonald's world, part of his peaceful demeanor, part of his ability to make beautiful cloth. "Thank you," she said. "Thank you very much."

He nodded and was silent some more. "Are you ready to try?" he asked after a while.

"Me?" Hazel was startled again. "Now?" She leaned forward in her chair.

"You'll have a wobble in your blanket, Donald," Marco spoke up from his position by the door. "It rarely works to have two weavers do the same piece," he told Hazel, who had looked over her shoulder in alarm at his words. "Everyone has his own tension and a change of weavers will show up on the finished cloth."

She sat back in her chair, her hands folded demurely in her lap.

"Och, Andrew. I dinna mind," Donald said mildly. "I dinna think of it as a wobble but as a reminder of this bonny lass. Come sit here, Miss Merriwether." He patted the bench next to him.

Hazel stood instantly and transferred to the bench. She cast a quick, happy glance at Marco, then turned her attention to the loom in front of her. "Are you sure it's all right?" she asked, fervently hoping Donald wouldn't say no.

He didn't. "Let me tell you what to do," he said. "Do you see these threads running from the beam in the back of the loom to this bar right here?" He waited for Hazel to nod. "This is the warp. The strand of yarn that gets passed from side to side in this wee wooden canoe called a shuttle is the weft." Again he waited for Hazel to nod her understanding.

"The warp is threaded through these long needles called heddles which sit in a frame called the harness. A loom must have at least two harnesses. This one has four. Every time I step on a treadle"—Hazel's eyes shot down to the bottom of the loom, where there were four pianolike wooden pedals—"one or several of the harnesses lift. It draws some of the warp threads up and pulls others down." He demonstrated with a rattle of heddles and waited for another nod.

"Now I throw the shuttle from one end to the other." It *whished* through the separated warp. "Then let the harness down and the weave is done. To make sure that the weft is snug and tight, I bring the beater forward and bang it into place." He pulled a wooden rail toward him, gave it two tugs, and released it. The blanket grew another thread bigger.

"Now I step on a treadle and lift another set of harnesses and throw the shuttle back. Let down the harnesses." They clunked "Beat it." *Rap, rap.* "Next pair of harnesses." *Rattle*. "Throw the shuttle." *Whish*. "Let down the harnesses." *Clunk*. "Beat it." *Rap, rap*.

He repeated the process several more times and stopped. "Do you understand?" he asked.

"Yes, I do," Hazel answered, itching to try it herself.

Donald slid off the bench and Hazel faced the loom alone. Nervous excitement seized her stomach. She stepped on a treadle, jumping when the harnesses rattled up. Then she slid the shuttle through the warp. It skittered a ways and stopped in the middle. "Oh, dear," she said, looking helplessly at Donald.

He chuckled and pulled the shuttle back to its starting place by the weft thread. "Try again."

Her next throw was more forceful. Too forceful. The shuttle went flying past her waiting hand and off the loom. "Oh, dear," she said again. Her glance at Donald was more anxious this time, afraid that he might be regretting his decision to let her work on his beautiful blanket.

"Dinna fret," he told her, picking the shuttle up from the floor. "It takes a wee bit of time to get used to."

Relieved, Hazel let the harness down, starting only a little when it clunked. She leaned forward to grab the beater and tug it against the weft, surprised to find it took a certain amount of strength. Donald had made it look so effortless. She found the next treadle and repeated the procedure, slightly less awkwardly this time.

After five or six passes Donald stopped her and showed her how to rachet forward the cloth beam. An inch or so of finished blanket advanced on the bolt and brought her line of work back to where she had begun. She was dismayed to see a lumpy ridge where Donald's weaving had left off and hers had started. "Have I ruined your blanket?" she asked Donald.

Smiling, he shook his head. "It's the most bonny bit in the piece," he said. "You weave a while, and I'll see about these tattie scones Andrew has brought." He touched her shoulder gently and went over to the hearth. "You'll have to move, Lev, laddie," he told the sleeping cat. "It's time for me to get tea."

Warmed by Donald's compliment, Hazel went back to work. With every throw of the shuttle the process got a little easier. She found the pattern, and the rhythm gradually gained a semblance of grace. She was sure she could keep weaving forever. It felt so good.

She loved the slow stretches and sweeps her body made as she beat and stepped and threw. She loved the *whish* and the *rattle* and the *clunk* of the loom, solid, comforting sounds in the quiet room. She loved watching the blanket build, thread by beautiful thread, each one carded and spun from sheep she'd seen grazing in the meadows. Each one dyed with plants and berries gathered in the Highland hills.

Her pleasure was compounded by the setting. By the drum of rain on the roof while they were warm and dry in the cottage. By Lev still sleeping on the hearth, his tail tucked around his head, and by Roger, his paws twitching as he dreamed alongside her bench. By Donald MacDonald spooning tea leaves into a chipped blue willow pot and setting out mismatched cups on the mantel. And by Marco. Hands clasped behind his curly head, big body tilted back in a chair, he just stared at her, an enchanted smile on his face. Hazel had felt deeply contented in her life. Now she felt euphoric.

# CHAPTER
## ⤌⤞ 5 ⤟⤍

"May we go back to Donald MacDonald's house today?" Hazel asked as she settled herself on the seat of the pony cart. Roger jumped in behind. The sky was blue this morning, and the sun was shining around scudding clouds. They didn't need the protection of the carriage.

Pleased with her eagerness and with the happy light in her eyes, Marco promised, "We'll go back tomorrow." He slapped the reins and the pony started forward. "Today I have something else I want to show you."

"What else can there be?" Hazel was puzzled. "What did we miss?"

"Nothing," Marco answered innocently.

Hazel looked at him quickly, searching his face for a sign of mischief. "Where are we going, then?" she demanded, suspicious of his satisfied smile.

The smile deepened. "It's a surprise," he answered. "Just sit back and follow me."

After a flicker of protest, Hazel sighed and decided to accept his advice. It was too fine a day to do otherwise. Besides, she'd come to realize, his surprises were usually quite intriguing.

They set off in a direction they hadn't yet taken, toward low, knobby hills at the end of the glen. As they drove, Marco quizzed her on her lessons. "What's a gimmer?" he asked.

"A one-year-old ewe," Hazel answered promptly.

"And a hogg?"

"A sheep from the time it's weaned in August until it's first shearing the following June."

"What does it mean to 'blend' wool?"

"To combine different grades or types of wool, usually for the sake of uniformity."

"When is it done?"

"During carding."

"Good."

Hazel wasn't sure why that one crisp word should give her such inordinate pleasure, but it did. She had enjoyed these past three days more than she ever could have imagined. The flood of woolly information not only filled her mind, it stirred her imagination. She found herself increasingly curious about all aspects of this fascinating fiber and proud of the knowledge she gained.

As had been the case yesterday at Donald MacDonald's cottage, the setting enhanced her enjoyment. She never tired of looking at the infinite stretches of empty hills, meadows, and sky. Nor could she ever get enough of the air, bracing and fresh and scented of the earth. She liked the plump pony and the homey little cart, she liked Roger leaning over her shoulder. And, she admitted more freely than ever before, she liked being with Marco.

She peeked sideways at him. His profile was impressive with his Renaissance nose silhouetted against the horizon. She quickly turned her gaze away.

"If there's something you wish to see, you shouldn't feel embarrassed to look," Marco commented.

Blushing, that's precisely what she did feel. "It was ill-mannered of me to stare," she said, wondering how he saw her slight glance. "I apologize."

"There's no need for apology," he replied. "I'm delighted to have you stare at me."

Her blush deepened, although she wasn't as disconcerted as she might have been a few days ago. "Nonetheless," she said, fixing her eyes straight forward and folding her hands in her lap, "it was rude."

"Rude. Ha." He gave a disgusted snort. "By whose standards?"

"By everyone's standards," she answered firmly. She was on sure ground when it came to etiquette.

"Not by mine."

"Well, by everyone else's," she retorted, a trace of exasperation disturbing her usual calm. She gave him a fast stare. "By the standards of polite society."

"Ah. The much hailed 'polite society,' " Marco murmured. "Since you are such a proponent of it, Miss Merriwether, perhaps you can explain how this noble institution arrived at its singular conclusion."

"It's very simple," Hazel said. Now she was beginning to feel confused. "It's the way it's always been. It's just *done*."

"Oh. I see."

Hazel risked another glance at him. His expression was grave. She didn't believe for an instant that his solemnity was more than skin deep. More determined, she tried again. "It's a question of consideration," she said. "While it may not bother you to be gaped at, it may make someone else uncomfortable or self-conscious. The considerate thing is to avoid such a possibility." She sat back, proud that she had thought of that explanation. It seemed unassailable.

Apparently Marco thought otherwise. "Do you think our self-conscious someone feels uncomfortable because of innate modesty," he theorized, "or because he also has been taught that staring isn't 'done'?"

This time Hazel turned on the seat to face him fully. "Really, Mr. MacGregor," she said. "I think you take a special delight in contradicting me."

Marco beamed. "As a matter of fact, Miss Merriwether," he said, "I do. With most people it's a tiresome and uninspiring exercise, but with you it's always rewarding. At the very least I'm treated to a flawless exhibition of poise. At the most I may even get you to rethink a thing or two."

Hazel's blush returned as she abruptly faced forward. "You're shameless," she decided, though a voice inside of her disagreed. His bold compliments dazzled her while his goading arguments did, indeed, make her say and think things that never would have entered her mind. He was unlike anyone she'd ever known, and being with him was a unique treat.

"Shame," Marco mused, rubbing his jaw. "That's another interesting concept. Would you say, Miss Merriwether, that shame dates back to Adam and Eve or only to the coronation of Victoria?"

Hazel gasped. A stimulating discussion was one thing, but this treaded on dangerous ground. "I think I would rather hear more about tweed," she said hastily. "Didn't you tell me that it was originally called tweel, but a clerk's error changed the spelling forever?"

"As usual, you've learned your lesson well," Marco responded, smiling, not at all perturbed by her swift retreat to the safe subject of wool. He knew that in the last three days she'd rethought more than one or two things, and he was sure she'd rethink many more in the future. Right now he just relished every moment he spent with her.

He chatted amiably about tweeds, describing the wool and the weaving and telling her about the finishing process, known in Harris as "waulking the cloth." Each length of tweed was made stronger and tighter by soaking it in soapy water, then passing vigorous double handfuls of it around a group of weavers. "It requires a bit of judgment to get it exactly right," he said. "In Harris their tweeds are always thirty-one inches wide when they come off the loom and always twenty-nine inches after they've been waulked."

After listening attentively to everything Marco told her, Hazel ventured an observation. "If this waulking process strengthens the cloth, wouldn't it make sense to use it for all types of woolens, rather than just for tweeds?" She looked over to see if he found her deduction foolish or thoughtful. She was glad that an approving grin appeared.

"Actually, most woolens do go through a shrinking process to finish them," he said. "Although it's generally referred to as 'fulling.' "

This information brought another flash of frustration. "I thought you told me there was nothing more to see," she protested. "You led me to believe it all ended with the weaving. Is that where we're going now? To see the fulling?"

Marco grinned again. "Perhaps I misled you a wee bit," he admitted. "Though strictly speaking, the cloth is seldom fulled at home. There are mills that do that. In fact, that was the first aspect of the textile industry to be done in a commercial mill, long before the invention of steam engines. So no, we aren't on our way to see cloth being fulled."

"What other details have you neglected to mention?" Hazel demanded. "I want you to tell me everything that happens to the wool from the time it leaves the loom until the time it's ready to be cut for a dress."

"Yes, ma'am," Marco said, feigning a salute. "Though, again, nothing else takes place at home. Fulled woolens are 'napped' and 'sheared,' but nowadays only by the machinery in a mill. In napping the fibers of the fabric are raised. In shearing they're shaved to a uniform height.

"And that's all. Now, Miss Merriwether, you've heard about or seen wool travel every inch of its journey from the sheep's back to the plaid draped over your shoulders."

"Is that everything?" she double-checked, half turning toward him.

"Absolutely everything."

"Are you sure?"

"Positive."

She turned back. "Then tell me where we're going."

Another smile crinkled the corners of his eyes. "Over that hill," he said, pointing with his chin.

When they crested the hill, Hazel was startled to see a large loch stretched at their feet. Its still, dark water was dotted with round, wooded islands, its distant shore crowded with tall trees. "How magnificent!" she cried. "It looks like the illustration for a fable." She glanced toward Marco to share her delight and was even more surprised to see a fleeting expression on his face that looked, incredibly, like relief.

"I'm glad you like it," was all he said.

At the bottom of the hill a bridge came into view, a narrow wooden walkway connecting the biggest island to the fern-filled bank. "*That* is where we're going," Marco announced, reining in the pony.

"Do you mean actually to the island?" Hazel looked at him again, alarmed this time. "Across that bridge? Is it safe? Will the cart fit?"

"Yes, actually to the island, Miss Merriwether," Marco said, descending. "Yes, across that bridge, and yes, it's safe. But no, the cart won't fit. We'll leave the pony on a tether and go over on foot." He came around and held up his hands to help her to the ground.

Hazel wasn't quite ready to make that commitment. Chewing her lower lip, she studied the bridge. It wasn't that long, but its pilings seemed slender and frail. Its railing was a single thin pole.

"You have my promise that I won't let you perish," Marco said, his arms still outstretched.

With a small sigh of resignation, Hazel reached down her hands and let herself be lifted from the cart.

Marco tethered the pony and shouldered a picnic hamper he pulled from the back. Then it was time to go across. It didn't help Hazel to see Roger set a tentative paw on the planks and sink into a cautious crouch. She stepped onto the bridge behind him, knuckles gleaming white on the rail. Roger slunk forward. She shuffled a few feet. The bridge swayed infinitesimally in the breeze. They both froze.

"A fine pair you are," Marco said at her back. "*Coraggio,* Miss Merriwether." He slid his arm around her waist to brace her.

The shock of his touch shot all the way through her, making her heart hammer uncontrollably. It cut off her breath and her ability to speak. It also made her forget her fear of the bridge. Without hesitation she walked its shaky length, aware only of Marco's strong arm tucking her against him. It was a more extraordinary sensation than being swept through the Palazzo Ducale linked to his elbow. More extraordinary even than being pressed next to him on the pony cart seat.

Once safely on the island, Marco let his arm fall away, but he found her hand and took it firmly in his. Thrilled, Hazel didn't attempt to dislodge it. Instead, her slender fingers curled around his. He gave them a light squeeze. Another shiver of pleasure shot through her.

She wasn't sure whether it was because of the way she felt or because of the island itself, but as they followed a windy path through the woods, Hazel was sure she was walking through a fairy tale. The June sunshine poked through the boughs of silvery birch trees and flickered off a carpet of violets and bluebells on the forest floor. With a rushing flap of feathers, a brightly colored pheasant flew up in front of them. A doe and her two spotted fawns, startled from a nap, sprang away behind a big mossy boulder.

"This is an enchanted island," Hazel declared. "It's a magical place."

"I think so," Marco said simply, looking, with his rosy cheeks and wild curls, like a woodland sprite.

She was even more convinced she was in the middle of a Brothers Grimm story when they emerged in a clearing on the top of a hill. There, overlooking the entire island, sat a cottage, a madcap combination of porches and gables and dormers, all dripping with gingerbread trim. After staring at the cottage in delight, Hazel glanced over her shoulder at the ground.

"What are you searching for?" Marco asked, glancing behind them too. "Did you lose something?"

Hazel shook her head. "I'm looking for the bread crumb trail," she answered. "Isn't this Hansel and Gretel's house?"

"No," he said, laughing. "It's Marco MacGregor's." He gave the hand he was holding a tug. "Come. Let me show you the inside."

The interior was even more intriguing than the outside. And more eclectic. Defying all common standards of decorating, it was, instead, an homage to Marco's taste and travels. In the parlor a painting by Mantegna hung behind a hooded straw chair from Orkney on whose seat was an embroidered silk cushion from China. On a hand-hewn kitchen dresser was a display of extravagant porcelain teapots, while a collection of carved shepherd's crooks stood in a fifteenth-century urn.

Finally disengaging her hand, Hazel walked over to the fireplace. "This is Venetian, isn't it?" she said, rubbing the green marble mantel. Without waiting for an answer, she picked up a long, pointed object made from a deer antler. It was polished by care and by use and had a design of hearts etched on one end.

"That's an old spindle," Marco said. "Before spinning wheels were invented, women spun out the wool with a distaff and spindle. It was a cumbersome and slow process, but one that wasn't easily surrendered. Up until fifteen or twenty years ago, most of the spinsters on Harris still used a distaff."

Hazel nodded and moved on to examine the small still life of Gorgonzola cheese and pears that stood on an antique Italian table. "It's all very beautiful," she said softly, running her finger down the stem of a Murano glass candlestick. Tearing her eyes away, she looked back at Marco and was surprised, for the second time that day, by his expression of relief.

Caught, he had to explain. "I was afraid you might not like it," he confessed. "Not everyone does, you know. One friend of mine, an old classmate, calls it the jumble mode of furnishing."

"How unkind," Hazel objected. "And how very untrue. There's a definite method here, quite a distinct pattern." Glancing around the room again, she nodded in confirmation. "I've never seen a house that more thoroughly reflected the character of its owner. If I can see it after only a short acquaintance, surely it should be bvious to someone who knows you well."

She walked over to get a closer look at a watercolor she sus-
ected was a Turner. It was a canal scene in Venice, shrouded in
mystical light. Suddenly she spun back toward Marco. "Now I
nderstand why you speak so mockingly of Strathdorna Manor,"
ne said, the thought spilling out of her mouth as soon as it popped
to her mind. "That 'pile of stones,' as you call it, is where you
ve, but this is your *home*. Isn't that so?" Her hands spread wide
o encompass the eccentric charm of the comfortable cottage.

"It doesn't feel precisely like the Highlands," she mused, try-
ng to capture its flavor, "but it isn't like Italy, either. Though I
ertainly see influences of both. A Scottish villa, perhaps. Or a
'enetian lodge." She shrugged, the appropriate architectural label
luding her.

"It's the blend of several cultures, the same as you. Like two
ifferent staples that are carded together to make a single wool.
'his must be the one corner of the world where you don't have
o be just Marco or just Andrew, but can be you, yourself, who
; both."

Marco's eyebrows raised. "Remarkable, Miss Merriwether," he
ongratulated her with an admiring dip of his head. "You're the
rst person ever to have understood the importance of this cot-
ige to me, let alone to have grasped its significance merely by
eeing it. You're absolutely correct. This is my sanctuary." He,
oo, spread his hands wide. "It's a perfect repository for all the
nings I collect on my travels, but it's also a much needed ref-
ge when those journeys begin to wear on my body and soul. I
ome here to refresh myself. To regain, as you suggest, my sense
f perspective. Yes, this is indeed the one corner of the world I
onsider my home."

Although she had come to the same conclusion and had blurted
ut as much herself, hearing that she alone shared the realization
vith Marco made it seem indecently intimate. She looked down,
tudying the Persian carpet at her feet. A faint flush of pink crept
ut from her high lace color and tinged the pale, silky skin of her
heeks. All at once, and without looking at him, she was very
ware of Marco's presence.

"But I shouldn't be surprised by your exceptional observation,"
e continued more softly, coming slowly across the room. He
topped a few feet in front of her. "I've always known that you're
n exceptional person."

In the silence that followed his quiet compliment, Hazel hear her heart beating loudly. She had to gulp to get enough breat to murmur an acknowledgment. "It's very gracious of you to sa so, Mr. MacGregor," she said, still not daring to look up.

"Not gracious, Miss Merriwether. Honest." He came anothe step nearer.

Without raising her eyes, she could see the bone buttons on hi corduroy waistcoat and his thumbs hooked in its pockets. Thi time she wasn't able to find either breath or response. She fe completely disconnected from the life she normally led. It wa almost as if she'd left it behind when she crossed the shaky wood en bridge. But she didn't know what to do or think in its place She gulped again.

"Miss Merriwether?"

"Yes?" she managed to whisper.

"Miss Merriwether, in a continuing spirit of honesty, I feel must warn you that I'm about to break the promise I made whe I plucked you and your sketch pad out of the field several day ago. Miss Merriwether, I'm about to lay a hand on you. In fact I'm about to lay two."

She watched as those hands unhooked from the pockets of hi waistcoat and as they moved closer to her face. They were larg hands with long, strong fingers, hands not unaccustomed to work Yet when they cradled her chin they were as gentle as down. Wit gossamer softness his thumbs slid across her cheeks, his right on lingering an extra moment on the tiny dot above her mouth. Eac light stroke sent waves of warm pleasure radiating through he whole body. Her heart beat even harder.

He lifted her face until she was staring into his eyes, but the were so intense and blue she had to blink. In the fraction of a instant that her eyes were shut, his head bent and his lips touche hers. It was just a brush, barely a kiss, but it turned the waves o pleasure from warm to hot. Her eyes flew open, her fingers fle to her mouth, feeling for the impression she was sure he'd lef "Oh, Mr. MacGregor," she gasped.

"Oh, Miss Merriwether," he replied. He leaned back a little an let his hands drop to her shoulders, a slow smile catching in th corners of his eyes. "Don't you think it's time we stopped callin each other Mister and Miss? I liked the way it sounded when yo said my name before. Go ahead." He gave her shoulders a sligh squeeze. "Say it again."

Hazel looked at him, letting her hand slip down, her eyes growing larger in wonder. He was so big. His body was large, his head was imposing, and his spirit was as vast as the sky. It was practically bursting from him, glowing in his cherub's pink cheeks, whirling out of his wild curls. It was in his smile, in his eyes, and in his galvanizing touch, light as a feather but vibrant with life.

"Marco," she said gladly.

He bent to give her another kiss. Not a brush this time, not a graze of the lips, but a full, deep, long, unhurried kiss. Inside of Hazel, the hot pleasure exploded.

She wanted to respond, wanted to urge him never to stop, but she didn't know what to do. She felt awkward and wooden, wrapped in the tartan shawl and planted in the middle of the room. She didn't know how to acknowledge the frantic pounding of her heart or how to react to the insistent pulsing of desire. It didn't matter. Marco showed her.

He pushed the shawl off her shoulders and let it fall to the floor, then draped her arms around his neck. Holding her tight, rolling his face against hers, he slid his hands up her back, leaving ripples of delight in their wake. His fingers inched higher and higher until he found her hat and its pin. A slight tug sent them down on top of the shawl. Another few tugs and her hairpins followed, releasing her hair in thick, shiny hanks.

Twining a smooth strand around his fingers, he held her off so he could examine every detail of her face. When he finally spoke, his voice was low and raw. "You're exquisite, Hazel," he said.

It didn't seem as though she could feel any more pleasure, but his words sent new shivers along the top of her skin. Mimicking his actions, she lifted a tentative hand to his head and took a single curl between two trembling fingers. It felt silky. And extremely personal. Her banging heart skipped a beat.

But emboldened by the sensation, she let go of the curl and brought her hand around to his face. For another moment she hesitated, startled by the brightness of his eyes. Then she looked at his cheeks. His high, flushed cheeks like a Renaissance angel's. Her hand hovered closer, longing, yearning, but shy.

Marco turned his head sideways and caught the tips of her fingers with a flicker of a kiss. "Don't be afraid," he murmured, reaching over to wrap his own fingers around hers. He brought them to his mouth and set a slow kiss on each one, then cupped them against his face. Her tingling hand burned.

"Marco," she said suddenly.

"Mmm?" he answered, turning his head again so his lips fit into her palm. His tongue traced her lifeline, then trailed away into the lace on her wrist.

She swallowed. "Nothing," she said faintly. "I was just practicing your name."

He smiled against her hand. "*Brava,*" he said. "You did a very good job. Try again."

"Marco."

"Perfect." He drew her hand to the back of his head and leaned forward to cover her mouth with his.

Hazel met him eagerly. Her hesitation evaporated as she finally gave in to the strong feelings within her. She was caught in a spell, bewitched by Marco MacGregor and his magic island, but she was, by no means, in a trance. She was neither dazed nor confused. Things had never been clearer. She crushed against him, her hands gripping his neck, her body aching with excitement.

After a moment he gently loosened her hold, letting her slip back a few inches. He kissed the tops of her hands and the tip of her nose and breathed, "*Bellissima,*" in her ear. Then, with his eyes fixed on her face, he unfastened the brooch on her blouse and tossed the pearl-studded pin on a table.

He carefully undid her uppermost button and carefully laid open her high collar. With deliberate slowness he bent his head and leaned forward to lay a hint of a kiss on her throat. That whispery touch went through her like a shock. Gasping for breath, Hazel arched back her head. Her eyes fluttered closed.

In one swift move Marco scooped her off her feet and carried her across the room and through a door. When Hazel opened her eyes again she was laying against a mass of eyelet-covered cushions in the center of a huge four-poster bed. Sunshine was pouring through the windows and Marco was pulling off her shoes. He smiled and sank down on the edge of the bed. She smiled and held out her hand.

They made love on lilac-colored linen sheets in a puddle of June sunshine. Giant blue delphiniums tapped on the windowpane outside. Marco made it seem like the most natural thing in the world. He made her forget everything except the intense pleasure of the moment. Everything except his lips and his tongue and his bare skin against hers.

"You're exquisite," he told her again, when they lay drowsy, their desire spent. "Utterly extraordinary." He traced a lazy finger down the slender curve of her neck and across the marble white skin of her breast. Leaning over, he gave it a light kiss.

Hazel hunched her shoulders at the tickle it caused. "I think you're quite extraordinary, too," she said softly. The magic had mellowed but the spell hadn't faded. She rolled on her side to look at him better. Her hand, unafraid, stroked the length of his chest. "There's so much of you," she added, a little bit awed. He looked as big without clothes as he did fully dressed, but now it was possible to see that he was rock solid, not fat.

"Well fed." He laughed. "I'm the result of a thirty-year passion for food. Which reminds me," he said, sitting up and swinging his legs over the side of the bed, "I have a splendid hamper in the kitchen. No, no." He stretched out his hand to prevent her from rising. "I'll go fetch it. We'll have our picnic right here."

Naked he went and naked he returned, this time with Roger at his heels. While Roger wagged his tail and settled in a sunny corner, Marco laid out lunch on the bed. Then propped against the pile of soft pillows, he fed her romantic compliments and morsels of food. The spell deepened.

Hazel had just followed a paper-thin slice of smoked salmon with a swallow of creamy dark ale when Roger jumped up and ran to the window, barking. "Has he heard a deer or a rabbit?" she asked as Marco set down a plate of pheasant terrine.

He shook his head. "Roger isn't a hunter," he said, getting up and going over to the window. "Damn!" he exclaimed. "It's your brother!"

"Cornelius?" Horror hung on that single word as Hazel suddenly clutched the sheet to her throat. She scrambled out of the bed and stumbled to the window, trying to keep from tripping on the lavender linen. She just caught a glimpse of Cornelius before he disappeared behind the trees on the path. He would be at the cottage in a matter of minutes.

The sight of her lanky brother didn't just break the glorious spell that had been building for four days, that had reached a crescendo on this wild island. It didn't just burst it as it happened in Venice when the gondola bumped against the mooring pole. It smashed it apart. Shattered it into ten thousand pieces. Hazel felt sick with shame, mortified beyond words. The feelings, both physical and emotional, that had seemed immensely enjoyable only moments before now seemed unspeakably wicked.

It was devastating enough to realize she had allowed Marco to lure her into his bed in the heat of desire, but to have then lain in languorous bliss while he fed her bits of lunch was unforgivable. What would her father think of his dolly if he could see her nibbling smoked salmon, naked, from the future Lord Strathdorna's fingers? What would Frederick say? *Frederick!* She hadn't thought of him in days.

"Dear God!" she cried. "What have I done?"

Marco whirled from the misfortune outside the window to the more alarming peril within. Hazel, the exquisite, extraordinary Hazel, was vanishing before his eyes. He reached out a hand to grab hold of her, but he was too late. She was already gone. She leaped from his touch as if he were a viperous snake, unable even to look at his face. Something inside of him turned ice cold.

Nearly sobbing with humiliation, Hazel yanked on her clothes. She crouched and twisted in an attempt to shield her body from Marco's view. Nor was she any longer interested in seeing his. She only wanted to flee as fast and as far from here as she could. Her hands were shaking as she fastened her buttons and as she ran into the parlor twisting her hair into its knot. She pulled her hairpins and hat from the pile on the floor, but left the MacGregor tartan where it lay. Jamming her bonnet into place, she reached the front door at the same moment as her brother.

"Cornelius!" she exclaimed for the second time in minutes. She tried to make her greeting sound pleasantly surprised, but it came out sounding desperate.

Cornelius didn't seem to notice. "Hello, Hazel," he said. If Hazel had been even a fraction more composed, she would have heard the worry in his tone. But she was concerned only with blocking his entrance to the cottage, unconsciously keeping him from the scene of her shame.

"What's wrong, Cornelius?" Marco asked quietly, behind her.

Hazel flinched at the thought of him being so close, but his question made her see the grim look on her brother's face for the first time. "What's wrong?" she echoed, though her words were heavy with dread. She was sure he had found out about her scandalous conduct and had come to drag her away.

"Hello, Andrew," Cornelius acknowledged his friend as he

bent to give Roger a pat. 'There's bad news from home," he said, straightening again. "There was a telegram waiting when we returned from Harris this morning. Papa's sent me to get you so we can start for Glasgow at once."

"Bad news?" Hazel raised her hand to her heart in new fear. "Is it Lucy?" she asked. "Or Frederick? Has something happened to one of them?"

As Marco was still standing behind her, Hazel didn't see the assessing look he gave her. If Cornelius saw it, it went over his head.

"It's neither of them," he reassured her. "It's the price of silver. It dropped below sixty-two on Thursday and made the market plunge. There was speculation that it would crash on Friday, but so far we haven't heard what's happened. Either way, though, I guess it's pretty serious. Papa's very anxious to get started for home."

Hazel was already on her way down the path, just as anxious as Edgar to depart. Her reasons, however, had nothing to do with the price of silver. In fact, she had very little idea of what Cornelius had said. Even if she had been her usual poised self, it's doubtful she would have understood the ramifications of the problem. It was just business talk. Edgar had told her much the same the evening he'd rattled the paper. More appalling was today's disaster.

She didn't listen as Marco cross-examined Cornelius or as her brother gave Marco vague answers. The grasp of the wool trade she'd acquired was suddenly irrelevant. Instead, she went over and over today's events in her mind. How could I have let this happen? she silently wondered. How could I have been so weak-willed? And poor Frederick, she thought, engulfed by guilt. How could I have behaved so vilely toward him when he's never shown me anything but esteem and devotion?

"Papa wants to pack up and drive to Garve tonight," Cornelius said, coming even with her on the path. Somehow the sun-dappled woods didn't seem as enchanting as they had.

"Yes, yes," Hazel answered absently. The plan was completely acceptable to her. She was glad they were leaving immediately. Now that the first shock of discovery was subsiding, she couldn't look at Marco without feeling a tiny twinge of attraction mingled with the enormous sense of shame. She couldn't wait to put this terrible temptation at an impossible distance. She wished she were back in Boston this instant. She needed the familiar comfort of her house, her friends, and her fiancé.

Frederick. She rubbed her forehead trying to conjure up his image. I'll make it up to him, Hazel silently vowed. We'll get married whenever he pleases. The day I get home, if that's what he wants. I'll be an ideal wife, thinking only of his happiness. And I'll never, ever betray him again.

# CHAPTER
## 6

"Welcome home, darling."

Looking up from her seat atop the steamer trunk, Hazel was amazed to see Frederick standing before her, a bouquet of roses in his hand. "Frederick," she said, "what on earth are you doing in New York?"

"I couldn't wait to see you," he confessed, setting the bouquet in her lap. Much affected by the flush of pink that suddenly colored her face, he leaned down and placed a polite kiss on her cheek. "You're such a sweet pet," he murmured. "I was right to miss you." Straightening, he added, "I decided that I ought to meet your ship and then ride back to Boston with you on the train. I thought it would give us a chance to catch up."

Hazel's blush deepened, though it wasn't caused by innocent excitement as Frederick suspected, but by immense guilt. *She* could have waited for this reunion. In fact, she would have preferred to have been comfortably resettled in Marlborough Street first. The crossing had been stormy and rough and her thoughts had been no less turbulent. She felt weary in every corner of her being. The idea of sitting with Frederick for six hours on the train was nowhere nearly as appealing as it should have been. But she was determined to keep the vow she had made.

"Dear Frederick," she said earnestly. "How very considerate of you to remember that I enjoy flowers." She made a show of taking a delicate sniff of the bouquet, while inwardly wondering what she was going to do with a dozen roses until she reached home—and a vase of water—sometime this evening. Marco, at least, would have given me more exotic blooms, she found herself thinking. Then appalled at the thought, her face grew redder still.

"Papa's gone to speak with the customs agent and Cornelius went in search of a newspaper with the latest baseball scores, but I know they'll both be thrilled to see you." She spoke quickly, as much to chase unwelcome images from her mind as to let Frederick know why she was sitting on her luggage, like an abandoned waif, in the middle of the bustling pier. "You're so clever to have thought of surprising us this way," she went on. "I know we're going to have a grand time on the train ride home."

But it wasn't as grand as Hazel predicted. Rather, it was tedious and long. Hazel asked for news of Lucy and the rest of their friends and listened while Frederick described the ongoing sea trials of the *Jubilee* which, he claimed, was looking more and more like a Cup contender every day. After that an awkward silence fell. For the life of her, Hazel couldn't think of a single thing to say. She felt desperate.

Edgar filled the void with terse questions about the state of the wool industry, the stock market, and the business climate in general. Frederick grew more sober as he answered, lines of tension narrowing his clear blue eyes. Hazel hardly heard the words, though, and the somber tones barely registered. Grateful to be relieved of the responsibility to make conversation, she leaned her head back and studied Frederick, trying to summon her excitement of his handsome looks. His blond hair seemed too fine, though, and his high cheeks seemed too pale.

With a small sigh, Hazel let her eyes close. I'm just tired, she thought. As soon as I'm rested, life will look right side up again.

To a degree it did. Being back in her own house restored a shadow of her usual contentment. It was reassuring to resume her pleasing routines in an atmosphere of refinement and comfort. But even at that, Hazel had the disquieting sense that the familiar texture of her life was starting to tatter and fray. At first she held herself accountable, sure that her unpardonable actions had somehow corrupted that ideal existence. Because her memory of the afternoon on the little island was so vivid, she was sure everyone else could see her lying naked and laughing in Marco's arms, too.

Only gradually did she begin to realize that the people around her were not reacting to an evil aura enveloping her, but to conditions and events she had nothing to do with. These were part of

the same financial rumblings that had brought them running home
from Scotland. Part of the same economic unrest that Frederick
and Edgar had grimly discussed on the train. For the first time in
weeks Hazel stopped brooding about her own problem and started
wondering what was upsetting the world at large. She knew it had
to be fairly serious if it caused her father to continuously walk
around under a black cloud. She wished she had paid more attention when those business discussions had taken place.

Hazel got her first hint of just how serious the situation was
at dinner almost a week after their return. Annie had no sooner
finished serving the fish course when Edgar exploded.

"What do you mean by having lobster in the middle of the
week?" he demanded. "Don't you know it's a frivolous expense
for just an ordinary family supper? Honestly, Hazel, I wish you'd
use a little common sense about planning the meals."

Stunned by her father's outburst, Hazel nearly choked on a bite
of lobster salad. Edgar never spoke to her that severely. "I'm sorry," she apologized when she'd stopped coughing. "I wasn't thinking of the expense when I asked Mrs. Harrigan to make it for this
evening, but only that it would be refreshing to have a cold dish
in this heat. I'll be more careful in the future. I promise."

"Hmmph," Edgar said, which was his way of indicating he
hadn't meant to yell at Hazel, but having done so, he was mollified
by her remorse.

In the silence that followed, the sound of silver forks scooping
lobster salad off porcelain plates reverberated like thunder. Hazel
held her breath when Annie brought the meat course. She didn't
know if her father would consider roast beef frivolous, too. To
tell the truth, she was a little bit vague about the cost of food,
always basing her menus on what pleased the palate rather than
on the price. She snuck a glance at Edgar, but he no longer seemed
aware of what he was eating. His attention was focused on some
distant place. She slowly released her breath.

"Have you heard about the new ruling that the National League
made?" Cornelius said into the heavy silence. "From now on flat
bats will be illegal. They'll all have to be round." It was obvious
from his hesitant tone that he was just trying to ease the tension,
but his remark had the reverse effect.

Edgar's fist banged down so hard the wine in his glass made
an angry splash on the tablecloth. "That's enough!" he roared.
"I'm fed up with this incessant drivel about baseball. It's time for

you to grow up and turn your mind to more important matters. If I ever hear you utter another word about that foolish game, you'll be out on the street, young man."

From the defiant thrust of Cornelius's chin, it seemed he was ready to take his chances, but Hazel quickly interceded. "This dreadful heat wave has been very hard on the nerves," she said soothingly. "I can't remember when it's been so oppressive, especially at night. It makes sound sleeping practically impossible." She cast a bright smile on the palpable gloom. "I'm sure it will be a big relief to go up to Marblehead next week. The sea breeze always revives the spirit."

"We won't be going to Marblehead next week," Edgar said abruptly. "I've put the cottage up for sale."

Complete astonishment wiped the conciliatory smile from Hazel's face and the mutinous glower from Cornelius's. They both turned to stare at their father, waiting open-mouthed for an explanation of his jolting announcement. None was forthcoming. Edgar jammed roast beef into his mouth until his plate was empty, then stood up and left the room.

"Will Mr. Merriwether be wanting his lemon pie, Miss Hazel?" Annie asked as she came to gather the plates.

Hazel looked back to the table. "I think not, Annie," she said calmly, dabbing her lips with the edge of her napkin. "Just bring dessert for my brother and me, if you please."

As soon as Annie had set down their wedges of lemon meringue pie and had disappeared down the back stairs, Hazel leaned forward. "What's this all about, Cornelius?" she demanded.

"I don't know," Cornelius answered, shaking his head. He stuck an exploratory fork into his pie. "It's the first time I've heard this news, too."

"I don't mean just the cottage," Hazel said with an impatient wave of her hand. "There's something more going on. Papa's been in a beastly mood ever since we came home. And he's *never* questioned the amount of money that's spent on food. Is business going very badly?"

This time Cornelius shrugged as he took a lemony bite. "I suppose it is," he said unenthusiastically.

"But why?" Hazel persisted. "Papa's so smart. He's always been successful. What's gone wrong now?"

"I don't know," Cornelius repeated, seeming more interested in his dessert than in the problem. "Papa's been in a foul mood at work, too, though. He's let go more than half the workers with no notice, and believe me, there's been some grumbling about that."

A cold knot of dread suddenly twisted Hazel's stomach. She sat back in her chair, her hands folded in her lap. "What's going to happen?" she asked quietly.

"I don't know," Cornelius said again. "But quite honestly, Hazel," he added, squinting over the top of a piece of pie shimmering at the end of his fork, "I don't care. I'm not interested in the business, and I hate being in that damn warehouse breathing in hot, woolly air. And while I'm at it, I'll tell you what else." He set down his fork and looked directly across the table at her.

"I don't care if Papa's selling the house in Marblehead, either," he told her emphatically. "I'm just as glad I won't have to play lawn croquet and tennis anymore. And I'm especially glad Frederick won't be able to drag me out yachting. I don't like boats."

Hazel gave a little gasp, but it was more a reflex than a heartfelt response. "Frederick is only trying to be nice to you," she said automatically.

With a snort, Cornelius returned his attention to the pie. "If he really wanted to be nice to me, he'd learn to place first base." He swallowed the last of his dessert in a giant gulp, then he stood up, too. "Say, sis, do you mind if I leave you here by yourself?" he asked. "I promised some fellows I'd pitch part of their game. There's still time to get in a few innings before dark."

"No, no. Go right ahead," Hazel said, waving him on his way. "Just don't let Papa know where you've gone."

"That's for sure." Cornelius laughed. Then he was out the door.

For a long time Hazel sat staring at her untouched portion of pie. Its stiff meringue was starting to wilt and slide down the side of the slice. "Well, I shall miss going to Marblehead," she told the melting confection. She pushed the plate away and rested her arms on the table. "I shall miss the air," she said sadly. "And the light by the sea. And the scent of wild roses in the balmy night."

"Were you talking to me, Miss Hazel?"

Looking up, Hazel saw Annie standing with a tray, waiting to clear off the table. Hazel laid her napkin neatly on the cloth and rose. "I was just commenting on the heat," she answered pleasantly. "It's been quite hot, don't you think?"

"A real scorcher, Miss Hazel," Annie agreed.

Hazel nodded and walked purposefully into the hall. Once there, though, out of sight of Annie, her steps flagged. Far from having a definite purpose, she felt bereft. The life that had been such a source of contentment was eroding around her. The world she had come hurrying home to, seeking refuge and reassurance, was collapsing, bit by gilded bit, and she didn't know why, let alone how to stop it.

"It's your *responsibility* to find the reason," someone said.

Hazel didn't look around for the speaker. It was Marco and he was inside her head. She slumped down on a horsehair bench, too discouraged even to chase him away. On the contrary, she grabbed guiltily for comfort from his large and healthy image. She remembered the sensation of tremendous security she had felt when he'd tucked her against him and guided her across the wobbly bridge. Against her will, the memory swelled her heart.

"But I don't know how to find the reason," she told him somewhat resentfully. "I can't ask Papa, and Cornelius neither knows nor cares." She ought to have known better than to expect sympathy in reply. Even when Marco was only a picture in her mind, he seemed to take pleasure from goading her into action with a combination of compliments and taunts.

"You're an intelligent woman with an extraordinary sense of perception," he said. "Surely you can figure out where to find the news of the world."

With a sigh, Hazel got to her feet and went off in search of the *Boston Evening Globe*. Inside her head Marco beamed. She sighed again.

"Frederick," Hazel said several days later, "do you think there's going to be a depression?"

"What?" Frederick was astounded. He crossed the parlor and sat down next to her on the sofa. "Where did you ever get that idea?"

Fighting the uneasy feeling that his closeness caused all too often these days, Hazel looked down at her hands. "I've been reading the newspapers," she said, forcing her fingers to lay neatly in her lap. "I don't understand most of the references, but there seems to be a great deal of talk about unemployment and a possible depression." She looked up then, her gray eyes anxious. "Do you think it will happen?"

"My poor, sweet pet," Frederick said fondly, picking up one of her hands and bringing it to his lips. He laid a light kiss across her knuckles before lowering it again and encasing it in both of his. "That's nothing for you to be worried about. The only thing you have to concern yourself with is our wedding. Did you decide on a date while you were away?"

Despite the cold grip that suddenly seized her heart, Hazel ignored his question. "Is it true, then?" she asked. "About the depression, I mean?"

"Darling Hazel," Frederick chided gently. "I told you not to fret about such matters. If you feel you must read the paper at all, you should open it straightaway to the page with the social notes and the features on fashion. Leave the rest to me. Don't you trust me to take care of you always?" He looked at her, waiting for an answer.

Hazel dropped her eyes again. After a moment she softly said, "Of course I do, Frederick." She found it difficult to breathe.

"Good girl," Frederick approved. "So shoo all that other muddle out of your head. It's too beautiful to be filled with such gloomy thoughts." He lifted a hand and waved it through the air like a carnival magician. "There," he pronounced, smiling. "Is it all gone?"

Still not looking up, Hazel nodded. She couldn't speak.

"Good," Frederick said again. "Now. Let's talk about happier things. Since you haven't been able to decide on a date for the wedding, I've come up with one." He didn't seem to notice that the hand he was holding had turned damp and chilly. "How does November the eighteenth sound to you? It's the Saturday before Thanksgiving, and the very start of the holiday season. I thought that everyone would be in a festive mood, but not yet tired out with endless parties."

A thousand excuses flooded Hazel's mind and clamored to be uttered, but she remembered the ardent promise she'd made on that day in Scotland: She would marry Frederick whenever he wanted. She nodded again.

"Really, Hazel," Frederick said, a trace of annoyance creeping into his tone. "You don't seem very interested in this. Ever since you've come home from England, you've been distracted. I could almost say that you left your attention on the other side of the Atlantic. Is that it? Are you still thinking about that baronial estate your father told me you visited?"

"No!" Hazel's head shot up as she vehemently denied that possibility. Her heart started beating rapidly in fear. "I'm not thinking about it at all. Not even a little. That is, only enough to write a thank-you note. Nothing more." She stopped herself when she saw the startled look on Frederick's face. With great effort and a deep breath, she steadied herself, then started again in a more normal tone.

"I'm sorry, Frederick," she said, tilting her head just a touch. "I'm afraid this heat is making me ill. It's so sudden, you know, after the cool air in Scotland and while crossing the ocean." She gave his hand a squeeze and showed him a brave smile. "I think November the eighteenth sounds splendid. I knew I could depend on you to think things through and come up with the perfect date. How fortunate I am to have you to rely on. Where would I be without you?" She wanted to believe it herself as much as she wanted him to.

It worked for one of them. Looking pleased, Frederick returned her squeeze. "Poor darling," he sympathized. "That trip was too much for you. I can see that it's worn you out. Didn't I tell you it was a foolish notion?"

"You did tell me so and you were right," Hazel replied with absolute sincerity. "It was a mistake to have gone. I should have listened to you."

Frederick nodded in satisfaction. "Next time you will," he said confidently. "But for now we must concentrate on getting you up to Marblehead. You'll feel much better by the sea."

"Oh," Hazel said, her quick flutter of enthusiasm fading. "Didn't Papa tell you? We aren't going to Marblehead this summer. He's selling the cottage."

"He's doing what?" Frederick exclaimed, suddenly withdrawing his hands. "What are you talking about? Where are you going instead?"

Hazel shrank back from his explosion of temper. "Nowhere," she answered cautiously. "We're staying here." After a pause she added, even more cautiously, "I think Papa's business is going badly."

"Oh, fine," Frederick snapped, rising and pacing the room. "How am I supposed to explain this to all our friends? Mother was planning to have a party after the Goelet Cup to announce our wedding date. We can hardly do that if you're sitting in town. And there's no point to doing it here. Everybody we know is at the sea for the summer. Except for the Eliots, who insist on going to the mountains. Now we'll have to postpone it until September. It's such a nuisance."

"I'm sorry," Hazel said softly.

Frederick stopped pacing long enough to look at her. "Of course you are," he said, his irritation abating. "Poor darling. It isn't your fault, is it?" He came over to the sofa again, but this time he remained standing. Hazel was forced to look up. "I might have known this would happen," he mused, fixed on a far-off thought.

"Might have known what would happen, Frederick?" Hazel asked, wondering as much at his cool tone as at his remark.

"Nothing, pet," Frederick answered, turning his gaze back to her. He smiled and brushed his finger down her cheek. "Now I know why you were asking me about a depression. But what I said before still holds true. You needn't worry. You have me, at least, to take care of you."

He left shortly after that, and Hazel couldn't help feeling relieved. Maybe she was imagining it, but there seemed to be a subtle change in Frederick's attitude. Even after he'd collected himself and chivalrously told her everything would work out, she thought she detected just a tiny note of condescension in his voice. And wasn't his touch a little bit bolder than before? Could she possibly have detected a hint of disrespect?

Completely drained, Hazel trudged up the stairs to bed. The strange puzzle of people and events wasn't getting easier to solve, it was getting more complicated. With what little energy she had left, she wished life were the way it used to be, when she'd known what to expect and what had been expected of her. And when those expectations had made her very happy instead of uncomfortable.

After I marry Frederick, life will be like that again, she told herself, hoping very much that it was true.

# CHAPTER
## 7

Hazel found that hope growing stronger as the summer went on and the situation at home got worse. Her father was increasingly gruff and withdrawn. He stayed late at his office, sometimes even missing dinner, an aberration of his inflexible schedule that would have been unthinkable not too long ago. Nor did he ever have an apology or an explanation for his absence. Once he came home just as Hazel was going up to bed. Without saying a word, he pushed past her in the hall. The odor of whiskey and tobacco remained after he was gone. Hazel's bewilderment bordered on despair.

Cornelius couldn't comfort her, even if he'd known what was going on. Taking advantage of Edgar's preoccupation, he was often away himself, sneaking out to play baseball. Besides, as he'd quite bluntly told her, he didn't care.

Despite Frederick's admonition not to, Hazel continued to read the papers. More and more of the news was sinking in and none of it was good. She didn't have to understand economics or politics to know that constant reports of the stock market "dropping," "suffering," "slumping," and being "hammered" weren't desired conditions. And R.H. White's advertisement for a "Great Financial Panic Sale" couldn't have made things plainer.

It was particularly disconcerting, though, to see that the wool market was "dull." Sales were a mere fifth of what they'd been at this same time last year. Manufacturers, beset by financial woes of their own, were buying less, leaving the dealers holding large inventories. As clearly as if he were sitting in her parlor, Hazel could hear Marco saying, "Wool is the currency of your life, Miss Merriwether." Now it was inescapably obvious that that currency was in trouble. What Hazel still didn't know was what it meant.

When she added the discomforts of heat and loneliness to the uncertainty and tension, it was small wonder that Hazel longed for an escape. She wandered through the dark and stuffy rooms of her house, whose heavy drapes had been drawn against the strong sun, yearning for the sound of laughter or Lucy's saucy chatter to break the deathly silence. Too distracted to sketch, too restless to stitch, she occupied her days wishing that this dreadful summer would come to an end.

Although Hazel pinned her hopes on her marriage to Frederick as a retreat to familiar ways, it sometimes seemed that Frederick was becoming less familiar and more of a stranger. With a lack of gallantry she'd never seen, he complained that her inconvenient stay in town was keeping him from his yacht. Yet from the tightness around his eyes and mouth, she suspected that he, like Edgar, was forced to spend more time than usual in his office tending to the matters of the business he would one day inherit from his father. Again she wished that the summer were over.

Eventually her wish was granted. August finally ended with a rise in the stock market and a drop in the temperature, a very welcome contrast to the way things had been going. When Hazel went to bed on the first Sunday in September, she felt more optimistic than she had in a long time. It was the last big weekend in Marblehead. Soon everyone would be back in Boston, and her normal routine would resume. Even Cornelius was cheerful because his beloved Beaneaters seemed assured of winning the pennant.

Sometime in the middle of the night Hazel was awakened by a banging on the front door. Though her room was three flights up and at the back of the house, the knocking was so loud and urgent it carried through the stillness. Next came the sounds of feet running back and forth along the carpeted hall and of low, hurried conversations outside of Edgar's and Cornelius's doors. Very curious and a little alarmed, Hazel scrambled out of bed, throwing on her dressing gown as she crossed the room.

She opened her door and stepped into the hall just as her father went racing by. His shirt was only half tucked in and his collar and tie were askew. He was struggling into his jacket as he ran.

"Papa, what's wrong?" Hazel called out. "What's happened?"

Edgar looked her way for less than a second, but even that quick glance was enough to send chills down Hazel's spine. His expression was fierce and his eyes, behind his glittering spectacles, were icy cold. "Get back to bed this instant!" he yelled at her, already gone.

Jarred to the core by his harshness, Hazel jumped back in her doorway but didn't completely obey her father's command. His extreme behavior only heightened her concern. When Cornelius dashed out of his room, stuffing his shirt into his trousers, Hazel was ready. She darted out in the hall and grabbed her brother's arm. "Tell me what's happened, Cornelius," she demanded.

"It's the warehouse," he answered briefly. "It's on fire."

Hazel's arm fell away and she went still in shock. "On fire?" she whispered.

"Cornelius, hurry up!" came Edgar's shout.

Cornelius gave a helpless shrug in the direction of the bellow. "Gotta go, sis," he said. He took a quick step away, then, on impulse, turned back. With more understanding than he'd ever shown, he dropped a kiss on her stricken cheek. "Don't worry," he advised.

But she did. She went back into her room and climbed onto her bed, but sleep was the last thing on her mind. Now that the initial horror of Cornelius's words was wearing off, a duller, more nagging fear was setting in. How big was the fire and how much would be burned? She searched her memory for what she knew of the warehouse and was frustrated to realize she knew nothing. Once or twice she had driven by it, but she'd never been inside. She could only speculate and guess.

Chewing her lip and clutching a pillow against her stomach, Hazel wondered if her father had valuable papers stored there. She had no idea what they might be, but it seemed as if reports of fires always mentioned the loss of valuable papers. Were these unidentified important documents kept in a safe? Could the safe withstand a fire? Or maybe there was money in it. That made sense. It stood to reason that he would have money to pay the workers.

The workers. Hazel suddenly tossed aside the pillow and leaped to her feet, propelled by another wave of horror. "What if there are people caught in the blaze?" she asked the room at large. "But what would people be doing there at this time of night?"

she counter-questioned the room, as she began to pace its length. Perhaps her father had a second shift, but somehow she doubted it, especially on a Sunday. A night guard, or guards, however, didn't seem unlikely.

A half an hour ticked slowly by while Hazel continued to pace and worry. At last, unable to stand the suspense any longer, she pulled on some clothes and sped down the stairs. She checked her pace only long enough to close the front door quietly behind her. Then she flew down the walk and swung onto Marlborough Street running. She had never been out this late before, and certainly never alone. It added to the unreal quality hanging in the predawn air.

On Commonwealth Avenue, out of breath and clutching a stitch in her side, Hazel was forced to go from a run to barely a walk. She was scanning the empty, sleeping street in deepening dismay, when she saw a hack plod away from the Hotel Vendomme in the block up ahead. Half scurrying, half hobbling, in an extra burst of effort, she caught up with the carriage and hailed the driver.

To her utter astonishment, he looked at her and kept on going. "Wait! Stop, I said!" Hazel cried, skipping to stay alongside. "I need to go to Summer Street immediately."

"Not in my cab, you don't," the driver replied. "I don't need your kind of business. Not at this hour."

"*My* kind of business!" Hazel gasped, outraged at his meaning. She stopped, plumped her hands on her hips, and looked around expectantly for someone to put this rude man in his place. When she realized that there was no one to help her and that, furthermore, she wasn't apt to find another hack at four o'clock in the morning, she dropped her hands and trotted after him again. "You don't understand," she called up to him. "My father's warehouse is on fire. I have to go there at once."

The driver gave a humorless laugh. "That's the first time I ever heard it put that way," he said. "I suppose you got to go smother the flames, eh?"

This time Hazel was nearly in tears as she said again, "You don't understand. It's a real fire, I promise you. Listen," she added, suddenly inspired. "I'll pay you double if it isn't."

"You'll pay me double either way," the man said, finally reining in his horses. "And I'll have your money *before* we start." He held out his hand. Hazel paid him and climbed gratefully into the carriage.

When they were halfway there, they could smell the fire. At five blocks away they could see the smoke against the gradually graying sky. At two blocks they could go no farther. The street was crowded with charging fire fighters and shoving onlookers. Hazel jumped down and ran the rest of the distance.

The closer she came, the more her fear grew. She could see the flames now, leaping wickedly from smashed windows and through black billows of smoke. It was deafeningly loud and ferociously hot and it gobbled the air as she tried to breathe. With every gasp she took, the stench of burning wool filled her nose and throat.

At last, jammed into a throng of shouting men, she could move no farther forward. Her pleading voice was lost amid the roar of men and flames, and her reaching hands were roughly batted aside. She tried to go back the way she'd come, but the crowd had closed around her, trapping her in the heat and stink and frenzy.

All at once the roof of the warehouse collapsed with a boom that eclipsed the already thunderous din. Great flames shot up, greedily sucking air, and a storm of sparks and embers poured down on the crowd. Frantic, Hazel beat them out of her clothes and shook them out of her hair. Her ears were ringing from the noise. Her eyes were raw and her mouth was parched.

With the break of dawn came a perceptible lessening of the pandemonium. Having consumed everything burnable, the raging fire subsided to a few angry hisses. And the riotous crowd, deprived not only of the blazing drama but also of the cover of night, lost its fervor and began to disperse. Free at last, Hazel wormed her way forward.

"That's far enough, miss," a policeman said, blocking her way with his nightstick. "Nobody goes beyond this line." He pointed his toe to show her an imaginary line in the soot.

"But I'm looking for my father and brother," Hazel explained. "My father owns the warehouse."

For the second time in hours someone doubted her position in the world. The policeman shook his head. "You'll have to look from here," he told her.

Too exhausted to argue, Hazel looked from there. She saw a huge brick building standing gutted and black, surrounded by puddles of murky water and piles of scorched debris. "Oh, dear God," she said softly. "Is everything lost?"

"It's not my place to say, miss," the policeman answered without emotion.

"There ain't enough wool left in there to knit a cap," announced a voice by her side. It held a certain note of satisfaction.

Turning, Hazel saw a husky youth with a pasty complexion and a garish houndstooth jacket. Before she could speak, the policeman interjected a noncommittal "Couldn't say."

The youth nodded vigorously. "I'd stake a week's wages on it," he said.

"Was anyone hurt?" Hazel asked.

"Nah," the young man answered, although he addressed himself to the policeman and not to Hazel. "They waited till everybody was out. They're saying it's revenge," he added with a knowing wink.

"Maybe yes, maybe no," the officer said.

Again the youth nodded. "I heard it was because the old man gave half his workers the boot. They decided to pay him back in kind. Today is Labor Day, you know."

"There'll have to be an investigation," the policeman responded, still refusing to render an opinion.

Hazel edged away, unnerved by the conversation. The policeman seemed indifferent while the youth seemed to revel in the destruction. But for both of them it was an impersonal matter, just another topic of discussion. It wasn't the business *their* fathers had built. It wasn't the currency of *their* lives.

"Papa!" she called suddenly, seeing Edgar in front of the burned-out building. Ignoring both the policeman and his imaginary line, she dashed across the street. "Papa, I was so worried . . . " she began, but her relief congealed before she could finish.

Seen up close, the warehouse was even more devastating than it had appeared from amidst the crowd. Wisps of steam rose with puffs of smoke from the soggy lumps of spoiled wool. Blackened bricks and beams lay scattered on the ground or propped at awkward angles. From within the building came the occasional screech of timbers still tearing loose, as well as the steady drip and slog of water dribbling down from the collapsed roof. The warehouse was ravaged, its contents destroyed. The air around it reeked of charred ruin.

But most frightening of all was her father. For one terrifying moment Hazel thought he'd gone mad. His forehead was so white and drawn his veins were visible. His bulging eyes seemed empty, as if she weren't there. "It's me, Papa," she said, stretching out a trembling hand to touch him.

"What are you doing here?" he demanded, his voice grating and cold. "What stupid notion possessed you to come? I told you to go back to bed. This is none of your business."

"I'm sorry," Hazel managed to whisper, her hand dropping to her side.

"You certainly are," Edgar said contemptuously. "Look at you. Your face is filthy and your clothes are full of holes. You look like a poor immigrant. If you'd stayed home as you should have, this wouldn't have happened."

"I'm sorry," Hazel said again, quickly smoothing her skirt and trying to straighten her hair. She pulled a handkerchief out of her reticule and scrubbed it across her face. She was rocked by her father's outburst. He'd been angry before, but he'd never been this vicious.

"Cornelius!" Edgar shouted into the warehouse. "Take your sister home!" He turned and stalked away, dismissing her completely.

"What are you doing here?" Cornelius asked, emerging through the door. Though his question was the same as Edgar's, his tone was surprised, not harsh.

"I was worried about you and Papa," Hazel answered miserably.

Nodding knowingly, Cornelius took her arm and guided her around the wreckage.

"It's quite serious, isn't it?" she asked

Cornelius nodded again.

Sitting in her bathtub a few hours later, Hazel let the tears stream down her face. No matter how hot she made the water, she couldn't make herself warm. She kept seeing the black and stinking building and kept feeling her father's frigid fury. A cold premonition filled her. There would be no going back to the old, contented times. Life was going to change. Summer was finally over, but a strange new season had begun.


"I've filed for bankruptcy today," Edgar announced at the end of a grim and silent meal several weeks after the fire.

Cornelius set down his fork, but he didn't say a word.

"What does that mean?" Hazel asked wildly, frightened by Edgar's ominous tone. She looked from him to her brother, but both faces were remote and closed. "What will happen?" she asked, her fear increasing.

Instead of answering her, Edgar pushed back his chair and stood up. He folded his napkin and placed it by his plate, then turned and walked away. His movements were controlled and deliberate, but as Hazel watched, his hands seemed to tremble and his step wavered. Her father, the foundation of her existence, was shaken.

"Cornelius," she said anxiously, swinging her gaze to her brother. She caught him in the act of rising, too. "No, don't go, Cornelius," she begged. "Tell me what bankruptcy means."

Cornelius sat down again, but he shrugged his shoulders. "It means Papa's out of cash," he answered simply.

"But how can he be out of cash," Hazel asked, the slang sounding odd in her mouth. "He's a successful businessman."

Again Cornelius shrugged. "I don't really know," he said. "He doesn't tell me anything, but I think he's had a lot of bad luck on the stock market. Then, with wool so slow this summer, he had to borrow a sack of money to cover his losses. Now his collateral has gone up in smoke, and the banks are probably calling in their loans. He's come to the end of the road. Everything's gone."

"Everything," Hazel repeated slowly. She rubbed her forehead. "Could you be more specific, please?" she asked. "Could you tell me what 'everything' is?"

This time Cornelius shook his head. "I don't know, sis," he answered honestly. "But I do know that it doesn't look too good."

As the days went on, it became apparent what "everything" was. First Edgar fired the servants. Within hours of their discharge, five of them were packed and gone. Only Mrs. Harrigan and Annie lingered as they tried to figure out what to do next. They stayed a week, but without the promise of wages, they hardly worked.

Next Edgar sold the horses and carriage, a loss that Hazel felt a little less. She had nowhere to go. She didn't dare go shopping, and she wasn't in the mood for museums or galleries. Most depressing of all, though, she made no social calls. Her friends were back from their summer vacations, but they ignored her as completely as if she'd died. There were no invitations to parties or dances, no notes to stop by for afternoon tea. She attended one dinner party, but only because it was at the Whitakers and only because she was Frederick's fiancée. Even Lucy looked the other way, her pretty face pink, when Hazel approached.

"What have I done to offend them?" she asked Frederick when he walked her home that evening. "Are they angry because I wasn't in Marblehead this summer?"

"It isn't what you've done," he absolved her, though there was an undercurrent of irritation in his voice. "It's your father. No one wants to be associated with bankruptcy. And whether you had anything to do with it or not, you're judged by your father's actions and reputation. You know that."

Hazel did know it, so she didn't bother to argue about the injustice of such a position. In fact, it was one she'd always accepted without question. What she did protest, though, was the judgment being made about Edgar. "Surely he can't be held responsible for the stock market," she said. "From what I've read, that's got to do with the Sherman Silver Purchase Act. And I've heard Papa speak quite forcibly against it. Nor does he have anything to do with the wool business being so sluggish."

"Oh?" Frederick said, his voice tightening. "Are you now an expert on financial affairs?"

Hazel's head dropped in acknowledgment of the reprimand. "No," she answered quietly. They walked in silence for a few minutes before she looked up at Frederick again. "But it isn't Papa's fault," she said pleadingly.

"Hazel." Frederick stopped and turned toward her. He took her hands in his and shook them gently. "It isn't the state of the economy," he said, with the patience of someone explaining things to a child. "It's Edgar. It's all that messy business about the fire and it being set as an act of revenge by a sacked employee. It was on the front page of all the papers and made quite a scandal. That's not the way we conduct our lives."

"I see," Hazel said, much abashed.

"And now there's this matter of your house being auctioned off and you going to live in some dismal bungalow in Lawrence. The whole situation is rather tawdry. It makes people uncomfortable."

"What?" Hazel exclaimed, jerking her hands free. "What are you talking about? You must be mistaken. Our house isn't being auctioned off. That's our *home*."

"Ah," Frederick said, put off by her abrupt reaction. "I gather your father hasn't yet informed you of his plans." He turned and started walking again. "Come along," he said, beckoning her to keep pace with him.

Hazel shut her eyes briefly to compose herself, then started anew. "Please, Frederick," she said. "Please tell me what is going on." She forced herself to speak calmly and to slip her hand through the crook of his arm, though she felt sick with dread.

Mollified, as always, by her show of demure deference, Frederick's tone changed. "Poor pet," he said, patting the hand on his arm. "This is all very trying for you, isn't it? You don't deserve to be treated so unhandsomely."

"What were you saying about the house?" Hazel prompted as mildly as she could.

"It's really Edgar's place to tell you," Frederick said, "but since he seems to be derelict in his duty, I suppose it falls on me." He patted her hand again, as if to brace her for the news. Hazel held her breath.

"The bankruptcy court is putting your house and all its furnishings on the auction block next Thursday," he told her. "The proceeds will be used to settle your father's debts."

Hazel stumbled and would have fallen if Frederick hadn't supported her. For the first time in her life she felt as if she were going to faint.

Nodding importantly, Frederick asked, "Do you see now why everyone is avoiding you?"

No longer interested in snubs or slights, Hazel asked a more urgent question. "What do you mean by 'all its furnishings'?" Her voice quavered as she spoke.

"Everything except your clothes," Frederick answered quietly.

"What about my sketch pads?" Hazel asked, barely above a whisper. "And my diary? And the photo albums?"

"You'll be allowed to keep those personal items. They have no value to anyone but you."

"Mama's silver?"

Frederick shook his head. "It'll be sold."

Hazel walked on awhile, sagging on Frederick's arm. "But where will we go?" she asked in bewilderment.

"I told you," Frederick answered. "You're to move to Lawrence. Edgar has arranged for a house there."

His voice seeped through a dark, dense fog that was enveloping Hazel's mind. She struggled to make some sense of what he was saying. The mill town north of Boston seemed like the other side of the moon. "Why Lawrence?" she finally asked.

Frederick sighed, a short sound that signaled his distaste for this discussion and his role in it. "The one asset that remains untouched is your share of the Great Stone Dam Mill, which we own in Lawrence," he explained. "If you remember, your father purchased it for you a few years back as some sort of acknowledgment of your friendship with Lucy." He shrugged, disinterested in Edgar's motives.

"It's worth comparatively little in monetary terms," he went on, "but we have to give some consideration to your father's position as a stockholder. Or rather," he corrected, with a nod toward Hazel, "as the trustee for the stockholder."

It was getting harder to form coherent thoughts, or to clear her mind of the daze. Completely disoriented, she leaned more heavily on Frederick.

"With that in mind," he continued, accepting her weight without a break in his stride, "we found positions in the mill for both Edgar and Cornelius. Edgar will be employed as a purchasing agent and Cornelius will be an assistant to the overseer on one of the operations floors."

This time Hazel stopped dead still. "The *mill*?" she said, her eyes wide with disbelief. "Papa is going to work in the *mill*?"

"It wasn't easy to find them jobs, you know," Frederick said, slightly offended by her failure to appreciate his benevolence. "The industry is slow right now, and there are thousands of men seeking work with no jobs to be had. We're firing more than we're hiring. It was only by special effort that we managed to contrive a means to employ Edgar and Cornelius."

Hazel hardly heard his words. Her mind was reeling. With her eyes fixed on the sidewalk, she slowly shook her head. "What's to become of us?" she murmured.

There was a limit to Frederick's tolerance for emotional distress, and he was approaching the end of it. "I can't answer for those two," he said shortly, "but I told you once before I'd take care of you, and I will." His tone was more dogged than affectionate. "After we're married, you'll come back to Boston, and life will be as it ever was. You'll have nothing to worry about."

At last Hazel looked up. "Yes, that's so," she said. Her voice grew stronger, though there was a note of desperation in it. "Yes," she said again. "Life will be as it ever was." She grabbed on to that thought and held it for all she was worth. It was the only hope in all this madness.

"Of course, now we'll have to postpone the wedding," Frederick continued more irritably. "We'll have to wait for the talk to die down and then have just a small reception. Mother will be chagrined to think of her only son being married in near anonymity, but there's no help for it. Anything else would be inappropriate, under the circumstances."

A few months ago Hazel would have been relieved to hear Frederick talk of postponing the wedding, but now she greeted the news with dismay. Suddenly everything was different. A delay in the wedding meant a delay in returning to the order and contentment of former times. It meant continuing to live in this nightmarish void. "How terribly disappointing," she said, in all sincerity. "I had November the eighteenth set in my mind."

"Don't tell it to me," Frederick said astringently. "Tell it to your father."

That's exactly what Hazel did as soon as she got home. At least, that was her intention. Even if it meant another blast of anger, she was determined to question him. She went straight into the parlor where she knew she'd find him with the evening papers. "Papa, I've heard the most terrible talk," she began, sinking into the chair opposite his. The rest of her speech dried up in her mouth. There was something strange about Edgar.

Though he was sitting in his usual chair with his usual stack of papers, they lay in his lap unopened while he stared absently into space. Hazel was shocked to see how old and worn he looked. She was suddenly aware of how much weight he'd lost and how his once neat clothes hung shabbily from his body. His hollow cheeks were poorly shaven and his mustache was untrimmed. Behind his spectacles the fury had faded from his eyes. His shoulders sagged. Edgar Merriwether was a defeated man.

"Papa!" Hazel cried, falling to her knees in front of him. She took one of his hands in hers. It was cold and limp. "Papa, are you all right? Do you feel ill? Papa, say something to me," she begged.

Edgar seemed to notice her for the first time. "Hello, dolly," he said. His voice was tired. "Did you have a pleasant evening?" He pulled his hand away and picked up a newspaper, holding it before his face. "We'll have to have a dinner here one of these evenings," he said as he turned the page.

Hazel sat slowly back on her heels, icy with horror. The newspaper was upside down. "Yes, Papa," she barely whispered, her throat choked with tears. Her world, her gilded, gracious, happy world, had crumbled bit by bit around her. Now its very foundation was not just shaken but was completely crushed. She was terrified.

At least I still have Frederick, she thought, fighting down the panic.

When Thursday came, their house was sold to the highest bidder and their possessions were carried off by strangers. Hazel sat for hour after grueling hour until the chair was sold from under her and her mind went nearly numb. Then they loaded their valises in a hired hack and went to catch the train to Lawrence. Edgar looked vacant. Cornelius was quiet and pale. Frederick was in Newport watching the *Vigilant* win the first race of the America's Cup. Eventually it won all three.

# CHAPTER
## 8

"Did you hear what I said, Andrew?" Murdo asked, waving his hand in front of Marco's eyes.

"What?" Marco started, his attention rushing back to the present. "Och, no, Murdo. I'm sorry. You caught me daydreaming. What did you say?" He shook his head to clear away all thoughts but those of sheep.

Satisfied that Marco was listening this time, Murdo pointed his crook at the fank. "I was talking about these ewe lambs," he said. "I think we ought to sell the lot to the lowlands. They'll not survive the winter up here."

Marco walked over to the gate and peered at the lambs milling and baaing inside the stone walls. "Probably so," he agreed. "They look small."

"Aye," Murdo said, nodding. "We had a late lambing this year. It dinna finish till nearly June, so some of the lambs were speaned too young." He shrugged his bony shoulders. "I canna help it," he said. "I canna ask each and every lamb its birth date before I take it from its mother. The second week in August is when the lambs have always been speaned, as long ago as I can remember."

Laughing, Marco clapped Murdo on the back. "Don't worry," he said. "I don't expect you to cross-examine all the sheep. We'll sell the lambs. I'll write tonight to the agent in Perth."

They took a last look in the fank, then started at a leisurely pace for the post were Marco had tied his horse and had left Roger to stand guard. As they walked, Murdo asked, "How is the American lass who was here at shearing time?" He sighed wistfully, adding, "She was a bonny one."

Though Marco's pace remained unhurried, a certain tension stiffened his body. "I imagine she's well," he answered.

His words were pleasant and his tone was friendly, but he didn't invite any further discussion of the "American lass." Nor did he mention that she was the precise subject of his daydreaming. He had been remembering how animated she had looked when she'd stood inside the pen, thrilled and excited by the flash of shears that cut away the sheep's wool. And how, when she'd knelt on the ground to run her fingers through the shorn fleece, she'd managed to look both innocently bucolic and elegantly polished. He sighed, too. She certainly was bonny.

"You've been away, Andrew," Murdo said, taking the hint and easily changing the topic. "Was it Italy again?"

"Yes. Venice," Marco replied as he reached his horse, a huge dapple gray named Winner's Dream. Roger rose, tail wagging, to greet him. *And Tangiers and Marseilles and Barcelona,* he added to himself. He'd been more restless that usual, moving from place to place searching for some sort of satisfaction. Despite diligent efforts to track down the best bouillabaise and paella, that satisfaction eluded him.

He swung up on Win and started down the road toward the Ferguesons'. It was a routine he followed whenever he'd been away for a while. He rode the width and breadth of Strathdorna, stopping at every croft to say hello and to find out what was new. It was why the Highlanders liked him so much. It was also why he knew more about sheep than any MacGregor since his grandfather Hugh.

Jean had just baked and there were oat bannocks lined up to cool on a board by the door. Although Roger's nose twitched and he strained in the direction of the aroma, he stayed at a wary distance, mindful of the rival dogs in the yard. Dismounting, Marco went over to examine the lumpy, round breads.

"I'll say this for you, Andrew," Jean said from the doorway, "you've always had a perfect sense of timing."

"It isn't me," Marco said, grinning. "It's your bannocks. They've lured me here from miles away."

"There you go again, making me out a sorceress," Jean reprimanded, shaking a stout, stained finger at him. "You would have had that nice Miss Merriwether believing I made magic brews in my kettles instead of just colors."

"To her, colors *are* magic," Marco replied, his grin fading. He remembered how fascinated "that nice Miss Merriwether" had been by Jean's mordants and dyes. How her face had lit up when she'd seen the stacks of richly tinted wool. It had been the same in Mantua, in the Palazzo Ducale, and in Venice, floating down the canals. The centuries-old colors of frescoes and buildings had caught her in a spell.

Eyeing him shrewdly, Jean said, "She's a charming lady." She stuffed a bannock in an old flour sack and handed it to him. "Bring her to see me again."

Ignoring her last remark, Marco thanked Jean for the bread, then swung up again on Win. Instead of pointing the big gray further down the road toward Duncan MacLeod's, as was logical, he backtracked to the fank and veered off to the left. Win moved effortlessly, his neck arching and his feet cupping, gliding like a carousel horse.

At Donald MacDonald's tiny cottage, Marco finally reined in the horse and slid to the ground. Roger flopped down, tongue hanging out, and regarded Marco reproachfully. "Sorry, Roge," Marco said, stooping to scratch behind his ears. "It's not our usual route, is it?" He stood up again. "It just seemed right to come here next," he explained, though he talked more to himself than to the panting dog.

Inside the cottage the scene was unchanged from his last visit. A kettle was steaming on the fire, and Lev lay curled up on the hearth. Smiling tranquilly, Donald MacDonald sat on the bench, making the loom go *rattle, whish, clunk, rap, rap*. The only difference was what he was weaving, a bolt of plain blue twill instead of a beautiful tartan blanket.

"Hello, Andrew," Donald greeted him, bringing the syncopation of shuttle, beater, and treadles to a halt. "You're just in time for tea."

"You stay there," Marco said, motioning him down on the bench. "I'll get it. I have a bannock from Jean Fergueson that's still warm from the oven."

"And there's a pot of blackberry jam that Morag MacTavish brought me last week. We'll have a feast." Donald resumed his weaving while Marco fixed tea.

For someone so large, and so accustomed to luxury, Marco moved around the small cottage with surprising ease. The fact was, he found as much pleasure in cooking as he did in eating. The kitchen was his favorite room in every house. Whether it was the tiled chamber at Strathdorna, replete with racks of copper cookware and a battery of cast-iron stoves, or this single hook and tripod over a pile of smoldering peat, he felt at home in a kitchen and was happy when preparing food.

"This looks lovely," Donald said, when he sat down to the simple fare. "What a pity Miss Merriwether isn't here to join us. I know she'd enjoy being here, though no more than I'd enjoy seeing her. She's a rare one, isn't she, Andrew?"

Marco took a swallow of tea before answering. He had turned Win around and had ridden back to Donald's because he had remembered how much Miss Merriwether had enjoyed her visit on that rainy afternoon. He remembered how he had rocked back in his chair and had watched, hour after hour, as she had bent and stretched with the movement of the loom. She had been so serene and graceful, so deeply contented with her task, that for a few moments in his life he had felt perfectly at peace. "Yes, Donald," he said quietly. "She's a rare one."

Nodding, Donald took a bite of bannock, slathered with blackberry jam. "She's got a natural feeling for wool," he said. "I'd like to show her some other patterns. Do you think she'll come back here again?"

Marco thought for a moment, then his shoulders and his eyebrows rose. "Who knows?" he answered, turning his hands palm up.

By the time Marco reached his house on the island the next day, he was ready to admit what it was he'd been searching for all summer. Hazel. His exotic destinations weren't as diverting as they used to be knowing she wasn't at the end of his journey but was back in Boston. And his perennial search for the quintessential experience wasn't as satisfying without her to appreciate his findings. He had dismissed her in disgust when she'd fled home to America in a prim and proper panic, but now he realized he couldn't rid himself of her so easily.

Walking around the parlor, he retraced the circuit Hazel had made. He studied the paintings and collections she had studied, ran his hands over the objects she had touched. He didn't see the teapots or the Turner watercolor, though. He saw her face, illuminated with pleasure in his home.

When he came to the table that held the still life of Gorgonzola and pears, his eye caught an object out of place. It was her brooch. The pearl-studded pin he had unfastened from her collar before laying a kiss on her luscious throat. Her skin had been warm and satin smooth. He had felt her pulse throb beneath his lips. His fingers curled tightly around the pin.

He went into the bedroom and sprawled on the bed, remembering how they'd made love in a pool of June sun. She had been exquisite to look at, sublime to feel. Her passion had thrilled his soul. They'd been so happy lying twined together on the lavender sheets. She had giggled, naked in his arms.

She had been happy and uninhibited. Until Cornelius had come striding up the path. Then she had changed with chilling speed, her delight turning to aversion. He had tried to grab on to her, to pull back the joy, but she had wrenched away, and he might as well have tried to hold on to smoke. He sighed, still feeling the intense disappointment that had clutched his heart.

A slight rustle made him turn his head, and he saw Roger peeking over the edge of the bed. "You miss her, too, don't you?" Marco said, reaching out to rub his nose. In reply Roger inched, paw by paw, onto the bed. He settled down and shut his eyes with his chin resting on Marco's stomach.

"What do you suppose this Frederick means to her?" he mused, absently stroking Roger's ears. "Did you hear how worried she was about him when Cornelius told her there was bad news from home?" When Roger didn't give so much as a flicker of his whiskers in response, Marco continued his speculation.

"She must have been referring to that Whitaker chap I met in Italy last summer. You can't believe what a bore he was." Roger yawned and pushed himself closer to Marco. "Right," Marco agreed. "Utterly dull. Still, he's got a handsome enough face, if you like those blond, chiseled type of looks." He stopped stroking and stared intently at Roger. "You don't suppose she's fallen for that pretty prig, do you?" Roger lifted his head and stared back.

Marco let his head fall against the pillows. It was startling to realize how much the thought hurt. He couldn't bear the idea of Hazel in Frederick Whitaker's arms, of her magnificent spirit quashed by Frederick's deadening mediocrity, and her beautiful body wasted on his ordinary gaze. He sighed again. "I guess I ought to go to Boston," he told Roger. Roger didn't answer. He was sound asleep.

• • •

"I've been thinking of taking a trip to America," Marco said at dinner that evening. He had made a special point of returning in time for the meal, something he rarely did unless there were guests. His passion for food did not extend itself to the overcooked joints of meats, his father favored.

"How nice, dear," Aunt Flora chirped nervously. It was her standard reply to all situations.

It wasn't Malcolm's. His reaction was just the opposite. "America?" he scoffed. "Why on earth would you want to go there? It's a beastly country."

"Have you been?" Marco asked pleasantly, though inwardly he fought to control his temper. It was always the same. Whether it was because he was embittered by his one foreign experience or just his disposition, Malcolm was disdainful of everything that wasn't British. Even at that, his tolerance was limited. It never failed to make Marco wonder how he could be related to such a man.

"Of course not," Malcolm snorted, reaching for his glass of claret. "Wouldn't go. Why do I need to stick myself in a backwoods colony?"

"The United States hasn't been a colony for one hundred and seventeen years," Marco retorted, losing the battle to contain his annoyance. "And I would venture to say it's as civilized as any country in Europe."

Having drained his glass in one breath, Malcolm refilled it from the decanter that stood by his plate. "That it is or it isn't makes little difference," he said, lifting his goblet and pointing it at his son. "What matters is that you've been traveling since early summer and you've only just got back. Really, Andrew"—he paused to take a hearty swallow—"you're going through my money like a cow through clover. Paintings, antiques, extended trips. Don't you think it's time you exercised some restraint?"

That's exactly what Marco was trying to do. With great difficulty he was keeping his mouth closed. To open it would mean a continuation of their eternal argument. He took a swallow from his own glass to calm his anger. It was useless to tell his father that without him watching out for the estate, as he'd done since Hugh had died, there would be no money for either of them to spend. Malcolm didn't understand.

He seemed to think that his fortune was a fixture of his position, like his title or the manor house or his seat in the House of Lords. Malcolm took it as his right that his coffers were full and was further convinced that they were immune to the predations that beset lesser men's money. He believed that only he or his son had the power to squander the vast sums and only by such time-honored aristocratic practices as gambling and high living.

Marco, however, knew better. For someone who found so much pleasure in the aesthetic, he was very clear-headed on the unlovely subject of money. He was under no illusions about what financed his life: the paintings, the antiques, the extended trips. It wasn't the fortune in sheep and land that Malcolm had inherited from Hugh. It was his own careful nurturing of it. Without his knowledge and vigilance, he knew it would all dribble away, lost not through profligacy, but through neglect.

"Actually, I'm considering this trip for business reasons," he said, struggling to make his tone neutral.

"Business?" Malcolm jumped on him instantly. "What business could you possibly have in America?"

Though Marco's knuckles were white around the stem of his glass, his voice was studiously calm as he replied, "Rumor has it that a bill is going to be proposed during the next session of Congress that could have a beneficial impact on us." He paused, but Malcolm made no comment, whether because he was waiting to hear what the legislation was or because he was again busy drinking his wine.

"Officially, it's going to be sponsored by William Wilson for its introduction in the House of Representatives," Marco continued. "But it really reflects the wishes of President Cleveland. It's an attempt to reform the American system of tariffs. In the proposed bill, wool, among other commodities, would be placed on the free list." Again Marco paused, and this time his father took advantage of it.

"Those Americans have a damned confusing method of governing," he complained, eyeing the sweet that the butler was serving. "Just when one thinks a law has been passed, it suddenly appears to have been defeated by the opposing half of Congress. Or vetoed by the president. One never knows where one stands."

"It's really not that complicated," Marco replied with forced patience. "Nor is it vastly different from the way we make laws. In this case, if Mr. Wilson's bill receives the approval of the House of Representatives, it will go to the Senate for a vote. If it passes there, wool will be allowed to enter the United States without a duty."

"Seems to be rather injudicious on their part," Malcolm commented, poking suspiciously at the pudding that had been placed in front of him.

"I believe it's President Cleveland's intention to create more advantageous conditions for the manufacturers," Marco responded, his voice now as tight as his fist. "Increased industry will, in turn, result in lower prices for the consumer. Whatever his reasoning, however, it could open up a new market for us."

His spoon imbedded in the custardy creation, Malcolm looked up at his son. "We've been selling our wool to Douglas Forbes for as long as I can remember," he said. "No need to change."

"Douglas died four years ago," Marco retorted, looking straight back at his father. "His brother Kenneth took over the business and has let it run down miserably. I've had it on my mind for some time to look for a different market."

"It's hardly necessary to go to America for that," Malcolm said, still exploring his dessert. "There are plenty of other agents here. British agents."

"I don't think we can afford to let any profitable opportunity pass by," Marco returned. "The world is in a state of economic malaise. Wool prices are plummeting. While we're fortunate not to have been affected so far, we mustn't get too smug. If we aren't careful, we could sustain heavy losses."

"Nonsense," Malcolm snapped, finally pushing the offending pudding to one side and reaching for his wine. "The only loss we are in danger of sustaining is from your gallivanting. I don't see why you don't just stay home and let this thing get sorted out by itself, instead of running off to trade with strangers."

"It is *not* nonsense," Marco snapped back, his meager supply of patience depleted. "Just pick up any newspaper and read what's happening. There are going to be some shocking changes of fortune before this crisis is over. The unlucky and the unwise will end up begging on street corners while those with imagination and shrewdness will end up way ahead.

"Besides," he went on, managing to moderate his tone, "I wasn't planning to trade with a stranger. I thought I'd go to Boston and look up that chap Edgar Merriwether. You remember him, don't you? He visited here last June. At the time he expressed interest in doing business with us. I just might pursue it."

"Merriwether?" Malcolm said vaguely, his objections suddenly forgotten as his attention was diverted. "Isn't he the one who wouldn't go out shooting? Odd fellow. Rather brash. And his son seemed gawky. The daughter was a beauty, though."

Only the flare of Marco's nostrils as he silently released his breath gave any indication of the depth of his relief. He took another gulp of wine to celebrate his victory. Yes, he thought. The daughter is a beauty.

# CHAPTER

## 9

"No!" Hazel wailed, her fists balling. "It's not fair!" In a completely uncharacteristic gesture, she reached back and gave the kitchen stove a resounding kick. It didn't help. A small cloud of soot dislodged itself from the inner walls and drifted out the open door, but the fire was still out, the coals cold. Now she had a bruised foot as well.

It had not been a good morning, even as mornings went these days. The milkman had refused to leave her order of butter and cream because she owed him two dollars and seven cents and her father had forgotten to give it to her. Then Fanny, the slow-witted serving girl they could barely afford to hire, had scorched the sheets she had been ironing. In exasperation, Hazel had sent her out to the grocery to buy a pound of cheese and a loaf of bread for lunch, despite Fanny's fearful protests that she would be kidnapped by spirits since it was All Hallows' Eve.

"For pity's sake," Hazel had said impatiently. "It's half past ten on a bright and sunny morning. There aren't any spirits abroad. You'll be perfectly safe."

Now it was half past eleven and Fanny still hadn't returned, even though the grocery store was only a short walk away. And the fire was out in the stove. The chicken stew Hazel had started for dinner was congealing, half cooked, in its pot. "It's not fair," she repeated, though her tone was less furious and more woeful this time.

Near to tears, she reached for a handful of kindling and snapped

140

it across her knee. That's when she noticed the streak of soot on her apron, left in the wake of her frustrated kick. One hand still full of kindling, she automatically tried to brush it off. It didn't disappear from her apron, but it smeared all over her cuff. Hazel was ready to throw the kindling at the stove and to stomp as far away from it as she could get, when a knock sounded on the front door.

"Finally!" she said. "That wretched girl has finally come back, and she's too lazy to walk around to the rear of the house."

She marched from the kitchen through the tiny dining room and down a dark, gloomy corridor that ran by the side of the parlor, ready to give Fanny a good scolding. "She probably thinks there are hobgoblins waiting behind the rubbish bins," she muttered, ignoring the smell of cooking cabbage that floated in from the upstairs tenants' staircase, on the other side of the thin wall.

"You'd better have a very good excuse," she said, yanking open the door. Then she froze in shock. It wasn't Fanny after all. It was Marco.

He looked wonderful. He looked big and healthy and bursting with life, unlike the pasty mill workers and the worried shopkeepers who inhabited Lawrence. He looked like Italian sunlight and Mantegna's cherubs and the vast and vibrant Scottish sky. After weeks of loneliness in this depressed mill city, he was a very welcome sight.

Then she remembered how she looked. Her eyes dropped in embarrassment as she surreptitiously searched for someplace to put the kindling still clutched in her fist. Finding nothing, she stuffed it into the pocket of her apron, then awkwardly tried to smooth its smudged skirt. She was suddenly very aware of the heavy smell of her neighbors' cabbage and of the peeling and stained wallpaper in the empty hall. There was more than miles that separated this grim, two-family house from Strathdorna Manor or the Hotel Royal Danieli. There was a whole quality of life. With shoulders hunched against his inevitable rejection of such a squalid scene, Hazel waited for Marco to mumble his regrets and leave.

She had forgotten, however, that Marco never mumbled. "Of course I have a good excuse," he said, stepping inside the door. He seemed almost too big to fit through the narrow entrance. "I missed you terribly."

Hazel's head shot up, her eyes wide with surprise. A warm wave of happiness swelled her heart. It was the nicest thing anyone had said to her in months. But as quickly as it came, the happiness died. He was probably just being polite. Probably just startled by the warning she'd barked when she opened the door. He couldn't really want to see her now that he knew how miserably reduced she was. Nobody did.

"You mustn't feel obliged to stay. . . . " she started. No, that sounded too rude. "I mean, that wasn't intended for you. About having an excuse, that is . . . " She was making it worse. "You see, Fanny . . . " She gave up.

"Hazel," Marco said, closing the door behind him, "I think you'd better invite me in for a cup of tea and tell me all about this Fanny and how she's managed to discompose you so severely. I want to be annoyed at her, too." Although he spoke lightly, he was extremely distressed by her state. When he'd prophesied to Malcolm that this panic would reverse the fortunes of many wealthy men, he'd never dreamed that Hazel would be one of the victims. She didn't belong in a dirty apron or a dismal house.

For two brief instants he'd seen a flash of gladness light up her face and lift her away from this fetid hall. Once when she'd recognized him and once when he'd told her he'd missed her. Then her shabby circumstances had grabbed her back, and that glorious joy had disappeared. It made him feel sick. "Shall we go in?" he suggested when Hazel didn't move.

She had good reason for staying put. She still didn't believe he would want anything to do with her when he realized the seriousness of her straits, and she would rather have his rebuff take place immediately than have it happen later when it could hurt more. "I can't offer you a cup of tea," she said bluntly, "because the fire in the kitchen stove has gone out, and of all the skills I've been required to learn recently, lighting the stove is the one at which I am least adept.

"Besides," she added, "there's no cream for the tea because we have fallen two dollars and seven cents in arrears with the milkman, and he has discontinued his service." She crossed her arms in front of her, sure that this dreary description would drive him away.

It didn't. Putting his hands on her shoulders, he turned her around, then gave her a gentle shove down the hall. "As it happens," he told her, "lighting a stove is one of the areas in which I excel. I'm also quite capable of drinking my tea without cream. We can pretend we're in Russia and strain very black tea through sugar cubes sitting on our tongues. You do have sugar cubes, don't you?"

"Yes," Hazel replied, her tone a little bit awed. Almost as wonderful as the feeling of his hands resting lightly on her shoulders was the knowledge that, having given him every opportunity to leave, Marco had chosen to stay. Not only that, he was already talking about Russia and pretending and food. His imagination and enthusiasm were an invigorating change from the daily routine of anxiety and disappointment and fatigue.

So great was her relief, it wasn't until she was halfway across the dining room that the full impact of his presence hit her. "Wait," she said, halting so abruptly he nearly walked over her heels. "What are you doing in America?" Life in Lawrence was so far removed from anything she'd ever known, it hadn't at first seemed that Venice or the Highlands were any more distant than Boston.

"I told you," Marco answered, his hand shooting out to grab the back of a dilapidated chair for balance. "I'm here because I missed you."

"No," Hazel said, turning to face him. "What are you *really* doing in America?" As refreshing and flattering as it was to hear him talk, her mind wasn't entirely lulled.

"I'm *really* in America because I missed you," Marco said, as gently as possible. It wrenched his heart to hear the new skepticism in her tone. "And to return something that is yours." He paused a moment, then shrugged. "I suppose it would be wise to make some business contacts in anticipation of the tariff reforms, too," he admitted.

"Ah," Hazel said, nodding, her suspicion justified. She turned to continue into the kitchen. Then the rest of what he said sunk in. "What have you got that's mine?" she demanded, whirling back toward him.

This time he was ready and waiting. "Ah," he said, mocking her knowing tone. But when she stuck her hands on her hips, indignant at his teasing, he reached into his pocket and held out her brooch.

"Oh," Hazel said, her hands falling to her sides. Astonished, she stared at the pin laying in pearly splendor on his palm. Then she remembered how she'd come to leave it behind.

"Oh," she said again, looking down, her cheeks red. She hadn't exactly forgotten that afternoon on the island, but in her thankfulness for his bright presence in the gloom of her life, she had pushed the scandal to the furthest recesses of her mind. Along with all its accompanying sensations. Now they came rushing back.

She remembered the June sun melting their bodies together, remembered the crush and caress of his weight. She remembered the feel of his lips as they brushed her bare skin, the feel of his hand sliding across her breast. Mostly, she remembered her absolute happiness as she leaned against the pile of eyelet pillows and let him put morsels of smoked salmon in her mouth.

"Thank you for returning it," she said primly, holding out her hand. Her gaze didn't meet his.

"No, no," Marco said, holding the brooch up. "I took it off; it's only fair that I should put it back on."

For a shocked instant her eyes flickered toward his face, then her blush deepened and her hand fell. "Very well," she said tightly, lifting her head and looking away.

"You needn't act as if I'm about to extract your teeth," Marco chided, carefully slipping the pin through her collar and fastening its clasp.

Although his fingers barely grazed her chin, she could feel his breath in her hair and could smell the sandalwood soap he used to scrub his glowing cheeks. She could feel her heart start to beat faster. As soon as the pin was in place, she turned quickly away and entered the kitchen. Behind her back, Marco grinned.

"There it is," Hazel said, pointing at the battered Glenwood whose door still hung open, letting the odor of dead coals fill the air. She was beginning to wonder about the wisdom of this visit.

"Hmm," Marco commented, glancing briefly at the tired-looking stove and then around the rest of the room. There was a shaky wooden table and four wooden chairs, a doorless cupboard, and an iron sink that was bleeding rust. His eyebrows raised.

"We've just moved in," Hazel said apologetically. "We haven't even been here a month. I mean to have it painted. I think that will help."

"Probably," Marco said briefly. There wasn't much else he could add. He knelt before the stove and fiddled with the dampers and rearranged the coals. Then he held out his hand expectantly. "Let me have the kindling in your pocket," he said. Hazel gave it to him. "And a match." She placed one in his hand. He struck it, stuck it under the twigs, and watched as the flames soared. After a minute the coal caught, too. He closed the door and stood up.

"It never does that for me," Hazel complained. "It always smolders and sputters and goes out."

"It's all in the dampers," Marco advised. "The fire has to breathe. Now," he said, going over to the sink to wash his hands, "shall we have tea or shall we proceed directly to lunch?"

It was Hazel's turn to smile. "I frankly had my doubts about a cup of tea and a cube of sugar being sufficient to satisfy you," she said, sitting down on one of the chairs. "However, lunch is even more hopeless than tea." She lifted her hands in the air. "There's nothing to eat." She suddenly felt more relaxed about admitting it.

"Nothing?" Marco said, looking at the few cans and crocks in the cupboard. "Possibly there is very little, but I can't believe there's nothing." He went over to the stove, picked up the lid on the pot, and peered in.

"That's dinner," Hazel said from her seat.

"Hmm." Marco's eyebrows raised again. He put down the lid and moved over to the cupboard.

"I sent Fanny to the store for some bread and cheese," Hazel explained. "But she's been gone forever. She's so slow, she probably forgot. That's who I thought you were when you knocked on the door."

"Ah-ha," Marco said, although it wasn't clear whether he was responding to her explanation or to some item he discovered on the shelves.

"What are you doing?" she asked, half rising and straining to see around his broad back.

"Making lunch," he answered, turning toward her, his hands full.

"With that?" she said suspiciously, settling back down. "That bread is two days old and that rind of cheese is as hard as a rock. Besides, there's no butter."

"No matter," Marco said, laying his plunder on the table and turning to rummage some more. He found four eggs, a can of tomatoes, and a few wilted sprigs of parsley. "*Zuppa Pavese*," he announced.

Hazel furrowed her brow.

"Pavian Soup," he translated. "It's the specialty of a very pretty city in the province of Lombardy named Pavia. The soup is made with chicken broth and poached eggs and toasted bread."

"Where are you going to get the chicken broth?" Hazel asked, her suspicion aroused again.

"From your stew," Marco answered calmly, approaching the pot with a ladle.

"No, you mustn't!" Hazel rose again in alarm. "That's all we have for dinner. Seriously. It took me half the morning to make it."

Marco's hand covered hers as she grabbed the ladle. "Hazel," he said quietly, "do you really think I would leave you hungry?"

She looked at him a moment, then her grasp on the ladle loosened. "No." She shook her head and went back to her seat.

"That's what the can of tomatoes is for," Marco said. "You'll see. It'll give the stew more flavor. Leave it to me."

Hazel followed his advice. Sitting in her chair, she watched as he moved knowledgeably and comfortably around her kitchen, straining broth, grating cheese, toasting bread. Not only did his skill amaze her, and his lack of self-consciousness, but also the very fact that he was here. In Lawrence. In her house. Chopping parsley.

Most of all, she was amazed by her reaction to his presence. She'd been variously glad, grateful, thrilled, and, for a few moments, embarrassed, but despite what had happened in Scotland, she hadn't been appalled or repulsed. Now she watched as he enlivened the drab little kitchen, doctoring her stew and preparing a savory-smelling lunch. It added a new dimension to the day. One, in fact, that he often seemed to inspire: delight.

"It's almost ready," Marco said, leaning over to sniff his soup. His nostrils flared in approval. "I've only to poach the eggs. Can you set the table?"

"Of course I can," Hazel answered, standing up immediately. "I'm not that lacking. Though there isn't that much to set. All the good dishes and linens and Mama's silver were sold."

Except for a brief glance at her, Marco seemed to ignore her last remark. "I didn't mean to imply that you were incapable," he said casually. "I suppose I ought to have said, '*Will* you set the table?' And *will* you set it in here? I know it isn't your habit to take your meals in the kitchen, but the dining room appeared excessively dark."

"It doesn't have any windows," Hazel admitted, shrugging resignedly. "I have no objection to eating in the kitchen. I usually do these days. You'd be surprised how my habits have changed."

"I can imagine," was all Marco said. For the moment.

Hazel spread out a plain white cloth, set out two plain white bowls, and filled two glasses with water from the sink. Marco's eyebrows raised again, but he made no comment. Instead, he laid thick slices of toast in the bottoms of the bowls, put a poached egg on top of each slice, and ladled chicken broth over it. "Traditionally, it calls for Parmesan cheese," he explained, as he sprinkled the chopped parsley and grated cheese in each bowl. "But this will do nicely." He finished with a grind of black pepper.

It was delicious. While they ate, the conversation was equally as enjoyable. Hazel asked after Roger and was told he was looking particularly sleek, having had a bath the day before Marco left. Marco asked about baseball and was told the Bostons had won the pennant for the third year in a row. They talked about sheep and the opera and food. Truffles were in season in the Piedmont region of Italy, and Gilbert and Sullivan's *Utopia Limited* had just opened in London.

"Now," Marco said, pushing his empty bowl to the side and resting his arms on the table. "Tell me about your life here."

The pleasure suddenly drained from the meal. The lovely scenes from better places and better times faded. Reality returned, even uglier after the temporary escape. "There's nothing much to tell," Hazel answered evenly. "It's a quiet existence."

"I'm not blind, Hazel," Marco said soberly. "I can see for myself that this isn't Buckingham Palace. It isn't even the house I went to on Marlborough Street in Boston."

"You went there?" Her tone was wistful.

"Yes. It was the address on your father's card. I was looking for you."

"It's a nice house, isn't it?"

"I didn't go inside."

"It was sold at auction."

"Yes."

She gulped. "So was everything in it."

Marco reached across the table and cupped his hand over hers.

The warmth of his touch was more than she could stand. She pulled her hand away and clenched it, with the other, in her lap. Despite this physical effort to hold in the pent-up horror, it suddenly came spilling out. "It's awful here," she choked. "Our house on Marlborough Street was so comfortable and this one is so miserable. Never mind that it's tiny. It's damp and it's drafty and it isn't even proper winter yet. But worst of all, I feel as though I live yoked to Mrs. O'Sullivan, upstairs. I can smell everything she cooks, which is mostly cabbage and potatoes. During the day I hear her babies crying, and at night I hear her arguing with her husband. And there's always some disgusting laundry dangling in front of my bedroom window, blocking the light.

"I spend all my days trapped in this house," she went on, passing her hands through the air to describe the boundaries of her life. "I've no one to visit and no one visits me. There are no museums or galleries here, and there's no point in going to the shops. There is a library, but I've no time to read."

"Have you kept up with your sketching?" Marco asked, steepling his hands beneath his chin and looking very grave.

"My sketching." She sounded particularly discouraged. "I haven't even unpacked my pads and paints," she said. "There's no place to put them and no place to work. The dining room has no windows, and Cornelius sleeps in the parlor. My room is too small, unless I sit on the bed, though there is still the problem of Mrs. O'Sullivan's laundry blocking the light. Besides," she added, shrugging, "I've no time for that, either."

"What is it that you do?" Marco asked, genuinely puzzled. "I understand that you no longer have a staff to bring you breakfast in bed, but this is a small house. It shouldn't be that hard to keep."

"Maybe it isn't if you know what you're doing," Hazel replied, smoothing the edge of the tablecloth with both hands. She looked up suddenly, her expression beseeching. "I don't mean to sound self-pitying," she said. "I know that we've fallen on desperate times and that I have to do my share, but I don't know *how* to do it. Keeping house on Marlborough Street meant *planning* the meals, not hunting for the least expensive ingredients and then cooking them. It meant telling the laundress that Papa's collars were too starched, not sewing on buttons and bleaching towels. It didn't mean carrying coal up from the basement or lighting the stove or heating water for baths or shoveling out ashes."

"But you have some help, don't you?" Marco said. "What about this Fanny person? Can't she do most of that?"

"Oh, her." Hazel dismissed the missing maid with a toss of her head. "She's even more inept than I am. I think the only reason we can afford her at all is because she's so dim. And that's another thing." Having undammed her problems, there was no stopping the flow.

"We're always worrying about money." Hazel sat back in her chair and shook her head hopelessly. "We have to ask the price of everything and then think very carefully, and often as not, we don't buy it. But I don't even know how much is too dear because no one tells me how much we have to spend. I only know that it's never enough."

The more she spoke, the more distressed Marco became. It hurt him to see her living in such cheerless conditions. It especially hurt to hear her sounding so bewildered. Before, she hadn't known where her comfortable life had come from. Now she didn't know where it had gone. He tried to figure out how to help her.

"I'm surprised that money is so tight," he said. "Edgar may have lost his business, but he didn't lose his knowledge or his skill. I should think that any number of mills would be glad to have someone of his experience. Surely he could command a decent salary."

Hazel hesitated, sitting up a little straighter. "I don't think Papa has been quite . . . um . . . *right* since the fire," she confessed. "I think he's still suffering the shock."

"What about Cornelius? Isn't he working?"

"Yes, he's working. Poor Cornelius." Hazel gave a small, sad smile. "He's an assistant overseer on the weaving floor of the Great Stone Dam Mill. He hasn't said anything, but I know he hates it."

"He may well hate it," Marco said unsympathetically, putting Cornelius's discomfort a distant second to Hazel's, "but he's earning a wage. Doesn't he contribute to household expenses?"

"Yes, of course he does. Everything he earns," Hazel said hastily. She was suddenly aware of how much she'd confided in Marco, answering his questions without thinking him nosy. It seemed natural to tell him what was happening, but enough was enough. She didn't want to sound like a case for the Church Charity Society.

"Please don't misunderstand me," she said earnestly. "We aren't starving or without shelter or even housed in a tenement. It's just by comparison with how we used to live . . . " Her voice trailed off as her memory wandered back. Then she shook her head to bring herself into the present. "We have meat every day," she continued briskly, "and all the coal we need. We have warm clothes and new shoes and I have my own room. Which is more than many families in Lawrence. It isn't so terrible. It could be a lot worse." She gave Marco a smile that she hoped would look bright.

He saw it as pathetic. "Poor Hazel," he said softly. Though he'd often been impatient with her pampered ignorance, he'd never wished her such a brutal awakening. "You've had a rough go of it."

The emotion in his voice stirred a strange feeling in her heart. It felt warm and wonderful, though she couldn't identify it. Moreover, she suspected that she shouldn't. It was probably dangerous to encourage his tenderness.

"How selfish of me to carry on like this," she said in her best company tone. "I'm behaving like a spoiled child whose toys are broken. We've had a slight setback in fortune, but it's only temporary I'm sure." She paused, then said more staunchly, "*Very* sure. Papa will get better soon, and he'll take care of everything. So will Frederick."

A shock shot through her. Frederick. How had she managed to forget about Frederick? How had she managed to let him slip so completely out of her head? Again?

She stood up abruptly and began to clear the table, stacking the dishes in the sink. More to the point, how could she have let Marco into her home? And back into her life? How could she have sat there, pouring out her problems, saying things to Marco she wouldn't dream of telling Frederick? She felt his eyes on her as she yanked away his bowl, but she refused to look up and meet his gaze. He had a way of turning her thoughts inside out, of making her act contrary to what she knew was absolutely proper. She wasn't going to give him the opportunity to work his charms on her again.

Too frequently she found herself in situations with him where she allowed her judgment to be overwhelmed by his dog or his repasts or his extraordinary manner and looks. And too frequently for comfort, those situations turned out to be scandalously intimate. Worse yet, somehow oblivious to the impropriety of them, she actually enjoyed them. Maybe today she wasn't naked in his bed, but well-bred ladies didn't each lunch alone in their kitchens with well-bred men.

She had sworn she'd have nothing more to do with him when

she'd fled from Scotland, but now here he was in her house, listening to her complaints and making her a meal named for a pretty city in Italy. Beguiling her, in short, with soup and sympathy. It was bad enough that he'd managed to creep into her mind in the months since she'd seen him last, goading her and delighting her in the privacy of her thoughts, but to let him do it in person was too much. Why in the world had she let him in the door?

"Frederick," he said, still seated at the table. His voice had a harder sound to it. "That name keeps coming up. Is he, by any chance, the same Frederick I met in Milan?"

"Yes," Hazel answered, not turning around, but busying herself at the sink. "Mr. Frederick Whitaker."

Marco stood slowly and walked around the table. "Mister?" he said, coming up behind her.

She heard the probing in his tone and meant to end his familiarity right here. She'd already divulged too many personal details. "Listen," she said, whirling around where she stood. And spinning into his arms. Her heart jumping, she looked up. He smiled down. Then he leaned forward and kissed her.

For a long moment she forgot what she was going to say. In fact, she forgot about Frederick and Lawrence and lunch. Marco's lips moved from her mouth to her cheek. His tongue traced the curve of her neck. He buried his nose, his regal Renaissance nose, in the silky mass of her hair, while his strong hands stroked the small of her back and circled her waist. For a long moment the only thing that existed was his touch and his taste and the tickle of his curls.

"I missed you, Hazel," he whispered into her ear. In response she crushed closer to him. It felt so good to be held, to be kissed, to have been missed. Her aching loneliness and misery disappeared. She'd missed him, too. Terribly. Her hands slid around his abundant body.

Then Mrs. O'Sullivan's baby woke from his nap and let out a howl. Though he was one floor away, he might as well have been sleeping in the sink. For the second time in minutes a shock shot through Hazel and jerked her back to reality. With a gasp she shoved Marco from her, then stepped quickly out of his reach. Her heart was beating very hard and her face felt hot.

"I see what you mean about the babies," Marco said ruefully, turning toward her.

"No!" Hazel said, holding up one hand while the other was

clapped over her chest. "And it isn't the babies. It's . . . it's the . . . " She couldn't quite say it.

"The kiss?" Marco offered.

She nodded vigorously. "It was a mistake," she said. "A dreadful mistake. I should never have allowed it to happen."

"Oh?" Marco's eyebrows raised.

"Yes," she said, plunging forward despite the heat on her cheeks. "What happened that afternoon in Scotland was horribly wrong. It was disgraceful, and I swore that nothing even approaching that would ever happen again. I shouldn't have invited you in this morning."

"You didn't," Marco said, his eyes narrowing at this show of piety. "I invited myself."

Lips pursed, she shook her head, refusing to be swayed. "It's no use, Marco," she said. "You must go and please don't come back." Something cold filled her stomach when she said those words, but she knew they had to be uttered.

"I don't believe you mean that," Marco said softly. He took a step in her direction. She took a corresponding step away. "You can't even look at me."

Hazel forced herself to look at him. "Please go," she repeated, though this time her voice wavered.

"But why?" Marco asked, spreading his hands. "Because I kissed you? You enjoyed it as much as I did. You know it's true."

She shook her head again. "I don't want to discuss it," she said. "You've got to go or people will talk. I'm engaged to be married, and I can't dishonor my fiancé with either deeds or gossip."

"What!" Marco exploded. Her words hit him like the kick of a horse. "What are you talking about? This is a prank. You're paying me back for all the times I've teased you. Right?"

"No."

"Then it's a piece of nonsense," he said, taking another step toward her. She moved around behind the table. "It's bound to be a desperate whim. How long have you been engaged?"

Head hanging, Hazel's answer was barely audible. "Since Christmas," she admitted.

"Since Christmas," Marco repeated flatly, starting to pace back and forth on his side of the table. "That's just fine. You were engaged when you came to Scotland, and you never mentioned a word about your future husband. He must have made quite an impression on your affections." His tone was sarcastic, and he stopped pacing long enough to glare at her.

Hazel didn't see the fury in his eyes because her head was still bent, but she could hear it in his voice and could imagine the blue turned to steel. "I told you," she said, "I made a mistake that afternoon."

"Your mistake wasn't in Scotland," he snapped back, pointing his finger across the table. "Your mistake was in agreeing to marry this man, whoever he is." He had started his pacing again, but stopped short. "Oh, no," he said with deadly quiet. "I do know who he is. He's *Mister* Frederick Whitaker, isn't he?"

Too stricken to speak, Hazel could only nod.

"Hazel." His voice was suddenly soft again. "Forget about Scotland. Forget about me. Frederick Whitaker still isn't the man you should marry. He has no spirit. No humor. He'll stifle the life from you. Your marriage will be a living hell."

"No," Hazel protested, finally raising her head. "No, that isn't true. It'll be an ideal marriage. Everyone says so. Our families have known each other for years. We have the same background, the same tastes, the same friends." Even as she said it, her words sounded hollow. While it may once have been the case, it was no longer so.

"And where are these friends now that you need them?" Marco demanded, giving instant voice to her doubts. He put both hands on the table and leaned across it. "How often do they come for tea and a comforting chat? For that matter, where is Frederick? I take it he hasn't fallen on hard times. What has he done to help you in your need?"

"He's done a great deal," Hazel replied, seizing a subject she could speak of with certainty. "You malign him, but he's really a very good man. Just because he doesn't have your sense of drama doesn't mean he isn't kind in his own way. After all, he found jobs for Papa and Cornelius when there were none to be had. His family owns the Great Stone Dam Mill, you know."

Far from being impressed by this information, Marco was aghast. He straightened slowly until he stood very tall. "Do you mean to say he owns the mill where your father and brother work, and he can't even pay them enough so his fiancée doesn't have to live in the shadow of Mrs. O'Sullivan's laundry?" He shook his head. "Doesn't he have any feelings for you at all?"

"Of course he does," Hazel said, faltering. She ignored his first question because she didn't know the answer and concentrated on the second question instead. It was suddenly very important to convince Marco of Frederick's worth. Possibly because she had to convince herself as well. "He's extremely fond of me," she insisted, searching desperately for an example to prove her point. "He calls me his darling," she said triumphantly. "And his sweet pet."

That didn't impress Marco, either. "His pet?" he shouted, resuming his pacing, this time jabbing his hand through the air. "You're not a pet. Roger's a pet. Aunt Flora's budgie is a pet. *You* are a person." He stopped to lean across the table again.

But Hazel had had enough. Maybe Frederick didn't make her heart pound with excitement, maybe he didn't delight her or thrill her or make her giggle, but he represented a time when she'd been deeply contented, and right now contentment seemed an exalted goal. She clung to it determinedly. "I'm going to marry Frederick," she said firmly. "And go back to leading a normal life."

Marco could have argued with her words, but not with her tone. It shut off all dispute. After a silent minute he shrugged and pushed himself up. "You seem to know what you want," he stated.

"Yes," Hazel said, although she already sounded less sure.

He took a deep breath. "Check the stew for salt," he said tonelessly. "It would also benefit from a bay leaf if you can find one." He rounded the table but didn't attempt to go near her as he headed for the door. "You stay here," he told her. "I invited myself in, I can show myself out."

The next instant he was gone. There was a void in the room in his wake. Hazel suddenly noticed the cold draft. And Mrs. O'Sullivan's babies and the dirty dishes in the sink. And the coal bin that needed filling and the fact that Fanny still hadn't returned. And the loneliness. It seemed even greater than before. She slumped down in a chair, her hands lying limp in her lap. "I'm going to marry Frederick," she repeated. "Then everything will be put to rights." The faucet dripped.

# CHAPTER

## —❧ 10 ❧—

"Dolly, tell the cook to prepare something special tonight," Edgar said when he and Cornelius returned from the mill that evening. "We're having company for dinner."

Hazel's hand froze in midmotion as she reached to take her father's top coat and hat. Coming in behind him, Cornelius looked shocked. Edgar had been behaving in an increasingly odd manner lately. No longer suffering the deep silence of depression, he now seemed to inhabit a world of his own. He often gave the impression that he was back on Marlborough Street, once again a wealthy businessman. Never, however, had that impression been so sharp.

In dismay Hazel saw her father's distant gaze behind his smudged spectacles and saw, also, that it was futile to try to bring it into focus. "Yes, Papa," she said, recovering her own balance. The only thing she could do was play along with his illusion. Smiling affectionately, she took the coat he handed her. "How many shall I tell the cook to expect?" she asked.

"Just one," Edgar replied, pulling his evening paper from under his arm. He walked briskly into the parlor, where he settled in the lone chair.

Hazel and Cornelius exchanged worried glances. They hung the coats they were holding on wooden pegs, then headed for the kitchen, meaning to discuss this matter at length. Edgar's next remark, however, froze Hazel in her tracks again.

"It's Andrew MacGregor. Do you remember him from Scotland?" he asked as he unfolded his newspaper. "He came to see me at my office this morning. I suspect he's gotten wind of the tariff talk and wants to make contacts in case it has a favorable outcome. He's a shrewd man. And he has a good product. I won't mind doing business with him at all." He lifted the paper, the conversation ended.

Hazel whirled back toward the parlor. "You mean you really invited him for dinner?" she exclaimed in alarm.

Setting down his paper, Edgar peered at his daughter. "I told you I did," he said. "I thought you understood me." He looked at her more carefully. "Are you all right, dolly?" he asked. "You ought to remember to take off your apron when you've finished your paintings. It looks messy." He went back to reading the *Lawrence Evening Star.*

"Yes, Papa," Hazel said automatically, though she left the apron tied to her waist. "You invited *Andrew MacGregor* to dinner?" she persisted, still not accepting the fact that Marco was going to be a guest. "Tonight?"

Edgar's paper came crashing down. "Yes, Hazel," Edgar replied, a touch of irritation in his tone. "I've told you twice now that I did. How could I not after all his hospitality? He'll be here at seven."

Hazel's eyes darted to the clock on the table. It said five minutes till. Her alarm grew.

"What'll we do, sis?" Cornelius asked in a low voice.

Hazel squared her shoulders. "Serve him chicken stew," she answered evenly. "I doubt that he'll object." More fiercely she thought, He'd better not. He made it himself.

"You mean you really believe that Andrew is coming?" Cornelius asked in amazement.

"Yes," she answered briefly. There was a knock on the door. She added, "He's here."

Cornelius looked at Hazel, too astonished to move. Edgar looked at Hazel, expecting their visitor to be shown in. In an uncommon display of annoyance and rebellion, Hazel turned around and walked into the kitchen.

"He knew the whole time he was here that he'd be coming back for dinner," she muttered, grabbing the sheet of baking soda biscuits she'd prepared and thrusting it into the oven. "It's just another one of his dreadful jokes, and he had the gall to chastise me for teasing." She slammed the oven door shut.

There was something else that was unnerving her, though, something she hated to admit. Despite wishing it were otherwise, she was glad he was there. As she'd been when she stepped off the train in Scotland, she was enormously relieved she hadn't chased him away for good.

She knew it was immoral and improper and, above all, disloyal, but she'd enjoyed this afternoon far more than she had any right to. First they'd chatted about trivialities, and then Marco had listened to her complaints, but she'd said everything on her mind on every single subject. She'd never known anyone she could talk to like that. Someone who not only accepted her thoughts, but expected—no, insisted—that she think.

"There you are, Miss Merriwether," came Marco's voice behind her. "How delightful to see you again."

She looked over her shoulder to see Marco standing with her brother, just inside the kitchen door. "Good evening," she said coolly, looking back at the stove, suddenly finding it imperative that she stir the stew. However much she enjoyed his visits, they were still wrong, and she meant to discourage them at every opportunity. She was engaged to marry Frederick, and that's all there was to it.

Unfazed, Marco advanced around the table. "I hope you'll forgive my modest gifts," he said. "They're just a token to express my pleasure at being your guest for dinner."

Reluctantly she looked at him again. He held out a huge bouquet of heather and a beribboned box of confections. "Thank you," she said, slowly setting down the wooden spoon and replacing the stewpot lid. Only then did she take the flowers and the package. "We'll have the chocolates for sweet."

"Not chocolates, Miss Merriwether," Marco corrected, his tone indicating his amusement with her pique, "*Marrons glacés*. Candied chestnuts. They're a specialty of the north of Italy, though I find the ones made in Milan by the Caffè del Teatro alla Scala to be incomparable. Nally Bellati makes sure I receive a dozen boxes every fall."

Hazel nodded, refusing to be enchanted by another of his food stories.

"Some people like to use them as the basis of fabulous desserts such as the whipped cream and meringue trifle called Monte Bianco," Marco went on blithely, "but I prefer to nibble them as they are, alternating with sips of a fine cognac."

"We haven't got any cognac," Hazel said, putting the box on the table and looking around for something to hold the flowers.

"Andrew's brought us some," Cornelius said happily. "As well as several very nice bottles of wine."

Glancing sideways at him, Hazel said politely, "How generous of you, Mr. MacGregor." Then she turned her back as she reached for a big pitcher.

"Not at all, Miss Merriwether," Marco replied, easily plucking the pitcher from its place on the top shelf and handing it to her. She took it grudgingly, but when she started to turn away, she found he hadn't let go. Forced to, she finally looked him full in the face. "It's I who am grateful for your generosity," he said, the corners of his mouth quivering. "You can't know how much I appreciate being able to join your family table. A hotel dining room can be a cold and lonely place."

"No doubt," Hazel said, giving the pitcher a yank. Suspicion suddenly outweighed her irritation. What was he up to now? she wondered. When he'd stalked out of the kitchen a few hours earlier, his expression had been ominous. Now here he was, plying her with presents, a grin lurking on his face.

It wasn't immediately apparent what Marco had up his sleeve, if anything besides an Italian linen shirt. He was the perfect guest. When they sat down to dinner, he pretended, along with the others, that they were having a seven-course feast instead of a bowl of biscuits and stew. And from their conversation about the social season now underway, he might have been on Marlborough Street, or at Strathdorna Manor, rather than in a two-family house in Lawrence, competing to be heard over Mrs. O'Sullivan's nightly argument.

Only when Hazel rose to leave the men to their after-dinner ritual did Marco break from accepted form. "Please don't go, Miss Merriwether," he begged, also standing. "It seems cruel to sentence you to solitude in the parlor while we sit merrily in here. I'm sure we have nothing to say that is unsuited for your ears. At worst, you'll be bored. But you may as well be bored in company as all alone."

"But your cigars," Hazel protested, though not very forcefully. Not only had she no desire to sit in the parlor by herself, it seemed an absurd gesture when it was only a few feet away.

"I, for one, am perfectly willing to forego that rite," he said, waving her back into her chair. "I've never been fond of tobacco anyway. It deadens the flavor of food, which to me, as you might imagine, is almost a crime."

"It shortens the breath, too," Cornelius added as Hazel sat down. "I've never understood how some fellows can smoke and play baseball. It's like coming up to bat with one strike against you."

"Cornelius," Edgar warned. "You know how I feel about baseball chatter." Mostly, though, he was upset because he'd been looking forward to a cigar.

With a disgusted shrug, Cornelius said, "I don't know what it matters anyway. After a day in the mill a little tobacco smoke couldn't possibly make a difference. It's got to be healthier than the air in there."

Hazel looked at her brother in astonishment. She had never heard him sound so cynical. Certainly she'd never seen him shrug off anything to do with baseball. Looking at him more closely, she realized how much he'd changed since the summer, too. Preoccupied with her own problems and worried about her father, she'd failed to notice that her baby brother had grown up. His shoulders had broadened and his face had lost its fuzziness, but most of all, he carried himself with an air of sureness. In the midst of calamity and crisis and depression, Cornelius had come of age. Hazel smiled. He was a fine-looking man.

"Now you sound like those troublemakers who are always agitating for a strike," Edgar said crankily. "They seem to think they're entitled to velvet-padded armchairs and glasses of champagne."

"They think they're entitled to safe and humane working conditions," Cornelius retorted. "And so do I." He picked up the glass of cognac Marco had poured for him and took a swallow.

"Nonsense," Edgar snapped. "Next you'll be mewling for the ten-hour day with the rest of the rabble-rousers."

Cornelius nodded. "It's a good idea. By the end of the day most of the workers are ready to drop from exhaustion. With what they're paid, they can't afford either decent housing or nourishing food. When they come in the next morning, they haven't properly recovered from the day before. And around it goes again, day after day, week after week, sucking the lint into their lungs, listening to the noise of the machinery, wearing down slowly, until one morning they can't get up anymore." He took another swallow of cognac.

"You're being melodramatic," Edgar scoffed.

"I'm being realistic." Cornelius leaned forward and tapped the table for emphasis. "There's a fellow on my floor who I could've sworn was forty-five or fifty. Today I found out that he's exactly my age. He's been working in the mill since he was nine." He leaned back and gave another shrug. "He'll be dead before he's twenty-five."

Edgar's own shoulders twitched irritably. "You're taking a very simplistic view," he said. "Running the mills on a shorter day or at greater expense simply isn't profitable. If there's no profit, there's no mill. Then where will your workers be?"

"Probably not much worse off than they are now," Cornelius growled, reaching for his glass again.

Turning her head from her father to her brother, Hazel's eyes grew wider with each exchange. Concerned only with learning to cook and keep house, she hadn't thought about what went on in the mills. They were simply there. The massive brick structures dominated the city. In fact, Lawrence had been built in 1845 for the sole purpose of making cloth. The mills employed thousands of workers, many of them, these days, immigrants from Ireland, Canada, Germany, Poland, and Italy. Those people who didn't participate in actual textile production worked in factories that made mill machinery or as mechanics who fixed it.

Hazel knew that life in Lawrence revolved around the mills and their foreign-born workers because she could see the human waves disappearing inside the immense buildings, or pouring back into the streets, at the sound of the factory bells. On the sidewalks, or in the shops on Essex Street, she heard the mixture of accents and languages. She knew the people were poor, because she saw how they dressed and saw the tenements where they lived, four, five, and six wooden stories up and jammed together on a block. But she didn't know what went on behind any of the facades.

She caught herself thinking that the mills were the new currency of her life, and that, once again, she didn't know anything about it. It was no longer a question of what paid for her paint boxes and bonnets, but of what put the chicken stew in her pot. Cheeks burning with guilt and embarrassment, she snuck a peek at Marco. His gaze was fixed on her, his hands folded across his stomach. His expression was thoughtful. She looked quickly away.

"The way things are going in this country right now, they should be grateful they have any jobs at all," Edgar said. "The cotton workers in New Bedford just took a ten percent wage reduction.

They were smart enough to accept the cut without squawking."

"They had no choice," Cornelius retorted, twirling the cognac in his glass. "They knew that the alternative is starvation. They had to accept what the owners dictated or risk being fired. Besides, the workers in New Bedford were making more than those in Lawrence to begin with. Even with the reduction, they're probably making more. Everyone knows that the mill operatives in Lawrence are the lowest paid in the state."

He sat back in his chair and took another swallow. "However, the mill *owners* in Lawrence," he added deliberately, "can still afford their fancy yachts."

Hazel gasped. That was a direct reference to Frederick, and it cast him as an ogre. She snuck another quick glance at Marco to see if it had registered with him. His eyebrows were raised. She turned back to her brother. "You must be exaggerating," she protested. "I'm sure the situation isn't as bad as you pretend." She felt obliged to defend Frederick, especially in front of Marco.

"Of course he's exaggerating," Edgar snorted. "The workers are uneducated. In most cases illiterate. Some of them can't even speak English. It's a romantic notion to expect them to earn as much as the owners, who have millions of dollars invested." He reached for his own glass and took a gulp.

"I am not exaggerating," Cornelius said hotly. "And I'm not 'pretending' that the situation is bad. The average mill operative doesn't earn as much in a year as Frederick spends every summer just varnishing his yacht. It isn't a 'romantic notion' to expect that a man has more value than a boat."

"But you heard Papa," Hazel returned primly, though inwardly she was amazed at her brother's fervor. She remembered being equally amazed when he'd spoken out against the Highland Clearances while they were having tea in London, surprised by his unexpected show of indignation. Then his outburst had been brief, however, and quickly quelled by Edgar. Now, whether it was because of the cognac or because of conviction, he refused to concede to anyone. Quite the opposite, the more they argued against him, the more worked up Cornelius became. Still, Hazel felt compelled to say, "It isn't fair to expect a laborer to earn as much as Frederick."

"Perhaps not as much," Cornelius shot back, leaning across the table toward her, "but if you use the word *fair* to mean just and decent, then it isn't 'fair' that any human being should have to work twelve hours a day to earn three hundred dollars a year Especially if he has to give two hundred of that to some larcenou landlord so he and his family can cram into one of those filth firetraps of a tenement. What's he got left to live on?"

Hazel may not have had the clearest grasp of household budg ets, but after a month of buying groceries, she knew that a hundre dollars a year wasn't going to feed a family. Never mind clothe or coal or other expenses. She was temporarily silenced.

Edgar wasn't. "You make it sound like an impossible dilem ma," he said. "You forget that in most families there is more than one wage earner. Usually the wife brings home a salary, too."

Cornelius looked at his father. "I haven't forgotten," he said quietly. "Nor have I forgotten that the children are forced to work as well. Small children who should be out in the fresh air and growing strong are stuck in mills. They're trading their young lives for a pittance, so their families can survive for another day or another week."

Edgar jabbed his spectacles up his nose, his irritation evident. "The children's jobs aren't that taxing," he said righteously. As an aside to Hazel, he explained, "They have to change bobbins or sweep up under the machines." Then, addressing his son again, he said, "It doesn't make economic sense to hire an adult, at extra pay, to do that sort of work. The owners have to exercise good business judgment."

"So we're back to what makes the most profit for the owners," Cornelius said bitterly. "And damn the effect on the workers." He lifted his glass and drained its contents.

"Watch your language," Edgar replied. "And I wish you'd real- ize that profit is what business is all about. It has to be the owners' chief concern."

"Papa!" Cornelius cried out suddenly, his voice filled with anguish. "How can you keep defending those men when, with all your knowledge, they pay you only fifteen dollars a week?"

If Cornelius had swiped his father across the face with his open hand, the blow couldn't have been more devastating. His words knocked the bluster out of Edgar and made him look old and shrunken. Hazel's heart wrenched.

"Really, Cornelius," she admonished. "I think you're being overly severe in your criticism."

"I'm not, Hazel," Cornelius retorted, slapping the table, his emotions still running high. "You don't know what goes on inside he mill. You can't even imagine the conditions. There's a total disregard for safety. Last week one of my weavers came within his much of losing an eye." He held out the very tip of his finger. "A shuttle got loose and went flying at his head. It happens all the time. People lose fingers or hands as a matter of course. I recently heard about a woman in another mill whose hair got caught in a machine. It pulled off half her scalp."

Involuntarily Hazel shuddered.

Cornelius nodded in agreement to her reaction. "If the machines don't get them," he went on, "the diseases will. Half the operatives on my floor are suffering from consumption, and the other half have bad hearts. Almost all of them are nearly deaf and their eyes are weak. It's because the lights are poor and there's no ventilation. That's the owners again—putting their profit first."

"I can't believe it," Hazel insisted with an anxious glance at Edgar. "I can't believe Frederick would allow unsafe conditions in his mill."

Frustrated, Cornelius slapped the table again, his cheeks bright from cognac and compassion. "If you could see it for yourself, you would believe it," he said. "If you could see it, you'd know it was true."

"That's a capital suggestion," Marco said, speaking up for the first time. All eyes turned to look at him. He beamed. "I'll go arrange for a mill tour tomorrow."

Not quite sure how her innocent remark on cigars had escalated so rapidly, Hazel found herself walking down Canal Street two days later, on her way to the Great Stone Dam Mill. Marco strode along at her side, commenting on the mild November afternoon and on the handsome row of trees that lined the canal, as if, for all the world, they were strolling on the Rialto in Venice. She had to keep reminding herself that this was an impersonal excursion, strictly for the purpose of seeing the mill.

"Quite an imposing structure, wouldn't you say?" he asked idly, nodding across the narrow strip of water at an enormous rectangle of bricks and windows.

Hazel nodded. The mill went on for hundreds of yards, and when it ended, another similar mill began. On and on, huge blocks of bricks with endless rows of windows, relieved only by a tall smokestack or an occasional belltower or a bridge. Even from here the sound of banging machinery could be heard.

"It's the Washington Mills," Marco said. "I was told that it' the largest wool manufacturer in the United States. They run ove eight hundred looms in six main buildings. This is just one."

"You've been here for three days and you already know how many looms each mill has?" Hazel demanded, miffed because sh had been here a month and didn't know one mill from another.

"Of course," he replied, laughing. "You know I'm a confirmed collector, obsessively searching out the essence of every place visit. The essence of Lawrence is mills, and since I don't think I'm ready to collect one of those yet, I have to content mysel with collecting information about them. But the Washington Mill are in the process of converting from woolen production to wor steds, and then I no longer know how it'll rank in the weaving world."

"I thought worsteds are woolens," Hazel said, curious despite her best intentions. He had a way, a certain air, that made everything he said sound like it was of the utmost interest.

"They are in the sense that they're woven from wool," he explained, "but in a somewhat different process that yields a different effect."

"Worsted is a tight, smooth fabric," Hazel interrupted. "I haven't spent half my life in dressmakers' salons without learning that much. I suppose, though, I assumed it was simply the result of the wool that was used. A Merino, perhaps, as opposed to a Black Face or a Cheviot." She glanced up questioningly.

Marco looked back at her with genuine admiration. "An excellent deduction," he applauded. "I can't tell you how much it pains me, therefore, to inform you that you're incorrect." He felt his heart leap at the pride that flashed across her lovely face with his praise, then sink as it abruptly faded with his subsequent remark. "Not completely incorrect, mind you," he amended, wishing that proud light would come back. It was particularly becoming.

"Worsteds usually do employ the finer down wools, because the goods are mostly used for clothing," he said. "But while woolens get their finish from fulling, worsteds achieve their flatness from the way the wool is carded. All the fibers have to be long ones and lay parallel to each other. It requires extra machinery in the mill. Your Frederick is set up for worsteds."

The mention of Frederick, as usual, made Hazel remember him with a stab of guilt. It didn't help that Marco referred to him as hers. She walked in silence for a few minutes, determinedly looking in every direction but at the man by her side. Which was where she really wanted to look. She never tired of his face, with its dramatic features and its exciting display of emotions. With forced interest, though, she examined the brick boardinghouses standing shoulder to shoulder the length of the street.

Following her focus, Marco said, "They were built by the mills back at the beginning of the city, when the operatives were mostly fresh-faced farm girls recruited from the hills of New England. There was a more paternal feeling among the owners then."

"Hmmm," Hazel said, turning the other way to study the canal.

"It's hard to believe that placid little ditch is what runs these gargantuan buildings, isn't it?" Marco commented pleasantly. That worked. Her head swung around and she looked at him, incredulous.

He nodded. "The water is let into the basement of the mills, where its sheer force spins giant turbines, which, in turn, spin shafts that drive the machinery. It's a very clean and efficient form of power, and it's all thanks to the Great Stone Dam that the city planners and boatloads of Irish immigrants put across the Merrimack River forty-five years ago."

Her gaze started to slide away. "At the time it was built, it was the longest dam in the world," Marco added. "Sixteen hundred and twenty-nine feet. It also gave your Frederick's mill its name."

"Stop calling him my Frederick," Hazel snapped, the strong feelings she was trying to contain bubbling over in irritation.

"Gladly," Marco answered. "As soon as it's true."

He didn't make any effort to interrupt the silence for the rest of their walk. There weren't that many people on Canal Street at this hour. Just brick mills on one side and brick boardinghouses on the other and a line of trees and a canal down the middle.

Well beyond the Washington Mills they crossed a short bridge spanning the canal. On the other side another mill stood, this one bearing the legend GREAT STONE DAM MILL spelled out in raised blocks. They walked down a narrow road and found themselves in a courtyard, a dark, grim quadrangle created by the giant huddle of mills.

Everywhere she looked, Hazel saw brick walls, tall, long, and humorless. Hundreds of arched windows stared down at her, unwinking. Through the cold glass came the sound of the machinery, much louder now, much harsher, relentless. A shiver ran down her spine. Had she been alone, she would have turned and fled. But Marco was there, guiding her unerringly through a door and into the Great Stone Dam Mill office.

Frederick was waiting for them. Another shiver ran down Hazel's spine. She hadn't considered the possibility of seeing him here. In the month that she'd lived in Lawrence, he had been to visit her only twice, each time briefly, before catching the train back to Boston at the end of the business day. She assumed he made the trip infrequently. The sight of him now, as she stood next to Marco, was extremely unsettling. In fact, it was a shock. "Frederick," she said.

"Mr. MacGregor," Frederick said, looking past Hazel. "What a pleasant surprise to see you." His voice sounded neither pleased nor surprised, however, but rather mistrusting. "When my agent told me you'd arranged for a tour, I was quite astonished to hear your name. I know our paths have the most uncanny way of crossing, but Lawrence was the last place I would have expected to see you. Especially," he added, "in the company of my fiancée." His cool gaze finally included Hazel. She felt her stomach knot.

"I must confess to giving coincidence a helping hand in this instance," Marco said easily, before Hazel could speak. "After meeting Edgar Merriwether when he was in London with his family last spring, I came searching them out on my journey here."

"Oh?" The single syllable managed to carry an inordinate amount of chilliness. "You never told me you had the occasion to see our Italian acquaintance while you were in London," he said to Hazel.

Her face white from his accusation, Hazel opened her mouth to stammer a reply.

"Unfortunately, it was only Miss Merriwether's father and amiable brother whom I encountered in London," Marco said smoothly, clasping his hands behind his ample back. "It's my loss that Miss Merriwether and I never came face to face. I would've been honored to point out some of the hidden treasures of the National Gallery."

Hazel closed her mouth. While Marco's answer stretched the truth, it wasn't a lie.

"Yes. Well," Frederick said, grudgingly accepting the explanation. His tone sharpened, though, as he added, "I do find it odd that you've picked a mill tour for entertainment while in America. Our museums and art galleries may suffer by comparison with those of Europe, but surely they contain some few pieces worth viewing."

"A great many," Marco assured him, waving a generous hand through the air. "In particular, I find the work of Winslow Homer quite appealing. But my interests include things other than paintings, and, in another remarkable coincidence, I've discovered that we're all concerned, in some way, with wool."

"Oh?" Frederick said again, with equal coolness.

"Yes," Marco said. "As it happens, I own a few sheep."

"I see," Frederick said, his tone distancing him from this farmer. He turned to Hazel. "I'm surprised to see you embroiled in this adventure, my dear," he said reprovingly. "I would hardly expect you to turn up at the mill."

Hazel was willing enough to leave at once. She had found the great, hulking building to be a dismaying size, and the noise rumbling through the windows had sounded ominous. Being in the office did nothing to encourage her. It was stark and unglamorous and painted a bilious shade of green. Worst of all, though, was the terrible tension between Marco and Frederick, magnified a hundredfold by her guilt. She would have gladly complied with the wish evident in Frederick's words.

Without perceptibly moving, however, and without taking hold of her in any way, Marco was suddenly blocking her escape. Wondering what he was up to now, she looked at him just as he started speaking again. His tone was still bland.

"We were discussing the wool manufacture at dinner the other evening," he said. "It soon became apparent that Miss Merriwether was unfamiliar with the process. Her brother very intelligently suggested that if she could see the operation for herself, it would increase her understanding immeasurably. I seconded the notion and volunteered to make an appointment."

"At dinner?" Frederick echoed, his blue eyes narrowing and a crimson flush coloring his cleanly cut cheeks. "Did I forget an engagement?" he asked Hazel.

For the first time since entering the office, Hazel had a chance to speak. "It was only an informal family supper," she said, her voice a surprising imitation of her usual calm. "It's a pity you weren't able to attend, Frederick. You know that you're always more than welcome at our home, but you're so seldom in Lawrence."

"I'm here three days a week," Frederick retorted.

It was Hazel's turn to say, "Oh?" She was stunned. How did it happen that she had only seen him twice if he was here three times a week? She knew that he felt uncomfortable in their dismal little parlor, but after all, it was only a house. They could have gone for a walk, if the situation was that unendurable, or for an ice-cream soda at Ketchum's Pharmacy. To simply ignore her was insulting.

Apparently Frederick realized his error. "I've been very busy," he said, by way of an apology. "It's a very trying time."

"Yes," Hazel agreed quietly. "It is."

"We won't delay you any further, then," Marco said heartily. "We'll be off on our tour and let you get back to work. All we want now is a guide. Perhaps Cornelius can be spared to show us around."

"I'll show you around," Frederick said, almost snapping at the thought of relinquishing his control. In his haste to assert his authority, he overlooked his disapproval of Hazel's presence in the mill. While Marco nodded in satisfaction, Hazel sighed. He had outmaneuvered them both.

Setting out at a brisk pace, Frederick led the way along a corridor connecting the office to the main building. It was a long, dimly lit hall whose narrow proportion did not permit them to walk abreast. "There's just the sorting and the dyeing in the basement," Frederick said over his shoulder. "You don't want to see that, do you?"

"Yes," said Hazel, who was right behind him, thinking about Jean Fergueson's colorful dye shed in the Highlands.

"Yes," said Marco, who was bringing up the rear. He had no intention of making this an abbreviated visit.

When they descended the stairwell at the end of the corridor, it was as if they had entered another world. Wool was everywhere. Great bins of fleeces sat side by side, stacked up to the ceiling. Men stood in front of benches, pawing through enormous piles, pulling out clumps and tossing them into various baskets. "This is the sorting area," Frederick told Marco, looking over Hazel's head. It was plain he felt uncomfortable describing any of the work to her.

"These men have years of experience," Marco said to Hazel. Obviously, he didn't have the same problem. "Do you see how fast they go? They aren't even thinking about it. Their hands just know the grade of the wool."

Hazel nodded, fanning herself with her hand. The air was warm and damp in here, made closer by Frederick's impatience and Marco's opposing persistence. She didn't linger by the sorting tables but kept walking along the paths through the bins. The scene on the other side, though, stopped her short.

Unblocked, the room suddenly stretched out, revealing the great length of the building. Huge vats, six feet across, ran in rows down one half. In the vats percolated sodden masses of wool, blue and red and green and brown. But the dyes were impressive only for their unbelievable volume. They lacked the richness and subtlety of the hues Jean rendered from her crottles and leaves. Still, Hazel was amazed at the scale, and she started walking again, going slowly and watching workers transfer lots of dyed wool to the drying machines lining the other half of the room. Her nose itched from the sharp chemical smell of the dyes.

"You really shouldn't be here," Frederick said fretfully. "The dyes can splash and you'll ruin your dress."

Hazel looked down at the neat folds of her skirt, unconsciously smoothing them. "I don't mind, Frederick," she said, meaning it.

Before Frederick could repeat his objections, Marco asked, "Don't you do your scouring yourself? I don't see any scouring trains. Or any picking machines, either, for that matter."

"We send the sorted wool out to a scouring mill," Frederick answered. "There isn't the space here for the trains. Nor is it a sensible expenditure for a small mill like this. At the Whitaker Mill, our other facility, we do all the work in our own plant."

"This is a *small* mill?" Hazel asked. To her it seemed vast.

"Yes, my dear, it is," Frederick answered, his good humor restored by her awe. "At the Whitaker Mill we have separate buildings for the dye works, the scouring, and the finishing."

If Hazel was awed by the basement, the first floor nearly overwhelmed her. The thing that struck her immediately, and very forcefully, was the din. The level of sound was monumental. And discordant. Hundreds of carding machines, connected by shafts spinning madly overhead, rattled and clamored as they raked and pulled and clawed the dyed wool into acceptable strands.

The second thing that struck Hazel was the size of the room. The basement had been shortened by the stacks of bins blocking off the sorting section. Here the view was uninterrupted from one end to the other. It was so long, it looked like a lesson in perspective from one of Hazel's art books, the far end being appreciably narrower than where they stood.

Frederick would have hurried through the room without commenting, not wanting to shout over the noise, but Marco bent next to Hazel's ear and yelled a brief explanation. "There are four steps to carding wool for worsted production. And four different machines to do it." He pointed to the machines as he roared out their names. "Carding. Gilling. Combing. Drawing. In succeeding stages, they create the appropriate roving."

Emboldened by the thrill of having his lips so close to her ear, Hazel shouted at Marco, "It isn't like Sarah Fergueson and her two combs, is it?" Marco smiled and shook his head.

In the relative quiet of the stairwell, Frederick paused to say, "Sequentially, the next operation is the spinning of the carded wool, but what you'll see next is the weaving. We do our spinning on the top floor."

"For the heat?" Marco asked.

"Yes."

"Wool spins best in warm, humid conditions," Marco translated for Hazel's benefit. It pained him to see the conflict on her face as she struggled between her natural curiosity and her resolute desire to please Frederick. He knew she wouldn't ask questions, so he supplied the answers. "Since heat always rises, the top floor is the warmest place in the mill."

"I understand," Hazel murmured, searching for an innocuous comment. "It must be very warm in the summer."

"Unbearable," Marco said shortly.

"It's part of the job." Frederick bristled at the implied criticism. "Besides, we have mostly Italian immigrants up there now. They're accustomed to the heat." Marco's eyebrows raised, but he didn't say anything as Frederick led the way onto the weaving floor.

Remembering the deep peace and pleasure she had found at Donald MacDonald's cottage, Hazel was eager to see it. Her illusion was shattered the instant she stepped through the door. Hundreds of looms sat side by side for dozens of rows. Thousands of warp threads stretched toward the vanishing point at the other end of the room. The mechanical cacophony made a mockery of Donald's cozy *rattle, whish, clunk, rap, rap*.

Frenzied workers, hollow-eyed and pale, raced back and forth with the nerve-racking speed necessary to keep up with their machines. The air was thick with lint and smelled of stale sweat. There was no place for Lev in this scene. Or for a peat-blackened kettle. Or for the excitement of seeing beautiful cloth growing strand by strand, rolling onto the drum.

The only thing she liked about the whole room was the sight of her brother coming toward her. She hardly recognized him, though. With a clipboard tucked against his chest, he looked so serious and intent.

"What do you think?" he shouted, bending closer.

She shook her head, too distressed to yell.

Cornelius nodded and pointed to a young boy with a handful of bobbins. He was thin and frail and his skin looked gray, but saddest of all were his eyes. They were blank. Hopeless. He was defeated by life before the age of nine.

Turning away, Hazel felt sick. If she could have, she would have run down the steps and out the door, gasping for a breath of clean air and a merciful moment of quiet. But she had nowhere to run. With one hand she rubbed her forehead. The other she pressed against her heart. She didn't have to work in the mill, jumping to attention at the clang of the bells, but the mill was, nonetheless, the ruling force of her life. It was the currency of her existence, and Cornelius hadn't exaggerated its horror one bit.

Forcing herself to continue, Hazel walked the length of the weaving floor, then ascended to the finishing room above. She took it for granted when Cornelius came along, staying by her side as they viewed the harried operatives at the fulling, napping, and shearing machines. By the time they reached the next floor, Hazel was almost too numb to see the drawers, menders, and warp dressers that Marco was pointing out, and too dazed to hear about the safety hazards Cornelius was describing. Although Frederick said nothing, throughout, the skin drew tighter across his cheeks.

Midway through the fetid heights of the spinning room, one last flight up, his annoyance finally boiled over. Unfortunately for Cornelius, he was the nearest and most acceptable target. "I've fired men for talking the way you are!" he shouted, waving a finger in Cornelius's face. "It's this kind of firebrand rubbish that stirs up the workers and causes trouble for everyone. In deference to your sister, I'll give you one more chance, but if I ever hear you spouting off again, you'll be out on the street and blacklisted from working in any mill in New England. Do you understand me?"

He stood back glaring. "Who gave you permission to leave your post, anyway?" he added. "Get down to your floor."

Despite the deafening racket, it was almost possible to sense the silence in the moment that followed. Afraid to breathe, Hazel looked from her brother to her future husband. Frederick was angry and offended, but Cornelius was still. He stood straight and looked directly at Frederick, neither cowed nor hotly resentful. Hazel could practically see him assessing the situation, weighing all the factors, and ultimately choosing the responsible course. Like the cotton workers in New Bedford who accepted the dictates of their employers rather than see their families starve, Cornelius went back to his post.

Hazel exhaled slowly. She was enormously proud of her brother for putting the welfare of his family in front of his own wishes, but it upset her that to do so he'd had to swallow his principles. It was obvious that Cornelius had turned a corner in that tense moment, but what surprised Hazel was that she felt she had, too. She didn't know how her life was any different than it had been the minute before, or even if it was better or worse, but she was certain that something had changed.

Without a word or a glance at either Marco or Frederick, she walked to the stairway and descended the four flights of steps. In the doorway of the mill she shivered at the blast of comparatively cold air, though she greedily gulped in its freshness.

"Hold up a moment, Miss Merriwether," Marco said, clambering down the steps behind her. "I'll walk you home."

"No, thank you, Mr. MacGregor," Hazel responded evenly, but without looking back.

"Hazel, darling, let me accompany you," Frederick said. "You mustn't go alone."

"No, thank you, Frederick," Hazel said, starting across the grim millyard. "I'm perfectly capable of finding my way by myself." And she was.

# CHAPTER

## ❦ 11 ❦

Although Cornelius resumed his rounds on the weaving floor with an expressionless face, his pulse was racing. In part it was due to Frederick. He had never liked him, but until Frederick had become engaged to Hazel, that dislike had been a vague and hazy emotion. Even at that point it had been more a sense of disappointment that his sister was going to be saddled with such a snob than of active antipathy. He felt that Hazel deserved someone better.

Only after he started working in the mill did Cornelius's feelings coalesce. He was outraged that the luxurious life Frederick felt was his right came at the expense of hundreds of workers. Though John Whitaker was the principal shareholder and president of the Great Stone Dam Mill, he had given its management into his son's hands, and Cornelius held Frederick personally responsible for the deplorable conditions that not only didn't improve, but actually got worse. It had been hard to refrain from telling Frederick what he thought of him just now, hard to remember that he needed this job to help support his father and Hazel.

But it wasn't only Frederick's ultimatum that had set Cornelius's heart pounding. It was also the sight, up on the spinning floor, of a pretty girl. She'd been small, probably a full foot shorter than his six feet, but there had been a feisty look about her, a look of spring-loaded energy that was absent from most of the other millworkers.

She'd worn her hair in two crinkly black braids, tied out of harm's way at the back of her head, though tiny tendrils had escaped

173

in every direction. Big, golden-brown eyes had defied the world from a round face sprinkled with freckles. Her lips had been full and bright pink and had twitched in the course of some animated inner conversation. In the few brief seconds that Cornelius had glimpsed her, he'd been totally captivated.

She stayed on his mind for the rest of the day and that night while he lay on his cot in the parlor. He kept remembering her stubborn air, as if she were determined that the mill wasn't going to defeat her. When her image remained just as vivid all the next week, he made it his business to find out who she was.

"Say," he said, falling in beside the overseer from the spinning room when the bell sent everyone streaming from their posts for lunch. "There's someone on your floor I've been wondering about." The rough-faced Irishman barely glanced his way.

"She's about this tall," Cornelius persisted, holding his hand level at his chest. He jostled around a group of spattered dyers in order to stay even with the foreman. "And she's about seventeen years old." Still no response. "She's got braids held together with a strip of cloth," he continued, twirling his finger behind his own dark head in example.

"Oh, yeah, her," the man said, finally acknowledging Cornelius with a leer. "She's got nice little titties, too. But it won't do you no good. Them Eye-talians is as strict as they come. Her father is up there, and he watches her and her two sisters like a hawk. He sees them even looking at a man, he starts jabbering at them and whacking them around."

"No, no," Cornelius said. "You misunderstand me." The man's coarseness made him feel ashamed. "I have someone leaving today, and when I saw this girl I thought she'd make a good weaver. She seems strong and quick."

"Uh-huh," the man said with a wink. "Quick." He pumped his fist back and forth.

"Is she a good worker?" Cornelius asked, trying to ignore both the foreman's suggestion and his own disgust.

The man shrugged. "I told you, her pa's got her locked up tight. Besides, she don't speak much English."

"What's her name?" Cornelius abandoned all attempts to keep this on a professional level. They weren't working anyway.

The foreman nodded knowingly. "She's called Agata Bell-occhio," he said, grinning. "Quite a mouthful, ain't it?"

"Will you approve an order transferring her to the weaving

room?" Cornelius asked, abandoning all attempts at finesse as well.

"Maybe so," the man answered, his grin fixed in place. "Maybe not. What's it worth to you?"

It was suddenly worth quite a bit to Cornelius, if for no other reason than because he couldn't bear to think of her at this man's mercy. "Three dollars," he said. He only made eleven dollars a week.

"I was thinking more like seven," the foreman responded.

"Four dollars," Cornelius countered.

"Six."

"Five."

The man's grin broadened. "Send up the transfer papers," he said.

Agata Bellocchio, Cornelius thought all day Sunday. Agata. The name suited her. It had a spirited sound. For once he actually looked forward to Monday morning, when he'd see her on his floor. He imagined bending near her to give her some instruction or to hear about some problem with the loom. The thought made him tingle.

Cornelius was looking his best when Agata approached with her papers grasped in her small hand. He had on a clean shirt and a crisply starched collar. He'd carefully knotted his tie and neatly combed his hair. And beneath his well-groomed exterior, his heart was beating hard.

She was even more appealing up close than she'd been at a distant glimpse. Though her brown dress was shabby and an uncomplimentary color, she seemed to sparkle nonetheless. Her freckles danced across her straightforward nose and over the clear skin of her high, round cheeks. She walked with her shoulders back, her chin up, and her small booted feet tapping smartly on the floor.

When she stopped in front of Cornelius and thrust her work card forward, he could see the bright intelligence in her eyes. "Good morning," he said.

"No speak English," Agata answered, without a trace of an apology.

Cornelius was instantly charmed. "That's all right," he reassured her. "I don't speak Italian, either." As soon as he said it, he was annoyed with himself. What a foolish remark. Agata didn't pay any attention to it, though, as she surveyed the room expectantly, ready to find her station and go to work.

"I'm going to put you with another weaver for a few days," Cornelius told her. "You can watch and see what she does. Once you get the idea, you can start with one loom and gradually add on more until you get up to the six."

Agata's gaze swung back to him, her black brows lifted in astonishment. It couldn't be from his words, which she didn't understand, so it had to be from his tone, patient, calm, respectful. She seemed to see him for the first time as a real person rather than as just another fixture of the noisy, dirty mill. She stared at his long, lean frame and at his clean, classic face, and at the dimples bracketing his engaging smile. Then she looked away. "No speak English," she repeated firmly.

"I know you don't," Cornelius said regretfully. "That makes it more difficult. But it doesn't make it impossible. Come with me." He beckoned her to follow him as he led the way down an aisle to a bank of looms. A scrawny woman with thin gray hair screwed tightly into a knot stood in front of them, waiting for the workday to begin.

"Good morning, Mrs. O'Connor," Cornelius said. "This is Miss Bellocchio from the spinning floor. She's going to watch you and learn how to be a weaver. Miss Bellocchio," he said, turning to Agata, "this is Mrs. O'Connor." But Agata wasn't looking at him. She was glaring back at the Irishwoman who was regarding her with open hostility. Cornelius sighed.

"She's Eye-talian," Mrs. O'Connor objected.

"Yes, she is," Cornelius agreed. "And she doesn't speak English, either."

Mrs. O'Connor's lips pursed in distaste. "How'm I supposed to teach her if she don't speak English?" she asked.

"I think you'll find Miss Bellocchio to be a ready learner," Cornelius replied. He didn't know how he knew that, but he was sure it was true. "If you just point things out as you proceed, I'm certain she'll pick up the routine."

Any other protests Mrs. O'Connor might have made were cut off by the clanging of the six o'clock bell and the subsequent roar as the driveshafts started spinning and the looms came to life. With more force than was necessary, the Irishwoman pushed Agata out of the way, then hurried the length of her machines. Agata's fists balled up, and she might have given Mrs. O'Connor as good as she got, if Cornelius hadn't tapped her on the shoulder and shouted, "Please just watch her."

When Agata turned a scowling face toward him, Cornelius added, "I know she's being nasty, but she's a good weaver. You should be able to learn what to do quickly. And remember, the sooner you learn, the sooner you'll have your own looms. I promise, I'll put you far away from her on the other side of the room."

He knew Agata couldn't understand what he was saying, and he wasn't even speaking loud enough for her to hear, but he hoped she might understand his intent. He pantomimed for her to watch and to store what she saw in her head. Eventually Agata gave a slight shrug and let her fists open up.

Cornelius nodded and moved a little ways off to observe. Not only was he concerned that the two women might pounce on each other, he was also worried that Mrs. O'Connor might obstruct Agata's view of the operation. He needn't have worried on the latter score. Agata made it her business to see what was going on. She followed her reluctant teacher at a safe distance, standing on her tiptoes to peer over Mrs. O'Connor's shoulder. She craned her slim neck to watch as the scrawny Irishwoman deftly tied broken warp threads or as she slipped fresh bobbins into the shuttles, sucking the loose thread through a small hole in the end. It was called the "kiss of death" because of the lint, dye, and diseases that got sucked into the lungs at the same time.

Only once did Agata get too close, and Mrs. O'Connor let her know it with a bony elbow. The Italian girl tensed and her scowl returned, but she stepped back and continued watching without further incident. Cornelius sighed again. He couldn't understand why people wasted so much time hating strangers for no apparent reason.

All I want from life, Cornelius thought, is to be left by myself and to play baseball. He watched another minute before turning away. No, that isn't the whole truth anymore, he admitted to himself, taking another look behind him at Agata's sturdy little body stretching to see the loom. Now I want to spend a Sunday afternoon alone with Agata, too.

For several weeks it looked as if his newest wish had as little chance of being granted as his other two. Agata seemed fiercely disinterested in her American boss, listening to his instructions, then abruptly putting her back to him. When he tried to catch her eye at the lunch bell or at quitting time, she marched past him without a glance. In fact, except for that first astounded stare, Agata refused to look at him.

Or did she? Just when Cornelius was completely discouraged,

he was startled to see her eyes dart away when he turned to her suddenly. His pulse leaped in excitement. "Miss Bellocchio," he shouted, impulsively bending close to her ear, "will you go for a walk with me on Sunday?"

Once again Agata wouldn't look at him. "No speak English!" she yelled, brushing past him to mend a broken thread on her far loom. She had picked up the routine as quickly as he'd known she would and was managing a full complement of machines within a week.

On her way back Cornelius was ready, his renewed hope not quite extinguished. Planting himself in front of her so she couldn't avoid him, he motioned a walk with two swinging fingers, then pointed at her and at himself. For the briefest of instants Agata's eyes met his. They were dark with suspicion. Then she raised her chin and walked around him. Sharp disappointment stabbed his heart.

He told himself to forget about her, that she wasn't interested in him. It was obvious that she distrusted him, and since they didn't speak the same language, there was no way he could convince her differently. But it wasn't that easy. She was on his mind constantly. During the day he found himself pulled to her row of looms by an almost magnetic force. At night he tossed on his cot, his body restless and hot. He couldn't remember ever wanting anything, even a spot on the Boston pitching roster, quite as intensely as he wanted to be with Agata. A Sunday walk with her became an all-consuming obsession.

In desperation he even stood on the corner of Union and Essex one blustery late November Sunday, waiting for the mass to let out at St. Lawrence's. He meant to fall in beside her when she came out of the church, to win her over with his persistence. In his haste to devise a plan, though, he'd forgotten to take into account the formidable presence of her family. Her barrel-shaped father, her worn-out mother, and her seven younger brothers and sisters. Nor had he prepared himself for her expression of shock when she recognized him in the crowd across the street. Then, in quick succession, her expressions of annoyance and indifference. Dejected, he went home.

It cheered him only slightly to see Andrew sitting in the parlor on his return. The big man seemed to overflow the cramped room, distracting from its seediness, giving it a temporary sense of warmth. "Are you here for Sunday dinner?" Cornelius asked, sprawling on his cot. It served as a divan during the day.

"I am," Andrew replied, setting down the book he'd been perusing. "With only one or two subtle hints and the bribe of a brace of pheasant, I've managed to obtain another invitation." He studied Cornelius a minute. "You seem downcast," he said. "Is it because you're sick of seeing my face across your table?"

"No, of course not," Cornelius answered, shaking his head emphatically. Then he added more ruefully, "I'd rather have you, Andrew, than anyone else I can think of."

"Thank you." Andrew's head tilted in acknowledgment of the compliment, and the corners of his mouth turned up in acknowledgment of its inference.

"Say, where is everybody?" Cornelius suddenly realized that Andrew was alone in the parlor. "Did they invite you here, then snub you?"

"I'm not insulted," Andrew answered with a chuckle. "The landlord came by to collect the rent, and your father dragged him into the bedroom to argue with him about the falling plaster. Your sister is in the kitchen fussing with dinner. She ordered me out when I suggested that orange peel might make a superb addition to her cranberry conserve."

"Is Hazel in there cooking the pheasant?" Cornelius asked with some concern. Despite his depression, his mouth had started watering when Andrew had mentioned pheasant. "It would be a pity to see them ruined."

"For shame, Cornelius," Andrew admonished, though he did so with a grin. "I think you underestimate your sister."

"No, I don't," Cornelius responded, shaking his head again. "I don't underestimate her at all. I think she's the best there is," he said with real affection. "But I also know she can't cook."

"True," Andrew murmured, his head dipping in concession. "However, you needn't worry for the safety of the pheasant. I tucked them into the oven in a bower of fresh sage. They should be roasted to perfection in another twenty minutes."

For the first time in weeks Cornelius laughed. "You're the only person I've ever met who comes as a guest to dinner and then cooks it himself," he said.

"Someone has to." Andrew shrugged deprecatingly. "And as you've pointed out, it's not one of your sister's many talents."

"But she tries hard," Cornelius insisted loyally.

"She tries hard," Andrew agreed.

"She'll do the potatoes well."

"No potatoes, today," Andrew corrected. "Instead, I've mad
polenta, which is a delicious cornmeal pudding and a practicall
inseparable companion of roast pheasant in Bergamo, a lovely
antique city in the north of Italy."

"That's right!" Cornelius cried, sitting up sharply. "I'd forgotte
that you're Italian, too."

"Too?" Andrew's eyebrows raised.

"I mean, uh . . . " Cornelius backpedaled. He'd been so de
lighted to make the connection between Agata and Andrew, sur
that it was somehow a means of reaching her, that he'd just bur
out. Now he wasn't sure how to explain her. "You see," he said
suddenly finding it necessary to examine his hands, "there's thi
Italian worker at the mill."

"Only one?" Andrew asked, his eyebrows still raised, his blu
eyes fixed on Cornelius.

"Oh, no," Cornelius amended. "There are lots. Especially in th
spinning room. But there's this one, uh, fellow, no, this weaver
on my floor who doesn't speak any English. I'd like to be able t
say something in Italian. You know"—he looked up at Andrew
silently pleading with him to understand—"to make this weave
feel more at ease."

"I see," Andrew said quietly, his eyes narrowing in thought.

"Do you think you could, Andrew?" Cornelius asked, his ow
eyes flicking away. "Tell me some words in Italian, I mean."

"Certainly," Andrew said, drawing himself up. "Although i
you're addressing my Italian half, I wish you'd call me Marco."

"Marco," Cornelius said obligingly. He nodded. The name some
how fit him better.

"We'll start with a greeting," Marco decided. "Say '*Buon giorno
signore.*' "

"*Buon giorno, signore,*" Cornelius repeated. Sort of.

"Yes. Well," Marco said, shrugging. "That means 'Good day
sir,' by the way. If you are speaking to the fellow's wife, yo
say '*Buon giorno, signora.*' "

"*Buon giorno, signora.*"

"Mmm. Better. Now, if you were to greet a young lady, yo
would say '*Buon giorno, signorina.*' "

"*Buon giorno, signorina,*" Cornelius said eagerly.

"Good," Marco said. "*Bravo.* Now, what other phrases woul
be useful? Would you like to say 'Do you need some help?' "

"No," Cornelius said slowly. "I can't remember too many al

at once. You can tell me that one next week. For right now, how do you say, uh . . . " His cheeks got pink. " 'I'd like to be your friend.' "

Marco nodded approvingly. "An excellent sentiment. You would say '*Vorrei essere il tuo amico*.' "

"*Vorrei essere il tuo amico*." Cornelius struggled with that one.

"Practice a bit," Marco suggested.

"*Vorrei essere il tuo amico*," Cornelius recited, over and over.

Marco listened for a while, correcting Cornelius's pronunciation, until he was satisfied he had it right. "Yes, you've got it," he said, pushing himself out of the chair. "You keep at it while I go make peace with Hazel." He started walking toward the kitchen, then paused, rubbing his chin. He turned toward the parlor again. "And Cornelius . . . ," he added.

"Yes?" Cornelius looked up.

"Cornelius," Marco said, his eyebrows furrowing delicately. "If, by any chance, you should ever have the occasion to tell an Italian girl that you love her, the words are *Ti amo*."

Cornelius turned bright red and didn't reply. Marco resumed his course for the kitchen.

At five minutes to six on Monday morning Cornelius stood at the center of the weaving room floor, greeting the workers as they trudged to their stations. When he saw Agata approaching, her pace brisk, her pretty face averted, he took a deep breath. "*Buon giorno, signorina*," he said.

The effect was immediate. Agata halted in midstride, her head snapping around, her brown eyes huge with amazement. She looked at him. Straight at him. Then, miraculously, she smiled. It was a charming smile, as sturdy as she was, that stretched her freckled cheeks and made Cornelius's heart leap. "*Buon giorno, signore*," she responded, continuing on to her looms.

Cornelius was left standing in the middle of the room, his clipboard clutched in his hands. He pretended to read the papers attached to it, to hide the excitement he felt. Really, he wanted to run down the aisle and jump in the air and let out a whoop of glee. She'd smiled at him! She'd even talked to him! He ran the glorious moment over and over in his mind, and each time he saw her face break into that smile, his heart took another leap.

The six hours till the noon bell had never seemed so long.

Although Cornelius walked by her station a dozen times, Agata looked up at him only once. Even that was an expressionless glance as she hurried to change the bobbins and get her loom back on line. It made Cornelius cringe to see her sucking the thread through the hole in the shuttle. He barely resisted the urge to rip it out of her hands and fling it far away from her. She was too full of life to be flirting with the kiss of death.

When the lunch bell finally rang, it caught Cornelius assisting a loom fixer on the other side of the room. He dropped what he was doing and ran back across the floor, his stomach knotting in dread, afraid that he would miss her after all. But Agata had taken a moment to relace her boot and was just rising as Cornelius came dashing down her row.

"Oh," he gasped, relief taking away his breath. And also taking away his memory of the phrase Marco had taught him. "Oh," he said again, in consternation this time. Agata looked at him, hesitated, then started to go around him. "No," he said desperately, holding up his hand. "Listen, I have something to tell you."

Agata stopped and looked at him again, her expression questioning. It hovered on the brink of suspicion, but unlike in the past, it now also held curiosity. "*Eh beh?*" she asked, cocking her head.

"Uh . . . " Cornelius responded, rubbing his forehead vigorously as he tried to remember the phrase. "Don't go away. Please," he begged. "It'll come back to me in a minute." He shut his eyes and tried to envision the scene in the parlor when Marco had clearly and carefully pronounced each Italian word. "Signorina," he said triumphantly. "Signorina Bellocchio."

"*Si?*" She looked at him expectantly.

Cornelius felt a flash of panic. What came next? "I wish you wouldn't distrust me," he burst out, miserable because he couldn't make her understand. "I have absolutely no bad intentions. I would like to be your friend." That was the trigger. The phrase jumped into his head. "*Vorrei essere il tuo amico,*" he said happily. Then he waited for her response.

Agata's eyes widened at his words, a look of wonder replacing the suspicion. She stared at him a long time, pondering his proposition. Finally some of the defiance with which she faced the world seemed to melt, and she came to a decision. With a little shrug she said, "*Mi piacerebbe.*"

Fresh alarm filled Cornelius. Now she'd given him her answer, and he didn't know what it meant. He shook his head hopelessly.

"*Mi piacerebbe*," Agata repeated, gesturing with her hand. When the tall American still looked blank, she simplified it even further. "*Si*," she said.

"*Si*," Cornelius echoed. He thought he knew what that meant, but for such a crucial point as this he had to be sure. "Does *si* mean 'yes'?" He nodded his head. "Or does *si* mean 'no'?" He shook his head.

"Yes, yes," Agata said, her hand waving through the air impatiently. How many times did she have to explain? "Yes," she said again. Then smiled.

Cornelius's spirits soared. A joyful smile spread across his face, too. For several moments they stood like that, smiling at each other, then Agata started to make her way to lunch. "No, wait," he said, reaching out his hand. He couldn't let her just walk away from him.

Agata looked back. "*Eh?*" she asked.

"Miss Bellocchio," Cornelius said, squaring his shoulders. "I mean, Signorina," he corrected. "Will you come for a walk with me on Sunday?" As he had before, he made walking motions with his fingers. Then he looked at her, praying her answer would be different than it had been then.

After a moment, she said, "*Forse*."

"*Forse*." Cornelius tried the word out in his mouth, hoping it would have some meaning if he said it. "*Forse*." It didn't. He looked at her, his eyebrows knitting.

"Maybe," Agata answered, spreading her hands wide.

"Maybe?" That took him by surprise. "You *do* speak English," he protested.

"No." Agata shook her head and her finger at the same time. "Yes. No. Maybe. Tank you. One, two, tree, four, fi'. *E cosi. Basta. Non più.*"

He found her accent charming. "That's very good," he complimented, beaming. Then remembering how Marco had praised him he added, "*Bravo.*"

Shaking her head again, Agata said, "*Brava.*"

"What?"

"*Brava*," she repeated, pointing to herself. "*Bravo.*" She pointed to him.

"Ahh," Cornelius said. "In that case, *brava.*"

"Tank you." Agata laughed. It was a low, pleasing sound, rich with humor. Cornelius liked it a lot.

"Will you come for a walk with me on Sunday?" he asked again, seizing the relaxed moment. "Don't say *forse*," he begged. "Say *si*."

Agata sighed and shifted from one foot to the other, rubbing her chin in thought. While Cornelius watched in anxiety, her pink lips worked, finally forming a word. "Yes," she said.

"*Brava*," Cornelius said, fairly floating.

If the six hours until the lunch bell had seemed long, the six days until Sunday seemed an eternity. He saw Agata only in the stifling atmosphere of the mill, amid the unspeakable din and the dull stares of the other operatives. When the noon bell stilled the looms, she hurried off to lunch. Although Cornelius would have gladly forfeited his midday meal to spend an hour alone with her, Agata's father and sister waited for her below, and she didn't dare be late. In fact, with words and gestures, she made him realize that the only way she could meet him on Sunday was to sneak out of the house while her family took an after-lunch nap.

The thought disturbed Cornelius. He had wanted to be completely open and honest. But he had snuck out of his own house enough times over the years, so he wasn't terribly shocked. Accordingly, he drew her a map with a meeting place circled, along the Merrimack River, beyond the mills. At half past two on Sunday he was there waiting. At three she came walking up. Something inside of him jumped.

She looked even prettier today than she did at work. Her Sunday dress, though a rough serge, was an appealing shade of blue. Cornelius could see the sleeves and hem of it as they stuck out from her coat. A clean strip of cotton tied back her black braids, and the cold, damp day had stung color between the freckles on her nose and cheeks.

"*Buon giorno*," he said when she came to a halt in front of him. "You look very nice."

"Good afternoon," she replied, not understanding the rest.

Suddenly overcome by shyness, Cornelius didn't explain. Instead, he started walking along the river path, and Agata took her place at his side. For a while they walked in total silence. After anticipating this moment for so long and so feverishly, now that it was here, Cornelius was chagrined to realize he felt awkward.

Regardless of the language barrier, he didn't know what to say. Or how to tell her what he thought of her.

When they rounded a bend and found themselves by a scrubby lot, however, Cornelius's reserve vanished. "It's a baseball diamond!" he exclaimed in delight. "It's not much of one, just for fooling around, but it'll do the job. Look," he said, pointing at an old feed bag in the dirt. "There's home plate."

Agata followed the direction of his finger, then turned back to stare at him. There was nothing about this little patch of earth and dead grass that looked at all appealing.

"It's for playing baseball," Cornelius explained. "It's the best game there is. Baseball."

"Bazeball," Agata repeated skeptically.

"That's right. *Brava.*" Cornelius laughed in sheer joy. "Come on," he said, grabbing her hand and pulling her across the outfield. "I'll show you."

It wasn't until they were almost to third that he felt the full impact of his spontaneous action. Her little hand was tucked securely in his, and she trotted next to him without a question. When he looked down, astounded by the situation, she smiled up at him, trusting. He felt his heart swell until it ached.

"This is home plate," he said, kicking the feed bag.

" 'Ome plate," Agata said, kicking it, too.

Cornelius threw back his head and laughed again. He felt so good. With Agata in tow, he made the rounds of the bases, naming each one as they stomped on it. Sweeping his free arm through the air, he described the territories in the meadow beyond. Right field. Left field. Center field. Catching his enthusiasm, Agata flung her own arm wide and repeated the name of each one.

On their way back to home, Cornelius spied a stick and a stone, which he picked up to use as a bat and a ball. While Agata watched and applauded with glee, he demonstrated how to play baseball. He was alternately the pitcher and the batter and even the catcher, then he ran out to the outfield to catch a few imaginary fly balls.

He told her about double plays and double headers and home runs and fouls, about strikes and balls and innings and outs. He told her everything he could think of because, in all the world, baseball was his favorite way to spend the day, and Agata was his favorite person to spend it with. He wanted her to like it as much as he did.

She seemed to. Though she finally cut off his flow of details which she could neither understand nor remember, she wasn't the least bit hesitant about trying her hand at the game. She swung the stick wildly when Cornelius tossed in the stone and raced around the bases when they pretended she got a hit. She jumped in the air to snatch a pop-up and ran after Cornelius to tag him out.

For an hour they played jubilantly, two children at recess. As they exercised their young bodies, they exorcised the mill, laughing and leaping until they forgot about the weaving room. They played baseball and they had fun.

The sky was getting early-winter dark when Agata rounded third, heading for home, determined to score another run. "You're out!" Cornelius shouted, his long legs eating up the ground behind her.

"No!" she yelled and dived for the plate.

"Out!" Cornelius shouted again, sliding in on top of her.

"No, *non è vero!*" she cried, laughing. She squirmed around to pound him with her fist. "Safe. *Io sono* safe."

"Out by a country mile," Cornelius insisted, laughing, too, and pinning down her arm.

Suddenly their laughter died away, leaving only two clouds of breath that joined and drifted off. They stared at each other, their faces inches-apart, their bodies sprawled together in the dirt. Cornelius was acutely aware of their closeness, of her chest rising and falling beneath him as she panted from exertion and excitement.

He slowly unclamped his hand from her arm and slowly moved it toward her face. With a tentative finger he brushed her freckles and smoothed an escaped tendril of hair. Carefully, gently, he lowered his head until his cold cheek touched hers. He gasped at the shock, then, wanting more, he rolled his face until his mouth found her warm, pink lips.

It was an inexpert kiss, unrefined, unknowing, but what it lacked in experience, it made up for in emotion. He pressed against her, his heart beating hard. When he finally broke away, it was only to raise himself on his elbows above her.

"Agata," he said, no longer a little boy, but every bit a man. "*Agata, ti amo.*"

Her golden brown eyes grew wide and a soft light filled them. Then they fluttered closed and her arms slid around his neck.

# CHAPTER

## 12

The slices of onion fell away from the knife in a pleasing design, distracting Hazel from her eternal battle to cook dinner. For a few minutes she played with the rings, arranging and rearranging them on the cutting board. It was a poor substitute for the mornings she used to spend in the Rose Parlor with her sketch pad and paints, but at least it was a momentary reprieve from the stew.

While her fingers doodled, her thoughts did, too. She imagined herself on a velvet-covered chaise, sipping tea and reading a novel. Or dressed in silk broadcloth, leisurely perusing the paintings in a gallery. She imagined herself in any number of scenes set with grace and beauty. Increasingly, though, Marco crept into the tableau.

She swept the onion rings into a pile and began chopping them vigorously, putting an end to the daydreams. After a moment her knife slowed, then stopped. She sighed, poking a disinterested finger at the mound of diced onions. Marco. What was she going to do about him?

He'd been to dinner twelve times since he'd arrived in America seven weeks ago, and that wasn't counting the first afternoon's lunch. Nor was it counting the times he'd "chanced" upon her while she was out, when he'd insisted on carrying her market basket and accompanying her on her rounds. And turning an otherwise dreary shopping trip into an amusing expedition.

"That's the trouble," she told the onions, running her hand through the pieces. "He always has some interesting anecdote, or a refreshing view that makes him impossible to ignore. And then there are all his presents." She attacked the pile again with her knife. "Flowers and candy are one thing. But pheasants? Or a basketful of wild mushrooms which he cooked with that delicious risotto? He knows very well it's too charming to resist.

"That's the trouble," she repeated, her knife slowing once more. "I enjoy being with him," she said wistfully. "The only thing I look forward to when I get out of bed every morning is the hope that he'll turn up at the door."

But as surely as every visit began with a delightful gift, it invariably ended in a fight. Although the object of the argument was usually trivial, like the matter of the orange peel in the cranberry conserve, the underlying cause was always Frederick. Frederick, who'd been to visit four times, compared with Marco's dozen. For none of those visits had he stayed to eat, never mind cook the meal.

"That's all right," Hazel said, defending her fiancé to the ever more finely chopped onions. "It's not important that Frederick come calling in Lawrence. What's important is that he take me back to Boston. Risotto is good enough while I'm eating it, but when it's gone I'm left here all day smelling Mrs. O'Sullivan's cabbage."

She gave the onions a final chop. "I wish Marco would realize that, instead of telling me that my marriage will be miserable. How could it be any more miserable than this?" She drew the knife through the air in a circle, taking in the paint flaking off the walls and sagging cupboard and the rust flaking off the sink.

"Anyway," she added, "I was happy when I lived in Boston, and I'll be happy there again." That's what she really missed. More than the maids and the cooks and the rooms full of upholstered furniture, she missed that deep, enduring sense of contentment. That's what she wanted to regain. That's why she was going to marry Frederick. And that's why she and Marco always ended his visits in an argument.

After they fought, he would storm out the door, his wrath as big and dramatic as he was. But the next day he'd be back, or at the most, the next week, full of new stories about what he'd seen and done and eaten on his trip to Boston or New York or Washington, D.C. For Edgar's benefit, he would also talk about the business possibilities he'd investigated, soberly describing the fragile state of the wool industry, indeed, of the whole economy.

Hazel scooped the onions into the stewpot and began to scrape the carrots. "I really ought to insist that he stop coming around," she said. Then she sighed again. She constantly teetered between her resolution to chase him away and her involuntary relief when she found out that she hadn't.

The sound of the front door opening ended her musings abruptly. Alarmed, she looked at the old clock on the windowsill above the sink. It ran slow, but even so, it was only midmorning, far too early for Edgar and Cornelius to be home from work. Marco was away again, looking at a mill in Maine. Besides, informal though he was, he wasn't rude. He always knocked.

"Hazel, can you come?" Cornelius's voice called out.

Her knife clattered to the table as she turned and raced for the parlor, her alarm growing. "What's happened?" she demanded, before she even got there. "Oh, no!" she exclaimed, when she burst into the room.

Cornelius was holding up Edgar, whose legs seemed too loose to do the job for him. There was a tear in his jacket and a stain on his shirt and his face looked unnaturally bright. "Howz my dolly?" he asked cheerfully, waving his hand. Then he passed out.

Leaping forward, Hazel reached to help Cornelius as he lowered Edgar onto the cot. "He's drunk," Cornelius said unnecessarily.

Hazel nodded, too shocked to speak. She'd never seen her father in such a state.

"He came in to work at half past nine," Cornelius told her, yanking off Edgar's shoes. "Then he started acting as if he were the owner of the mill. Ordering people around. Sitting in Frederick's office. He even threatened to fire one of the clerks." He pulled off Edgar's tie, unsnapped his collar, and unbuttoned a few buttons so he could breathe.

"The agent sent for me and told me to take Papa home." He threw a blanket over his father's unconscious form and turned to look at his sister. "It's a good thing Frederick wasn't there," he said. "There would have been a different ending to the story."

Nodding again, Hazel sank into the chair, staring at the man on the cot. "He looks so frail," she said, as much to herself as to her brother. "He used to be so robust."

"His world collapsed," Cornelius said briefly. "He doesn't know how to live in another one."

Hazel looked at Cornelius, her surprise at his observation overcoming her shock. "But you do, don't you?" she said quietly.

"You've been steady and strong, while we've flopped around helplessly."

Cornelius shrugged. "I've been living in someone else's world all my life," he said. "It's not so difficult to exchange one for another."

"Poor Cornelius." Hazel was suddenly filled with sympathy for her little brother, who'd had to grow up so fast. "It's very hateful, isn't it?"

"Yes," Cornelius admitted, "but probably no more hateful than what you have to do all day. It can't be too enjoyable for you to do the wash and the ironing and cook the meals." He paused, then added ruefully, "Not if the way they taste can be taken for a guide."

His remark made her laugh and that thawed the lump congealed in her chest. "Ingrate," she chastised.

Grinning, Cornelius came over to the chair. "I have to get back to the mill," he said, bending over to plant a kiss on the top of her head. "Will you be all right, sis?"

It had been a long time since he had called her that. Or since he'd set a kiss in her hair. In fact, she hardly ever saw him lately. He was at the mill all day and in bed after dinner and he disappeared every Sunday afternoon. He's probably found a baseball game somewhere, she decided. The thought pleased her. He deserved some diversion.

"I'll be fine," she assured him, smiling.

He squeezed her shoulder. "Don't sit there too long. Papa's just going to sleep." He was almost to the hall when he looked back. "I don't think you're helpless," he said. "I think you've been very brave."

Despite Cornelius's advice, Hazel did sit there awhile, staring at the still figure of her father. Now that her brother had gone, that short moment of warmth had also vanished, and she again felt lonely and cold. It had been one thing to see her father old and defeated; it was another to see him act like a drunken fool.

Once she'd thought him invincible, his wisdom absolute. Once his world, irrefutably, had been hers. But that had been before Scotland. No, really before Venice. Before Marco had started goading her with questions and drilling her with facts. Before tiny doubts had started building one on top of the other in her mind. Seeing her father now, the foundation of her existence, lying on a cheap cot in a shabby room, made those little doubts grow huge. If the collapse of his world left him in a drunken stupor, where did it leave her?

Rubbing her forehead, she finally stood up. There was still the stew to start and five shirts to iron and now Edgar's jacket needed mending. Fanny had never come back and no one had ever been hired in her place. Never mind that Hazel didn't have time to read or paint, she didn't even have time to brood.

Before she left the room, she removed her father's glasses and carefully set them on the table by the bed. Edgar looked more vulnerable than ever, but instead of feeling sorry for him, Hazel felt a stab of resentment. "How could you do this to me, Papa?" she asked.

In response, Edgar snored.

Shoulders hunched against the draft in the parlor and the chill in her spirit, Hazel went back to the kitchen. Cornelius had called her brave, but she didn't feel it. Instead, she felt lost and afraid.

By the next morning Edgar was sober, and he returned to the mill looking pale and shaky and even more beaten. Heavy with sadness, Hazel set about her own work. She stoked up the fire until it was roaring, then heated all her kettles filled with water to do the wash. She scrubbed one set of sheets, four shirts, a petticoat, and Cornelius's underwear, then rinsed them and wrung them and hung them on the line by the back door. She dusted the dining room and the parlor and swept the floors. She made her bed and her father's and emptied the ash bin. She was standing in the kitchen prepared to start dinner, wondering if she could possibly duplicate Marco's risotto, when she heard a knock on the front door. Her heaviness instantly lifted.

"Oh, good," she said happily. "He's back. I'll ask him how to make it."

Hurrying across the house, she smoothed her apron and brushed a strand of hair from her cheek. There was a glad smile on her face when she opened the door. It faded in momentary surprise, then determinedly reappeared. "Frederick," she said. "How lovely to see you."

"Good morning, Hazel," he replied. "May I come in?"

"Of course," she said, jumping back and swinging open the door. She'd been so startled to find him standing there that all other thoughts had fled. Now her manners returned. "You're just in time for tea," she said as he squeezed past her and walked down the hall. A faint smell of bay rum clung to his clean face.

"No need to go to any trouble. I apologize for not giving you any notice of my call." His tone sounded stiff and formal.

Hazel's brow wrinkled in puzzlement. How many times had he stopped by on Marlborough Street, without announcement, and thought nothing of it? Perhaps it was just a trick of sound because his back was to her. "It's no trouble at all," she responded. "The kettle's already hot. I've only to pour the water into a pot. Come sit in the parlor while I fetch the tray. I won't be a minute."

She made sure he was settled before she went back to the kitchen, shaking her head at how uncomfortable he looked. As she reached down the teapot and spooned in some tea, she couldn't help remembering how at ease Marco always seemed. He didn't perch rigidly on the edge of the chair, as if he were afraid that if he leaned back he'd spoil his cashmere coat. Nor did he contrast starkly with the threadbare room. Rather, he filled it so its dreariness was no longer obvious.

That isn't fair, she told herself sternly, banishing the image. And it's also besides the point. It's only natural that Frederick should be uncomfortable. After all, it's an uncomfortable house and Frederick is accustomed to luxury. She refused to remind herself that Marco was, too. Instead, she ferreted out the cups with the fewest cracks and set them neatly on the tray. Then she opened a tin of shortbread that Marco had brought her once and that she'd been saving for a special day.

As she arranged the biscuits on a plate and filled the sugar bowl and creamer, she managed to work up quite a bit of sympathy for Frederick. It has to be very difficult for him, she thought. Just imagine, his home and all his friends and social life are in Boston, while I'm stuck way up here in Lawrence. What a trial it must be.

"I'm sorry I kept you waiting," she said warmly, whisking into the parlor and setting the loaded tray on the table by the cot. It wobbled, but didn't fall.

"You oughtn't've bothered, Hazel. It really wasn't necessary," Frederick said. He still hadn't removed his coat.

"Nonsense," Hazel replied lightly. "It's never a bother to have tea with you. I can't think of a more delightful way to spend the morning. Shall I pour out?"

"Yes, if you must," Frederick answered. "Though I really can't stay for long."

His words were brief and unexceptional, but there was something in his tone, something about his demeanor, that suddenly filled Hazel with dread. In silence she poured his tea and added his sugar and dribbled in a spot of cream. After giving it a stir, she handed it to him. "Biscuit?" she asked calmly, passing the plate of hoarded shortbread.

He shook his head. "No, thank you," he said.

Hazel poured her own tea, then sat gracefully on the cot. "There's a feeling of snow in the air," she said. "Do you think we'll have some today?" She took a sip of tea.

"More than likely," Frederick answered. "I felt a few flakes already. And the temperature seems to be dropping." He took a swallow, too.

"Not too much, I hope. Not like last week. That cold wave was quite a shock. At one point the temperature was eighteen below. Did it get that low in Boston?"

"Hazel," Frederick said, setting his half-emptied cup on the tray, "I've something to discuss with you." His eyes didn't quite meet hers.

"Yes, Frederick?" Though her tone remained mild and her expression smooth, her mouth suddenly felt dry. She took another sip of tea, but it made no difference.

"It pains me to say these things, my dear, but they must be said." There was a note of genuine regret in his voice, though it was hard to discern if it was on her behalf or on his own.

Hazel took a deep breath. "If they must, they must," she said practically. "Please go on."

Frederick looked at her then, a little surprised by her attitude. "I'm sure you're aware of the incident involving your father yesterday morning," he said more coolly than before.

"The incident," Hazel repeated, thinking of Edgar stretched unconscious on the cot. "Yes, I am."

"If he had been anyone other than your father, he would have been fired on the spot." Irritation was starting to work into Frederick's voice.

"I see."

"In fact, I had a bit of a time convincing *my* father that Edgar shouldn't be let go."

"I see," Hazel murmured again. She looked at her teacup, but left it sitting in her lap.

"Frankly, Hazel," Frederick said, sitting forward on the chair,

"I'm not sure I can keep defending your family. It's becoming an embarrassment to mine."

This time Hazel had no response. She just stared at Frederick in amazement.

"And it's not only Edgar's half-mad behavior," Frederick continued, his annoyance now freely released. "It's also your brother. He allied himself with the troublemakers, complaining about working conditions when he ought to be grateful he has any work at all. You heard him yourself on your tour of the mill. Despite my warning that day, he hasn't stopped agitating the operatives. And now there's even a rumor of his liaison with one of them. Some immigrant girl."

"What?" Hazel burst out. That was one accusation too many. "How ridiculous. It's just cruel gossip."

"It is, nonetheless, the gossip surrounding your family," Frederick responded icily. "And while we're on the subject of gossip, I think it's appropriate to mention this MacGregor fellow. It's been said that he spends an inordinate amount of time in your home. I realize he bought us refreshments in Italy, but our debt of hospitality goes only so far. I think you're exceeding it."

"But you seemed to enjoy his company while we were abroad," Hazel protested, though a surge of guilt blunted her objection considerably.

"He was an amusing bit of local color," Frederick replied. "He added a harmless dash of eccentricity to our holiday, but that isn't the sort of acquaintance I seek at home.

"I know he's had some education and that has you fooled," Frederick went on, "but it's obvious from his looks and manner that his breeding is poor. He's just a sheep farmer who has come into some money." For a moment his tone softened as he leaned over and squeezed Hazel's hand, lying limp in her lap.

"Poor darling," he said. "You're too innocent to know about these things. You'll have to trust my judgment."

Hazel could barely refrain from pulling her hand free as she struggled to find something to say to cover her distress. She considered telling Frederick that Marco was the son of a baron, but she was afraid he'd be furious, not only because his judgment had been disproved, but also because she hadn't told him before. "Papa likes to have him here," she finally said. "They can go on for hours about the wool industry."

Frederick sat up abruptly. "That's exactly what I'm referring to," he said, his irritation returning. "That farmer is here far too often. It presents the wrong image to society."

"Society?" Now Hazel was incredulous. She set her cup on the tray, too, and turned back to look at Frederick. "Is that what this is all about?" she asked. "About what society thinks? Because if it is, Frederick, you needn't worry. Society has forgotten that we exist."

"I know," Frederick said tightly, holding himself very still. "Which is why my father has suggested that I might end our engagement."

Hazel felt a wave of cold wash over her that had nothing to do with the draft. "Oh?" she managed to say.

"He feels I might find a more suitable wife than the daughter and sister of millworkers."

This time she didn't say anything. Her hands were clenched together in her lap.

Frederick studied her a moment before he continued. "I've convinced him, however, that once your name is Whitaker instead of Merriwether, people will forget about your family." He hesitated slightly before adding, "Especially if you sever your association with it."

Hazel stared at him again, her gray eyes huge. "What are you saying, Frederick?" she asked quietly.

"I'm saying that we should get married very soon and that you should leave all this"—he waved his hand around the dingy parlor—"behind you for good. Forget that it ever happened. That you ever lived here. Or that you ever knew anyone who did."

"But I *do* live here, Frederick," Hazel said, unwilling to believe what she was hearing. She must have misunderstood him. "So do Papa and Cornelius. And more than likely they'll continue to live here after we're married."

"Yes."

Silence followed his single syllable. Hazel swallowed. "Are you asking me to desert my family?" she asked finally. "To forget about *Papa* and *Cornelius*?"

"They'll only bring you down, Hazel," Frederick said, leaning toward her, his handsome face earnest. "You're too good for them. Too beautiful. They'll ruin you with their commonness. I can give you everything you need." He held his hand out imploring her to accept it.

She drew back from it in horror. It shocked her to think she had once wanted to marry this man, that she had happily and eagerly consented to be his wife. How could she have been so blind? Even after she'd admitted to herself that he didn't make her heart pound with excitement, she still had yearned for the life he represented. A life, she now realized, that meant abandoning her family. The thought was too awful to contemplate.

"Tell me something, please," she said with deadly calm. "If it's so painful for you to acknowledge my family, why do you want to marry me at all? Why not accept your father's suggestion to terminate our engagement?"

Stung by her rebuff, Frederick sat back. "I pledged myself to marry you," he said without affection. "We were formally engaged. We announced it in public. If I break it off now, people will talk. There will be a scandal. An unpleasant scene."

"Oh, I see." Her voice remained lethally even. "So we've come back to what society thinks." She nodded, digesting that fact. After a minute she went on. "Do you know, Frederick," she said, cocking her head, "I never realized you were so concerned with other people's opinions. Someone once told me that I'm an exceptionally perceptive person, but he must have been mistaken, because I completely failed to perceive your need for society's approval. You'll go to incredible lengths to keep your image from being tainted."

"It's too late for that," Frederick snapped, enraged by her criticism. "Thanks to you and your family, it already is. Either way I turn, I'm caught. If I break off with you, I'll be condemned for my actions, and if I marry you, I'll be haunted by Edgar and Cornelius."

"Quite a dilemma," Hazel agreed, just barely keeping her control. "But perhaps I can make it easier. Papa needs to be cared for while he recovers from his setbacks. I can't leave him now. And I won't leave Cornelius, either. There. I've helped you to decide."

"I think not," Frederick said, springing to his feet and towering over Hazel. "I've come to a different decision." He stalked around behind the chair and leaned across its back to deliver his verdict. "I've decided that I want you for my wife. You are easily the most beautiful woman in our set, and your disposition and manners are extremely refined. You have excellent taste, an admirable knowledge of art and music, and your skills as a hostess are well known. I'm convinced that once this business with your family is forgotten, ours will be a marriage that is held up as an example."

Hazel was speechless. Far from being flattered by his list of her accomplishments, she was disgusted. He had recited them as he would recite the characteristics of a prized yacht. She was just an object, another element in the perfect design of his life, like a precious painting or an antique vase or a house at the proper address. He had picked her for her physical charms, for how she would appear to society. His only interest in her was as the image she presented. An image that would bear his name and, thus, reflect back on him.

It dawned on her that that was the way it always had been. There was no difference between being Edgar's dolly and Frederick's sweet pet. She was still valued in the same manner. Her worth was as an accessory to someone else's life. Like Cornelius, the world she inhabited had always been someone else's world, but unlike her wise younger brother, she hadn't even known it until this minute.

Rising, she walked over to the window and looked out. It was snowing, a light, wet snow that wasn't sticking. It was making the road muddy, though, and was probably soaking the laundry she'd hung on the line.

Suddenly she was very angry. Her life had been taken out of her hands. It was simply an exhibit, a display for the front hall showcase in whoever's house she lived. What was worse, cushioned by the elegant furnishings and civilized conversations, she'd not only let it be taken from her, she'd contentedly given it away. In the back of her mind Hazel heard Marco say, "You're not a pet. *You* are a person."

She turned back to Frederick. "Perhaps you didn't understand me," she said to him. "I'm releasing you from your promise. Our engagement is off."

"I understood you perfectly well," he replied, standing up very straight, his cheeks flushed. "But perhaps you didn't understand me. I've chosen *not* to end our engagement. In fact, I've set a date for the seventeenth of February."

"How dare you—" Hazel started to protest hotly.

"That's two months from now." Frederick's voice rose slightly and hardened, drowning her out. "Mother felt she needed that much time to plan the reception. Under the circumstances, it will have to be small, but it can't be too small or people will talk."

"Frederick—"

"I would advise you to think twice about this little show of the sulks, Hazel," he cautioned, his face growing redder. "You would do well to remember that I'm tolerating Edgar's drunkenness and Cornelius's troublemaking only because you're my fiancée. Should our engagement be broken, I would no longer feel that obligation."

Hazel gasped. "You can't be serious," she said. Cold before, she now felt frozen. Unless she married him, Frederick would fire her father and brother.

It wasn't a toothless threat he was making. They needed those jobs in the mill to pay for basic food and shelter. With the country in an economic depression and Edgar in a mental one, there was no chance he would find other work. There was little likelihood that Cornelius could, either. The ideal marriage she had once envisioned had degenerated into blackmail. Her shoulders sagged.

"I'm very serious, my dear," Frederick said. His flush faded when he saw he'd regained the upper hand. "May I assume that the seventeenth of February meets with your approval?"

The anger that had flared up in Hazel slowly smoldered out. She'd made her discovery too late to regain control of her life. If she didn't marry Frederick, her father and brother would suffer. She remembered how Cornelius had manfully swallowed his condemnations of the deplorable conditions at the mill and had gone back to his station, placing concern for his family above his personal convictions. Now it was her turn to do the same thing.

"The seventeenth of February will be fine," she said in a voice devoid of emotion.

"Excellent!" He gathered up his hat, his spirits restored. "I can't stay any longer, I'm afraid. I must get back to Boston. Thank you so much for the tea, my dear." He walked over to her and stroked her cheek. "You're upset now," he told her. "But after we're married, you'll realize I was right."

Hazel didn't answer, nor did she move to show him out. She just stood by the window shivering and thinking about the bitter irony of the situation. Where once she'd regarded marriage to Frederick as her salvation, as her last link to the life she used to enjoy, now she regarded that life as a prison and her marriage as the key that locked the cell door.

As the days went by, the despair stayed with her, putting shadows under her eyes and stealing her appetite. Cornelius watched her for a time, then, one evening, finally asked her what was wrong.

"Nothing," she reassured him, forcing a smile. "I'm just a little sad. Maybe it's Christmas. It's coming up next Monday, but I'm afraid it won't be very festive this year." Last Christmas, in a swirl of silks and jewels and candlelight, she had become engaged to Frederick. Her smile disappeared.

Cornelius accepted her excuse, even though he didn't completely believe it. He kept watching.

When there was a knock on the front door the next morning, Hazel went reluctantly to answer it, afraid it was Frederick with more arrangements to announce. When she opened the door, though, Marco stood there, a crockery jug underneath his arm.

"You've been keeping a secret from me, Hazel," he said reproachfully.

Hazel's pulse raced in confusion. How had he found out? "A secret?" she asked, playing for time.

"Yes." He held up the jug, beaming. "Maple syrup."

She laughed shakily. "That's no secret," she said, relieved. "Everybody knows about it."

"Every American knows about it," Marco corrected. "Or perhaps every New Englander. But I promise you, it's a delight that's unknown beyond your shores. Although," he mused, laying a thoughtful finger alongside his nose, "it could be a worthwhile venture to ship some back to England." He nodded brightly. "In addition to making a profit, I would have the satisfaction of knowing I had brought enlightenment to Great Britain."

"Marco MacGregor, the Maple Syrup Savior?" she offered.

"Oh, yes, I like the sound of it," Marco responded, coming in. He shrugged out of his coat as he walked down the narrow hall, tossing it on a peg on the far wall. He turned into the parlor and threw himself on the cot, still gripping the jug.

"Seriously, Hazel," he said. "It's an awe-inspiring concept. Just imagine, this ambrosial syrup is the lifeblood of a tree. Sap." He shook his head in amazement. "And do you know how they extract it?" He didn't wait for her to answer as she sank into the chair, but went right on talking.

"They insert taps into the trees, and the sap flows into a bucket like water into a sink." He described the process with his free hand, twisting it through the air. "Then huge caldrons of it are boiled down to make a tiny bit of syrup. It's done in the early spring when the nights are frosty and the days are thawing. We must make an expedition to watch this miracle being performed. They call it 'sugaring off.' A lovely phrase, don't you think?"

He looked at Hazel for confirmation, then sat up straight. "What's the matter?" he demanded.

Hazel shook her head. She had been listening to his story happily, grateful for the distraction, until his suggestion for a sugaring expedition. By the time the sap ran in the maples again, she would be Mrs. Frederick Whitaker. She would never accompany Marco to watch the syrup being made. For some reason, that drove in the reality of her situation like nothing else had. She bent over, her hand pressing the pain in her chest.

"Don't say no," he told her. "Something's wrong. The color just drained from your face, and you look as if your best friend died." He set the jug on the floor and leaned forward in concern. "Is that it? Has something happened to Edgar? Or to Cornelius?"

She shook her head again. "They're fine," she said faintly.

Marco reached across and took one of her hands in his. "My God, Hazel," he exclaimed. "You're freezing cold." He stood up and pulled her up, too. "Come. I'm going to make you a cup of hot milk and brandy." He wrapped his arm around her shoulders and guided her into the kitchen.

His attempts at comfort didn't make it easier. They made it worse. The feeling of his arm around her made the pain in her heart almost unendurable. She couldn't imagine never feeling him hug her again, never feeling his big, warm body next to hers. It was impossible to think she would never see his face again, with its Renaissance nose and cherub cheeks. Never see his eyebrows raise. Never see him beam. Never again hear him recount his gastronomic adventures with an enthusiasm bordering on rapture. Never hear him compliment her and criticize her and goad her into thinking. Then she admitted it. She was in love with him.

Marco sat her down on a kitchen chair and went to put a pan of milk on the stove. As he worked, Hazel watched him in anguish. She was in love with him. She probably had been since that afternoon in Venice.

While Marco waited for the milk to warm, he knelt in front of her and chaffed her hands. He didn't say a word, but there was worry in his eyes. What a difference between Marco and

Frederick, she thought. Why hadn't she seen it before? Marco's vitality filled this drab little house. Frederick's facade made it littler and drabber. Marco hadn't let its meanness deter him from visiting at every opportunity. Frederick, fearing a smudge on his image, had hardly called at all. Marco cared about her. Frederick cared about himself.

When the milk was ready, Marco folded her hands together and set them in her lap. Then he went to pour the milk into a cup and liberally lace it with brandy. "Drink it all up," he ordered as he handed it to her. Pulling another chair so close to her that when he sat their knees nearly touched, he watched her like a mother hen until she had drunk every drop. "Better?" he asked.

She nodded.

"Good. Now tell me what's troubling you."

She gulped. Then burst into tears.

"Hazel, what is it?" Marco asked frantically, gathering her into his lap. He cradled her against him, rubbing her arm, stroking her back. "Tell me, tell me," he whispered, burying his nose in her hair. "Let me help."

Hazel sobbed until she choked, until she gasped for air. It didn't do any good. She still felt as if her heart were being ripped in two. How could she tell him she'd been in love with him all these months and hadn't even known it? And how could she tell him that now that she knew it, she could never do anything about it? It was too late. The most glorious moments in her entire life had been there for her to seize, and, instead, she'd turned her back on them, consumed by decorum and guilt. There was nothing she could tell him. There was no way he could help.

Eventually her sobbing ceased and she leaned, exhausted, against his chest. "I've ruined your jacket," she said dully, but didn't pick up her head.

He shrugged and held her closer. "That's what tailors are for," he replied.

She let him wipe her tears away with his monogrammed linen handkerchief. Then she let him soothe her reddened face with feathery gentle kisses. He placed each one with exquisite care, just barely touching his warm lips to her cheeks. To seal it, he blew softly on her skin. What was a breath of a sensation on the outside of Hazel was a bittersweet shock within. She knew she shouldn't let him kiss her, but she did.

He trailed the tips of his fingers under her jaw and lifted up her chin with his thumb. "Where does it hurt, Hazel?" he asked, his voice low and rough.

"Here?" He put a tender kiss on her nose.

"Here?" With his lips, he brushed the line of her brow.

"Or here?" His mouth came down on hers unhurriedly. It lingered, caressing, but questioning.

In answer Hazel crushed against him. She twined her arms around his neck and clung to him, straining as close as she could get. Her love for him became an overpowering need that burned through her body and swept all else from her mind. "Marco," she whispered. "Please don't let me go."

"I won't," he promised hoarsely, tightening his hold. One hand slipped up to cup her neck while the other spread across her back. When he laid his warm cheek to hers, the clean scent of his curls filled her nose and the heat of his breath filled her ear. "I won't," he said again.

He turned his head slowly, drawing his lips across her face, stopping when they came to the tiny dot above her mouth. First he kissed it. Then he touched it with his tongue. Hazel caught her breath sharply. Inside of her, desire exploded.

He lifted her in his arms and carried her into her room, laying her down with her head on the single pillow. As he had once before, he unpinned her brooch and set it on the table. With sure fingers he unbuttoned her blouse. His nostrils flared when it fell open to reveal the lush skin of her breasts peeking out from the lace of her camisole. He bent forward to slide his lips across them.

Suddenly panicking, Hazel held him there. Her fingers tangled in his hair as they pressed his head to her chest. She wanted to hold on to him forever. If she let go, she was afraid he'd disappear. It was an unbearable thought.

After a moment Marco disentangled her fingers, but instead of letting them drop, he drew them up to his mouth. His blue eyes were bright and large. "I'm here, Hazel," he told her, giving each finger a kiss. "I'll always be here."

Turn by turn, he undressed them both, his jacket, her skirt, his shirt, her blouse. When their clothes lay in a pile on the floor, he slid under the quilt and into Hazel's waiting arms. On plain muslin sheets, not lilac linen ones, in the gray shade of Mrs. O'Sullivan's laundry, not a puddle of Scottish sun, they made love.

It wasn't like the last time when it had been joyous and exploring, when it had been magically alive and full of promise. Now Hazel felt as if she were saying farewell, that this wasn't the beginning but the end. It was almost as if she were desperately storing this moment away for the bleak future, as if she were memorizing every abundant inch of him.

Her eager fingers felt the bump in his nose and the smooth skin of those high, rosy cheeks. Then bolder, more greedy, they searched him all over, stroking the muscles in his arms, rubbing the length of his long, strong legs. She followed her hands with great gulping kisses, oblivious to everything but her hunger for this man.

Marco responded with titanic passion, exciting her body, stirring unimaginable sensations. His kisses were deep and moist and uninhibited. His touch gave her pleasure she never knew existed. He responded to her mood, trying to loosen the fear gripping her spirit and fueling her ardor. Despite the intense thrills he aroused, though, the fear wouldn't recede.

Even when, after a while, her devouring need had been satisfied, the fear remained. So did her love for him. Without the distorting influence of desire, though, cold reality reasserted itself. It was too late. She lay on her back staring at the ceiling, while Marco lay on his side running his fingers down her face.

"You're filled with misery," he said quietly. "There's more bothering you than just this house or the mills. Why can't you tell me what it is?"

She couldn't answer. Without taking her eyes from the cracks overhead, she shrugged.

He put his hand against her cheek and turned her face toward him. "Look at me," he insisted, giving her head a little shake. "Whatever it is, I can help you make it better."

No, he couldn't. Hazel pulled his hand away and shoved his arm off her shoulders. Her destiny had been decided by others than herself, and those mighty men had neglected to include Marco. She rolled on her side and started to stand up.

A strong arm dragged her back down on the bed. "Don't be silly, Hazel," he said more forcefully. "Something is eating you whole. You've got to tell me about it. You can't keep it inside yourself."

In response Hazel slipped out of his grasp and swung her bare feet onto the cold wooden floor. She stepped into her bloomers and put on her camisole and petticoat before turning to look at Marco. Propped up on an elbow, he had a puzzled expression on his face. "This was a mistake," she said briefly.

"Och, Hazel!" he cried, sitting up abruptly. "You've said that to me before."

"I was right then, and I'm even more right now," she replied, buttoning her blouse. "I'm not blaming you. It was my own fault, but it can't ever happen again. In fact"—she hesitated only slightly—"I don't want you to come here anymore." Her voice was steady and her tone was flat.

"I know I've told you that before, too. But this time I'm very serious. I should never have allowed myself to believe that your visits were harmless." She slipped her skirt over her head. "I ought to have insisted, then, that you leave me alone."

"That isn't what you said a little while ago," Marco said pointedly. "A little while ago you asked me not to let go of you. I'm inclined to think you were more sincere then than you are now."

Hazel's hands faltered only infinitesimally as she fastened her skirt around her waist. Not wanting to sit on the bed again, she leaned against the wall to pull on her stockings. "I told you," she said, without looking at him. "I made a mistake."

"*This* is the mistake you're making," he roared, leaping out of the bed. Magnificently naked, he glared at her across the room.

"No." She shook her head firmly, reaching for her shoes. "I'm engaged to marry Frederick Whitaker, and on the seventeenth of February I'll become his wife. Surely you can understand that there's nothing more to be said."

"So that's what this is about!" Marco exclaimed. "You've finally set a date to marry that tedious fool, and the thought of it is making you sick. And no wonder. It isn't so much a marriage as a life sentence."

"Don't be ridiculous," Hazel replied. Her voice was still calm but inside she was raw. She'd decided the same thing herself. "We shall be very happy together."

"I'm not being ridiculous," he retorted. "I'm being honest. If you aren't thoroughly disenchanted with Frederick on your wedding day, I predict that you will be within a year. He's incapable of making you happy. How can he when he'll never know or understand you? He's a dullard, Hazel, an unimaginative drone. It's impossible for him to conceive of a mind or a spirit like yours. And what Frederick can't imagine, he won't accept."

"You're being unfair," she said doggedly. "Frederick's a good man."

"Good at what?" Marco shouted, stabbing his finger through the air. "Good at sailing his yacht? Good at exploiting the workers in his mill? Good at patting you on the head and calling you his 'sweet pet'? Frederick may be good at a number of things, but he isn't good for you. Don't marry him, Hazel. Marry me instead."

"Now you're being absurd," she replied, hardly realizing that Marco had just proposed to her. The way he said it, sliding it into his tirade with his other heated remarks, made it seem far less momentous than it was. Failing to absorb its significance, she treated it as an offhand suggestion. "Everything's been settled. Our marriage has been announced. There was even a notice in the *Globe* on Wednesday. Frederick clipped it and sent it to me. So you see," she concluded, turning her hands palm up, "it's too late to change our plans. People will talk." It was an unconscious echo of what Frederick had said, and as soon as she heard her words she flinched.

Marco's reaction was considerably stronger. "*People?*" he bellowed. "I thought you'd gone past that mindless obsession with 'polite society.' What the devil do you care what *people* say? *People* don't have to live your life." He pounded the bed with his fist. "*People* don't have to marry Frederick. *People* don't have to face him across the breakfast table for the next fifty years. *People* don't have to share his bed or have his children. *You* do.

"Hazel," he said, his voice dropping in controlled wrath. "Let people talk. Let them say you have two heads and twelve toes. Let them say anything they damn well please, but don't let their petty gossip ruin your life."

He made a majestic figure, naked and outraged, but Hazel refused to look at him. She knew what she had to do and why she had to do it and she couldn't let herself be distracted by either his powerful looks or his equally powerful words. "A stirring speech," she said politely. "Thank you for your concern."

Marco slowly blew out his breath. He could fight against anger, he could rant against stupidity. He could argue, plead, and cajole against any flicker of opposition. But he was helpless against her stony silence. It was almost as if her elegant calm, the serenity that soothed his spirit and balmed his soul, had turned to marble. He put on his clothes and left.

# CHAPTER
## ❦ 13 ❧

The Sunday afternoon baseball game became a ritual. All through December, Agata and Cornelius slipped away from their families and met at the deserted diamond by the river. Instead of the stick and stone they used for the first game, Cornelius brought his bat and ball. Agata took to the game immediately. With her bright eyes and sturdy little body, she was soon connecting with the ball and slamming it out. To his delight, Cornelius was able to really pitch instead of just tossing.

Under his tutelage, Agata's English began to improve, too. In no time at all, though, her baseball vocabulary was absolutely perfect. "Put it here!" she yelled, tapping the outside corner of the plate with her bat. "*Penso che voglio* hit it up the middle."

Out on the mound Cornelius grinned. It didn't seem possible that she could be any more endearing, but every minute he spent with her, his love for her grew. Not only was she pretty and forthright and funny and spirited, but her enjoyment of baseball was almost as great as his. If he'd tried to invent a perfect girl, he couldn't have come any closer than Agata. Certainly she was miles ahead of the beribboned younger sisters of Hazel's friends. "Watch out for the twister," he called, sending in his curve ball. She popped it foul.

Walking home afterward in the winter twilight, warm and contented from an hour or two of exercise, Cornelius put his arm around her and pulled her near him. "What are you thinking about?" he asked her, rubbing his chin across the top of her head.

Wind and exertion had made dozens of crinkly black tendrils spring up from her braids.

"I am tinking about *mio papà*," she confessed ruefully, sliding her arm around his waist. "He is very *arrabbiato*."

"Thinking," Cornelius corrected automatically, trying to figure out what she said.

"Tinking," Agata repeated.

"Thhhinking."

"Thhhinking."

He nodded. "Good. Why are you thinking about your father?" he asked. "What's *arrabbiato*?"

"Grrrr," Agata explained, scowling and shaking her fist in the air.

Cornelius nodded again. "Angry," he translated.

"Angry," Agata said carefully.

"Why is he angry?" Cornelius was concerned.

"*Perchè* . . . No. Because," she amended, remembering the word. "Because I go out like this—" she let go of Cornelius and set a tiptoeing pose—"when he sleep."

"He's angry because you sneak away from the house?"

It was Agata's turn to nod. "Yes. Sneak." She started to slide back into the circle of Cornelius's arm, but he halted suddenly and turned to her, his gray eyes serious. "*Che*?" she asked, cocking her head.

He'd been bothered from the first by the secrecy of their meetings. It seemed to imply that his intentions were dishonorable, and that couldn't be further from the truth. "I think I should go talk to your father," he told her.

"No, no, no," Agata said, waving both hands in alarm. "No good." She shook her head, too.

"But I want to tell him how I feel about you," he insisted. "I want to let him know that I admire you and respect you and would never do anything to hurt you."

"Pff," Agata scoffed. "How you going to tell this to *Papà* when *I* don't understand what you say?"

That stopped him. She was right. He knew only a few phrases in Italian, and Agata's father knew only a few phrases in English, all of which were related to millwork, not courtship. He had no means of communicating his feelings to Signore Bellocchio. But he could make Agata understand.

"I said that I love you," he told her tenderly. He slipped his

arms under hers and hugged her to his chest. "I love you a lot."
Drawing her even closer, he bent his head and whispered in her
ear, *"Ti amo."*

Agata looked up at him, her round face flushed. *"Amore mio,"*
she responded in a husky voice. *"Anch'io, ti amo."* She lifted her
lips to his. "I love you, too."

Cornelius let himself be persuaded not to approach Agata's
father, but the honorable intentions he'd wanted to tell Signore
Bellocchio about increased in intensity daily. At the mill he often
found himself stalled by Agata's station, watching her animated
face with helpless fascination. There was little opportunity for
them to touch, or even to talk, and Cornelius was just barely able
to resist the powerful urge to grab her up and flee far from the noise
and the heat and the disease-filled air of the weaving room.

Standing at home plate on Christmas Day, he presented Agata
with a bag of chocolates and a little gold pin. He'd thought a long
time about what to give her. There were any number of things he
wanted to buy, but most of them he couldn't afford. Besides, he
didn't dare. How would she explain a music box or a challis shawl
to her father? He'd finally decided on the chocolates because they
could eat them on the spot, and on the simple pin with its single tiny garnet because it was something she could wear over her
heart, but hidden under her dress.

*"O che bello,"* she said, touched nearly to tears. "It's beautiful."
She kept staring at it with brimming eyes, then cradled it next to
her cheek. "I keep it forever. Always." She finally tore her eyes
away from it and looked up at him. "For you, *caro* Cornelius, I
have *niente,"* she told him sorrowfully. "Nothing."

He shook his head, his throat suddenly full, too. "You've just
given me the best gift I've ever gotten," he said.

"Yes?" She looked at him in amazement. "What?"

He set a hand on each of her shoulders and pulled her forward
until their cold noses touched. "Your love," he answered.

Agata's hands slipped around his back and she laid her face
against his chest. "Pff," she said into the wool of his jacket. "I
give you my love every day. It's not a Christmas gift."

One Sunday in late January, when a blustery wind blew a flurry
of snow on their baseball game, they couldn't bear the thought
of giving up any of their precious time together and going home

early. Instead, they cracked open the back door of Elgin Bros.
Livery, snuck inside, and crept up to the hayloft. There was no one
around on this miserable afternoon except the horses, drowsing in
their stalls or poking halfheartedly at their feed buckets.

By comparison with the bleak outdoors, the loft was cozy, especially when they snuggled under a layer of hay with their heads
on a pile of burlap sacks. Cornelius took Agata's bare hands and
tucked them between the buttons of his jacket. "Cold?" he asked,
rubbing her cheek with the back of his hand. He worried because
she had neither muffler nor hat and because the cloth of her old
coat was so thin.

"*Un po'*," she admitted, shivering. "In Calabria it is never snow."

"It isn't so bad if you have warm enough clothes," he said,
wriggling closer, with a rustle of hay, and throwing his arm across
her. "Or if you're sitting by a fire drinking hot chocolate. Then it
can be rather pretty."

"Hot chocolate?" Agata asked. She buried her nose against his
neck. "*Cioccolato caldo? Che cos'è?*"

"Don't you know what hot chocolate is? Don't you have it in
Calabria?"

"I don't tink so."

"Thhhink," he corrected, pressing his mouth against her cheek
so she could feel the way he pronounced it.

"Thhhink," she repeated, pressing her mouth against his.

"Mmmm," he said. "It's delicious." Although for a long moment he didn't specify to which he was referring. When he finally broke away from her kiss, he explained, "It's made with hot
milk and cocoa powder and sugar and sometimes vanilla or cin-
namon."

"Mmmm," she agreed, still nuzzling his lips. "Maybe someday
I drink."

"Not maybe," Cornelius replied. "Definitely." Suddenly all his
honorable intentions came together, and he was filled with resolution. "Someday we'll be able to spend the entire day drinking
hot chocolate, if we want to," he told her.

"Yes?" she asked idly, kissing the bottom of his ear.

"Yes," he answered firmly. He took her face in his hand and
held it away so he could look directly into her eyes. "Someday
we're going to go away from here," he said. "We're never going
to work in the mills again. We're going to be able to play baseball
and drink hot chocolate and be together all the time." He touched

his finger to his lip and then to hers. "I promise you that, Agata," he said solemnly.

"Yes?" she asked again, though this time she was incredulous.

"Yes," Cornelius repeated, even more positively than before.

For a moment she didn't respond, then she started to say, "But, *Papà*—"

Cornelius cut her off before she could go any further. "He can't say anything when we're married."

"Married?" Agata inched back to get a better perspective of his expression. "*Sposati?*" she asked, wanting to make absolutely sure she understood what he was saying.

He nodded. "*Sposati*. If that's how you say married in Italian." To illustrate, he plucked her left hand from his jacket and slipped an imaginary ring over her fourth finger.

Agata stared at her finger as if she were seeing an actual wedding band. "*Sposati*," she whispered to herself, trying to absorb that fact. Then she flung herself against him, covering his face with jubilant kisses. "*Amore!*" she cried. "When? When? When? When?"

The euphoric grin that had formed on Cornelius's face began to fade. For another minute he held her close to him, savoring her elation. Finally he had to admit, "I don't know." He could feel the excitement flow out of her, and she lay limp and still on top of him.

Brushing bits of straw from the collar of her coat, he tried to explain. "If I were alone, I'd take you away tomorrow," he said. "No," he amended. "I'd take you away today. This afternoon. Right this minute." Her body grew tense in his arms as she waited to hear the rest.

"But I have to think about my family," he went on. "There's my sister, Hazel, and my father. Papa isn't well. I can't just leave him. They'd be helpless without me."

Agata finally raised her head and drew away from him in the hay. "*Ho capito*," she said quietly. "I understand."

"No, you don't," Cornelius said miserably, clutching one of her hands and trying to pull her back. "You think I'm making an excuse so I don't have to keep my promise. But that's not true." He ran his thumb across her freckled cheeks and under her sad brown eyes. "I love you, Agata," he told her. "I want to marry you. You are my life."

After a moment Agata gave him a little smile and an apologetic shrug. Sliding across the straw again, she said determinedly, "We wait. Someday we marry, *amore mio*."

Grateful for her patience, Cornelius clasped her to him. "It won't be long," he vowed. "I'll think of a way to make it happen soon."

Confident again, Agata kissed the worried furrow in his brow. "Yes," she said. "I know."

"Hazel's going to be married next month," Cornelius thought out loud. "Maybe after that Frederick will help her take care of Papa."

"*Ecco! Si,*" Agata pounced. "Yes, yes. Frederick will help with Papa. I tink so." With a guilty glance upward, she caught herself. "*Ola.* I mean, I thhhink." She pressed her mouth to his again.

Cornelius responded to Agata's kiss without hesitation, although he had very serious second thoughts about Frederick's cooperation. Happy in her embrace, however, he gave a shrug of his own. Something would happen.

It wasn't what Cornelius expected. When he came to work on Thursday morning, he was shocked to see Agata standing in front of her looms, her face raw from weeping. His distress was made that much greater by his inability to question her about the cause of her tears. Thwarted by many curious gazes, he could say no more than "Good morning, Miss Bellocchio. Is everything all right?"

In reply Agata gave only a tight nod, unable to look at him as she fiddled with the shuttle in her hands. It took every ounce of Cornelius's willpower to pretend that he was unconcerned as he slowly sauntered down the aisle greeting the other workers. Over the next six hours his feverish mind came up with a dozen desperate scenarios. He imagined everything from a death in her family to her father having found out about their baseball games. During his many passes by her station, though, Agata never gave him a clue. In fact, she resolutely kept her reddened eyes averted.

When the noon bell finally rang, Cornelius was planted at the head of her row of looms and waiting, afraid she might be so upset she would try to slip by him without explaining. He needn't have worried on that score, however. As she had done once before while her fellow weavers filed out to lunch, Agata found a shoelace that needed retying. She was just standing again when Cornelius came dashing down the empty aisle and seized hold of her hands.

"My God, Agata!" he exclaimed. "You've got to tell me what's wrong."

In the course of the long morning, Agata's swollen face had settled into a stoic mask. All it took was Cornelius's touch, however, to make her break into tears anew. She slumped in his grip, her body wracked with sobs.

Completely unconcerned with who might be watching or listening, Cornelius gathered her against him. As he rubbed her back, he swayed to and fro in solace. "Agata, Agata," he murmured in her ear, while nesting kisses among the crinkly tendrils escaped from her braids.

When at last she managed to regain some semblance of speech, her voice was so broken, Cornelius could scarcely understand her. "*È terribile,* Cornelius," she sputtered.

"What?" he asked. "What are you saying?" He mopped her wet face with the palm of his hand until he remembered his handkerchief. He pulled it out and was daubing at her eyes when Agata took it from him. "Did you say that something was terrible?"

Nodding as she blew her nose, Agata answered, "*Sì. Terribile.*"

Cornelius's anxiety increased. "What is it?" he asked desperately. "What happened?"

This time Agata shook her head, unable to speak for fear of dissolving in another flood of tears.

"Are you sick?" Cornelius probed, fighting to retain his control. She continued to shake her head as he ascended the list of tragedies he'd outlined in his mind. "Are you hurt? Is your *papà* hurt? *Mamma? Fratello? Sorella?*" When it seemed that everyone in her family was whole and healthy, Cornelius took a deep breath. "Has your *papà* found out about us?" he asked quietly.

"No," she answered briefly.

"No?" Now Cornelius was puzzled.

Shaking her head again, Agata clicked her tongue against her teeth in denial. "More bad," she gasped.

"If no one is sick or has died, what could be worse than that?" Cornelius asked. Panic suddenly gripped him, and he in turn gripped Agata. "Tell me what it is," he insisted.

She inhaled sharply, then released the breath in a long, slow shudder. "Is me," she said simply. "I marry my cousin."

For a fraction of a moment Cornelius felt absolutely numb. But it was only a tenth of an instant before a searing pain shot through him. "What?" he exploded, shaking the little body he was holding.

He barely saw her frightened face, barely saw the tears begin to flow. All he knew was that he'd never hurt so badly in his life. His heart felt white hot.

"You told me you loved me," he said savagely. "You told me we'd wait until we could be married. That wasn't even four full days ago. Did you really have so little faith?"

"No, *amore*, no," Agata choked, trying to pry his iron fingers from her arms. "I don't want. I *must. Capisci?*"

When he finally absorbed her words this time, when he finally realized she was as distraught as he was, some of his blinding rage drained away, though his heart continued to ache. He loosened his fierce hold of her, but he didn't let go. "No," he answered. "No, Agata, I don't understand. Tell me what's going on."

In tearful fits and starts, half in Italian, half in English, Agata explained that her father's second cousin had arrived from Italy last night, reviving a vow made nineteen years before. Close friends in Calabria, the cousins had married in a double ceremony on Easter Sunday and had pledged that their firstborn son and daughter would be joined in marriage. She had thought that promise void when her family immigrated last year, but it had come back to life to haunt her. She was to become the bride of Tomasso Garofano on March twenty-fifth. "*È Pasqua,*" she concluded. "Easter."

There was another moment of stillness when Agata finished her story, a moment when Cornelius was too stunned to speak. When his reaction set in, it wasn't the fiery explosion it had been the last time, but rather a stumbling refusal to accept the situation. His hands finally dropped away from her and hung by his side. His gaze wandered. "It's not possible," he said. "It can't be true."

Now Agata reached out to him. Taking one of his limp hands in both of hers, she carried it to her lips. "*È vero,*" she said, placing a kiss across the knuckles. "Is true."

Her kiss seemed to jolt him out of his daze. As his fingers flipped around and tightly grasped hers, he focused intently on her face. "I won't let it happen," he told her. "I'll go see your father tonight. After work. I'll tell him you can't marry your cousin because you're going to marry me." He grabbed her other hand, too. "If I have to, I'll take an interpreter," he went on more wildly. "I must make your father understand that we love each other and that *we* are going to be married. You and I. Us."

Tears were running down Agata's freckled cheeks by the time she stopped him. "Is no good," she said, gulping for air. "My *papà* and *papà* of Tomasso make a promise before God on the day they marry. *Papà* must keep the promise or it is *una disgrazia. Una vergogna.*" For a moment she hunted through her mind for a suitable translation. Finally she threw up her hands and cried, "I don't know how to say in English."

"It doesn't matter," Cornelius said, grabbing her hands again. "And it doesn't matter about that promise between your father and Tomasso's father. They have no right to pledge away your life. Your life belongs to you."

Agata shook her head miserably. "No," she said. "In Calabria, I must do what *Papà* say or it is *una disgrazia*. How do you say this in English?"

"We aren't in Calabria now," Cornelius protested, ignoring her question. "This is America. Girls marry whomever they choose." When she started to shake her head again and to click her tongue against her teeth, Cornelius clapped together the hands he was holding. "Listen to me," he pleaded.

"We don't have to ask your father. We don't have to ask anyone. We'll run away and get married and then it'll be done. We can live at my house in the beginning. It'll be a bit crowded, but we'll work it out. Hazel won't mind. Honestly. She has a very good heart. She'll make you feel welcome and comfortable. You'll see that that's the way she is."

Agata had to press her hand to his lips to make him stop this time. "No, *amore*," she said, fat tears sliding down her face. "I cannot. Don't you understand? *È una disgrazia.*"

Cornelius stared at her for a long moment, then his shoulders sagged. He could love her until the day he died, but he couldn't change the way she was raised. Her fate had been decided before she was born, and she was bound by duty and honor to accept it. "Disgrace." He supplied the word dully. "It would be a disgrace for you to break the pledge."

"*Si. Una disgrazia.*"

By the time the other weavers straggled back to their machines, Agata and Cornelius were standing at their stations, their faces sad but composed. Inside, though, Cornelius was torn apart. He still couldn't believe it was true. To lose Agata was to lose the purpose in his life.

# CHAPTER

## ⟞⟩ 14 ⟨⟝

"Did you hear what I said, Hazel?" There was an edge of annoyance in Mrs. Whitaker's voice.

Starting guiltily, Hazel turned so quickly the dressmaker's pin stabbed her rib. She flinched slightly but otherwise ignored the prick. "I'm afraid I've been daydreaming," she apologized to her future mother-in-law.

"Which is natural with your wedding only ten days away," the dressmaker interjected, readjusting the pin. "I can't tell you how many brides I've seen go all aflutter just before the big day. Some get so excited their feet seem to leave the ground."

"*Are* you listening to me, Hazel?" Mrs. Whitaker demanded.

"I'm sorry," Hazel apologized again. Mrs. Whitaker's faded face was pink with impatience. "What were you saying?"

"I was telling you about the flowers for the tables," she answered, only partly mollified. "We're going to have white roses and lilies of the valley in a crystal vase tied with a white satin ribbon. Frederick said you're fond of roses."

For a moment Hazel didn't respond as she imagined the banal bouquets. "There are very few flowers I dislike," she finally answered. "I'm sure the effect will be lovely."

Further annoyed by Hazel's lack of enthusiasm, Mrs. Whitaker unleashed her irritation at the dressmaker. "Aren't you ready yet?" she snapped. "You've been dawdling over that jabot for half an hour. I'll be late for my luncheon if you don't hurry."

"Almost ready, ma'am," the dressmaker replied, her fingers

moving faster. Another pin stabbed Hazel's skin. This time in the breast.

Ignoring that prick was a little more difficult. As was ignoring the fact that Mrs. Whitaker meant to dash off to a luncheon, leaving Hazel to find her way back to the train, unfed and by herself. Nonetheless, her voice was pleasant as she said, "If you have an appointment, don't let us delay you. We can finish up after you're gone."

"Really, Hazel," Mrs. Whitaker complained. "This is an expensive gown. I have to make sure it's being done properly."

Hazel's hand swept down to stay the dressmaker's busy fingers. She turned to fully face Mrs. Whitaker, sitting on the velvet sofa of the salon. "I was having my clothes made, without supervision, since I was fourteen years old," she said quietly, a flush creeping up her cheeks. "Are you suggesting that I now have neither the taste nor the judgment to be fitted for my own wedding gown?"

"Oh, dear," Mrs. Whitaker responded, thoroughly nonplussed by this display of defiance, however composed. "No, no. Of course not," she backpedaled. "I'm sure you're quite capable of fitting your dress. Anyway," she added, "these are just the final adjustments. Yes, in that case," she decided, "I think I'll be off." She rose quickly to leave. "I'll see you next week. Don't forget, you're to come to us on the Thursday before the wedding."

Hazel waited until Mrs. Whitaker was out the door before she turned back to face the dressmaker. "Please excuse my mother-in-law's brusqueness," she said a trifle wearily. This was happening too often.

"Don't you worry," the dressmaker soothed. "It's natural for mothers to come undone, too. I see it all the time." She fiddled with a few more pins, then stepped back. "There. How does that look?"

A big oval mirror in a gilt-edged frame was tilted to reflect every inch of the ivory peau de soie gown, from the puffed, mutton-leg sleeves to the tiny waist to the swirl of the long train. Hazel sighed. The dress was very rich, but it wasn't what she would have chosen. There was too much fussy lace on the neck and bodice and trailing down her hip. It was a style more suited to Lucy's dainty prettiness than to her own elegant beauty. "Very nice," she told the woman.

As the train chugged back to Lawrence, Hazel lolled her head against the seat and stared out the window. The woods and pastures, looking bare and stark in the winter sun, perfectly matched her mood. It wasn't so very long ago, she thought dispiritedly, that she would have been consulted about the wedding arrangements, rather than informed of them. Her taste and opinion would have been admired and esteemed, not mistrusted.

She shut her eyes as she acknowledged the painful truth: Even if she still yearned for her old life on Marlborough Street, her marriage to Frederick would never bring it back. She would always be treated like a poor relation by his family. And probably by the people she had once called friends, too.

She squeezed her eyes tighter to hold back a flood of tears. Marco had been right, she thought. He'd known it long before she'd been willing to admit it to herself. This marriage, in his words, was going to be a living hell.

"Ticket, miss," the conductor said, interrupting her brooding.

Sniffling, Hazel opened her eyes and reached inside her reticule. She handed the man her ticket, then watched him punch it and hand it back. Instead of moving on, however, the conductor lingered. "Are you all right, miss?" he asked hesitantly.

Surprised, Hazel looked up at his broad, sympathetic face. "Thank you," she said. "I'll be fine in a minute."

He nodded and pulled a small tin from his pocket. "Have a lemon drop, miss," he offered, holding out the open box. "It'll help to cheer you up."

Oddly moved, Hazel accepted the candy, thanking him again for his kindness. After he'd continued down the aisle, though, doom recaptured her spirit. It'll take more than a lemon drop to help me, she thought glumly. I'm in the deepest of dungeons.

What was worse, the dire mood seemed contagious. Poor Cornelius had been walking around for almost a week, his eyes hollow and tragic. What little conversation she made over dinner, she had to repeat twice for his benefit. Even then, he hardly heard her. Edgar was no better. He had been sunken inside himself ever since the "incident" at the mill, though Hazel wasn't sure whether her bleakness could be blamed for that.

It was responsible for Marco's disappearance, however. The thought brought a fresh threat of tears. Hazel crossed her arms over her chest and riveted her face to the window. Obviously Marco had finally believed her harsh words and cold tone. She hadn't seen or heard from him since before Christmas. Not a postcard. Not a peep of gossip. He had gone back to Venice or Scotland or someplace beyond. Vanished completely from her world. Which was what she'd wanted. Wasn't it?

Swallowing hard, Hazel fought back the tears. Despite having deliberately and purposefully chased him away, not a day went by that she didn't long for him and miss him and wish he would magically reappear. Nor did a day go by that she didn't wonder about his proposal. If that's what it had been.

However many times she reviewed that scene in her mind, she came up with a different version. Sometimes it sounded as if he'd wanted to marry her. Other times it just sounded as if he didn't want her to marry Frederick. It had been such an angry moment, and he hadn't mentioned love, she couldn't be sure if he'd meant it or if it had been a whim born of frustration.

Maybe he'd never returned because he regretted uttering those words and was afraid she'd take him up on them. Or maybe his proposal was a charitable act, provoked by pity. Maybe it was just a tease. Maybe it wasn't. Maybe he really wanted her. Maybe he didn't. Maybe it was only her imagination and he hadn't asked her to marry him at all. Maybe he had. Maybe.

Hazel hugged herself tighter and leaned her head against the window. Why hadn't she questioned him about it further? Why hadn't she asked him to repeat what he'd said after his fury had subsided? For that matter, why hadn't she reconsidered his proposal in a less agitated state? It had all happened so swiftly, in such hot and cold bursts of emotion, that what could have been the beginning of the happiest time in her life had instead been the end of it.

Lawrence was coming closer now. Hazel could see the river and the buildings and the hulking mills that gave the city its life. She greeted its approach with mixed feelings. On the one hand, she hated returning, knowing what a dismal house and a dreary routine awaited her. But when she thought about where she would be in only one more week, the immigrant city of overcrowded tenements seemed a sanctuary.

As the train crossed the Merrimack, and then the canal, Hazel stared vacantly down the line of mills, trying to pick out the one in which her father and brother worked. Using the massive Washington Mills as a landmark, she counted down until her listless gaze came to the spot where the Great Stone Dam Mill stood. Her heart suddenly leaped to her throat.

A great cloud of dust rose above the brick building, which was no longer a solid rectangle, but sat with one corner collapsed. Windows were wrecked, the glass was shattered, the slate on the roof was sliding free and sailing to the ground in lethal slabs. Even from this distance, Hazel could see people jumping from windows and pouring from the door, their bodies rigid in panic. She sat bolt upright, her insides turned to ice.

It was obvious that everyone else in the car had seen the same frightening sight. They jammed against the windows, buzzing with shock and speculation. Amid the exclamations of horror, there sounded a refrain. "Remember the Pemberton Mill?" it went. "It completely collapsed in eighteen-sixty." "The iron columns were badly cast." "Ninety people killed."

Hazel sprang from her seat and rushed for the door, ready to hurl herself from the train as soon as it stopped at the depot. "Ninety people killed." The thought reverberated in her mind. With each echo her fear grew more enormous. Unlike the night of the warehouse fire, when Edgar and Cornelius had gone to the site aware of the danger that lay within, this time the danger had struck unawares while they were trapped inside. She was nearly frantic with worry by the time the train made its lethargic way into the station.

Without waiting for it to come to a full halt, she clambered down the steps past the conductor who had been concerned about her happiness. "Wait, miss," he called as he tried to catch her arm. Hazel pulled away and landed on the platform in a sprawl. In an instant she was up and running, her skirt bunched in her fists as she raced through town toward the mill.

It was a good distance and she had to stop more than once to gulp cold air into her burning lungs and to let some strength dribble back to her legs. After a brief rest, though, her icy anxiety drove her on. By the time she arrived at the mill, her breath was coming in painful gasps and her body was trembling with fatigue. As she stumbled through the throngs of people milling in the yard, she was buffeted and jostled and nearly knocked to the ground.

Despair and a touch of panic were added to her fear. There were hundreds and hundreds of people here, some bruised or battered, some simply scared. But they formed a noisy, shouting mass that she was too weak to penetrate. Clutching the stitches in her sides, she made feeble leaps in the air in an attempt to see over the top of the crowd. All she saw was a blur of people. Where, in this impassable mob, were Papa and Cornelius?

"Hazel!" In the din she barely heard the shout. "Hazel!" it came again. Desperate, she looked around for its source. A few yards away, and pushing steadily toward her, was Marco. In another instant she was in his arms.

She had been glad to see him any number of times, even immensely relieved on some occasions, but never, ever had she been as thankful as she was right this minute. She had no idea where he'd been or how he came to be here now. She knew only that he was a welcome refuge. All around chaos reigned, but hiding against his body, she felt safe. As his hands kneaded her back and hugged her to him, she absorbed his strength and courage. Gradually she caught her breath and her pulse returned to normal.

"All right?" he asked, his head bent close to her ear.

Nodding, Hazel pulled away from his secure embrace. "Have you seen Papa or Cornelius?" she asked, casting another glance around the crowded millyard. She stretched on tiptoe, holding on to Marco for balance.

"Not yet," he replied. "Here, Hazel. Let me lift you up so you can get a better look. Even I'm not tall enough to see above this confusion."

Without waiting for a reply, he grabbed her around the knees and hoisted her to his shoulder. Clutching onto the collar of his coat, Hazel scanned the sea of people for a familiar face. She never gave her undignified position a second thought.

"Who do you see?" Marco called.

"No one," Hazel answered, shaking her head in renewed despair. That wasn't exactly accurate. She saw scores of people. They were being carried out of the mill now. Broken and twisted bodies with limbs hanging at odd angles. Her stomach lurched in a combination of fear and horror.

"What's happening?" Marco yelled more impatiently. "Tell me what you see, Hazel."

Gulping back the alarm that this dreadful scene aroused, she tried to describe it objectively. "They're bringing people out on blankets. No, they aren't blankets." She stared more intently. "I think they've cut lengths of wool from the bolts being woven. They're using them as stretchers."

"What else?"

Peering around again, Hazel saw a space being cleared for the injured workers. They were being laid side by side on the cold stone blocks of the millyard. "Over there!" she shouted, pointing at the opening. "That's where they're bringing the people who've been hurt."

Marco started moving in that direction with Hazel still sitting on his shoulder. As the crowd bumped and shoved against him, Hazel clung to his coat with both hands, her knuckles white, though she never ceased searching for her father and brother. "There's Frederick!" she yelled suddenly. One hand flew out to point again, then quickly snatched Marco's curls. She had forgotten about Frederick, forgotten that he might be in the mill, too.

Marco seemed to stop for a moment, but that could have been because his way was blocked. Finally he shouted, "Is he hurt?" He turned in the direction she had pointed. "Do you want to go to him?"

Hazel shook her head. "No," she answered in response to both questions. "He's all right," she called down. She was glad he wasn't injured, but beyond that she didn't care. Concern for Edgar and Cornelius outweighed everything else. "He's wearing his top hat." Marco turned back.

When at last they broke through to the edge of the clearing, Hazel put her arms around Marco's neck and slid to the ground. She started across the area, then stopped abruptly. Seen up close, this field of crushed and bloody millworkers was appalling. Some people were dead, some were dying, some screamed and moaned in agonizing pain. Clothes were torn, and so was flesh. Raw, gaping wounds were exposed to the pale winter sun.

Hazel clapped her hand to her mouth to hold back a wave of nausea. With this sickening sight, though, came a new level of fear. Her eyes raced down the rows of bodies, looking frantically for her father and brother. When faces were turned away or rendered unrecognizable, she checked for familiar clothes. Rather than feel relieved when she failed to find them, she felt a rush of panic. What if Papa and Cornelius were still inside the building, crumpled beneath a pile of bricks or smashed under a huge machine? She lunged for the mill.

"Wait!" Marco shouted, grabbing hold of her arm.

She spun around to stare at him, her eyes huge with fright. "But Papa . . ." she started to say.

"You can't go in there," Marco told her. He took her by the shoulders and shook her until some sense returned. "You stay here," he ordered. "I'll go look for them. But you have to stay exactly here," he repeated. "Promise me. I must know where to find you again." He waited for her to nod before he let her go and moved off.

The minutes passed like hours once Marco was gone. Something else gave way in the mill with an ominous rumble and another cloud of dust. The shrieks from the crowd that accompanied this aftershock only fanned her frenzy. Now she was afraid for Marco's safety as well.

Her dubious patience was nearly gone, her promise forgotten, when she suddenly saw her brother emerge from the mill. "Cornelius!" she cried, relief making her giddy. "Cornelius, over here!" She jumped up and down, waving her hands, but he didn't see her in the crowd and couldn't hear her calls. Cradled in his arms was the body of a small young woman whose long, black braids dangled down his side.

Without hesitation, Hazel started toward him, stepping around the injured people laying on the ground and out of the way of rescuers bearing more on the makeshift stretchers. As she went, almost light with happiness, she kept glancing toward her brother to make sure she didn't lose him. Her gaze flicked his way as he gently set his burden down. Then, when he didn't release his hold, she watched more closely.

To Hazel's amazement, Cornelius carefully brushed the dirt from the young woman's face and tenderly smoothed some escaped crinkles of hair. But when her baby brother bent down and laid a kiss on top of a swelling bruise, Hazel stopped still to stare. Her astonishment increased when the young woman's eyes fluttered open and instead of shrinking from Cornelius, she pressed closer to him. Their arms around each other, they hunched together on the cold millyard stone.

Uncertain of whether to go forward and interrupt this intimate embrace or to retreat unseen, Hazel shifted from foot to foot, increasingly overwhelmed by everything that was happening. In a matter of minutes her emotions had been sent spinning. They had gone from wild anxiety to excited release and now to incredulous surprise. It was too intense and sudden. She was having difficulty thinking straight.

While she stood there trying to gather her thoughts and reach a simple decision, she had yet another shock. She saw Marco come out of the mill with Edgar in his arms. Her father had lost even more weight in the past few months and had seemed to grow even older. Seeing him now, a small, frail bundle clasped against large, hearty Marco, he looked unbearably withered and still. Raw fear flooded through Hazel.

This time she didn't stop to ponder what to do. This time she picked up her skirt and raced for her father. She reached his side and sank to her knees just as Marco set him on the ground. "Papa!" she gasped. Her hand hovered near his face but she was afraid to touch him. His skin was gray and dull. His eyes were shut. He didn't move. She looked at Marco in terror.

"He's alive," Marco said briefly. With grim efficiency he went to work, unsnapping Edgar's collar and loosening his tie. He tucked his cashmere muffler under Edgar's head, then shrugged out of his great, caped topcoat and spread it over Edgar's unstirring body.

"What happened to him?" Hazel whispered from her frozen crouch.

"I found him in the sorting room," Marco answered. "A stack of bins had fallen on top of him." Even as he said it, he picked a tuft of wool from Edgar's hair. "He isn't conscious, but he has a pulse."

With cold, stiff fingers Hazel smoothed the wisp of hair that Marco had dislodged. She straightened her father's glasses, which, miraculously, hadn't been cracked. Then she twisted her hands together in her lap. "Will he be all right?" she asked in a very little voice.

After a moment's silence Marco finally said, "I don't know."

Hazel looked down at her father, the knot in her stomach hard. She no longer heard the commotion all around her, no longer saw the milling crowd. She was aware only of Edgar's face, of his sunken cheeks, which barely moved with breath. "Please, Papa," she begged. "Please wake up."

Edgar's eyelids slowly lifted. His gray eyes slowly shifted toward his daughter. He didn't seem to see her, though his gaze was dim and unfocused. "I'm right here, Papa," Hazel said in a quavery voice. She reached under the capes of Marco's coat and found one of her father's hands. Squeezing it hard, she repeated, "I'm here."

Edgar's lips moved as if to speak, but there was no sound. Only a bright trail of blood came out, ran down his face, and splashed, in fat, red drops, on the gray stone beneath his head.

"No!" Hazel cried. "No. No." She dabbed at the blood with her bare fingers until Marco stuffed his handkerchief into her hand. Though she wiped the vivid line from Edgar's chin, blood still rimmed his mouth. "No," she moaned again.

"Hazel," Marco said.

She glanced at him for a fraction of an instant, for less than the beat of a heart. By the time she looked back to her father, however, Edgar had died.

In the days that followed, when Hazel tried to reconstruct those moments, she was never sure what had happened next. She remembered feeling distant and numb, as if she were floating on the edge of sleep. Somehow she had come to be standing, and somehow Marco had held her up. From wherever they'd been, both Cornelius and Frederick had appeared, one on the heels of the other. She remembered Marco's voice ringing in her ears as he had explained to them what had happened. At least, that's probably what he'd been saying. She couldn't be sure. She hadn't heard the words.

She did remember him instructing Cornelius to take her home. And she remembered Frederick's angry voice snapping, "Aren't you overextending your authority, sir? I believe Miss Merriwether is my responsibility."

As Cornelius's arm had settled around her shoulders and he had started to lead her away, she remembered Marco responding with frigid civility, "I assumed you would be too preoccupied to leave the mill at this crucial time. I was sure you would want to concern yourself with the many other victims of this tragedy."

For one lucid moment Hazel had looked around and had seen the faces of all three men. Cornelius's had been pale and grimly sober. Marco's had been a mask of sorrow. And in Frederick's face there had been both dismay and annoyance, as if he didn't wish to concern himself with this tragedy at all, but rather as if he wished he were sailing on his yacht. After that, apparently, Cornelius had taken her home.

# CHAPTER

## ᴼᴼ᭠ 15 ᭠ᴼᴼ

"He was a fine man, struck down by a terrible accident before he had the chance to fulfill his life's dreams," the minister told the small group of people huddled around the open grave. A steady, cold rain fell as he spoke, splatting on black umbrellas and sending muddy rivulets onto the coffin.

"He was a man dearly loved by his family and friends and deeply respected by his fellow workers. This man, uh . . . " The minister glanced quickly at the paper in his hand, looking for Edgar's name. He had already buried six mill operatives today, and he was growing weary. "This man," he repeated. The rain had soaked his notes and had made the ink run. "Uh, Edward Merrill, will be missed by all whose lives he touched."

Behind her, Hazel could hear Marco's hiss of breath. Without turning, she knew his nostrils were flaring in outrage. Not only was the eulogy inaccurate and bland, Edgar wasn't even identified correctly. It was the final indignity, ending his life as anonymously as it had begun, his achievements forgotten and ignored.

Hazel knew what Marco was feeling, but she didn't feel it herself. Apart from being cold, very cold, both inside and out, she felt very little. The daze that had descended on her in the millyard three days ago continued to blanket her mind. What few thoughts filtered through the fog were dim and disconnected, as if they belonged to someone else.

It didn't seem possible that Edgar was gone and that with his death the last remnants of his world had disappeared. However objectionable that world had come to be, it had, nonetheless, given her life its direction. Nor did it matter that she no longer accepted that direction willingly and contentedly. The fact remained that she still accepted it. It was the only direction she had ever known, and she had no other to take its place.

Beside her, Frederick coughed slightly and pulled his silk muffler more tightly around his throat. Hazel looked over at him, only vaguely registering his red nose and rigid posture. Unlike Cornelius, on the other side of her, and Marco behind her, Frederick was the only representative of the world being buried with Edgar. She clung to that image as she clung to other mementos of her father, his watch, his spectacles, the last newspaper he read, anxious to keep his memory from sliding into oblivion. Disoriented by shock and confused by grief, she looked at Frederick with a hazy renewal of hope. Frederick, however, looked straight ahead.

The minister came to the part of his service where he usually asked for a hymn. Skeptically eyeing this small, grim band, he instead directed, "Let us pray in silence for the soul of our friend and loved one." Of the five faces before him, only Mrs. O'Sullivan's dropped. The others continued to stare at him until he mercifully ended the ordeal by tossing an icy clump of mud onto the coffin and intoning, "Earth to earth, ashes to ashes, dust to dust . . ."

They filed out of the cemetery mostly isolated from each other by their umbrellas. Only Hazel and Cornelius were linked under one. "They ought to have had the decency to come today," Cornelius muttered.

Momentarily startled from her fog by the intensity of his tone, Hazel asked, "Who ought to have?"

"The rest of Frederick's family, that's who," Cornelius answered bitterly, though neither his gaze nor his voice carried beyond the circle of their umbrella. "Mr. and Mrs. Whitaker. Lucy. Even Charlotte."

"Yes, I suppose they ought to have," Hazel answered slowly. She hadn't thought about it before. If she didn't feel so numb, or weren't becoming accustomed to their snubs, she might have been as offended as Cornelius. As it was, however, she just shrugged. "I suppose the weather was too miserable for them to make the trip up from Boston," she said, fading back into her fog.

"Awkward of Papa not to have died on a nicer day," Cornelius said, muttering again, his eyes fixed forward and his grip on the umbrella handle white. "Of course, if they cared as much about the safety in the mill as they did about the size of their bank account, Papa might still be alive. Along with the fourteen other workers who died." He turned to stare at Hazel fiercely, the umbrella tilting and letting a sheet of rain drench her arm.

"Oh, Cornelius," she murmured, absently wiping away the water. She heard what he was saying, and she knew what he meant, but she couldn't summon the passion to care.

"Oh, Cornelius, nothing," he retorted. "They jammed too many heavy machines on every floor, then cut away supports to squeeze in a few more. It's a wonder the whole building didn't collapse instead of just a corner. It's a wonder we weren't all killed."

This time Hazel had no answer, but his words lodged uncomfortably in her mind. What if he had died, too? The thought was unimaginably awful. Despite her numbness, she shivered and clutched her brother's arm a little harder.

"They ought to have attended every funeral," Cornelius added gruffly, understanding the extra pressure. "And they ought to have visited every single person who was hurt."

When they reached their house and were closing their umbrellas, Mrs. O'Sullivan said, "I've baked a lemon cake for you. I'll go up and fetch it."

Surprised again from her trance, Hazel said, "How kind of you. In that case I'll put the kettle on for tea."

While Mrs. O'Sullivan disappeared through her door, the others followed Hazel down the dismal hall. Marco and Cornelius hung their damp coats on the pegs next to Hazel's, but Frederick, as he had done in the past, kept his on. He also remained where he was while Marco and Cornelius carried chairs from the dining room to the parlor, saying, "May I have a word with you in private, Hazel?" He looked around the small house as if he thought that were impossible.

"Of course, Frederick," Hazel answered, unpinning her hat from her hair and setting it on the dining room table. "Why don't you come into the kitchen with me while I make the tea?" She turned and started for the kitchen without waiting for him to reply.

"I'm afraid there's no place to sit," she said mechanically as she bent to poke the coals in the stove to life. "The kitchen chairs were in the dining room, which were the ones that were brought into the parlor."

"I don't mind," Frederick said stiffly, closing the door behind him. "Although," he added, "perhaps I ought to bring a chair for you. What I have to say may cause you some distress."

"Oh?" Hazel's tone was polite as she filled the kettle in the rusty sink.

Frederick looked at it distastefully and kept a careful distance. In fact, he held his coat close to him as he edged around, as if afraid to let it brush against any surface. When he finally found a spot in which he felt relatively safe, in front of the doorless cupboard, he stopped and began his speech in a rehearsed tone.

"I'm sorry if I appear to be insensitive to your grief, my dear," he told her.

"I don't think you have been, Frederick," Hazel forgave him as she shoveled a few more lumps of coal onto the fire.

"No. Quite so." He obviously hadn't counted on her interruption, and it took him an instant to retrieve the thread of his address. "I was speaking more in the future tense, you see."

"I see." She set the tray on the table and turned to him. "Frederick, would you reach down the sugar bowl and creamer, please?"

"Hazel, *are* you listening to me?"

His words and tone, identical to the ones his mother had used just the other day, jarred her. Folding her hands in front of her, she answered quietly, "Yes, Frederick, I am."

"Good." Frederick gathered himself up, appeased. "As I was saying, what I have to tell you now might appear to be insensitive. But I'm confident that you will, ultimately, come to realize that my timing is not entirely inappropriate."

He had her full attention now. Little hints of feelings were starting to prick the daze in her mind. "Go on," she said softly.

Drawing a deep breath, Frederick plunged forward. "Since Edgar's death makes it necessary for us to postpone our wedding anyway," he said, "I think this is the ideal moment to break off our engagement."

Hazel's hand flew to her mouth in shock. "What are you saying?" she demanded.

"I can see that you're upset," Frederick observed, "but if you would just consider the situation for a moment, I'm sure that you'll see I'm right. By the time your year of mourning is over, our romance will have receded in society's memory. The resulting scandal will be minimal. In fact, it may be no more than a bored whisper or two as people try to remember what happened." He nodded, pleased with his logic. "It's the ideal moment," he repeated.

Hazel listened to his explanation with increasing consciousness. She felt as if she were coming awake for the first time since that horrifying moment in the millyard. And, as is often the case when fingers or toes begin to thaw, fiery sparks shot through her mind. "How dare you attempt to justify your behavior," she raged, her eyes as gray and stormy as the sky outside. "How dare you preoccupy yourself with the effect of your actions on society."

She pointed an accusing finger at him. "You don't *appear* to be insensitive, Frederick," she told him. "You *are* insensitive. Cloddish. Ill-mannered." She paused a moment, her finger trembling, before she hurled the final reproach. "Common."

Bright color jumped into Frederick's face. "You're overwrought," he told her tightly, finally reaching behind him for the sugar bowl and creamer she'd requested. "You're not reviewing the situation rationally."

"Rationally?" Hazel echoed, jabbing her hands on her hips and ignoring the dishes Frederick held out. "You have a most interesting definition of rational," she scoffed. "I'm curious to hear what you consider to be a rational explanation of your actions."

"I already told you," Frederick replied, thrusting the bowl and the creamer farther toward her. "It will diminish the scandal and gossip if we do it now. Really, Hazel," he added when she continued to glare at him, "you can't possibly expect me to go on as I have for another year.

"I'm constantly forced to refuse invitations because you can't accompany me. I was willing to overlook quite a bit and to wait for you when our wedding was imminent, but if it goes on like this much longer, people will forget to invite me altogether. Here." He shook the creamer and sugar bowl irritably. "Take these things."

Hazel snatched them out of his hands and plunked them down on the tea tray. "That isn't a rational explanation, Frederick," she snapped. "That's a selfish one. And it's entirely in keeping with my initial perception of you as common. It's the sort of behavior I might expect from someone with inferior instincts and education."

"I wouldn't be so hasty with my insults, if I were you," Frederick retorted, his face flaming. "I was trying to be as chivalrous as possible under the circumstances, but I can see my efforts are unappreciated. As long as you brought up the subject of coarse behavior, let's discuss your conduct on the day of the mill accident." It was his turn to stab a finger at her. "You made a hoydenish spectacle of yourself riding around on that MacGregor fellow's shoulder. It was an appalling display. It was the sort of behavior that *I* might have expected from a mill operative, not from my fiancée."

Too stunned to respond, Hazel stood there, her eyes wide with disbelief.

"What?" Frederick asked archly, crossing his arms. "No saucy remark? No pithy comment?"

"I was looking for Papa and Cornelius," Hazel finally protested, still incredulous. "You can't expect that I would exhibit my tea party manners in the middle of a catastrophe like that."

"I would expect my future wife to exhibit perfect manners in every situation," Frederick replied icily. "As I would expect her to heed my warnings about her associations." He turned to pace imperiously, but after a single stride he remembered where he was and turned back abruptly.

"I told you that I found your friendship with that half-caste sheep farmer to be inappropriate," he continued, even more irritated. "Yet you persist, to this day, in maintaining cordial relations with him. It's given him very grand ideas. Look at the outrageous way he spoke to me at the mill the other day." Frederick threw out his hand to illustrate his point. "To say nothing of his audacity in seizing control of the situation.

"He had no business ordering you and Cornelius to go home, then putting himself in charge of Edgar's body. Nor did he have any business inserting himself into the family group at the funeral today." Clasping his hands behind his back, Frederick leaned forward to deliver the rest of his lecture.

"Men like that aren't capable of discerning between a kind word and genuine acceptance," he admonished her. "And as a result of your failure to sufficiently discourage him, he has presumed too much familiarity."

Hazel pressed her suddenly cold hands to her hot brow, her head reeling. She felt as if she had stood up too quickly. Not only had her blood rushed to her brain, but all her thoughts and feelings had, too. This whole situation was growing more fantastic by the moment, from Frederick's insensitive use of her father's death as an excuse to end their engagement to his callous treatment of Edgar's funeral as a measure of social rank. From his misconception of Marco's background to his miscalculation of Marco's relationship to her. "He was only being helpful," she finally responded faintly. "He was a friend of Papa's. And he's fond of Cornelius, too."

"Then there's Cornelius," Frederick pounced, seeing her body slump and hearing her voice weaken. He wagged his finger at her again. "From the way he embraced that immigrant girl in the millyard—she was Italian, I think—there can be no doubt that the rumors of their liaison are true. It was disgraceful." He nearly shuddered at the memory.

"I should probably expect no better of him, however," Frederick went on, reclasping his hands behind his back. "He's repaid me for my generosity in providing him with work by being a troublemaker since the day he started in the mill. All that talk about the conditions, always agitating for higher wages and shorter days. Now he's aligned himself with the operatives at the Washington Mills who are going out on strike next week." He shook his handsome head in disgust.

Hazel straightened. She might have been on slightly shaky moral ground where Marco was concerned, but there wasn't a trace of guilt in her mind about her affection for her brother. "The Washington Mills operatives are striking because their wages have been reduced," she stated firmly, defending Cornelius's position. "It's a completely reasonable grievance on their part, and it's admirably compassionate on Cornelius's part to support it."

The flush that had started to fade once again filled Frederick's face, pushing beneath his blond hair. "You don't know what you're talking about, Hazel," he said nastily. "And neither does Cornelius. But whereas your ignorance is merely annoying, Cornelius's is dangerous. I've given him ample warnings, but he still insists on stirring up the workers. Well, I've had enough of that." He pulled his gloves out of the pocket of his coat and slapped them against his palm. "When the mill is repaired and resumes operations, there will be no position in it for Cornelius. I'm firing him."

For a long moment Hazel just stared at him. Then she squared her shoulders and drew in her breath. "I can see that today is your day to disencumber yourself of Merriwethers," she said at last, her voice calm. Deadly so. "You've buried one, jilted another, and fired the third. To borrow a term from Cornelius's baseball, three strikes and we're out."

Frederick had the grace to look regretful. Sliding his gloves back into his pocket, he said, "I can understand that you would be distressed, Hazel. . . ."

"Can you?" Hazel interrupted, her voice gathering rage. "Can you really? Somehow, Frederick, I think you are incapable of understanding. Your only thoughts are of yourself and how you will be affected by any given circumstance. By how society will judge you." She paused, forcing her fury back under control, folding her arms in front of her.

"I don't care if Cornelius is an embarrassment to you," she told him. "In fact, I'm glad he's a nuisance. Moreover, I won't let you dismiss him so easily. You forget that I'm still a stockholder in the Great Stone Dam Mill. I'll use my power to prevent you from firing him, just as you've used your power to make me do as you wished."

There was no hint of regret on Frederick's face now as he spat out, "Impossible!" Beneath his crisp collar, a vein throbbed angrily. "You've no power over me. That silly bit of stock is a pittance. A vulgar gesture on Edgar's part. We pretended to take it seriously out of pity, but in reality it gives you no authority."

"In that case, I'll sell it immediately," Hazel exploded, her hands flying through the air. "I've no need in my life, ever again, for something—or someone—who gives me no authority. Nor do I want any pity. I've relinquished control of myself and my possessions too docilely in the past. It won't happen again. I'll begin by ridding myself of my stock in your despicable mill."

At first Frederick said nothing, though his jaw was rigid with disdain. "It was my hope," he finally told her in a tone as stiff as his posture, "that we would be able to end this in a civilized manner. But obviously that was expecting too much."

"Civilized?" Hazel exclaimed, pressing a slender hand to her heart. "What could you possibly know about civilized behavior?" She shook her head in wonder. "I don't know how your precious society will judge you for this day's work," she said, "but I can tell you that I think you have violated every accepted standard of decency and honor. Your actions are inexcusable."

Frederick's finger started to point as he framed an angry response. But after a second glance at Hazel's eyes, intensely gray n her marble-white face, his arm dropped. Instead, he adjusted he lapels of his coat, turned, and walked out.

After he had gone, leaving the door flapping ajar, the hot emotion rushed out of Hazel. Suddenly weak and breathless she sagged against the kitchen table for support. What had she done? What had she said? She wasn't even sure. It had all happened so quickly. One minute she'd been muffled in a numbing cocoon of grief, the next minute she'd been yanked from her fog to be cruelly abused and abandoned.

She had reacted instinctively, responding to the raw feelings that had raked her heart. Only one thought stood out amid the mixture of fury, confusion, and hurt: She was tired, mightily tired, of other people telling her what to do with her life. She wanted the control of her destiny to lie in her own hands. Of everyone in the world, she alone knew what was best for herself.

When a few minutes passed and her breathing slowed, Hazel took a cautious step away from the table. Her legs were wobbly, but they held her. Moving slowly, she walked to the stove. The kettleful of water had nearly boiled out. She carried it to the sink and refilled it. Every motion was wearily executed. Maybe she had just declared her independence, but this certainly wasn't any Fourth of July. It had been a very hard day, and she felt battered and drained.

Just as Hazel set the kettle back on the stove, the kitchen door flew open and Marco strode in. There was nothing reluctant about his entrance, or about the path he cut across the room. In fact, where Frederick had seemed uncomfortable, he seemed completely at home. "Isn't the tea ready yet?" he asked, coming over to inspect the kettle for himself. "We've just about run out of conversation with Mrs. O'Sullivan. I left poor Cornelius asking the names and ages of all her babies while I came to see if you needed some help."

"The water boiled away," Hazel explained dully, going back to lean on the table while she waited for the fresh kettle to heat.

"Shall I top up the sugar bowl, then?" he asked, poking around on the tea tray to see what needed doing. "Fill the creamer? Get a plate for the cake? Mrs. O'Sullivan is holding it in her lap."

"Yes, if you like."

He studied her a minute, then went over to the cupboard in search of a spoon. "You know, Hazel," he said, rummaging in the drawer, "it's not too late to break off your engagement to

Frederick. It's obvious that he's not the man for you. Look at
how miserable you are after your 'private talk.' He isn't capable of
comforting you when you're sad, and he'll never share your joys.
You shouldn't just postpone your wedding, you should cancel it
altogether." After finding a spoon, he turned back to the table.
And stopped short.

Hazel was standing up straight. Very straight. Her eyes, listless
the moment before, were bright and intense. "I've listened to as
many of your opinions as I care to!" she shouted, punching the air
with her fist. If Marco had said anything else, if he had commented
on the rain or the new moon or the muddy ruts in the road, she
might have fallen into his arms seeking the same safety she had
found three days before in the millyard. But in her present frame
of mind, his words were exactly wrong. Drained though she was,
she still determined to control her own destiny. She was through
with living in someone else's world. And with being left all alone
when that world collapsed.

"I don't need you or anyone else to tell me what I should do
and what I shouldn't. With whom I should associate and whom I
should shun. I can make those decisions for myself." She banged
her fist on her chest for emphasis.

It took only a hint of an unleashed temper for Marco to respond
in kind. "You ought to be able to make those decisions," he
shouted back, "but when you choose Frederick Whitaker for a
husband, I have to doubt your ability." Coming closer, he stabbed
the spoon in the sugar. "It's an utterly senseless choice," he roared.
"An idiotic decision based on ridiculous codes of etiquette and a
misguided sense of loyalty."

Fists clenched at her sides now, Hazel leaned angrily toward
him. "Don't you tell me what it's based on!" she yelled. "You
know nothing about it."

"I certainly do!" he bellowed, leaning forward, too. "I know
that there isn't a damn thing he can offer you that I can't offer
you as well. Except perhaps a lifetime of priggish manners and a
passionless marriage." He wagged his finger at her, only inches
from her face.

"If it's a grand house you want, I can give you a manor in
Scotland and a *palazzo* in Venice. I'll even buy your old house
in Boston. Or another one. Or several. I'll give you houses all
over the world, if it'll make you happy. I'll give you exquisite art

and fine food. Fascinating travels. Jewelry. Dresses from Worth. Anything you desire."

Hazel swatted away his finger. "I don't want you to give me anything," she snapped. "I don't want to be seduced like some sloe-eyed courtesan, my favors purchased with ropes of pearls and cloths of spun gold." She pointed her own finger at him. "I won't be bought, do you hear me? And I won't be collected like one of your rare treasures."

Had Marco paused to truly absorb what she was saying, he probably would have been thrilled. In his present rage, though, he dismissed it with a giant swipe of his hand. "Bah," he scoffed. "You're being absurd. You know I'm not trying to buy you. If anyone is, it's your darling Frederick. He's the one who measures people by what they possess. And now that you're poor, his measure of you has dropped considerably. Don't shake your head. It's true. He'll go through the rest of his life feeling that he's married beneath him. What's more appalling to contemplate, he'll make you feel it, too."

He slapped his palm on the top of the table. "That's what I came back to Lawrence to tell you. To stop you before it's too late. Do you realize that I no sooner reached Strathdorna than I turned around and came back to warn you? I hadn't been there a week, barely time to scratch Roger's head, before I was on my way across the Atlantic again, afraid the whole voyage that I wouldn't get here in time to keep you from making the biggest mistake of your life."

"By *your* assessment," Hazel stormed, slamming her hand on the table, too. "It's what *you* think. What *you* have decided. Without ever once asking me or taking time to consider that it's *my* life."

Marco's nostrils were flaring, his curls were wild. "That's simply not so, Hazel!" he shouted. "I have asked you what you could possibly see in that humorless boor, and all I've gotten in response is a stone wall."

"Now, *that* is simply not so!" Hazel cried. "I have answered you. I've given you my reasons, but you've chosen not to accept them. You seem to feel that you know better than I."

"That's because Frederick doesn't love you. *I* do." He jabbed his chest with his finger. "And you don't love him. You love *me*."

An uneasy silence followed his furious statement as Hazel shifted from foot to foot. His words, however angrily uttered, had a startling effect. "You seem fairly sure of that fact," she said cautiously.

"I am," he growled, taking his cue from her lowered voice. "You can't deny it."

The thin thread of reason that stretched tentatively across her mind instantly snapped. Told again what she couldn't do, think, or feel, she most certainly did deny it. "You're imagining it!" she yelled, stomping her foot on the floor. "You're inventing something that doesn't exist."

It was Marco's turn to be startled into silence as he stared at the woman in front of him. Her gray eyes were enormous in her beautiful face, flushed and taut with wrath. "You don't really believe that," he finally told her.

Further goaded, Hazel hissed, "I do. Absolutely."

"Look at me and tell me you don't love me," he demanded.

There was a pause, then Hazel said evenly, "I don't love you." Her eyes were fixed on his.

Marco seemed huge as he slowly inhaled. "Very well," he said, turning to leave. "Marry whom you please."

If Hazel had felt drained after Frederick's departure, now she felt destroyed. It wasn't enough to lean against the table. She slumped to the floor and braced her back against its leg. How she had longed to hear him tell her he loved her, but when he finally had, she'd sent him away. Instead of rejoicing in his declaration, she'd scorned it. She'd succeeded in gaining control of her fate, but at what cost?

After a while, she forced herself to stand up. She filled the cream pitcher and the sugar bowl and dumped boiling water into the pot. Then, taking a deep breath, she carried the tray into the parlor, where she had tea with her brother and Mrs. O'Sullivan. Her numbness had returned.

# CHAPTER
## —⊷ 16 ⊷—

"That was quite an argument that you and Marco had," Cornelius commented carefully. He stacked the teacups on the tray and carried it into the kitchen.

"Oh dear," Hazel said, again shaken from her daze. "Did you hear it all?" she asked anxiously, trailing behind her brother.

Setting the tray on the table, he shrugged. "Not what you said, so much as the tone," he answered. "The closed door sort of distorted your words, though the volume came through all right." He unloaded the dirty dishes into the sink, stuffing another piece of cake into his mouth as he did so. "It was nice of Mrs. O'Sullivan to bake this for us, wasn't it?"

"Yes, very nice." Hazel chewed her lip in the silence that followed, knowing that Cornelius was curious to hear what had happened. He couldn't have been very happy to see Marco stalk out of their house.

"It's a long-running argument," she finally said, not entirely untruthfully. "It goes back almost to Venice. And I suppose it didn't help that I'm feeling particularly touchy at the moment." Someday, perhaps, she would explain it to her brother, but not now. First she had to understand what had happened herself. That, too, though, was for another day. She was feeling not only touchy at the moment, but also utterly exhausted.

More or less accepting her explanation, Cornelius nodded. He finished putting away the tea things and set another kettleful of water on the stove to heat for washing the dishes. Nothing left to do, he sat down on the corner of the table. "Sis?" he said tentatively.

"Hmm?" Hazel was standing by the kitchen window looking out. The rain had stopped and it was nearly dark, a cold and bleak winter evening. It perfectly matched her mood.

"I've been thinking."

"Yes?" She turned to face him, forcing herself to pay attention. Once again she found herself thinking what a fine-looking man Cornelius had become. His face was clean and clear, even if it was far more serious than it ought to be at his age. She hadn't seen that engaging grin of his in far too long. "What have you been thinking?"

"About our situation."

"Ah."

"It's not too good."

Hazel sighed and came over to sit on the opposite corner of the table. "I didn't think it was," she admitted. "But I hadn't gotten as far as thinking what to do about it."

"I have," Cornelius said quietly.

She just looked at him, waiting.

Cornelius looked away. "I think I should leave you here and go back to Boston to find work," he blurted out.

For a moment Hazel thought her heart had stopped. Her whole body turned icy cold. "Leave me?" she whispered. She had no one else.

"Hazel, I know it seems awful," he said, sliding over and grasping one of her cold hands. He looked straight at her now, his expression earnest. "There isn't any other way, though. There's no work here. Mills are either laying off operatives or closing altogether. I've even heard that Frederick Ayer, who owns the Washington Mills, is glad about the strike so he has an excuse to shut down production for a while. And I can't sit around waiting for the Whitakers to rebuild the Great Stone Dam Mill. It could take months. We have to eat in the meantime."

"Yes, of course, you're right," Hazel said hollowly, looking down at the hand holding hers. It was slender, like hers, but strong and capable.

"A year ago I would have punched anyone who said I'd leave you all alone in a place like this," he told her, giving her fingers a squeeze. "But a year ago our lives were very different. We could afford to concern ourselves with nice behavior. We didn't have to worry about simply surviving then."

"Yes, you're right," Hazel said again, rubbing her forehead with her free hand. "I mustn't be silly and vaporish about this," she added more desperately. "It took me by surprise is all."

"You aren't being silly," Cornelius said fondly. "You've every right to be upset. Believe me, if there were any alternative, I'd take it. But I can't think of a single one. I have no way to earn money here, and I can't take you with me. I may not even find work in Boston. I may have to move on. Maybe out West."

Hazel drew a sharp breath. "Oh, no," she said quickly, grabbing on to his hand. "That's too far away. It's bad enough that you have to go to Boston, but I couldn't bear to know that you were thousands of miles from here. Promise me, Cornelius. Promise me that you won't go out West."

Cornelius hesitated for a minute while he rubbed his fingers across her knuckles. Then he said, "I can't honestly make that promise." He looked at her steadily. "I'll promise you only that I'll try my best to get a job in Boston or somewhere nearby."

After a while she nodded miserably. He would do whatever he had to.

"Come on," he said, rising suddenly and giving her a hug. "It won't be so bad. There's enough money to get you through another few months. Maybe more, if the weather is mild. By that time I'll surely have found some sort of employment and will be sending you my wages."

Arms around his waist, Hazel clung to him tightly. "I'll miss you," she said in a broken voice.

Cornelius planted a kiss on the top of her head. "I'll miss you, too, sis," he told her. "But at least I'll know that you have Frederick to look in on you. And I'll wager that Marco stops by occasionally, too."

Her face against his vest, Hazel froze. In her mind she saw each of those men as they'd stormed out of her life for good. For an instant she considered telling Cornelius that neither Frederick nor Marco would be calling, but immediately rejected the thought. What was the point? He would only worry more about leaving her alone. And it had to be done. As he'd said, there were no other alternatives. She pulled away from him and forced a smile. "The water must be hot by now," she said. "I'll wash if you'll dry."

His dimples appeared for the first time in weeks. "Fair enough," he said, picking up the towel.

Hazel had rolled up her sleeves and soaped up the dishrag when another image flashed through her mind. "Cornelius," she said, turning to him, her hands full of bubbles, "what about that girl I saw you with in the millyard the other day? It seemed as if she was someone very dear to you."

His elbows on the drainboard, his long body bent in half, Cornelius had been watching her lazily. Now he looked down abruptly. The towel twisted between his fingers, and his mouth twisted as he tried to form words. "She is," he finally said, his face turned toward the floor. "I never realized how dear someone could be until I met her."

"Oh," Hazel said in a hushed tone. From the emotion in his voice, she felt as though she had blundered into someplace very private and sacred.

"Her name is Agata."

"Agata. That's lovely."

"It suits her. She's wonderful." He looked over at Hazel for the first time, her hands hanging limp in the dishwater. "You'd like her," he said, his eyes imploring.

"I'm certain that I will," Hazel said encouragingly. "I'm certain that we'll be the best of friends."

"No," Cornelius said, his voice hoarse. Looking down again, he rested his head on his arms. "You'll never meet her. She's going to be married on Easter Sunday. Her father arranged it before she was born. His first daughter and his cousin's first son."

"Oh, no," Hazel moaned, taking her hands out of the dishwater and going over to wrap them around her brother. She laid her cheek against the back of his head, feeling the silkiness of his hair. "Poor Cornelius," she commiserated. "It hurts very much, doesn't it?" He nodded. She knew. She hurt, too.

When Cornelius left the next morning, a single satchel in his hand, Hazel felt a burst of panic. It wasn't that she hadn't been alone all day in the house before. It was the thought that she'd be alone all night as well. And the next and the next for as far into the future as she could see.

She fidgeted around the house all day Sunday, inventing chores where there were suddenly none to be done. There was no laundry to wash and iron, no meals to prepare, no one to notice if the house was dusted or not. There was no one to take care of. Except me, she thought. From now on I have to take care of myself.

It was a scary idea. Despite her fierce avowals of independence, she wasn't sure she knew how. Yes, she could cook and scrub and clean. Even lighting the stove wasn't the battle it once had been. Now, though, she had to shape the boundaries of her life as well. Unfettered by father or fiancé or lover, she finally had what she wanted: Her destiny was her own. The problem was, while she was certain of what she didn't want it to be, she'd never really had the opportunity to think about what it was she did want. Flung instantly free, she felt lost.

That night her sleep was uneasy. The house was alive with creaks and groans she'd never heard before. When Hazel rose on Monday morning, she felt raw and jumpy. For one fearful moment she even considered writing to Frederick, begging his forgiveness and asking to be taken back. That did it. No sooner had the thought formed than she was horrified by it. As her back stiffened in indignation, her panic disappeared.

*She* had done nothing that needed forgiving. It was *he* who had behaved in a reprehensible manner. Just when she was at the lowest point in her life, instead of reaching out to help her, he'd deserted her. Never again, she promised herself, renewing her vow. I'll never again trade control of my life for a little bit of luxury.

After a visit to her banker later that morning, however, Hazel's defiance deflated. She asked Mr. Mason to help her sell her Great Stone Dam Mill stock, and eager to help a beautiful woman, he agreed. It brought such a small amount of money, though, she felt another surge of panic. With careful planning, she might make it through the summer. But what would she do next winter? What if Cornelius couldn't find work? What if he went West and she never heard from him again?

It didn't help her state of mind that the temperature dropped and the wind began to blow that afternoon, and by evening they were in the throes of a blizzard. Every shriek outside and every bitter draft within emphasized her loneliness and anxiety. Where was Cornelius on this miserable night? Was her baby brother safe? When she looked out the window, all she could see were dense white swirls, isolating her house from the rest of the world. Even the reassuring noise of Mrs. O'Sullivan's babies and fights was missing, drowned out by the storm. In her life Hazel had never felt so alone.

The snow continued most of Tuesday while Hazel huddled, sip-

ping tea, by the kitchen stove. On Wednesday, despite biting air
and huge drifts of snow, she went outside for a walk. Without
any special errand, for once, she wandered away from her usual
route past the stolidly respectable shops along Essex Street. What
she saw on the walk did nothing to relieve her.

The tall wooden tenements looked especially grim in the cold.
Drippy-nosed toddlers peered from soot-frosted windows and laundry hung frozen on lines out back. In front, in the snow-clogged
streets, the destitute paced, raggedy, thin children and filthy,
gaunt adults. The voices changed from street to street, from
Italian- to Polish- to Irish-accented English, but the message was
always the same. Help.

Hazel fled back to her house, shivering as much from despair
as from the cold. She knew what a thin margin separated her from
that wretched poverty. Please God, she prayed. Not me.

On Thursday and Friday she hid at home, but by Saturday afternoon she was so desperate for human contact, she again ventured
out. Today, though, she confined herself to walking up one side
of Essex Street and down the other, stepping over gray lumps of
snow and pausing to peer in the windows at Stearns' and Oswald's
and Cahill's. It wasn't much of a comfort, but it took the edge off
her dismal lonesomeness.

Preoccupied with her thoughts and the simple routine, Hazel
didn't notice the crowd gathering until the sidewalks were full.
Suddenly it was hard to move forward as hundreds of people
jammed the wide walks, staring at the street. Pressed against a
building, Hazel craned her neck to see what was happening. She
saw only the backs of heads.

No one seemed frenzied or terrified, as they had at the mill on
the day of the accident. Puzzled, Hazel inched her way through
the mob until she arrived at the curb. The street was empty. "What
is it?" she asked the young man standing next to her. "What is
everyone looking at?"

"They wait for the parade," he replied in a heavy German
accent. "The Washington Mill strikers is going to march. Fifteen
hundred or more of them."

Curious, Hazel waited with the rest, stamping her feet to ward
off the cold. She heard the sound of the brass band at the head
of the parade before she saw it coming. Then, to the cheers and
applause of the crowd, the first section passed by. Weavers and
menders and warp dressers and examiners marched purposefully,

holding aloft hand-lettered placards. "A FAIR DAY'S WORK FOR A FAIR DAY'S PAY," one read. "THE LAST PILL TOO BITTER TO SWALLOW," read another. "WE ARE HUMAN BEINGS, NOT BEASTS."

Behind the weavers came a lively drum corps, then another section of workers. The scourers, carders, combers, and drawers carried more signs urging, "DON'T BE A SUCKER OR A SCAB, BUT STAND UP FOR YOUR RIGHTS LIKE A MAN." The applause grew stronger, and swept up in the spirit, Hazel clapped along exuberantly. Then, out of nowhere, the orderly enthusiasm surrounding her became an angry eddy.

Stimulated by the excitement of the crowd and a bottle of wine, two Italian workers began taunting the German youth standing next to Hazel. He responded with a shove that provoked the temper of a French Canadian, which attracted the attention of a trio of Irish boys. Before she knew what was happening, Hazel found herself pushed into the middle of a fighting pack.

A vile-smelling man crashed against her chest, knocking out her breath and making her fall into the person behind her. Furious, he jabbed her erect with an elbow in the back. It catapulted her into another man, who stabbed a fist in her shoulder. With each violent blow Hazel felt a flash of pain and terror, but hemmed in by the mob, she was unable to escape.

In her rising fear she instinctively fought back, flailing her arms and thrashing out. That only made it worse. Rock-hard fists smashed against her ribs and glanced off her head. Her hat was ripped, pin and all, from her hair. She wasn't an intentional target, but, caught in the middle of this wild melee, the brutal punches found her all the same. Her heart was pounding frantically and dry sobs filled her throat, yet she couldn't draw a breath.

Suddenly a small hand grasped hers and yanked her free of the fight. With a cry of pure fright, Hazel spun to face her newest attacker. It was a girl with crinkly black braids and a round freckled face. She was the girl that Cornelius had carried out of the mill. Agata.

Though Hazel was still trapped in the crowd and another vicious blow had just staggered her, at the sight of Agata she nearly wept with relief. At least now she had an ally. With the rush of relief came a measure of reason, and clutching Agata's hand, she was able to follow her lead. They wormed their way out of the shouting crowd and stumbled into an empty doorway, where, backs against a display window, they slid to the ground.

Her hands gripping her upturned knees, Hazel sucked in great greedy gulps of icy air. Every breath hurt. They made her head reel. She leaned against the glass and shut her eyes against the pain.

"Are you all right?" came the sound of Agata's voice, wobbly and distant, as if through a long tin tube.

In response, Hazel's head lolled and her eyes stayed shut. She felt Agata's tentative finger dabbing at her lip and only then realized it was split and bleeding.

"You must go home," came Agata's voice again. This time it sounded a little closer. "I help you."

"In a minute," Hazel gasped, still struggling for breath. In the background she could hear the sounds of the parade as well as the sounds of the fight. One was determinedly cheerful while the other was decidedly ugly, but both were born of the same frustration. Slowly the wrenching heaves calmed. Slowly she opened her eyes again.

From a weak slit they flew wide. "What happened to *you*?" she exclaimed, lifting her head. On closer inspection, Agata's freckled face was grimy, her crinkly hair was matted. There was a welt on her forehead, though it was faded and receding. "Did they get you, too? Are you hurt?"

"Eh?" Agata asked, trying to keep up with Hazel's English. "This?" She patted her forehead and cocked her head questioningly. When Hazel nodded, she shrugged. "From the mill," she said offhandedly.

"The mill? But that was . . . " Hazel started. Then she stopped. That terrible accident had happened only ten days ago. It seemed like a lifetime had passed since that point.

"Now I remember," she said. "That's the bruise that Cornelius kissed."

"You saw?" Agata's brows knitted with worry.

Hazel nodded again as her mind filled with that tender scene. "It took me by surprise," she admitted.

"You think is bad?" Agata's expression was even more worried, and her sturdy body hunched forward.

"Oh, no," Hazel said, putting a reassuring hand on Agata's threadbare sleeve. The movement caused a shot of pain, but she tried to ignore it. "I thought it was very sweet. I was only surprised because Cornelius hadn't told me about you then. Up until that moment I thought his sole interest in life was baseball."

Relief cleared Agata's face of anxiety, and she sat back against the window, wriggling her shoulders as she phrased her next thought. "Tell me, please, where is Cornelius?" She glanced sideways at Hazel as if wondering if this request was pressing her luck.

"Believe me," Hazel answered, leaning her own head against the glass, "I would tell you if I knew, but I'm really not sure." She rolled her head and met Agata's glance honestly. "I'd like to know myself. I can tell you only that he left for Boston last Sunday morning to find work, and I haven't heard from him yet."

"Boston?" Agata sat up again, dismayed. "When does he come here?"

Hazel studied her a moment before she answered. "I don't know," she said finally. "Agata, what's wrong?" She knew that life in the tenements was primitive, at best, but from the look of Agata's chapped and dirty face, it didn't seem as if she'd been enjoying even that dubious shelter.

Agata shrugged, though, dismissing the question with a toss of her head. *"Non c'è niente,"* she said.

*"Niente?"* The word sounded familiar. Hazel pulled herself up a little straighter and tried to remember the phrases she'd learned in Italy. "I've forgotten what that means."

"Nothing. It means 'nothing.' " Agata avoided her eyes.

In the instant that Hazel debated whether she had the right to pursue the issue or should politely let it drop, one of the fighters was knocked down and landed in a sprawl in the doorway. Agata was on her feet at once and reaching down to haul Hazel up. "I take you home," she announced. "Come."

It was easier said than done. It couldn't have been more than five minutes that they'd been sitting there, but Hazel's body was already stiff. The freezing air had seeped into every sore muscle and bruised rib, making it difficult to stand and torture to walk. Involuntarily she moaned.

"Put your arm here," Agata ordered, tapping her shoulders. When Hazel obeyed, Agata slipped her hand around Hazel's waist for support. "Now we go." They slowly hobbled through the crowd.

After a few steps Hazel no longer felt as if her legs would collapse, but she was still miserably sore. Out of the protection of the doorway, the chill wind cut through her coat, making her shiver. Tears welled up in her eyes and froze on her lashes. "Oh, dear," she said, trying to be brave, though her voice sounded shaky. "A hot bath would feel awfully good right now."

"Yes?" Agata was skeptical. Every bath she'd ever taken had been in a washtub. They'd been brisk and efficient, hardly blissful.

"Yes." Hazel was wistful. She remembered her tub on Marlborough Street. It had been long and deep and had held gallons of steamy, scented water.

They limped along in silence, turning left after City Hall and right by the Common. On Maple Street they both automatically turned in. Only then did it occur to Hazel that she hadn't given Agata directions. "You know where I live?" she asked, mildly surprised.

Agata nodded. "Cornelius tell me."

"Of course. I wasn't thinking."

After another minute of silence Agata added hesitantly, "I come every day to wait for him, but I only see you."

"You've waited for him on the street?" Hazel asked, aghast. "It's been bitter cold all week. You should've knocked on the door."

Again Agata shrugged and avoided Hazel's eyes.

When they reached Hazel's house, Agata delivered her to the door, then started to back down the steps. "Oh, no," Hazel said, fumbling in her pocket for the key. "Don't leave now. Come in and have tea with me."

"You sure?" Agata attempted to smooth her braids.

"Very sure," Hazel said firmly, unlocking the door and pushing it open. "I'd be grateful for your company. I'll show you photographs of Cornelius when he was small," she added as a bribe. As she stood back to let Agata enter, another thought struck her. "Unless you think your family would object."

"Pff," Agata replied with a flick of her hand. She climbed back up the steps, but gestured for Hazel to go in first. At the end of the hall she helped Hazel out of her coat, her eyes widening at the sight of Hazel's clothes. Though twisted and rumpled by the fight, they were still more beautiful than any she had ever seen up close. The skirt was made of a fine blue wool, and the waist was a delicate stripe in silk. Somewhat self-consciously, Agata shed her own coat and hung it on a peg.

In the kitchen Hazel sank down on a chair. "I just have to rest a minute," she apologized. "Then I'll make the tea."

"I do it," Agata offered. "Tell me how."

"The fire needs more coal, I think," Hazel said, accepting gladly. "And you can fill the kettle at the sink. Or would you prefer
hot chocolate? There's plenty of milk." To her astonishment, tears
jumped into Agata's eyes and she abruptly turned her back.

"Hot chocolate," Agata choked. "I have never drink."

Hazel was puzzled by her reaction, but didn't probe. "The bottle
of milk is keeping cold on the windowsill," she said smoothly.
"The tin of cocoa powder is in the cupboard. It's on the second
shelf. The one that says Baker's on the front of it. No, not that
one," she said as Agata reached for the tin of tea. "The one next
to it." When Agata's hand still wavered, she said, "The one with
the painting of the girl in the white apron. That's it. There's a
pan on the shelf underneath."

Following her instructions, Agata combined the cocoa powder
with sugar and milk in the pan. Then she sliced a loaf of bread,
toasted it, buttered it, and spread it with jam. She fetched the photo
album from a box under Hazel's bed and set the table with cups,
saucers, napkins, and plates. With every new direction Agata grew
more reserved and quiet. When she finally sat down at the table,
she kept her head bowed and her hands in her lap until Hazel
encouraged her to begin. Then she ate only what was offered to
her and not a crumb more.

At first Hazel was worried that she had unwittingly insulted the
Italian girl, but as she showed her the pictures in the family album,
she realized Agata was not offended, but awed. Although Hazel
considered this house to be dismal, her existence dreary, evidently
Agata considered them both exalted. The realization completely
nonplussed her. What could Agata's life be like if a cup of hot
chocolate and a leather-bound book of photographs rendered her
speechless in reverence? Hazel couldn't even begin to imagine.

"Did you like the hot chocolate?" she asked.

Agata nodded. "Good," she said. "Thank you." She sat so rigidly, she didn't even touch the back of the chair.

"Would you like another cup?"

Agata shook her head. "No, thank you."

Hazel looked around for something else she could give her
guest. It was so heart-wrenching to think about the meagerness
of Agata's life, she felt compelled to lavish her with treats. "Would
you like, um . . . " There wasn't much on the shelves. Not like
the days when Marco cheered her with tins of biscuits and boxes

of candied chestnuts. "Would you like some maple syrup?"

Agata looked at her. "Maple surp?" she asked.

"Maple syrup. It's made from the sap of maple trees." When Agata continued to look mystified, Hazel tried to further explain. "The sap is the juice of the tree, and it's boiled down until it's thick and sweet. Well, here." She hauled herself out of her chair, ignoring the stabs of pain that her movement caused. Yanking the almost empty jug of syrup from the cupboard shelf, she took a few steps back and collapsed again in her chair. She tipped out a spoonful of syrup and handed it to Agata.

"Try it," she urged. "It was brought to me by an Italian friend who thought he'd discovered manna from heaven."

"Mmm," Agata said. "*Buono*." She licked the spoon. "Is the same friend who teach Cornelius to speak Italian?"

"Did he?" Hazel asked, oddly moved by the thought. She could just see those two dark heads bent together, one wildly curly, the other silkily straight. She could just hear Marco's voice, filled with humor and affection, as he gave her little brother Italian lessons. An unbearable longing for him overcame her.

"I know," she said. "Would you like to see some more photographs? I have some from Italy. I can show you our friend."

This time Agata nodded. "Yes," she accepted.

"Oh, good." Hazel was pleased. "But I'll have to ask you to get them, if you would. They're in the same box under my bed. They're wrapped up in a square of cloth and tied with a blue ribbon."

When Agata returned with the bundle, she looked at Hazel uncertainly. Finally unable to contain the question on her mind, she blurted out, "Only you sleep in that room?"

"I'm the only one who sleeps in the entire house at the moment," Hazel answered ruefully.

Agata sucked in her breath, her lips twitching in silent amazement.

"Why?" Hazel asked as she untied the bow. "How many people sleep in your room?"

"Ten people. Two rooms," Agata answered, sliding back onto the edge of her seat. Her eyes fixed on the pile, waiting for it to be unveiled.

But Hazel's hands had left the photographs and had flown to her chest. "Do you mean to say there are only two bedrooms for a family of ten?" she asked, appalled.

"No, no." Agata looked up, wagging her finger. "Two rooms is the whole house."

"Oh, my," Hazel breathed. That was worse than she'd thought. "No wonder you think this horrid house is a palace."

"Palace?"

Hazel reached back into her memory of Italy more successfully this time. "*Palazzo*," she translated.

"*Si*," Agata agreed.

"No, it isn't. Look at some real ones." She flipped away the cloth and pulled out pictures of Venice. Lining them up, she let Agata inspect them while she continued to hunt for one particular photo. "Here it is," she said, finding Marco posed on the roof of the Duomo.

She studied it a long time before she passed it to Agata. Even in the stillness of a snapshot, Marco looked magnificently alive. It made her ache that much more. Lonely and hurting as she was now, she forgot the reasons she'd sent him away, remembering only how he'd filled her house and her heart with life.

Agata looked at the photograph, then looked at Hazel shrewdly. "Is *molto simpatico*," she commented.

It was Hazel's turn to nod in agreement. Though there was no exact English equivalent, she knew what Agata had said. *Simpatico* meant that Marco was charming and likable with a touch of some undefinable air. She sighed and picked up the next photo in the pile.

"This is in front of the Palazzo Ducale in Mantua," she said. "Now, that's what I call a palace. It has over five hundred rooms." She was about to toss it aside and select another, when she saw Agata's intent stare. "What is it?" she asked, reexamining the photo.

"This man?" Agata pointed at the stiff figure in the picture.

"Oh." Hazel's cut lips pursed. "He's Frederick Whitaker."

"He owns the mill, yes?"

"Yes."

"*This* is your Frederick?" Agata was incredulous. "This is the man you marry?"

"Not anymore," Hazel replied. "He broke off our engagement."

"What does that mean?" Agata demanded, her eyes darting between Hazel and the photograph.

"It means he changed his mind," Hazel told her. "It's over. No wedding. *Niente*."

"Ahh." Agata tsked. "*Peccato*."

"And what does *that* mean?"

"Is too bad."

"Oh, no," Hazel hastily corrected. "Not at all. I'm quite glad to be rid of him. He's an unpleasant man."

"Yes?"

"Absolutely," Hazel said firmly, putting the photo facedown on the table.

"Me, too," Agata confessed. "No more wedding. Tomasso 'broke off our engagement.'"

"What?" Hazel exclaimed, turning to stare at Agata. "I thought it was decided before you were born. I thought it was some sort of sacred promise that couldn't be undone."

Agata lifted her eyebrows and shrugged. "It was undone," she said. "But is all right," she reassured Hazel. "*Niente peccato*. He is 'unpleasant man,' too."

"No wonder you're so eager to find Cornelius," Hazel said. "He'll be ecstatic when he hears what happened." She thought a moment before delicately adding, "What did happen?"

Agata's eyes dropped and she rubbed the bruise on her forehead. Finally she said, "Someone tell Tomasso that Cornelius kiss me. And that I kiss him. At the mill."

"The day of the accident?"

Without looking up, Agata nodded. "Tomasso call me a *puttana* and say he never marry me. The wedding is *finito*."

"A *puttana*?"

"Not nice lady."

"What a dreadful thing to say! But what about your father? And Tomasso's father?" Hazel pressed. "I thought they were the ones who arranged this. Surely they objected."

"Pff," Agata said, though her remark didn't carry its usual disdain. Under the dirt her cheeks were flushed. "Papa call me a *disgraziata*," she said in a low voice, still not looking up. "A disgrace." She paused for a long, long time before continuing in almost a whisper. "He tell me to leave his house. Never come back. I am not his daughter anymore."

For a stunned moment Hazel struggled to absorb Agata's story. It seemed unspeakably barbaric until an even more horrifying thought struck her. On a slightly cruder level it was exactly what had happened to her. Like her, Agata had surrendered her fate to her father and her fiancé, trusting she would be taken care of in return for her loyalty. Instead, like her, Agata had been abandoned.

"When did this happen?" she asked.

"Sunday." Agata's sturdy shoulders were drooped.

"Where have you been living since then?" Hazel's voice was hesitant. She was almost afraid to hear the answer. Anyway, she probably knew. Agata's matted hair and grimy face had already told her.

"On the streets," Agata admitted. "I sleep in the church."

"Well," Hazel said, drawing a breath. She didn't ask for any more details of Agata's ordeal. They would keep for some other time. "You'd best put some water on to boil for a bath while I go find some clothes that might fit you," she told her calmly. "From now on, this is where you live."

Agata's head finally shot up. "No," she protested. "I cannot. Is too much."

"Pff," Hazel responded, pushing herself to her feet. "There are two bedrooms here and only one person." While she held on to the table to gain her balance, she added, "Besides, maybe you can teach me how to make risotto."

"Oooo," Agata moaned, genuinely stricken. "I don't know how. Risotto is from Milano. I am from Calabria." She'd failed in her first chance to help in exchange for this miracle. "I make *pasta fagioli*," she offered desperately. "Is very delicious."

"Good. We'll have that for dinner tomorrow night," Hazel decided with a smile. "The washtub is behind the stove. I'll be right back with some towels." She turned to hobble out of the kitchen.

"Hazel." Agata's voice stopped her. Hazel turned back. "*Grazie mille*," the girl said from her heart. "Thank you one thousand times."

"You're welcome," Hazel responded sincerely. "You're very welcome." As she went into her bedroom to gather together some linens and lacy underwear, she thought how close she was to Agata's state of extreme destitution. Only inches separated her from life on the streets.

"Never again," she told an embroidered nightgown, repeating the pledge she'd made before. "I'll never again put myself in a position to be cruelly deserted."

They spent Sunday snug in their house. Agata tried on clothes, and for the first time in weeks, Hazel laughed. "Ow," she said, clutching her ribs, though she couldn't stop giggling. "I'm not being mean," she gasped. "But I wish we had a mirror so you could see how you look."

"No good?" Agata asked anxiously. The fine fabrics were celestially soft on her skin. They made her feel as elegant as Hazel appeared.

"They will be," Hazel assured her, wiping the tears of laughter from her cheeks. "We just have to make a few adjustments. Right now you look like a little girl dressing up in her mother's clothes."

On Monday the postman stuck a letter through their slot. "It's from Cornelius!" Hazel cried, ripping it open. Five dollars dropped out. "He must have found work." She quickly scanned the brief message. "He's been shoveling snow. Nothing permanent. He never was one to write long letters," she added, handing the page to Agata. "And no return address, either."

There was a mist in Agata's eyes as she took the letter. Her fingers passed over Cornelius's few lines, then pressed it to her lips. She gave the letter back.

Hazel took it, studying Agata thoughtfully. Finally she asked, "Agata, can you read?"

The freckles on Agata's round face jumped out when she blushed. "No," she answered simply.

Hazel nodded. "We'll adjust that, too."

As winter grudgingly gave way to spring, Hazel spent her days paring down clothes, giving Agata English lessons, and teaching her to read. She was a willing and apt student. And a natural cook. What she lacked in experience, she made up for in instinct. In short order she took over the kitchen.

There was another letter from Cornelius and another five dollars. He'd had a job knocking down and carting away an old shed. Still nothing permanent. Nor an address to write back to.

The days went by in a certain routine. While she was pleasantly occupied, Hazel pushed her worries out of the way. In fact, life went so smoothly, she even pulled her sketch pad and pencils from the box under her bed. Flipping through the pages, she showed Agata her drawings of Italy.

"You made these?" Agata asked, her eyes wide.

"Yes. They're good, aren't they?" Hazel answered, almost as

amazed as Agata. She hadn't looked at them in nearly a year. What a different person she'd been then, though these sketches gave a hint of what had been hidden inside her. The strength, the conviction, even the passion she'd discovered since that time, had poured out through her pencils and paints without her being aware they existed.

But Marco had known. He had spotted them immediately, standing behind her in the sun-baked Piazza del Duomo. Her memory of that day was suddenly so vivid, she could almost feel the heat trapped beneath her clothes. She remembered her first sight of him and the cool shivers that had run down her spine. He'd been so big and dramatic against the hot Italian sky, like a Renaissance masterpiece come to life.

That's enough, she told herself sternly. It's over. Out loud, she said, "Yes, I was good." She spoke quickly, in an attempt to close Marco out of her mind. "Let me see if I can do it again," she added determinedly. Then she busied herself arranging a still life with a plateful of Agata's raviolis, some spoons, and a wedge of cheese.

# CHAPTER

## —✦17✦—

They were sitting in the kitchen one March morning, basking in the sliver of weak spring sunshine that fell across the table, when a knock sounded on the front door. A pencil gripped in her fingers, Agata looked up from the exercise book in which she was carefully printing her name. "Will I go?" she asked.

"Shall I go," Hazel corrected. "Yes, please, if you would." She lacked only a few stitches to finish the hem of a tartan tafetta skirt she was shortening for Agata. "It's probably Mrs. O'Sullivan returning the cup of sugar she borrowed on Saturday."

Agata bounded away but was back in a minute, her brown eyes big and bright. "Who is it?" Hazel asked. In reply Agata handed her a visiting card.

MARCO MACGREGOR, it read.

Despite her best intentions, Hazel's heart started beating hard. With only one stitch left to sew, she dropped the needle, thrust the skirt from her, and stood up. Suddenly it was hard to swallow.

"I put him in the parlor," Agata whispered excitedly. "He is very large."

"Yes, yes. Good," Hazel responded nervously, smoothing her hair. Almost to herself, she added, "I wonder what he wants." Their last meeting, after Edgar's funeral, had seemed harshly final.

"I don't know." Agata spread her hands and shrugged her shoulders. Then she plopped into her chair, saying conspiratorily, "Go find out. I'll stay here."

Halfway to the door Hazel spun around and returned to seize Agata by the wrist. "Oh, no," she said, shaking her head. "You're coming with me. Don't you dare leave me alone. Even for a minute." Despite her agitation, she hadn't forgotten the hard lessons she'd learned in recent times. She wanted Agata present to keep from being distracted.

With a wide-eyed Agata at her heels, Hazel swept into the parlor. Then stopped. The sight of Marco made her catch her breath. However vivid she thought her memories were, they couldn't compare with his actual presence. It was impossible to capture his tremendous spirit and to store it in her mind. When he stood up to greet her, Hazel felt something melt inside her that she hadn't even known was frozen.

"Hello, Hazel," he said.

Hazel forced herself to move forward and willed her voice to be calm. "Hello, Marco," she responded. "May I present to you Miss Agata Bellocchio?"

"I'm very pleased to meet you, Miss Bellocchio," Marco said, bowing low. He straightened, took Agata's hand in his, and looked intently at her. "Would you, by any chance, be Cornelius's *signorina*?"

Never in her life had anyone bowed to her. Utterly dazzled, Agata could only tilt her head back to stare at his face and answer, "*O si.*"

"*Devo fare i miei complimenti a Cornelius. Mi sembra che c'ha molto buon gusto.*"

Agata gasped.

Smiling, Marco turned to Hazel. "I was telling Miss Bellocchio that I must make my compliments to Cornelius. It would seem he has shown very good taste."

"I'll have to agree with you," Hazel said, going over to the cot. "Agata has become a dear friend." She sat down gracefully and folded her hands in her lap. Agata came over and sat on the edge. "What a surprise to see you," Hazel went on politely. "I assumed you would be back in Italy or Scotland by now."

"I leave tomorrow night," Marco replied, dropping into the chair. "The Royal Mail Steamship sails from Boston for Glasgow. It couldn't be more convenient. I'll be home in a trice."

"Tomorrow?" Hazel echoed in involuntary alarm. It didn't matter that five minutes ago she'd imagined him to be gone already. Now that he was here, her stomach knotted at the thought of him leaving.

"Yes." Marco didn't seem to notice her dismay. "I want to be home in ample time for lambing. It doesn't start for another month or more, but it's vitally important that good, rich hay is laid out now that the graze is poor so the ewes will deliver healthy lambs."

"Of course," Hazel murmured.

"And speaking of poor graze," Marco went on, "I've just come from a trip to New Mexico. I tell you, Hazel, that is the most extraordinary country. You haven't lived until you've seen the mesas at sunrise. Here." He reached down to pick up a parcel by the side of the chair. "I've brought you a present."

While Hazel took the package and untied the strings, and Agata craned her neck to watch, Marco continued chatting. "In places it seems as if there is nothing for the sheep to eat but sand and a few twigs of brush, yet they seem to thrive. The people thrive on a different diet, too. There's a strong Mexican influence. Have you ever heard of a tortilla?"

Before Marco could launch into a full description, starting with how the sun-dried corn was rolled with a stone, Hazel pulled back the paper to reveal a thick, woven wool rug. "How beautiful!" she exclaimed. "What unusual designs. They look almost mystical. Is it Egyptian?"

Smiling again, Marco shook his head. "Navajo," he answered. "It's fascinating to watch the Indian women sitting cross-legged in front of their vertical looms creating these works of art." He shook his head in admiration this time. "Just look at the colors."

When he leaned over to run his fingers across the burnt red and yellow geometric patterns, Hazel caught a whiff of his sandalwood soap. Taking a steadying breath, she remarked, "They have a much different feeling than the colors that Jean Fergueson makes with her crottles and weeds."

"Yet these are made with plants and berries, too. It's impossible to achieve the same effects with chemical dyes. It's the land that makes the difference." He sat back again. "These are the colors of New Mexico. The colors of adobe houses and mesquite and chili peppers drying in the sun."

"Peppers," Hazel said, setting down the rug, her memory jogged. "We have some wonderful pepper biscuits that Agata baked yesterday. May I offer you tea?"

Marco's eyebrows raised. "Calabrese?" he asked Agata. When she nodded, his eyes sparkled. "It sounds like a treat," he accepted.

"I'll go make the tea," Agata volunteered, jumping up.

"No, no," Hazel countered, instantly rising. "You stay here. I'll go."

"I know," Marco said, also getting to his feet. "Why don't we all go into the kitchen? It's much cozier than the parlor."

Hazel wasn't sure she was prepared for him to be cozy or familiar, but before she could protest, Marco took Agata's arm and led the astonished girl away. Despite her thrill at seeing him and her dread at the thought of him leaving, despite the real pleasure she found in hearing descriptions and observations of his trip, she hadn't forgotten her pledge. She wasn't going to be bewitched by a Navajo blanket and tales of tortillas.

In the kitchen Agata disengaged herself to run and fill the kettle, while Hazel hastily cleared the table of their morning activities. Marco's sharp glance took in the exercise book and the sewing and, to judge from his expression, drew conclusions without asking any questions. Fingering the taffeta skirt, he commented, "I remember you wearing this, Hazel, but I think the green and yellow plaid is more suited to Miss Bellocchio. You look better in the MacGregor tartan."

Yanking the skirt away from him, Hazel started to retort, but Marco had already moved easily over to the cupboard. "Are these the *biscotti*?" he asked, opening the lid of the tin without an invitation. "Oh, my," he admired, examining the hard, pepper-specked cookies within.

"They look delicious. An uncle of mine had a cook from Calabria. She used to send me huge packages of these biscuits while I was at school in England. I don't think I would have survived Eton without them. Shall I put them on a plate?" He reached down a platter before either Hazel or Agata could answer.

Behind his back Hazel threw up her hands.

As Marco arranged the biscuits, he snuck a broken piece into his mouth. "*Eccezionale*," he praised. "Cornelius is a lucky man. By"—that reminded him—"where is Cornelius? I took a stroll along the canal before coming here and noticed that the Great Stone Dam Mill is still closed for repairs. Has he found another job?"

When his casual question was greeted by silence, Marco turned around to see if he'd been heard. Agata was wringing her hands. Hazel looked sober. "What is it?" he asked, alarmed. "Has something happened to him?" He set the plate down and moved closer.

"No, he's fine," Hazel hastened to reassure him. "At least, hope he is," she amended. Squaring her shoulders, she told hi "Cornelius went to Boston the day after Papa's funeral to fir work. There isn't any here, and he had to do something."

"Has he found a job?" Marco asked instantly. There was not ing amiable about his tone now.

"Well," Hazel hedged, centering a chair at the table. "Nothir steady," she finally admitted. "But he's had a few odd jobs ar has sent some money."

"Where is he?" Marco demanded. "*I'll* give him work. He ca just drift around."

"I don't know where he is," Hazel answered. "Honestly," sl insisted, seeing Marco's skeptical look. "He just sticks some mo ey in an envelope and scribbles a few lines promising to wri soon. There's never a return address."

"What are you living on? How are you paying the rent? Haze this is mad. You can't stay here alone."

"I'm not alone," Hazel replied, her chin rising. "Agata is wi me. And we're managing. Papa put by a little money." She turn to Agata before he could ask her how much.

"I think the water's hot," she said. "Will you make the tea whi I get the sugar and milk?" As she went to fill the pitcher from t milk bottle on the window, she looked at Marco and ordere "Stop seething and set the table." He glared at her, exasperate and then he complied.

After they were seated and Hazel had poured out, the three them sat there without saying a word. Hazel finally broke the sto silence by politely inquiring, "Did your stay in America yield t business opportunities you hoped it would?"

"Yes," Marco answered succinctly. There was another mome of silence, then he gave a shrug of resignation. "There's nothir firm yet," he said, picking up the conversation. "I'm still waitir for the Wilson tariff to be enacted. From all I can tell, that w be sometime this summer. I'm going to hold this year's clip unt it happens."

"You must feel it's fairly certain to become law."

"Of course, nothing is ever absolute," Marco conceded, "b from what I see now, I think it's worth the risk. It's passed throu; the House of Representatives with strong support, and though tl Senate is taking its time, the outcome will be favorable for m The import duties on raw wool will be dropped. With the price cottish Cheviot wool hovering around thirty-six cents a pound, should do rather well."

"Is that high?" Hazel asked. Then, seeing his empty cup, said, Would you like some more tea?"

"Yes on both counts," Marco answered, pushing his cup across ne table. "Scottish and English wool, alone, is holding steady n the market, or rising. The price of domestic wool has fallen ramatically in the past year. The New Mexican clip, for example, as gone from fourteen cents to nine."

Hazel refilled his cup, then held the pot out to Agata. When \gata shook her head, she topped up her own cup. "It would eem, then, that your trip has been a resounding success."

"Not really." Marco reached for a biscuit. "It will probably rove financially beneficial, but that wasn't my entire goal." :lbows propped on the table, he held the cookie in front of im while he fixed his eyes on her face.

Neither his stare nor his pointed comment brought a response. Iazel calmly added sugar and milk to her tea, then gave it a stir. Ier eyes remained fixed on her spoon.

His shrug was slightly less resigned this time, and there was an dge to his tone as he continued to fill the void with conversation. If I were really serious about making a huge success in business, would consider buying a mill. There are a number that have gone •ankrupt. Without meaning to circle like a vulture, I'll have to say hey're an excellent buy."

Now Hazel looked at him, her expression astonished. "But hey've gone bankrupt for a good reason," she objected. "There's . depression and there isn't any business. How could you possibly xpect to overcome those odds?"

"I wouldn't expect to overcome them," Marco told her, taking bite of the biscuit in front of his nose. "I would expect to outwait hem. The depression won't last forever. Eventually the politicians nd captains of industry will stumble on corrective measures. They lways do. As a long-term investment, it could be quite profitable. \t least, that's my guess," he added, dunking the remainder of the •iscuit in his tea. "Just idle speculation." He popped the saturated norsel in his mouth.

Hazel set down her spoon and pushed her teacup to one side. 'I can understand your wanting to find the best market for your vool," she said, "but it's beyond me why you would consider nvesting in a mill. You don't seem to approve of conditions in them any more than Cornelius does. Or Agata."

"True," he agreed, helping himself from the plate again. "As
said, it's something I would do only if I were single-minded abou
making money. Although"—he paused to nibble thoughtfully o
the biscuit—"it might be an interesting experiment to see if a mil
could be operated safely and profitably. *And* pay the workers
decent wage." He wagged the chewed biscuit at her. "Not lik
the business your fiancé, Mr. Frederick Whitaker, runs."

Silence followed his statement. Agata looked back and fortl
with increasing anxiety. Finally she burst out, "He is not her fianc
anymore. The engagement is broken."

"Agata!" Hazel cried. But the damage was done.

"Is it?" Marco pounced, dropping the biscuit. "Hazel, that'
splendid! Now you can marry me."

"No, no. Wait." Hazel held up both hands.

Marco reached across the table and seized them. "Why didn'
you tell me immediately that you'd given him the boot?" h
boomed. "You just sat there looking devastated when I told yo
I was leaving tomorrow. For heaven's sake, Hazel, I can cance
that ticket. It means nothing. Murdo can see to the ewes."

"I didn't give Frederick the boot," Hazel responded, strugglin
to free her hands. "He gave it to me."

Some of the joy on Marco's face was submerged by his outrage
"Then he's not only a fool, he's an unforgivable villain. But that'
not news," he added contemptuously. "I told you months ago tha
he was a snake who'd bring you nothing but misery." Then h
dismissed Frederick with a toss of his big head.

"*We* will have an extraordinary marriage," he told her, givin
the hands he was holding a squeeze. "We were meant for eac
other. You'll see. The angels will come down from heaven t
applaud at our wedding."

Finally succeeding in pulling her hands out of his grasp, Haze
set them, away from his reach, in her lap. "I think you're bein
a little bit hasty," she started to say.

"You think we're ill-suited because I'm so blustery and you'r
so calm, don't you?" Marco interrupted with a fond smile. "Bu
that's just the facade. Inside we're the same. We take differen
routes, but we have identical destinations." He crossed his arm
on the table and leaned toward her. "Our days together will be
constant source of pleasure."

"You're not listening to me," Hazel stated more forcefully

"You don't understand what I'm trying to tell you—"

"Of course I do," Marco interrupted again, his face glowing even more than usual. "I understand you better than anyone else in the world. Sometimes even better than you do yourself." He turned to Agata for support. *"Di la che siamo perfetti insieme,"* he encouraged as Agata's mouth fell open. "Tell her that we're perfect together."

"Stop it!" Hazel's hand flew out of her lap and slammed on the table. "Stop telling me what I think and feel and want!" she shouted. "You don't understand me better than I do myself. Do you hear me? It's a presumptuous mistake on your part to think that you do."

Marco's eyes narrowed. "What are you saying, Hazel?" he asked, leaning back in his chair. "Are you saying that even now that you're free, you don't want to marry me?"

"I'm saying," Hazel answered tightly, straining to regain a hold on her temper, "that I don't want you to decide that question for me. It's for me to answer." She shut her eyes a moment and drew a breath. When she spoke again, her voice was nearly normal.

"It's perfectly possible that I would enjoy being married to you," she told him. "That I would enjoy going from a *palazzo* in Venice to a cottage on a Scottish lake. I might very well find pleasure in searching out the most delicious strawberries and the most exquisite art. But Marco, don't you see?" she implored. She pressed her hands together and held them under her chin. "It's a decision that *I* want to make. In fact, I want, no, I intend to make *all* the decisions about my life from now on."

"Fine," Marco said flatly, flinging an arm over the back of the chair. "So decide. Which would you rather? To molder away in this miserable little house or to marry me and be comfortable and happy?"

Hazel's tenuous patience snapped. Despite her veneer of tranquillity since Agata had entered her life, beneath the surface she was still suffering the shock of having her world turned upside down. "You refuse to understand what I'm saying!" she exploded. "You're convinced that you know better. You're positive that you and your possessions are my only hope for happiness. Well, let me tell you something, Marco MacGregor." She tapped her finger on the table. "I've arrived at a different decision. I've decided that I will never again be so swaddled in comfort and blinded by luxury that I relinquish control of my life. Now do you understand *that*?"

Frustrated, Marco's voice rose, too. "I understand that you're being very stubborn," he stormed, swinging his arm back onto the table. "I understand that you're being unreasonable and unrealistic. Put aside marriage for a moment." He swiped it out of the way with his hand. "You can't continue to live as you are. You're on the thin edge of complete poverty. And believe me, Hazel, there is nothing brave or ennobling about being poor."

He stood up abruptly and stalked to the end of the kitchen. "Poverty doesn't lead to enlightenment," he growled, turning to face her. "It doesn't liberate your spirit. Just the opposite. It shackles you with despair and disease and death. You don't have to take my word for it. Ask your friend." He gestured toward Agata. "Ask her what her life was like in her village in Calabria. Why she left to come to the United States. And ask her what it's like in the tenements. Find out if people sit around being proud of their independence and wisdom or if they sit around being hungry and sick." He shook his head. "You can't keep going like this."

Hazel was in no mood for his lecture, especially when she'd already drawn the same conclusion herself. "I told you," she said angrily, rising, too, "we're managing. We have a few resources."

"Bah." Marco snorted in disgust. "That's a fantasy. A romantic notion." He started treading back and forth in front of the cupboard. "How long do you think Edgar's savings will last? A month? Two?" His hand slashed through the air with every question. "Then what will you do? Get a job in the mill? Work twelve hours a day to earn seven dollars a week? Your wages wouldn't even pay the rent on this house.

"And don't think that Cornelius is going to rescue you. However good his intentions—and I don't doubt they are—if he's doing odd jobs as you say, I'll wager everything I own that he's earning no more than a dollar a day. How can he support himself on that and support you, too?"

Marco stopped his caged pacing and came over to lean on the edge of the table. "If you won't accept my offer of marriage," he said, "at least accept my offer of help."

"No." Hazel answered him instantly, gripping the other end of the table. The exact same questions had gone round and round in her mind until she was dizzy. But she wasn't about to admit it. Or to give in to him. "I've told you over and over that my life isn't for sale. Other people have made me promises, too. They've assured me, just as sincerely as you are now, that they would always keep me safe and comfortable.

"Leave it to them," she mimicked bitterly. "Don't let ugly thoughts sully my beautiful head. I trusted them. I fulfilled my half of the bargain. And what did I get in return?" Her eyes were huge and dark against her deathly pale face. "This." She swept her arm around the cheerless kitchen.

"You're talking about Frederick now," Marco accused, pointing a finger at her. "I'm not Frederick and you can't even begin to compare me with him. Aside from the fact that he's a heartless snob, he's never loved you as I do. And you've never loved him. Don't scowl at me, Hazel," he said, shaking his finger and scowling himself. "You know very well that it's true."

"There you go again!" Hazel cried, flinging her hands in the air. "You insist on telling me how I feel. Where do you get the gall to presume to know what's inside my heart?"

"In this case, it doesn't take gall," Marco retorted. "It only requires an ounce of perception. It's easy for me to sense what's inside your heart because it's the same thing that's inside mine." He suddenly dropped his scolding finger and leaned across the table again.

"That's what this is really all about," he said. "It's all about love." His voice became rich and coaxing.

"Never mind the *palazzo* and the art collections," he said, brushing them off the table. "What I can buy doesn't matter. It's what I feel that does. What we feel for each other. The longing, the desire, the sense that the world is empty and that life is only an exercise in breathing when we aren't together. It's these feelings that count more than anything else."

He straightened slowly. "That's why I can't understand why you won't marry me."

Hazel straightened, too, folding her arms in front of her. It was so quiet in the kitchen she could hear Agata's braids rubbing across the back of her blouse as she turned her head from one to the other. "It should be fairly simple to deduce," she said finally, her voice level. "It must be because you're wrong. It must be because I don't love you after all."

Marco stared at her. "You don't mean that," he stated.

Hazel stared back. "Obviously I do."

There was another moment of silence. Then Marco turned and left.

Hazel stood where she was until she heard the front door slam, then she sagged into her chair and dropped her face in her hands. A tremendous sense of loss swept over her. A sense, as Marco had said, that the world was empty. She felt cold and hollow. Her limbs felt weak.

# CHAPTER
## —◦❧ 18 ❧◦—

"Hazel?" Agata's voice was a whisper. Her hand was tentative as it touched Hazel's arm. "Are you all right?"

After a minute Hazel nodded, though she didn't raise her head. Agata dragged her chair over and sat down so close their knees bumped. She waited quietly until Hazel finally lifted her face, her hands falling listlessly in her lap.

"Are you very sad?" Agata asked anxiously.

Another minute passed by before Hazel shrugged. "I don't know," she answered dully.

"I think you are," Agata decided. "Signore Marco is *molto simpatico*. I think you are sad to see him go."

Her words fanned a dim spark inside of Hazel, making her sit up straighter. "Whether I am or I'm not," she said with a little more spirit, "I'm better off that he's gone."

"Oh." Kneading her hands together, Agata tried to digest both that thought and the force with which it had been uttered. "But it's true, you know," she finally blurted out. "It's true what he said about being poor. It's not nice. You wouldn't like it."

"I'm sure I wouldn't," Hazel freely admitted. "I already don't. I know that what Marco said about it was true. But, Agata"—Hazel reached over and held the girl's twisting hands still while she looked at her intently—"what I said was true, too. From now on I have to make decisions about my life for myself. Do you understand?"

"Yes," Agata said, nodding, desperate to please Hazel. Then she shook her head. "No," she said, because she didn't.

Hazel let go of Agata's hands and sat up. "I know you think this house is quite comfortable," she said slowly, searching for a way to explain. "But compared with where we used to live, this house is a stable. Agata, we had five floors of big, beautiful rooms just for our family and servants." She leaned forward in an effort to make Agata see such glory. "We had damask-covered sofas and silk-tasseled lamps. We had a French porcelain dinner service for twenty-four guests."

Deciding that Agata looked properly impressed, Hazel leaned back again. "In six months' time it all disappeared," she went on. "First the house and the dishes. Then Papa. Then Frederick. And here I am." She lifted her hands in the air. "I'm left with nothing." Her fist suddenly pounded into her palm. "Nothing! Not only no money, but, more important, no knowledge of how to survive. If I'd ever asked such a question, I would've been told, 'Don't worry. Go buy a new bonnet.'"

Shaking her head in amazement at her helplessness, she said, "Can you believe that when I got to Lawrence, I didn't even know how to cook?"

Agata shook her head, too, though she was doubting the possibility that Hazel could have a flaw.

"Of course," Hazel continued, with a trace of a smile, "if you ask Cornelius, he'll tell you I still can't cook."

"No," Agata protested instantly. She didn't want to contradict Cornelius, but she couldn't let that insult pass.

"It's true," Hazel admitted, shrugging. "I don't have a knack for it, the way you do, although at least now I can nourish myself." Then she dismissed that issue with a flick of her fingers.

"The point is, I can't ever let myself be so mesmerized by a pretty set of china or a rare Persian rug that I'm left without a prayer when it's pulled from under my feet. Don't you see, Agata?" She leaned forward again and squeezed hold of the girl's hands.

"I have to know what's happening to me. Not only what, but why and how and when. I have to be the one who decides how to react. What to do. What to think. What to say. I can't give up that right for the sake of a luxurious home. And," she added, giving Agata's hands a shake, "I can't love someone who expects me to."

Agata stared at her in awed silence. Then she breathed, *"Brava."*

Hazel dropped Agata's hands and leaned her arms on her knees, her chin hanging nearly to her chest. *"Brava,* indeed," she said in a muffled voice. "Bravado is more like it."

"What does that mean?" Agata cried, alarmed by Hazel's sudden deflation.

Hazel lifted her head, though her body stayed bent. "It means," she said bitterly, "I just made a very stirring speech that, as Marco so gallantly pointed out, is totally unrealistic. I can't live on stirring speeches. What can I do to survive? I don't know anything. I'm a product of my upbringing. I'm just a fetching toy."

"That isn't true," Agata denied. "You know many, many things."

Hazel's neck arched as her head sank again. "Such as?" she asked dispiritedly. "Such as buying bonnets? Such as pouring tea? Of the two of us, Agata, you're the one with the greater chance of surviving."

"I don't think so," Agata maintained, shaking her head so vehemently her braids swung over her shoulder. Impatiently she pushed them back. "Every day I learn something new from you. Two, three, five things. But there is not even one you learn from me."

"That's sweet of you to say." Hazel's voice was muffled again. "Although I think you are confusing pretty clothes with skills that can earn a living."

"No," Agata said stubbornly. "A skill, that is easy to get. Any *idiota* can learn a skill. The workers in the mill have a skill. But that's all they know. They know how to stand in front of their machines until they drop on the floor and die. Like me, before I met you and Cornelius. I had three things in my head: eat, sleep, and operate the looms.

"But you"—she grabbed Hazel's shoulders and pushed her upright—"your head is full of more wonderful things than I can imagine."

Despite herself, Hazel felt a warm flash of comfort at Agata's continued admiration. Shifting self-consciously in her chair, though, she challenged, "Name one."

Without hesitation, Agata answered, "You make beautiful pictures."

"Well," Hazel temporized. "Yes," she finally admitted. "I guess I have some talent for drawing. But there aren't many artists who make a living. Unless they sit in parks doing portraits of people, and I'm not very good at portraits. You'll have to think of a better skill than that."

Agata was ready immediately. "You know how to talk very nice."

"Now, you see?" Hazel said, wagging her finger. "That's just the sort of useless accomplishment I was referring to. Pretty manners. What good are they?"

"*Molto*," Agata replied, nodding wisely. "Try to get work without them."

That silenced Hazel for a moment. "All right," she conceded. "And you can read and write."

Hazel started to downplay that ability, too, until she realized the same criterion applied. Illiterate workers hadn't a chance of success. Grudgingly, she agreed.

"You see how many things already?" Agata said happily "We should go on." She jumped up. "I'll make a fresh pot of tea."

While Agata stoked the stove and refilled the kettle, Hazel drew the demolished plate of pepper biscuits closer. Despite the chill in her heart, she felt herself being swept along by Agata's enthusiasm. "Maybe I should make a list," she said in jest. "How will we ever remember so many valuable abilities?"

"What's a list?" Agata asked, turning away from the stove.

"It's a series of items written down on a piece of paper," Hazel explained. "Usually in a column."

"*Ecco. Perfetto.*" Agata ran to get her exercise book and pencil, then ran back and plopped in her chair, holding them out to Hazel.

"Oh, no." Hazel lifted her hands in the air. "I think you should make the list. After all, you're the one who thinks I know so much. This way, you can learn it, too."

"But I don't know how to spell any words," Agata demurred.

"I'll spell," Hazel said firmly, shoving the book in front of Agata. "You write. Ready?"

"*Si.*"

"One. D-r-a-w-i-n-g."

Agata slowly printed the word.

"Do you think we should include painting with drawing, or put it separately?" Hazel mused, teetering between taking this list seriously and treating it as a joke.

"Number two," Agata answered, pencil poised.

Hazel spelled *painting*, then *reading, writing*, and *manners*. "Next?" she asked.

"You know about beautiful dresses."

"Oh, Agata, really," Hazel admonished. "That's just plain foolish."

Unintimidated, Agata demanded, "Spell, please."

"C-l-o-t-h-e-s," Hazel spelled, shrugging. She got up to make the tea. "Now what?"

Rubbing her chin with the end of the pencil, Agata thought about it for a moment. "When Signore Marco talked about what the sheeps eat and what is the price of wool, did you know what he said?" she asked.

"Yes, mostly." Hazel had a sudden vision of the Highlands, of the dramatic empty hills and the vast, tempestuous sky. She saw Roger joyfully rounding up a flock of sheep and Marco, clad in tweed jacket and corduroy knickers, explaining about staples and breeds and fleeces and grading. The University of Sheep, he'd called it, taking her for classes at Murdo's fanks, and Jean Fergueson's dye shed, and Donald MacDonald's loom. As she fussed with the teapot, a smile stole across her face.

"Spell *sheeps*," Agata instructed.

"S-h-e-e-p. There's no *s* on the end. It's the same word for the singular and the plural."

"*Wool?*"

Hazel brought the teapot back to the table. "I'm not sure I know enough about that one to put it on the list," she said doubtfully. She'd only scratched the surface on her tour.

"*Wool?*" Agata insisted.

Hazel sighed. "W-o-o-l. I know the next one," she added, sliding onto her chair. When Agata cocked her head, Hazel said, "You."

"Me?" Agata sat up straight and stared.

"Yes, indeed," Hazel replied, smiling. "Your faith in me is worth more than all the rest of those silly items."

Squinting her eyes, Agata thought about that statement. After a minute she hunched over the book again and printed her name without any help.

The entire pot of tea was gone, as well as the remaining pepper biscuits and several slices of toasted bread with cheese, before they ran out of possible entries. When they were done, three pages of Agata's exercise book were covered with her plain block letters. The list enumerated everything from Hazel's knowledge of art to her trips to Europe, from her petit point pillows to her consummate poise. It included talents as particular as waltzing and as ephemeral as good taste.

"The question is," Hazel summed up, reviewing the final inventory, "what does all of this mean?"

"It means you know many things," Agata said stoutly, taking the book out of Hazel's hands and banging the print-covered pages in illustration. "Look how many."

"Oh, *molto*," Hazel agreed, mocking, trying to hide her disappointment at the unpromising results of their search. "Which of those many accomplishments, do you suppose, is going to help me pay the rent? The dancing? Or maybe number seventeen: flower arrangements?"

"Maybe." Agata thrust out her chin. She refused to be dissuaded. "Maybe all of them together."

"Together? Hmmm. Let's see." Hazel took back the list and studied it, her brow furrowed in pretend concentration. "I know. I can draw pictures of clothes for sheep."

"Hazel," Agata warned.

"No? Then perhaps I can make petit point pillows for European travelers with good manners."

Agata snatched the book away. "*Basta!*" she commanded. "Stop it. You think this is worth nothing, but you don't know what nothing really is. Think what you would do if there was no list. You would have one hope only. Go to work in the mill. But here"—she shook the book at Hazel—"you have many chances."

Agata's stern tone jarred Hazel. The immigrant girl was right. Without all the refinements Hazel had scoffed at, her options in life would be nil. Taking hold of herself, she reviewed that compilation of aptitudes and abilities more closely. Maybe there wasn't a clear-cut career on that list, she concluded, but there was a recurring theme. The sum total of her accomplishments showed a certain amount of specialized knowledge and definite evidence of an artistic eye. What she needed now was a method of exchanging them for money.

"Let me see that again," she said, reaching determinedly for the book. She stared at it and stared at it until Agata's fat letters began to blur. "I can . . . " she began, hoping the sentence would finish itself. "I can . . . " Nothing else came out.

In an attempt to force the thought along, she started at the top of the list. "I can draw . . . " Nothing. She peeked fearfully over the edge of the book at Agata. "I can draw sheep eating flowers," she said very fast. Then ducked.

Agata's napkin went sailing over her head. "*Buffone!*" she shouted, though she was laughing as she did so. "It's not funny."

"I know it isn't," Hazel apologized with a wide smile. Twisting around to retrieve the napkin, she added, "It's just that I honestly can't make any sense of this jumble. Here." She tossed the book back across the table. "You try."

It was Agata's turn to stare. She squirmed in frustration, first because she couldn't read the words, despite having written them, and second because she couldn't find a solution. "Maybe you can . . . " She scratched her head with the point of her pencil. Finally she giggled. "Maybe you can draw flowers eating sheep?"

"Ah." Hazel nodded sagely. "An excellent idea. Now, why couldn't I have thought of that?" Propping an elbow on the table, she leaned against her palm. "At least we both agree that my fortune lies in my being able to draw something."

Feeling a little giddy, Agata suggested, "Maybe you could draw flowers *on* sheep."

"There's a good thought," Hazel said, laughing. "Think how much time it would save if the design were applied directly to the sheep." Feeling a little giddy herself in the wake of this tumultuous day, she elaborated. "The dyeworks could be eliminated completely since the color and print would be in the fleece. It might get lost in the carding and spinning, but as soon as it was woven, it would reappear. Oh, yes, Agata, this could revolutionize the textile industry."

As she laughed, she could see the floral wool emerging, thread by thread, on Donald MacDonald's loom. Suddenly she stopped laughing, though the design kept growing. There were thistles, bristling pink, and stalks of mauve-colored heather, and a few sprigs of pale blue butterwort for good measure. It was a soft, fine wool, almost like a challis. It kept inching along, peacefully, serenely. *Rattle, whish, clunk, rap, rap.*

"If you made the pictures very small on the lambs, do you think they would grow with the sheep?" Agata wondered in the same giggly vein. Glancing at Hazel in anticipation of an equally silly response, she was surprised by the thoughtful expression on her face. "What is it?" she demanded, instantly sober. "What did you think?"

Hazel sat up. "Do you suppose," she asked quietly, not wanting to acknowledge the excitement that was building inside her, "that I could possibly draw designs for woolen fabrics?"

After a long pause Agata gulped. "Draw designs?" she questioned carefully. While she could sense that Hazel was in earnest about this idea, she wasn't sure she felt the same way. "Aren't there men at the mill who do that?"

"Are there?" Hazel wasn't visibly dismayed. In fact, she seemed even more enthusiastic. "Yes, they would be men," she decided, dismissing them with an impatient gesture. "That's why most woolens you see are drab and dark. They're imagining their own somber suits. How would men know what a woman wants to wear?"

As she talked, her spark of an idea caught fire. "I remember when I used to have my clothes made," she told Agata, edging forward in her chair until their knees again bumped. "I could never find exactly the goods I wanted. Either the design was too dreary or the wool was too stiff. Something was always wrong. More often than not, I wound up ordering a fabric imported from Paris that was probably wildly expensive, but still wasn't completely right."

She grabbed the exercise book off the table and waved it in front of Agata's face. "Don't you see?" she asked eagerly. "It's all here. These are the things I know best. Look." She pointed to each item as she read it off. "Drawing. Painting. Clothes. Art. Good Taste. Wool." She put the book down a minute and gave a shrug. "Well," she admitted, "I don't know a great deal about wool. But I know a little. And after years of going to dressmakers, I know about the finished product."

Dismissing that small problem in her rush to explain her larger vision, she picked up the list again. "Even the little things seem more significant," she went on, scanning the page with her finger. "Like flower arranging," she selected. "I could use my familiarity with flowers in the designs I do. And here. This one." She pointed. "European trips. I've seen how fashionable women dress in the most sophisticated cities in Europe."

Suddenly she threw the book on the table and leaned forward

o clutch Agata's knees. "If I could reduce the first twenty-four ears of my life to a single concept," she said, her tone and her xpression both intent, "it would be this. I was elegant." She sat ack abruptly. "Add to that my ability to draw and the fact that ve're stuck in a city whose entire reason for being is to weave vool." She lifted her hands in the air. "The conclusion is ines-apable. I should draw elegant designs for wools."

She sat forward again. "What do you think?" she asked anx-ously.

Agata exhaled slowly. "*Perfetto*," she said, stunned. Even hough it was she who had kept insisting that Hazel was brilliant nd talented, she was awed by this result. In her whole life she ad never known anyone who'd done anything besides scratch he earth for a bare living or stand behind the machines in a nill. With the possible exception of Cornelius, though even he ad been imprisoned in the weaving room. "You will sell these lesigns to the mills?"

"I hope so." Hazel gave a worried laugh and started to chew ner lip. "They've reduced production," she acknowledged. Then she argued, "But they have to weave something. It might as well be a beautiful pattern as an ugly one."

Agata nodded her agreement.

"They have their own employees who make designs," Hazel further acknowledged. "But maybe they can be persuaded to try something that women would like."

Agata nodded again and picked up the exercise book from the table. "Number five," she said, tapping the page. "Manners. You talk very nice."

Hazel gave another laugh, this one tinged with nervous excite-ment. Despite the obstacles and risks apparent with this plan, she liked the idea very much. It meant using her mind and her imagi-nation to create something not only lovely but functional. It meant that her collection of socially correct accomplishments and polite proclivities wasn't a waste after all. Mostly, though, it meant that she could really control the course of her life. With hard work and some luck, she would make her own way, and then she would be beholden to no one. The hollow feeling inside her, left by Marco's departure, began to fill.

"Let's go shopping," she said, jumping up. "There's still plenty of time before the stores close."

"Shopping?" Though she was obviously surprised, Agata stood

up obediently. "I think we have enough food for dinner," she said following Hazel to the front hall.

"We aren't going shopping for food," Hazel explained, pulling on her coat. "We're going to Essex Street to buy samples from the best bolts of wool we can find, so I have something to use as a guide. Then we're going to buy some new pots of paint, as mine are either dried or used up. And finally, we're going to stop at Ketchum's for the latest issue of *Harper's Bazaar* and a cherry soda."

"So much money," Agata murmured, wrapping herself in the heavy shawl she used as a coat. Hers hadn't survived her week on the streets, and it was beyond Hazel's tailoring to cut one down.

"Don't think of it as an expense, Agata," Hazel said grandly as she gathered up her reticule and swept out the door. "Think of it as an investment."

Hazel wasn't quite as blithe the next afternoon when she stared at the single design she'd struggled all morning to make. It had proved to be more complicated than she'd originally imagined. After studying her samples, she'd realized that she couldn't just paint some flowers on a page. She had to take into account spacing and weave and the repetition of pattern. She had to think about dyes and fibers and the final product. For example, butterflies were hardly appropriate for a fabric destined to be an overcoat. She knew just enough to know how little she knew.

She crumpled up the paper in front of her and tossed it on the floor. Her rendering of vines and berries was just as ordinary as any of the wools she'd bought at Stearns'.

"No," Agata protested, setting down her rolling pin and bending to pick up the wad. "Why did you do this? It was a pretty picture." She straightened the paper.

"Maybe," Hazel said glumly. "But it wasn't a very good fabric design. If you think what it would look like as a skirt, it would be either quite boring or unspeakably garish."

"Tsch." Agata clicked her tongue against her teeth and laid the wrinkled page on the table. Then, turning back, she continued to make ravioli.

Slumped in her chair, Hazel watched Agata work. She watched as the Italian girl rolled the pasta paper thin, then as she placed little mounds of chopped meat and spices at even intervals on the dough and as she covered it with another layer the same size. She watched as Agata pressed the two sheets of pasta together, then cut neat squares, each with its own mound of filling.

Picking up her pencil again, Hazel started drawing. She drew neat little squares, evenly spaced across the page. In the center of each she shaded a mound.

"I like the other more," Agata stated, walking around the end of the table to look.

"As a picture, yes," Hazel agreed, feeling a rush of yesterday's excitement. "But as a design, this one is better."

She spent another hour working on the idea until, again, she threw down her pencil in frustration. It was a good design, but it wasn't a great one. There was something missing. Some sense of magic. Pushing her pad aside, she went out for a walk.

The next morning Hazel alternately stared at the blank paper and watched as Agata rolled up her sleeves and kneaded flour and yeast for bread. Occasionally she took hold of her pencil, determined to pursue a flutter of a thought, but she invariably set it down again. The thought had fluttered away.

When Agata stuck the bread on the back of the stove to rise and sat down to quietly practice her letters, Hazel had to look for a new diversion. Pulling an old sketch pad out of the art supply box on the floor beside her, she idly flipped through the pages. Scenes of Venice jumped out at her. Beautiful *palazzi* and footbridges over canals. She smiled as she remembered the incredible city.

And the incredible afternoon she had spent with Marco. Closing her eyes, she could practically recreate the sights and sounds of their tour. She could see the pottery pitchers full of lush green basil on the copper-covered bar in the *osteria* where they had eaten grilled sardines and sweet baby clams. She could see the weathered whiteness of ancient marble madonnas in their niches and the faded pastels of centuries-old walls. She could hear the carillons chiming through the mellow air of a late, summer afternoon and the soft lap of water against the gondolier's long oar. Mostly, though, she could sense Marco next to her. Big. Dramatic. Full of life.

This time when she picked up her pencil, she put it to use. She drew the mooring poles, their stripes and flames reflected on moonlit waters, and louvered shutters, closed for a noontime nap. She drew Venetian awnings and bunched curtains and minaret windows, columns and mosaics and arches. The next day she painted them, mixing the colors she saw in her mind.

The next day and the next she made more drawings, and the days after that she again transformed them with paint. In ten days time she had dozens of paintings. Selecting three, she began the exacting work of turning them into fabric designs. First she decided on their application, then she chose a wool. Then, with a ruler and paper, she carefully plotted them out. She drew them and painted them with painstaking care and attached a sheet of paper with copious notes.

For two months she proceeded the same way. Sketching, painting, and selecting a few patterns for finished designs. She found her inspiration in bowls of wild strawberries under a grape arbor in Mantua and in the marble fretwork atop Milan's Duomo. In the endless miles of stone walls dissecting Highland meadows and in tweed-jacketed shepherds roaming the rugged hills.

As she worked, though, there was always Marco. He stood peering over her shoulder, hands clasped behind his back, as on that first day in the hot *piazza*. Alternately, he admired and criticized, his eyebrows raising or his nostrils flaring, but he never disappeared. He was as much her inspiration as Italy or Scotland, and his voice sounded constantly in her head. "Without passion the imagination is dry," he said. Remembering him, her fingers danced over the pages.

It took great presence of mind, therefore, to tell herself that was all in the past. That now he was just another bright memory. That now she no longer loved him.

# CHAPTER
## ❧19❧

"Which do you like the most?" Agata asked, thumbing through the pages in the portfolio where Hazel kept the completed designs.

Hazel finished washing her brushes in the sink and came over to stand behind Agata as she flipped the sheets. Drying her hands on the towel, Hazel studied each one thoughtfully. It amazed her to see them. Not only were they intriguing patterns and appealing colors, they looked so . . . so professional. A thrill ran through her. They were beautiful designs and she had made them herself.

"Which one?" Agata insisted, coming to the end of the group.

"I don't know," Hazel answered, smiling. "At the risk of sounding immodest, I think they're equally fine. No, that isn't true," she instantly amended. "I like this one the best."

From the stack she pulled the design for a heavy brocade of dark green ferns brought to life by a scattering of tiny, bright purple violets, half hidden in the feathery leaves. She wasn't sure if it was her favorite because she actually imagined wearing the finished product or because, while she had drawn it, she had imagined Marco's enchanted island and the magical afternoon she had spent on it.

Out loud, though, she said, "I think a winter coat done in this fabric would be magnificent."

"*Magnifico,*" Agata agreed, pulling another design from the group. "Me, I like this one, too."

"Yes," Hazel said, eyeing the design for a midnight-blue cashmere shot through with ribbons of gold-colored silk, inspired by the nighttime view from her window at the Hotel Royal Danieli. "It would make a very handsome suit for you. Perhaps trimmed with deep blue velvet and gold braided buttons."

"*Ola.*" Agata giggled. "I will be a *grande signora.*"

"We'll both be wearing rags if I don't pry myself away from the kitchen table and go out and start selling," Hazel corrected ruefully.

"It's time?" Agata asked, putting the two sketches back in the portfolio and carefully straightening the stack. "You have enough?"

"Past time," Hazel answered. "Whether I have enough or not is beside the point. Even though I'd much rather sit here doodling and dreaming and admiring my work, I can't afford to make any more designs. Our funds are running perilously low, and I don't dare spend any more of them on sheets of paper or pots of paint."

"Don't think of it as an expense, Hazel," Agata deadpanned. "Think of it as an investment."

Laughing and gently swatting Agata with the dish towel, Hazel replied, "If we don't see a return on our *investment* very soon, there won't be anything left to think about at all."

Although they both continued laughing and making light of the situation, grim thoughts of destitution lingered in the recesses of their minds. Nor did either of them wonder aloud about Cornelius, though they each had their private worries. After a long interval he'd sent another letter, this one containing only four dollars. Now they hadn't heard from him in weeks.

For Agata, more distressing than the thought of poverty, was the thought of being cast adrift on the streets before Cornelius returned. How would he know where to find her, or even that he should look? For Hazel, though, poverty was a horror beyond and apart from her concern about her brother's safety. Despite the defiant front she had presented to Marco, it was too frightening to contemplate. Whatever their individual fears, however, both women were united in an ardent hope that the fabric designs would be a success.

On Monday morning Hazel spent hours agonizing over how to dress. She tried on outfit after outfit in an attempt to find the perfect one to wear on her selling expedition. "I have to look fashionable," she told Agata, who sat on the bed watching this show cross-legged and wide-eyed. "After all, they'll see me before they see my work. It's important that I give an impression of stylishness and taste. Otherwise, they'll never believe my designs could be worth anything."

"This one is very beautiful," Agata encouraged, nodding at the rose silk walking costume that Hazel was modeling.

"On the other hand," Hazel fretted, reaching behind her back to undo the mother-of-pearl buttons, "if I look too richly dressed, they won't believe I'm serious. I'll give the impression of being a dilettante instead of a professional artist."

"It's very difficult," Agata commiserated, though she'd never before encountered such a problem.

At ten o'clock of the cool, mid-May morning, Hazel finally stepped out of the house. In a soft gray serge suit with black soutache trim and a white tucked blouse underneath, she achieved exactly the image she'd sought. Elegant but serious.

"*In bocca lupo!*" Agata called from the doorway.

Hazel turned around. "What did you say?" she asked.

"In the mouth of the wolf," Agata translated. "It means good luck."

Hazel gulped and nodded, then resolutely turned forward again. With her leather-bound portfolio and composed expression, she looked the picture of confidence. Inside, though, she was extremely nervous. Her stomach kept twisting in knots and her pulse made erratic bounds.

It wasn't that she regretted embarking on this course, because just the opposite was true. What had started out as a simple attempt to make money had ended up being something much more personal. In the past two months she had felt a sense of satisfaction grow in direct proportion to the number of designs she drew. It was a strong and deeply rooted feeling that swelled her heart with pride. It wasn't unlike the pleasure she'd had weaving at Donald MacDonald's loom. In her own way she was making beautiful woolens.

The enjoyment she got in spending her days painting and planning went beyond mere amusement. For the first time in her life she was putting her mind and her talents to the pursuit of something useful. In the process she was calling on every memory and observation, every bit of information she'd ever possessed. And what she didn't have stored in her head or her soul, she made a point of searching out. It was mental stretching. Creative exertion. Like a vigorous round of jumping jacks, it made her feel awfully good.

It made her feel, in fact, as if she really had taken control of her life. By assembling her abilities into a gratifying occupation, she had made a start at shaping her fate. Even if she never realized a single penny from the attempt, she felt enormously enriched for having tried.

Unfortunately, she knew that she couldn't afford spiritual fulfillment unless it was also accompanied by financial reward. That's why, as she approached the Washington Mills, her stomach was churning nervously. This was the crucial moment in the project, the proof of her success or failure. Now she would find out if her designs for sumptuous woolen fabrics were the beginning of a career or just the end of a folly.

"Yes?" the clerk asked indifferently when Hazel walked into the office. It was much larger than the office at the Great Stone Dam Mill, but otherwise it looked much the same. Austere.

Without setting down his pen, the balding man stared at her, waiting for a response. Three other clerks glanced up incuriously. A score more remained bent over their work. Hazel was acutely aware of the enormous size of this business. The Washington Mills had miles of machinery. Thousands of workers produced millions of yards of goods. Even in here she could hear the muffled roar of wool being carded, spun, and woven. Suddenly Hazel felt very insignificant. The designs in the portfolio under her arm, which had seemed so sophisticated moments before, now seemed amateurish.

"Yes?" the clerk repeated impatiently.

"I would like to see the agent, please," Hazel responded calmly. There was no hint in her voice of the dryness in her throat.

The clerk set down his pen. "Do you have an appointment?" he asked.

Hazel's rapidly pounding heart skipped a beat. "No," she answered. "But I'm prepared to wait."

Shaking his head at such foolhardiness, the clerk picked up his pen again. "Mr. Chapin is in Boston today," he told her, going back to his writing. "If you want to see Mr. Jeffries, his office is the third door down." He pointed over his shoulder with the end of his pen, then continued copying numbers.

Hazel hesitated, wondering who Mr. Jeffries was, but the clerk seemed disinterested in giving any further information. Her cheeks a little pink, Hazel walked through the gate and down the indicated hall. At the third door she stopped and took a deep breath. Then she knocked softly.

"Yes?" came the ubiquitous question.

She opened the door and entered. A young man with a pasty complexion sat behind a plain wooden desk in a windowless room. The air was stale. "Mr. Jeffries?" she inquired, approaching the desk.

The young man shook his head. "I'm Mr. Jeffries's secretary," he answered. "May I help you?"

Hazel doubted it very much. In fact, she was beginning to suspect that no one at the Washington Mills could help her. Still, she didn't give up. "The clerk in the outer office suggested that I see Mr. Jeffries," she explained.

He pulled a watch out of his pocket and looked at the time, then turned to squint speculatively at the door behind him. "At eleven-thirty," he decided, turning back to Hazel.

"Very well," she said, nodding.

"There's a bench in the hall," he added. "I'll call you when he's ready."

The pink on her cheeks got a little deeper as Hazel returned to the corridor. She found the bench, a short way down, and sank onto it, discouraged. Did you think they would be waiting for you with an unfurled carpet? she asked herself. In response, she shrugged. Maybe she hadn't expected that would be the case, but she certainly had hoped so.

It was eleven-fifty by the watch pinned on Hazel's jacket when the clerk finally poked his head out the door. "Mr. Jeffries will see you now," he announced. Hazel rose and followed him into the office.

Mr. Jeffries was a weedy-looking man behind another plain wooden desk beyond the inner door. There was a window in his office, but it looked down a long, stone yard between two interminable brick mills. "Yes?" he asked.

"How do you do, Mr. Jeffries," Hazel answered, crossing the small office toward him. "Thank you so much for seeing me."

Mr. Jeffries gave a grudging dip of his head. He had pink-rimmed eyes and a permanently irritated look.

"I have some designs for woolen fabrics," Hazel continued, far more smoothly than she felt. She lifted her portfolio onto Mr.

Jeffries desk. "May I show them to you?"

"Designs?" Mr. Jeffries asked impatiently. "Why would I want to see designs? I have nothing to do with production. Only with sales. You'll want to see Mr. Coleman. He's upstairs, fourth door on the right."

With flagging spirit, Hazel went to see Mr. Coleman, but he had just stepped out to lunch. She waited on another bench until he returned and until he finished two previous appointments. When she was finally ushered into his office, a replica of Mr. Jeffries's, it was twenty-five past one. Somewhat dispiritedly she stated her purpose, though this time she didn't lift her portfolio to the desk. It was just as well. Mr. Coleman wasn't interested.

"Do you realize, young lady," he lectured, "that the strike has only been over for one week?"

Hazel nodded. She was well aware of it. The broken workers had gone back to their machines without having gained a penny.

"We have three months' backlog to catch up with," Mr. Coleman continued. "How could you possibly expect us to be interested in your designs?"

Hazel didn't answer. She just wanted him to finish his scold so she could politely leave. As she listened, she idly noticed that Mr. Coleman's slash of mustache was identical to his twin slashes of eyebrows.

"Besides which," he went on, "we have our own designers on salary. We've no need to look elsewhere for our patterns."

"Thank you for your time," Hazel said, seizing the opening when he paused for breath. Quickly turning, she went out.

Back across the canal, Hazel leaned against a budding tree in relief. Despite the rejection, she was glad to get away from the oppressive atmosphere. The Washington Mills was a huge corporation, run by monotonous men in ugly offices. There was no place in it for her, or for her handful of designs inspired by heather-covered hills and ancient Venetian *palazzi*.

She was about to flee back to the safety of her kitchen and the solace of Agata's unquestioning faith in her when a stern voice stopped her. Where do you think you're going? it asked. You can run back to your house, but you can't escape the consequences if you fail. How much will Agata admire you when you're both sleeping on the street?

But I'm hungry, another self protested weakly. I haven't had any lunch.

You'll be missing a lot of meals very soon, the first voice answered ominously.

Sighing, Hazel pushed herself away from the tree and started plodding down Canal Street. Maybe the Washington Mills was too big, she decided. Maybe she would have more success in a smaller company. With more spring in her step, she turned around and headed for the Wilcox Mill. It was a tenth the size of the Washington Mills and still owned by a single family.

The clerk at the Wilcox Mill stood up when she entered the office. This show of manners immediately heartened Hazel. The fact that Mr. Ames, the agent, greeted her cordially and shook her hand gave her further encouragement. Her heart beating faster in hope, Hazel explained her purpose.

"Designs, you say?" Mr. Ames mused, his stout fingers stroking both of his chins. "Well, it can't hurt to have a look. If they're as pretty as you are, I wouldn't want to miss them. Come sit here," he said, pulling a chair up. "Let's see what you've got."

After just an instant of hesitation, Hazel went around behind the desk and sat down next to the portly agent. "I certainly appreciate the opportunity to show you my work," she said sincerely.

"My pleasure, Miss Merriwether," Mr. Ames replied. This close, his breath smelled like old cigars.

Ignoring that smell, and the smell of his hair tonic, too, Hazel eagerly opened her portfolio. This was the first time anyone beside Agata had seen her designs. In fact, this was the first time they'd been out of her kitchen. Folding back the protective tissue, she revealed one. It was a fine worsted mosaic in shades of ivory and beige.

"Hmm," Mr. Ames commented. "Very nice."

"Thank you," Hazel said, glowing. It *was* nice. It didn't look amateurish at all. Even in the harsh context of a mill office, it looked technically adept and aesthetically rich. Once again she felt herself swelling with pride. "Here's the same pattern in grays," she said, carefully turning the sheet. "I've also done it in deeper browns. I feel this design calls for neutral tones."

"Quite right," Mr. Ames agreed. "You've got a good eye."

Another surge of pleasure flooded Hazel. "Now I have a series of challis-weight florals," she said happily, easing the sheet over.

"Oh, yes," Mr. Ames complimented, leaning closer. "Lovely." His arm brushed against Hazel's.

Undisturbed, Hazel shifted out of his way. "This one has three

different varieties of heather," she explained. "I've interspersed
branches of bog myrtle for contrast."

"Lovely," Mr. Ames repeated. He reached out to brush a speck
of dust off the paper. When his hand dropped, it landed on the
edge of Hazel's chair.

This time Hazel visibly flinched away. "I've included this
design of butterflies and hummingbirds with the florals," she
said, eyeing the agent more cautiously. "It seems to have the
same flowery feeling."

"Very nice," Mr. Ames murmured. "Very soft." His hand slid
over Hazel's thigh.

She stood up abruptly, her face burning. "I can see you aren't the
least bit interested in my work," she said, her voice quivering with
disappointment. With trembling fingers, she shoved the designs in
a stack and slammed the portfolio shut. "You've been deceitful
and unkind."

"Don't go getting all self-righteous on me," Mr. Ames snapped,
also standing up. "What am I supposed to think when you come
into my office selling pictures? I've only known females to sell
one thing."

Her portfolio clutched under her arm, Hazel banged the door
behind her before the agent could tell her what that one thing
was. She ran out of the building and ran over the canal bridge,
coming to rest again against a tree. Gasping for breath and choking back tears of humiliation, Hazel tried to regain her composure. Mr. Ames's reaction was far worse than the cold rejection
of the Washington Mills. At least there they'd dealt with her on
a businesslike basis. Those unimaginative men had been honest,
if brusque, about their disinterest in her designs. It hurt much
more to have her hopes crushed after Mr. Ames had dishonestly
raised them.

After a while her strength seeped back. She no longer felt as
though her knees would buckle. Slowly she stepped away from
the tree and slowly she made her way home.

Agata took one look at Hazel's face and twisted her hands in
her apron. "It's bad?" she asked, hunching her shoulders against
the news.

"Terrible," Hazel responded grimly. She dropped her portfolio
on the floor and dropped herself in a kitchen chair.

"I'll make you some tea," Agata said, stooping to pick up the
case of precious designs. She laid it reverently on the table. Half-

way to the sink with the kettle in her hand, she stopped. "No, I can't," she apologized, turning back to Hazel. "The tea is *finito*. We drank the last for breakfast. Will I go to the store?"

"Never mind," Hazel answered, too weary even to correct her. She rubbed her forehead. "I'll just have a slice of bread and some cheese."

"I'll toast it," Agata volunteered, anxious to find some way she could help her friend.

Three slices of toasted bread and cheese and Agata's solicitous hovering put a modicum of starch back in Hazel's spine. It was a trip to the grocer's later that afternoon, though, that really made up her mind. Counting the few coins of change she received, she knew she couldn't afford to hide in the house and lick her wounds. Until she had exhausted every possibility for selling her designs, she couldn't afford the luxury of giving up. "Pride goeth before a fall," she told Agata.

"What does that mean?" Agata wrinkled her brow.

"It means that tomorrow I have to put on a clean waist and try again."

Which is what she did. Yesterday's nervous anticipation was replaced by dread as she methodically made the rounds of Lawrence's woolens and worsteds mills. At the first mill she didn't get past the clerk in the front office. At the next two she was sent to see assistants to the agents who dismissed her as soon as they heard her purpose. At the fourth mill, she waited for half an hour and was finally shown into the office of the head designer, but suddenly suspicious of his motives for wanting to see her work, she left without opening her portfolio.

It wasn't until she forced herself to enter the office of the fifth mill, late in the afternoon, that she encountered a bit of civility. The man to whom she was directed was Mr. Snow, the manager in charge of production. In his early fifties, Mr. Snow was a small, neat person with appropriately graying hair and a forthright expression. He asked Hazel to sit, then listened attentively to her perfunctory recitation. To her surprise, he neither instantly banished her nor tried to steal her ideas.

Instead, he said, "To tell the truth, Miss Merriwether, the Duck Bridge Mill isn't able to buy a spool of yarn right now. If I were to guess, I'd say that the company will declare bankruptcy before the week is out."

"Oh, I see," Hazel murmured, taken aback by this blunt state-

ment. She rose to leave. "In that case, I won't waste any mor
of your time."

Mr. Snow rose, too. "On the contrary, Miss Merriwether,
you have some time to spare, I'd be very curious to see you
designs. Even though I can't buy them, I might be able to hel
you. I've been in this business for nearly thirty years, and I know
my way around. Perhaps I can steer you down the right road."

His offer further surprised her. For a long minute she stoo
there staring at him, trying to find some clue to his kindness i
his face. His regular features and unwavering gaze were open an
sincere, but her experiences in the past two days had taught Haze
to distrust even upstanding appearances. "It's very generous o
you, Mr. Snow," she finally said, "but I'm frankly puzzled as t
why you should want to help me."

Mr. Snow smiled. "I appreciate your qualms," he said, noddin
his approval. "You're wise to be cautious. However, my reaso
for helping you is very simple. I recognize that you're needy o
work and trying to make your way in a depressed industry. B
next week it's quite likely that I'll be in the same position. If
give you good advice now, perhaps I'll be rewarded for my effort
by someone else giving me an opportunity."

His explanation made perfect sense. Returning his smile, Haze
sat down again. "I'd be pleased to show you my designs, Mr
Snow," she said, setting her portfolio on his desk and untying
the strings.

Mr. Snow kept his eyes on the designs as Hazel slowly turne
the sheets, and he listened, without comment, as she explaine
each one. When she reached the end, he leaned back in his chai
and crossed his arms. While Hazel waited anxiously for the ver
dict, Mr. Snow gave the situation careful consideration. Finally h
spoke. "I foresee several problems in marketing these designs," h
began.

Hazel felt her heart sink. Suddenly faint, she looked down a
her lap.

"Although neither of them is insurmountable," Mr. Snow wen
on. Desperate hope grabbed Hazel's heart. She lifted her head t
hear what he had to say.

"The first problem is the manner of presentation," Mr. Snow
told her. "Normally a design is presented with a pattern care
known as a draft." He reached behind him and pulled a piec
of graph paper from a shelf. It was covered with tiny symbols.

"You see," he said, pointing, "this shows where each thread has be set in order to achieve the desired effect. Accompanying the aft is a 'layout,' which gives such details as how many harnesses the loom, how many threads in the full width of the warp, and w many threads in one inch of weft. It tells the type, quality, d grade of the stock—that is to say, of the fiber being used— d it usually gives it by its stock number."

With each detail Mr. Snow mentioned, Hazel felt her brief surge hope fade away. She barely recognized the terms he was using, t alone know how to calculate them for every design. Yester- y's assessment had been right after all. She was just an ama- ur.

"As I said, however," Mr. Snow continued, unaware of Hazel's esawing hope, "this problem is not going to deter a truly inter- ted buyer. It's essentially a technical detail that a competent raftsman can resolve."

This time Hazel held her rebounding excitement in check. "And e second problem?" she prompted.

"The second problem is a little more difficult to overcome," Ir. Snow admitted, resting his elbows on the arms of his chair nd knitting his hands together.

Hazel sighed. Now she was done.

"Your designs are highly specialized," Mr. Snow said, "and ey require a highly specialized mill. Offhand, I can only think f one or two mills in the country that produce these types of voolens. Most of the really fancy goods are still imported from urope."

His words fell like bricks, crushing her last bit of optimism. "I nderstand," she said dully, starting to gather together the worth- ss designs. Her fingers felt clumsy, but she no longer cared if he got the sheets wrinkled.

"It's a question of economics, you see," Mr. Snow explained. Take this design for example." He leaned forward and laid his and on the sheet of paper that happened to face up. It was Hazel's avorite brocade of ferns and violets.

Tears sprang to her eyes as she thought of that long-ago June fternoon, holding Marco's hand in his fairy-tale forest. There ad been just the two of them and some pheasants and fawns. Jo mills. No fears. No struggle for survival. Blinking back the ears, she said, "I'm sorry. What did you say?"

Mr. Snow looked at her sympathetically. "I was just telling

you the cost involved in producing this brocade. Aside from th
expensive stock needed, the run on a fabric like this is small.
the hundreds of yards. Most mills in this country are set up
run thousands of yards at a time. Weaving fancy goods is to
particular a task for the average American mill."

Unable to speak, Hazel just nodded.

"But that's not to say there aren't a few around," he added mor
encouragingly. "And the best way to find them isn't by trampin
from mill to mill, but by going to the commission houses in Ne
York and Boston. More often than not, they're the ones wh
decide on the designs anyway. They handle all the business
their mill client, from advancing capital to selling the finishe
product. Here," he said, reaching for his pen and some pape
"I'm going to write down a few names." For several minute
there was no other sound in the room.

Hazel finished putting her designs back in the portfolio and sli
it down on the floor next to her chair. Then she waited numbl
while Mr. Snow continued to write.

"Take heart, Miss Merriwether," Mr. Snow said, finally hand
ing her the completed list. "You just might have some luck wi
these houses. Please feel free to mention my name if you think
will help. But frankly, I think your designs will speak for them
selves."

His words caught Hazel in the middle of mechanically foldin
the paper and stuffing it into her reticule. Her head shot up. "Yo
do?" she asked incredulously.

"Yes, I do," Mr. Snow answered, looking vaguely surprised b
her amazement. "Didn't I say so? Heavens, don't tell me I wa
so engrossed in my gloomy forecasts that I forgot to tell you
think your designs are truly remarkable."

"You never mentioned it," Hazel murmured, sitting up straight
The numbness was gone. Now every nerve tingled.

"I apologize," he said, tilting his head. "Perhaps I thought
was obvious. You're an extremely talented woman. I think you
designs will make beautiful goods."

"Thank you, Mr. Snow," Hazel said from the edge of her chair
"Thank you very much." Her smile was radiant.

"You're welcome, Miss Merriwether," he replied, also smiling
He held out his hand. "I wish you the best of luck."

Hazel shook his hand, then stood and started for the door, th
cumulative discouragement of the last two days nearly forgotten

Her hand was on the knob when he hailed her again. Turning, she saw him standing behind his desk. "Yes, Mr. Snow?" she asked.

Looking more somber, he said, "I also meant to tell you that I was very sorry to hear about your father."

"You knew Papa?" Hazel exclaimed, taking an astonished step toward him.

"I told you I've been in this business a long time," Mr. Snow answered. He shook his head pensively, as if looking back through the years. "Your father and I started out in wool during the war. He became a knowledgeable broker and as good as his word. What a shame he got pulled down by the current state of affairs."

With another shake of his head, he turned his attention back to Hazel. "That, of course, is the biggest obstacle you have to overcome," he said. "The woeful condition of the wool industry at present."

When Hazel finally left his office, she felt neither effervescent nor daunted, but a stable balance of the two. While reveling in Mr. Snow's compliment, she was realistic about the problems he'd outlined. As he himself had said, though, there were ways around all of them if she was determined. And she was.

By lunchtime on Wednesday that determination was starting to sag again. Not wanting to waste a minute of time, she had boarded the 8:20 A.M. train to Boston and by 9:45 had presented herself and her portfolio at the first commission house on Mr. Snow's list. After an hour of waiting, her reception had been less than overwhelming. At the second house she'd actually opened her portfolio, but hadn't been able to carefully turn the sheets and explain each one. The man she'd been sent to see quickly flicked through them, unconcerned about ruffling the edges of the paper.

"I can't sell these," he complained, shoving them away. "Find me a customer for such fancy stuff first, then come back and see me."

On top of everything else it was considerably warmer than it had been, the kind of sudden spell of heat that May can bring. Inside her gray serge suit she felt as if she were boiling. If she'd known the temperature was going to climb, she would have worn linen. Hot and discouraged, she collapsed on a bench in the Commons to nibble on the sandwich that Agata had stuck in her purse.

As she ate, she glanced absently at a newspaper that the previous occupant of the bench had left behind. Its screaming headline arrested her in mid-bite. MORE THAN 160 DWELLINGS BURNED, it read. TREMENDOUS WAVE OF FLAME ON AND NEAR THE BOSTON BALL GROUNDS. Hazel put her sandwich on the bench and picked up the *Post* instead. With mounting dismay, she read about the fire that had started under the twenty-five-cent seats in the right-field bleachers the preceding afternoon and had rapidly devoured the entire ballpark and almost five blocks of Boston as well.

No one had died, though eight people had been injured, and four hundred others had been left homeless. And the South End Grounds, the site of her brother's youthful dreams, had been demolished. Poor Cornelius, she thought. Wherever he was, he must be grieving. In less than a year he'd lost first his home, then his father. He'd been forced to leave his sister behind and to give up the woman he loved. Now the lone symbol of his boyhood was gone, his last illusion of happiness had burned to the ground.

Dropping the newspaper on top of the forgotten sandwich, Hazel stood up. It wasn't so very different from what had happened to her, she realized. At the very same moment that the ball grounds were burning, she had been sitting in Mr. Snow's office, listening as he exposed her last daydream to the stark light of reality. The thought gave her little cheer. Doggedly, she returned to her rounds.

By four o'clock she'd been to every commission house on the list. Most calls hadn't taken that long, and all the houses were near each other, on or around Summer Street. No one had given her the slightest hope, though one man had shaken his head sadly and said, "If this were two years ago, I might be able to rouse some interest. Not today, though. Not with the industry in the state it's in."

Trudging back toward North Station along Temple Place, she passed by the door to Baily's. All at once she had an overwhelming desire for a butterscotch sundae. The temperature was still high and her spirits were low, and the thought of something cold and sweet was irresistible. Turning so quickly she almost collided with a woman walking behind her, she retraced her steps and entered the ice cream parlor. She knew she shouldn't waste precious pennies, but the temptation was too great. She leaned her portfolio against the wall and slid into a wire-backed chair at a small, round marble table.

Her sundae arrived in a splendid cloud of whipped cream and cherries, set in a fluted glass atop a lacy paper doily. It looked like a confection created in heaven. For the first time that day, Hazel felt a flutter of anticipation. Spoon hovering happily, she was trying to decide where to plunge it when a voice said, "What a coincidence." Simultaneously someone else's trilled, "Hazel!"

Her head jerked up and her spoon hand fell to the table as her heart gave a lurch, then froze. Looming above her was Marco, and on his arm, of all people, was Lucy Whitaker. It took only an instant for two things to happen. The first was for her heart to unfreeze and start racing. The second was for her to cease feebly pretending to herself that she didn't love Marco. Because seeing him in front of her she knew that she did. And always would.

She knew she would always feel a thrill when he entered the room and her breath would always catch when he spoke to her. She knew she would never stop delighting in his magnificent face or reveling in his exuberant embrace of life. She knew that she loved him, but now she doubted that her love was returned.

It caused her more pain than she could possibly imagine to see her former best friend clinging possessively to his arm. And to know he was back in America, but hadn't bothered to call on her in Lawrence. Apparently he preferred to eat ice cream in Boston with a tractable beauty like Lucy. In the same moment that she admitted that she still loved Marco, Hazel also realized she'd lost him.

Swallowing hard, she forced herself to say, "It's a small world, isn't it?" She looked down at her ice cream sundae without really seeing it. She didn't want an answer to her question. She just wanted them to go away. There was a limit to how much disappointment she should have to endure. Surely today she had exceeded it.

Instead of making the obligatory small talk and moving on, though, Marco pulled up two chairs, seated a reluctant Lucy, and sat down himself. "I haven't yet decided if the world is actually small," he said, "or if certain lives are just fated to intertwine. Perhaps there's a magnetic force that pulls people together regardless of their attempts to resist."

"What an idea!" Lucy laughed. "You make us out to be no better than marionettes."

"Perhaps we aren't," Marco mused, propping his elbows on the little table and leaning forward. "What do you think, Hazel?"

Hazel leaned back, determined to resist his particular magnetic force. "Perhaps," she said neutrally.

Marco's eyebrows arched. "Well, I'm glad we've settled that," he said. "Now you can tell me how you've been."

"Perfectly fine, thank you," Hazel answered politely. A whiff of his sandalwood soap drifted under her nose and made her draw her breath sharply.

"And the charming Agata?"

"Also well, thank you."

There was a pause in which Lucy shifted uncomfortably and Marco stared across the table at Hazel. Miserably uncomfortable herself, she refused to meet his eyes.

"Your sundae is melting," Marco finally commented, sitting back. Hazel silently expelled her breath. "Is it butterscotch?" he asked, eyeing it critically. "Don't you find that too sweet? Next time you ought to try hot fudge on coffee ice cream. It's enormously refreshing without being cloying."

"I thought I wanted something sweet," Hazel said, defending her choice. She set the spoon she was still holding on the table and folded her hands in her lap. "I was just walking past the door when the idea jumped into my mind."

"You see?" Marco pounced, sitting forward again. Hazel hastily retreated. "That's proof of my theory. If you had kept on walking, our paths would have missed by inches. Instead, the forces of fate, acting through the intermediary of a butterscotch sundae, drew us together."

Though she still looked away, Hazel could feel him staring intently. Her heat-flushed cheeks turned a deeper pink. What did he want from her? If he didn't love her, why couldn't he leave her alone?

"What a lot of fuss about a bowl of ice cream," Lucy said, pouting. She felt forgotten and didn't like it.

A flash of annoyance crossed Marco's face at her interruption, but Hazel didn't see it as she turned to the dainty blonde, glad for the distraction. "And how have you been, Lucy?" she asked in her best Marlborough Street tone. "It seems ages since I've seen you."

"I've been madly busy," Lucy replied with a delicate wave of her hand. "We've been getting ready to go to Marblehead next month. You know what a whirlwind that is. I've been traipsing back and forth to the dressmaker almost daily. On top of that,

Mother and I decided to redecorate the house at the shore and
now we're bustling to finish it in time for a christening party
or Frederick's new yacht. You know, the first regatta is—" She
stopped abruptly, remembering that Hazel was no longer a part
of that world.

For a moment she wriggled awkwardly, then, unable to control
herself, blurted out, "Don't you miss it?"

"Miss Marblehead?" Hazel considered the question, unperturbed by its lack of tact. "No," she decided, surprised to realize it was true. It had been months since she'd thought about
Marblehead. In fact, she suddenly realized, she no longer missed
her life in Boston, either. Her aimless pursuit of genteel plea-
sures was a thing of the past. She now required more satisfying
endeavors. To be sure, she would gladly welcome a return to
the financial stability she used to enjoy, but only on different
terms.

Shaking her head, she repeated, "No, I don't miss it at all. I
used to enjoy the light by the sea and the sweet smell of wild
roses in the salt air, but there are other lovely places in the world
and more interesting things to do."

Miffed by this response, Lucy's tone turned catty. "I forgot
you went to Scotland last summer," she said. "I suppose you'll
be summering there from now on."

Hot color leaped back into Hazel's cheeks, and she snuck a
quick peek at Marco. He was grinning, immensely enjoying the
joke. Obviously, Lucy still didn't know who he was. It briefly
crossed Hazel's mind to wonder what Frederick's reaction would
be if he could see his sister now, in the company of the "half-caste
sheep farmer" and the fiancée he had disowned. That thought got
pushed aside, though, when Marco spoke.

"They say the Highland hills are glorious in August when the
weather is in bloom," he commented with seeming innocence. "If
you haven't already made your plans, you'd do well to give Scotland some serious thought."

A spark of anger flashed through Hazel. This joke had gone
far enough. Lifting her chin, she stated loftily, "I'll be attending
to business this summer. I won't have time to be idle."

"Business?" Lucy echoed incredulously, her china-blue eyes
wide.

"What business?" Marco demanded, abandoning his guileless
air. He leaned on the marble table again, his expression intent.

Too late Hazel realized the mistake that she had made. Marco never had been one to be silenced by a grand remark, and Lucy was always on the alert for possible gossip. "Just a little business I've started," she said evasively. "Oh, look. Isn't that Marian Chapman?" She peered beyond their shoulders at a familiar figure on the other side of the room. "What a lovely bonnet she's wearing. Do you suppose the cherries are silk or wax?"

It worked for Lucy. She quickly turned to look for her friend and to inspect her hat. Marco, however, was distinctly disinterested in Marian and what was on Marian's head. "What does this little business do?" he asked, without even glancing around. "Who's helping you with it?"

If Marco had stopped after his first question, Hazel might have given another vague answer. But his second question rekindled the anger. "No one is helping me with it," she snapped. "I don't need any help. I'm doing it by myself."

Marco's eyebrows rose. "Very well," he conceded impatiently. "You don't need any help. But what exactly is it that you're doing by yourself?"

On the verge of telling him that it was none of his affair, Hazel caught a glimpse of Lucy's face. Drawn back to her present companions by their heated exchange, she waited for Hazel's answer with an expression of morbid curiosity. Sure that Lucy thought she was washing clothes or scrubbing floors, Hazel sat up straighter and proudly replied, "I'm designing woolen fabrics."

Marco's eyebrows shot up again, this time in admiration, but before he could say anything, Lucy laughed. "Come now, Hazel," she chided. "Don't tell me you call that a business. Surely anyone can decide which bolt will be red and which will be green and which will have navy-blue stripes. I doubt that Father has a designer for his mills."

Though Hazel's hands were clenched in her lap, her voice remained absolutely level. "I'm not concerned with common fabrics, Lucy," she said. "My designs are for fine woolens."

While Lucy looked cross and Hazel looked cool, Marco reached out his long arm and snagged the corner of her portfolio. "Is that what you have in here?" he asked, sliding it toward him. "May I see?"

"No." That one calmly stated word stopped him as still as the slender hand she laid on the other end of the case. For a very quiet moment they stared at each other across the little table, each with hand on the portfolio. From her steady gray eyes and perfect composure, it was impossible to tell that Hazel's heart was beating abnormally fast.

Finally Marco released his hold, in fact, raised both hands in the air. "Very well," he conceded again. "I won't look. But how will I know if they're good?"

If he had hoped to goad her into relenting, this time he had misjudged her mood. Sliding the portfolio back against the wall, she told him, "When the fabrics are on the market, you may choose to buy them or not."

Made cautious by her rebuke, but by no means stopped, Marco leaned back in his chair and folded his arms on his chest. "That sounds positive," he observed. "May I take it, then, that you've had success? When may we expect to see the fruits of your labor?"

Wishing that she had never let herself get pushed this far, Hazel sought to withdraw with as much dignity as possible. "I've only just begun showing the collection," she explained, running her finger along the smooth edge of the marble. "Until now I've been working on the designs themselves. It takes more time than one would suspect to create a single pattern. . . . " Her voice trailed off, and she looked up at her audience.

Marco's eyes were narrowing, and a smile was forming on Lucy's face. Whisking her hand into her lap, Hazel straightened up in her chair. "I have some very good leads, however," she said firmly. When their expressions didn't change, she added more desperately, "In particular, Mr. Snow at the Duck Bridge Mill has expressed great interest in my work."

Though that information didn't affect Marco's scrutiny, at least it wiped away Lucy's smirk. Encouraged, Hazel elaborated. "I'm trying to get a sense of the industry before I commit myself to any one place. It's such a tentative time for wool manufacturers, one has to be extremely circumspect." That gave her an idea.

"It would seem the tariff bill you've been anxiously awaiting has gotten bogged down in the Senate," she said conversationally, directing herself to Marco. "Senator Gorman is having a heyday proposing amendments. At last count there were several hundred and no end in sight."

Only an infinitesimal crinkle in the corner of his eyes showed that Marco knew she was trying to change the subject. "I'm still prepared to take the risk," he said agreeably, allowing his attention to be diverted. "I have faith in its favorable passage. What they're tinkering with now are the ad valorem duties on manufactured goods. So far, no one has appeared unduly exercised about raw wool being on the free list."

"Perhaps not," Hazel rebutted, "but if President Cleveland vetoes the bill, as he's threatened to do, free wool will perish just the same. For better or worse, its fate seems linked to the Sugar Trust."

Marco tipped his head in respect. "You've been informing yourself, haven't you?" he congratulated. "Nonetheless, my Washington sources tell me that Cleveland won't offend his party with a veto. More likely, he'll let the bill become law without his signature."

Cheeks flushed by his compliment, Hazel was ready with another reply, but Lucy broke in. "Wool, wool, wool," she complained. "That's all everyone talks about these days. We can't get through a single meal without Father or Frederick bringing the boring subject up. You'd think there was nothing else in the world but wool."

There was another silence following her outburst. Marco's finger tapped slowly on the table as he watched for Hazel's reaction. Looking down at her hands, now still in her lap, Hazel thought for a moment before she spoke. She remembered a long-ago day on the seat of a pony cart with a silky black dog on her lap. "Wool is the currency of your life, Miss Merriwether," Marco had admonished. How painfully she'd learned he was right.

Finally looking up, she fixed her eyes on Lucy. "There may be other things," she told the pretty blonde, "but in *your* world, there would be very little else without wool."

"Tsch." Annoyed by this remonstration, Lucy turned sharply away from Hazel to rest her gaze on Marco, looking up at him through her lashes. "You promised you'd take me to see the fire," she reminded him.

"The site of the fire," Marco corrected absently, his fingers still drumming. "It's been thoroughly extinguished." He looked at her. "Yes," he acknowledged, "I suppose I did." Turning forward again, he leaned on the table. "Look what a soggy mess this has become," he said, wagging a finger at the sundae. "Eat it up, Hazel, and come with us."

Even if her sympathy for Cornelius weren't still fresh in her mind, there was small likelihood she'd willingly go along on this tour. Hazel hadn't any desire to be the third person who made their company a crowd. "No, thank you," she declined, her calm one again giving no hint of the roil of emotions inside. "I don't wish to see it."

Marco didn't protest. Instead, he asked simply, "What of Cornelius?"

Aware of Lucy's inquisitive stare, Hazel answered simply, "He's fine."

For a minute it looked as if Marco wanted to say something else, but Hazel maintained her impenetrable poise. Shrugging, he pushed himself back from the table. "Are you ready?" he asked Lucy.

In response she stood up. "So nice to see you, Hazel," she trilled, already wending her way through the scattering of tables toward the door.

Marco's eyebrows lifted as he gave the table a final tap and rose. "So nice to see you, Hazel," he echoed with a regretful smile.

Unable to speak, Hazel just nodded. Then, as if the little interruption were over and forgotten, she returned her attention to her sundae and picked up her spoon. As she carried the first melted bite to her mouth, she heard Marco walk away. Her appetite was gone and her throat was tight, but afraid he might glance back, she opened her mouth, slid in the ice cream, and swallowed. He was right again. It was too sweet.

It was all Hazel could do to plod to the station, to buy her ticket, and to board the six o'clock train. She sank into a seat and lolled her head against its back, just as her legs gave out and her eyes closed shut. As the train coughed and bucked and started chugging toward Lawrence, dozens of images drifted across her mind. She saw Marco as he'd been today, leaning across a table, but in a Venetian *osteria* and under a grape arbor in Mantua. She saw him raising his eyebrows on the other side of a bowl of *gelato* in Milan and on the other side of a platter of mutton at Strathdorna Manor. She saw him with a jug of maple syrup tucked under the capes of his coat, with a pepper biscuit in his fingers, with smoked salmon in his bed.

Tears welled up under her closed eyelids and squeezed out through the lashes. Since the day she'd met him, the best moments of her life had been in his presence. The afternoon in Venice, the wool lessons in Scotland, the lunches he'd cooked in her kitchen. He had teased her and comforted her, made her laugh and made her think. He had inspired the passions in her soul. While the rest of her world had crumbled around her, her love for him had grown stronger.

What a waste, she thought. I let those moments slip by. I even resisted them. If I knew then what I know now, it would've been different. I would've reveled in those moments. I would've . . . In her mind she hesitated. Then she admitted it. I would've married him, she thought. Only now it's too late.

Opening her eyes and wiping away the tears before they rolled down her cheeks, Hazel knew that in her foolishness she'd succeeded in chasing Marco away. There were only so many times he could listen to her reject his proposal. Only so many times he would return after her denial of love. Three strikes and you're out. She'd lost him. If not to Lucy, then to somebody else.

Seeing the portfolio lying across her lap, Hazel forlornly untied the strings and peeked inside. It dawned on her then that if she'd married Marco, she never would have made these designs. She would have gone from a life of luxury to a life of luxury, with only a very brief stop in hardship. She never would have had to assess herself and figure out what it took to survive. The responsibility for her life would have been ceded to someone else. Again.

Fingering the beautiful designs between the sheets of tissue, she remembered the tremendous pride and satisfaction she'd felt at their creation. There had been a feeling of accomplishment, a sense that she had plumbed the depths of her being to combine all her talents and knowledge into a useful skill. A sense that she had shaped her own fate.

Hazel closed the portfolio and retied its strings and folded her hands sadly on its top. There was no warm rush inside at the thought. No triumphant sounding of trumpets. No jubilant chorus. She had done what she had fiercely sworn she would do. She had taken control of her life. But it suddenly seemed that without someone she loved to share that life with, it was only half a victory. Life without love wasn't enough.

Sighing, she closed her eyes again. She had chosen to pursue her destiny by herself. Now she had to live with the results. By herself. Well, she thought glumly, at least I have Agata for company.

But when she disembarked from the train and dragged herself home, she was greeted by an empty house.

# CHAPTER
## —•✷ 20 ✷•—

As the train drew closer to Lawrence, Cornelius could see the wall of mills barricading the city, stern and cheerless. Despite the warm May sunshine, a shiver ran through him. Whatever else happened, he was thankful he was no longer cooped up in one of them. It turned his stomach, though, to think of Agata still imprisoned in the foul air and merciless cacophony of the weaving room, shortening her life with every lint-filled breath she took. Either there or crowded into a stinking tenement, scrubbing her new husband's clothes.

He turned abruptly away from the window, unable to endure the images the sight of Lawrence conjured. If the truth be told, that was what had kept him away this long. It caused him unbearable pain to be so close to Agata and yet not be able to be with her. Worse, to be visibly reminded of the misery of her existence and to know that he was helpless to give her any comfort.

Not that he'd really been able to afford to come back. Until a few weeks ago he'd been living from hand to mouth, finding odd jobs during the day and paying two bits for a bed and a blanket every night. The money he'd sent to Hazel had been arduously scraped together. In between those paltry offerings there had been some desperately meager times.

Still and all, he was just as glad to be away from Lawrence. The only thing that troubled him was that he was out of touch with his sister. It would have eased his mind, and his conscience, too, if he'd been able to supply Hazel with an address to which she could

write. He would have liked reading her letters and imagining h
was listening to her calm voice.

But though he'd missed her a lot, and felt guilty about the scan
notes that had accompanied the money, he hadn't been seriousl
worried about her welfare. She was a lot more capable than she'
been a year ago. This crisis had seemed, somehow, to give he
strength. Besides, there was always Frederick. However much h
disliked his future brother-in-law, Cornelius was sure Frederic
could be trusted to help.

Yesterday's fire, though, had thrown things into a different light
Seeing the terrible devastation it had wreaked in a matter of minute
had given him a sobering reminder of the fragility of life. He'd bee
through fire before when his father's warehouse had burned, whe
not only a business had been destroyed, but also the man who buil
it. That fire had been the beginning of the end for Edgar and ha
changed forever the course of Cornelius's life.

After yesterday's destruction he was overtaken by the urge t
talk to Hazel. Sticking a letter in a mail slot and waiting three o
four days for an answer simply wouldn't do. He had to see he
in person, had to reassure himself she was still there. He had t
give her a hug and plant a kiss in her hair.

She was the last person in the world he was really close to
Sure, there were the fellows he played ball with, and he like
Marco a lot, but Hazel was his sister. His entire family. Feelin
shaken and vulnerable, he'd asked for the day off, and Mr. Selee
feeling shaken himself, had given it to him.

Now, descending from the train, those feelings were on th
verge of being overwhelmed by the painful memories of Agata
As he walked to the house on Maple Street, that sense grew mor
forceful. He caught himself looking around, hungrily, for a familia
freckled face, then felt cold inside when he realized the futility
Head down, he continued walking, trying to ignore the atmospher
of tenements and immigrants that pervaded the city and provide
such a vivid reminder of Agata.

Once, though, he heard a voice call out "*Buon giorno, signora,*"
and looking up, he saw the back of a small woman with a pair o
black braids wrapped around her head. His heart leaped in hope
and he felt himself burn hot. His hand reached out, propelled by
longing. The next moment the woman turned and he saw her face
It was old and haggard and drained of life. As quickly as his hear
had started racing, it froze. His hand dropped.

Great though his disappointment was, it seemed mild compared with the depression that gripped him next. When he thought about the years of drudgery Agata would have to live through to end up looking like that old woman, it was almost more than he could stand. He actually turned around and was ready to run back to the railroad station, to flee forever from Lawrence. Only when he remembered he was here to see Hazel could he make himself turn again and keep going.

When his soft rap on the front door brought no response, he opened it and entered. The narrow, dark hall with its peeling paper was empty and silent, though from within he heard the faint sound of water running. Tossing his straw hat on a vacant peg, he went through the dining room on his way to the kitchen. Despite his grim thoughts of a few minutes before, a smile began to brighten his face. She'll be surprised, he thought, imagining Hazel's astonishment. Then he stepped through the doorway. He halted instantly as his heart stopped and his mind went blank.

Instead of his sister's tall elegant form, he saw a sturdy little person standing at the sink. Two crinkly black braids hung down her back and were tied at her neck with a ribbon. This was no old woman worn out by life. No mirage on the corner of the street.

"Agata?" he whispered just as she sensed his presence and turned to have a look. "Agata!" he cried as her eyes opened wide and she flew across the kitchen into his arms. "Agata," he murmured, crushing her close to him and pressing his lips against her head.

"Agata, Agata," he repeated, hardly believing the warm body in his arms was real. He ran his hands down her back and rubbed his cheek in her hair, reveling in the pleasure it gave him. It was like holding a dream, like having his deepest desire fulfilled. Stroking her, caressing her, feeling her hands tightly circle his neck, the months of anguish inside him disappeared.

Then she lifted her head, and he saw the dear, round face that he loved was flushed and streaked with tears. "What's wrong?" he demanded, suddenly seized by fear. Panic filled his throat.

"*Niente*," she answered, twining her fingers in his hair. Her wet cheeks bunched as she smiled. "Now everything is perfect, *caro mio*. I'm just too happy, so I cry."

The panic vanished and his heart felt so full he thought it would burst. "Not happier than I am," he told her as he lowered his head, thrilled when her eager lips met his. Their kiss was long and deep and filled with joy, and they clung to each other as if they'd never let go.

# CHAPTER
## ❦ 21 ❦

Bewildered, Hazel walked through the house again. It was unlike Agata not to be home waiting for her. On her second tour of the kitchen, Hazel looked more intently for some clue to Agata's absence. Nothing. Everything was as neat as a pin. As Hazel unfastened her hat and shrugged out of her jacket, she chewed her lip in puzzlement.

The thought crossed her mind that Agata might have gone to the store for a forgotten ingredient, but that idea was discarded almost immediately. Agata never bought anything without first explaining its absolute necessity. Besides, there was no sign of interrupted food preparation. It next crossed Hazel's mind that Agata's father may have tracked her down and come to claim her. That thought caused considerably more alarm.

She was just about to go ask Mrs. O'Sullivan if she had noticed any unusual activity, when she heard the front door close. Relieved, Hazel dumped her hat and jacket on the table and collapsed on a chair, her temporary worry yielding to her fatigue. A moment later Agata came bounding into the kitchen. And Cornelius was hard on her heels.

For a fraction of an instant Hazel just sat there, astonishment striking her dumb. Then she leaped up, crying, "Cornelius!" and her brother, laughing, swung her into a hug. Once again her low spirits vanished, replaced this time by delight. When Cornelius finally set her down, Hazel hung on to his hands and told him, "I'm so glad you're here."

"So am I," Cornelius said, smiling and giving her hands a squeeze. His eyes slid over to Agata and the brackets around his smile deepened.

Following his eyes, Hazel saw the excitement on Agata's face. She also saw her sunburned nose and the disarray of her hair, as if she'd been outside running. Another glance at her brother gave Hazel the same impression. Then she remembered Agata telling her about their Sunday afternoon ritual. They'd probably gone to their baseball diamond for a few commemorative innings. Looking back and forth, Hazel saw something even stronger. She saw utter devotion and love.

A wave of melancholy broke the bubble of jubilation within her. In the presence of such obvious intimacy, Hazel felt alone and excluded. Cornelius and Agata had each other to share their lives with, but she was all by herself. The desolation lasted only a moment, though, before she resolutely pushed it away. After all, this was exactly the happy ending she had wished for her brother and friend. Just because she was foolish enough to have chased away the man she loved didn't mean everyone else should have to suffer.

Forcing herself to smile, she said, "We should do something special to celebrate. Maybe we'll have an extravagant dinner. How does that sound?" Without waiting for an answer, she went on, building genuine eagerness as she spoke. "Agata is a wonderful cook," she told Cornelius. "So this will really be a treat. What would you like to eat? Veal chops? Salmon? Pick whatever you fancy. There's just enough time to run to the store. I think we even have a bottle of wine left. Let me check."

Disengaging her hands, she went over to the cupboard and would have started rummaging through its contents if Cornelius hadn't stopped her. "Don't bother, sis," he said regretfully. "I can't stay for dinner. In fact, I've got to get going right now."

Arrested as she was reaching to look behind the canister of coffee, Hazel turned to stare, her arms still lifted in the air. "Where on earth are you going?" she asked, amazed. Had she been mistaken about the devotion she thought she saw? "You only just got here."

"I got here this morning," Cornelius corrected gently. "Our trains must have passed midway. Now I've got to get back to Boston in time to grab my satchel and be on the night train to Philadelphia."

Hazel's arms dropped. "Do you have to go so far?" she asked, disappointed. "Is it because you have the promise of some work?"

The brackets around his grin started to reappear. "You migh{ say that," Cornelius answered.

Mystified, Hazel cocked her head. "What does that mean?" sh{ asked. "Do you or don't you have a job?"

"I do," Cornelius replied, his grin getting even broader.

"Well, what is it?" Hazel demanded, exasperated by his eva{ siveness. She jammed her hands on her hips. "And why do yo{ have to go to Philadelphia to do it?"

"Because I'm on the mound tomorrow," Cornelius said. The{ he could contain his glee no longer. "Sis," he exulted, "I'm { pitcher for Boston."

Hazel's hands flew off her hips and clapped together under he{ chin. "Cornelius, that's marvelous!" she exclaimed. "It's wha{ you've always wanted. You must be treading on air."

In response Cornelius moved over behind Agata and wrappe{ his long arms around her little body. "I am now," he said. Whe{ Agata turned her face up, smiling, he put a kiss on her nose.

"I just tried out on a whim," he explained, looking back t{ Hazel. "I didn't have anything else to do, and I'd been gettin{ a lot of practice this spring. When Mr. Selee signed me, I wa{ pleased enough and I've had a grand time playing. But that wil{ elation I always imagined I would have was somehow missing{ Do you know when I finally felt it?"

"When?" Hazel asked dutifully, though she thought she alread{ knew.

"When Agata promised to marry me as soon as I come bac{ from this trip." He gave the happy girl in his arms a hug. "Havin{ her makes all the difference in how I feel about playing ball. An{ everything else, too."

"I understand," Hazel said softly, feeling another waft of melan{ cholia. She had identified it herself only an hour ago. Life withou{ love wasn't enough. Now her brother had both.

"Say," Cornelius continued more guiltily, "I'm sorry I haven'{ written or come sooner. We were on the road until last Friday{ and I didn't get paid until Monday."

Rousing herself from her lonely reflections, Hazel smiled fondly{ "Don't worry about it," she said. "What matters is that you're her{ now."

"Oh, no," Cornelius said, suddenly remembering his train an{ letting go of Agata. "I'm not here now. I've got to run." He shove{ his hand into his pocket, pulled out a handful of bills, and tosse{

them on the table. Then he hurried to kiss both Hazel and Agata before he went racing out the door. "I'll be back in two weeks!" he shouted over his shoulder.

"Happy?" Hazel asked Agata with a smile after Cornelius had gone.

Agata's answering smile was so bright it lit up the entire room. "*Molto*," she said. "*Moltissimo*." Grabbing Hazel by the hand, she led her in an impromptu dance.

The money that Cornelius had tossed on the table wasn't exactly a fortune, but it certainly was a blessing. Hazel's other funds were nearly depleted. What hadn't been spent on rent and food had gone for paints and paper. Relieved as she was to have the wolf staved away from the door, though, it didn't diminish Hazel's need to sell her designs. While it was no longer a financial necessity, her self-esteem was at stake.

She had chosen to take control of her fate at great and painful expense. Determined not to let her life be bought, she had given up Marco. She wasn't about to let that sacrifice be wasted just because the roof over her head was paid for. Besides, however much she loved Cornelius and Agata, the idea of being the spinster auntie in their household wasn't hugely appealing.

"This doesn't change anything," she informed Agata as she reviewed her portfolio, carefully turning each sheet.

"No, of course not," Agata agreed. Although for her, everything was changed. These days she was practically floating. She hummed as she peeled potatoes.

"I still have to find a buyer for my work." Hazel stopped at the green brocade and ran her fingers, lightly, over the ferns and violets. "I can't just stick them under the bed and pretend I never made them." She studied the design for a moment more then looked up at Agata. "Can I?" she asked a little anxiously.

"No, no," Agata assured her, pushing the peels aside and starting to slice the potatoes. "They are too beautiful to put under the bed. Also"—she glanced at Hazel and nodded wisely—"it makes you happy to draw and paint."

"It's true," Hazel admitted, looking back at the brocade and remembering not only the afternoon in the Scottish woods, but the pleasure she'd had in interpreting it on paper. "I've gotten more satisfaction from doing these designs than from anything else I've ever done. They aren't just pretty pictures, you know," she told Agata, whose eyes flicked away from the pile of potatoes to give the design a quick inspection. "They have a purpose."

"*Si*." Agata nodded again. "Woolen goods."

"Woolen goods, yes," Hazel confirmed. "But they also represent a means to earn my own way."

"*Brava*," Agata approved. Pushing aside the potatoes, she went to work on the carrots. As she briskly scraped their skins, she snuck a peek at Hazel. "How you going to make them do that?" she asked.

"Aha." Hazel gave a rueful laugh. "That's the rub. How indeed." Shoving the portfolio out of the way, she propped an elbow on the table and leaned her head against her hand. "There are still a few commission houses on the list," she said, thinking out loud. "They're all in New York, except for one in Philadelphia. I suppose I could write to them explaining what I have."

"Good."

"And I suppose while I'm writing, I might send letters to a few of the big fashion houses. Maybe they would be interested in telling the mills what they want instead of vice versa."

"Good," Agata said again.

"I should look through *Harper's Bazaar* to see if I can find addresses."

For a few minutes there was silence as Agata continued to scrape and Hazel continued to think. Finally Hazel spoke, still speculating. "Mr. Snow might have a few more ideas hidden in his head," she said. "I wonder if I dare go back and see him?"

"I think you do dare," Agata decided, starting to chop the carrots.

Laughing again, Hazel looked across at her loyal supporter. "I've become very brazen. Is that what you're trying to say?"

"I don't know brazen," Agata answered, shrugging. "But I think you have *molto corragio*."

"*Corragio?*" Hazel questioned. "Is that courage?"

"*Si*. Courage."

Despite Agata's assessment, Hazel wasn't sure she was quite courageous enough to ask Mr. Snow for more help. Instead, she wrote to the names she had, or was able to glean from magazines. She spent two days doing it, laboriously composing just the right letters, then neatly copying them, sealing them, and bringing them to the post. Then she waited for replies.

A week went by. None came. Hazel's hope started to fade. Another four days passed. Finally the mailman dropped a letter through the slot. It was from a decorating house in New York. While Agata fidgeted excitedly by her side, Hazel opened it. Her hands were shaking slightly, and she found herself holding her breath. As she read the message inside, though, she slowly expelled. It was a rejection. Turning to Agata, she tried to make light of it. "The fortunes of war," she said.

"What does that mean?" Agata demanded, snatching the letter from Hazel and straining to read it. Unable to do so, she thrust it back. "Tell me what it says."

"It says they aren't interested in seeing my work."

"*Idioti*," Agata said scornfully.

When the next day again brought no responses, Hazel decided that courage or no, it was time to go see Mr. Snow. She was rapidly running out of options. All the way to the Duck Bridge Mill she rehearsed her speech, polishing phrases until she struck the appropriate tone. Needing some assistance, but not desperate.

Her practice was in vain, however. When she reached the mill, the office was locked. Mr. Snow had prophesied correctly. The business had gone bankrupt. Truly despairing, Hazel returned home.

That evening she was distracted by Cornelius's return, flushed with victory after beating both Philadelphia and Pittsburgh. "It's my twisters," he told them. "They even fooled Big Ed Delahanty, and he's last year's batting champ. This year he's hitting four hundred."

"Pff." Agata dismissed that awesome statistic. No man was too great for her Cornelius. "Your fast ball is very good, too," she reminded him. "And you have a slow drop on the outside corner that is a beauty."

While Cornelius laughed in delight, Hazel shook her head in amazement. Agata really was the perfect match for her brother. Not only did she inspire him and admire him, she loved baseball. Though still somewhat envious, Hazel was touched.

The distraction lasted all the next week as Hazel helped Agata prepare for her wedding. It was going to be a very simple ceremony, with only Hazel in attendance, followed by lunch for the three of them at the Shawsheen House. Then Cornelius would have to dash for the 1:15 train because there was a 3:30 game to be played in Boston. "Still and all," Hazel decided, "every bride should have a special dress." Although Agata felt that her entire wardrobe was a miracle, she allowed Hazel to cut down a gown of pale yellow silk on which she lovingly fastened the tiny gold and garnet pin that Cornelius had given her for Christmas.

It was only after the wedding and after Cornelius started daily commuting that Hazel's despair returned full force. Her brother talked about moving them all back to Boston. It was closer to the ball field and, really, why did they need to stay in Lawrence? Agata had gone to see her mother to ask her to come to the wedding, but her mother had kissed her cheek and said she couldn't. There was nothing to keep them there.

Hazel knew it was the practical solution, but the idea filled her with dread. It was awkward enough living with the newly married couple in a house, however dismal, that was *her* home. She didn't want to think what it would be like losing even that last, small dignity.

Redoubling her efforts, she visited mills she hadn't tried, and instead of just stating her purpose, she attempted to talk the agents into taking a chance on her designs. She composed more letters, writing to everyone she could think of, from dressmakers to clothing manufacturers. On a whim she even wrote to Worth of Paris. No responses.

Dragging back one hot June day, she passed the postman on the corner of Elm and Lawrence. She forced a smile and would have kept trudging if he hadn't touched his cap and said, "Left a letter for you today, Miss Merriwether."

Hazel straightened up instantly, her heart leaping in hope. "Thank you very much," she remembered to say before almost running the rest of the way home. Don't get so excited, she cautioned herself as she hurried along. It's probably just another rejection. Despite that admonition, she skipped every few steps and her heart refused to stop hammering.

Agata was waiting on the steps, the letter clutched in her hand. "What is it? What is it?" she asked, waving the envelope when Hazel was still twenty feet away. "What does it say?"

"I don't know," Hazel said, laughing as she came up the steps and pushed Agata through the door. "Let's go inside and read it."

"Who's it from?" Agata demanded, handing the letter over her shoulder as she raced down the hall for the kitchen.

Taking it and peering at the return address, Hazel answered, "The West Atlantic Mill?" She slowed down, truly puzzled. "I never wrote to them," she said, examining the envelope again. "I've never even heard of them."

She tossed her portfolio on the dining room table as she went past, then carried the letter into the kitchen and sank into a chair. While Agata watched anxiously, Hazel opened the envelope, pulled out the paper inside, unfolded it, and scanned the page. Her eyes opened wide.

"What?" Agata cried. "Tell me."

Incredulous, Hazel read every word out loud. "Lawrence, Massachusetts. June twenty-seventh, 1894," she read. "Dear Miss Merriwether, As I hoped, my small favor to you last month was richly repaid. I am now the agent for a new enterprise, the West Atlantic Mill Corporation.

"If you have not already placed your designs, we may be able to help each other again. I would appreciate the opportunity to meet with you, at your convenience.

"I look forward to your reply, and I remain, Respectfully Yours, Horace Snow."

Hazel looked up at Agata, at a loss for another word, and for a moment Agata was speechless in both English and Italian. Then they burst out laughing, and Agata found her voice. "*Ce l'hai fatto!*" she exclaimed. "You did it!"

"Not so fast," Hazel protested, though she couldn't stop grinning. "I haven't done anything yet. For all I know, he may just want to chat in the ephemeral hope that we'll pass some good luck back and forth. Or maybe he remembered a name that he forgot to put on the list. Maybe even some place I've discovered on my own. So you see," she concluded, waving her hand, "it may be nothing at all."

"I don't think it's nothing," Agata maintained. "I think it's a home run."

Laughing again, Hazel said, "We'll see."

Despite her studied skepticism, it was hard for Hazel to keep from snatching up her portfolio and bolting out the door. As it was, she barely took the time to remove her hat before getting out her stationery to write an answering note. Ever mindful of appearing too eager, she suggested an appointment for the following week, Monday, the second of July.

Friday's post brought a letter of confirmation, and Hazel spent the weekend in a state of nervous anticipation. "You should have gone at once," Agata fretted. She relieved her own agitation by making miles of spaghetti, which she hung around the kitchen to dry. With Cornelius on the road, it was impossible for them to consume it all fresh.

Monday morning finally came, and at ten A.M., punctually, looking elegant and composed, Hazel presented herself at the West Atlantic Mill. It was the Duck Bridge Mill, with a new sign above the door. Today there was no waiting on benches or dealing with indifferent clerks. Today she was shown instantly and courteously into Mr. Snow's office.

"Miss Merriwether," he said, rising to greet her. "What a pleasure to see you again. I've begun to think of you as my lucky charm."

Although Hazel smiled and shook his hand, her hopes plunged at his words. Her suspicion had been justified after all. She took a deep breath to steady her voice. "I'm delighted that things have been resolved for you," she said, without a hint of the disappointment she felt. "How fortunate that the mill should be revived by new owners. At least, that's what I presume has happened," she added hastily.

"Absolutely correct, Miss Merriwether," Mr. Snow reassured her, coming around the desk to hold out a chair. Hazel sat down. "The West Atlantic Mill Corporation bought up the mill, lock, stock, and barrel, as it were, including many of the old employees. It intends to continue the Duck Bridge Mill's worsted manufacture for the short term. However, for the long term, its plan is quite different. That's why I've asked you here. I'm glad to see you've brought your portfolio."

With these words Hazel's spirit started to climb back up. "You've intrigued me," she said as Mr. Snow settled himself on his side of the desk. "What precisely do these plans entail?"

"Simply put," Mr. Snow answered, folding his hands on his blotter and leaning forward, "the corporation intends to produce fancy woolen goods."

For a moment Hazel was so stunned she couldn't think of a thing to say. It was as if her most fervent wish had been granted. As if her fairy godmother had waved her magic wand. Only with tremendous effort could Hazel suppress her utter excitement. Willing herself to be businesslike, she said calmly, "I'm even more intrigued."

"I thought you might be," Mr. Snow said with a smile. "There aren't a great many mills capable of this kind of production."

"I've discovered that for a fact," Hazel responded, unable to stop a giddy laugh from escaping. "Your news is heaven-sent. It's almost . . . " On the verge of blurting out its perfection, another thought struck her, instantly deflating her euphoria. "It's almost too good to be true," she finished more soberly.

Suddenly cautious, she mused, "Given the problems you outlined the last time we spoke, the small runs, the expensive stock, and so forth, I have to wonder why such a venture is being attempted. Especially in the middle of a depression."

Unruffled, Mr. Snow replied, "That's a valid question. However, for every rule there are exceptions. Let me see if I can explain." He swept an imaginary speck of dust from the blotter, then refolded his hands.

"As you might know, the Wilson tariff bill, which should pass Congress any day now, will put raw wool on the free list and lower the ad valorem duty on finished goods. The fact that raw wool will come in cheaply would be a boon for this sagging industry, if it weren't for the fact that, with the same stroke of the pen, European woolens and worsteds will also be less costly. The market will be flooded with inexpensive imports, which will further debilitate our American manufacture."

When he paused, Hazel said, "You paint a very grave picture." Her first spark of doubt was becoming stronger. "It more than ever leaves me wondering why someone would want to start up a mill in this bleak situation."

"Because of the exception to the rule," Mr. Snow told her, aligning his letter opener and pen. Nothing was out of place on his desk. Satisfied, he leaned back in his chair and steepled his hands under his chin.

"It's the corporation's thought that the manufacture of luxury woolens will be this exception," he went on. "It feels that the consumers of fancy goods are not as interested in saving nickels and dimes as they are in obtaining quality pieces. With the free list making the finer foreign stock more available, the corporation is convinced that it can manufacture a product that will give the European woolens stiff competition."

"An interesting theory," Hazel murmured, her doubt beginning to dissolve. What Mr. Snow said made sense.

The agent nodded. "The corporation is backing its belief in that theory with a serious financial investment. Special looms have been ordered from England, and arrangements are being made to bring some master weavers here to train our operatives. They've even instructed me to offer wages nearly double the accepted standard in order to attract and retain a highly skilled and motivated work force."

Dipping her head, Hazel acknowledged, "Very impressive." Maybe this was true after all. A tiny hope again took root.

"The only thing lacking for the production of these goods is the design."

As Hazel inhaled sharply, that tiny hope grew huge.

Mr. Snow leaned forward. "When the corporation outlined its plan, I immediately thought of you. I remembered that not only were your designs exceptional, your choice of fibers was as well. You seem to have an instinct for this particular manufacture."

Hazel opened her mouth to reply, but no sound came out. Clearing her throat, she tried again. "Am I to understand," she asked, a trifle unsteadily, "that you're interested in buying some of my designs?"

"Not exactly," Mr. Snow answered, realigning his letter opener and pen.

The pounding in Hazel's heart stopped cold.

"It would be more accurate to say I'm interested in commissioning a collection of designs. The corporation, quite rightly, I believe, wants to present a line of goods that represents a consistent aesthetic sense rather than a random sampling of tastes." Mr. Snow paused and looked across the desk at Hazel. "Are you still intrigued, Miss Merriwether?" he asked.

Hazel had to swallow hard before she could answer. "Very," she finally said, sitting at the edge of the chair.

Mr. Snow nodded again. "There is one small problem," he admitted.

Despite the warm day, Hazel felt her skin turn icy.

"I spoke to the board of directors about you," he continued slowly. His gaze flicked away from her face. "It seems they have some fellow they favor. But I saw his work," he added more quickly. "It's nothing extraordinary. And I'm convinced that the success of this venture depends heavily on having outstanding designs."

"Surely they have to understand that," Hazel said desperately, seeing her last chance about to disappear.

"They do understand that part," Mr. Snow said, still not looking directly at her. "The problem is, you see . . ." He hesitated, his cheeks turning bright pink. "You're a woman," he finished rapidly.

This time Hazel couldn't suppress her gasp. "Why should that be problem?" she asked in shock. "If anything, I should think it would e an advantage. After all, women are the ultimate purchasers of the oods. Who better than a woman to know what they would like?"

"I agree with you," Mr. Snow said. He sounded embarrassed. But you must understand the corporation's concern. Business projections set a long course. The directors are afraid you'll jump ship idway to marry and raise a family."

The nervous emotion that had been tensing Hazel suddenly rained away. An unexpected sadness filled her as she fell back gainst her chair. "If that's their chief fear," she said quietly, "you ay tell the directors not to worry. There's little danger of that appening."

Looking relieved, Mr. Snow said, "I think that information will ase their minds. Although," he added, his cheeks flaming again, I find it difficult to comprehend for a woman of your beauty and alent." It was his turn to clear his throat then, as he put that elicate business behind him.

"Now," he went on in a surer tone, "the only thing that remains s for me to show your work to the directors. They meet on Thursday n Boston."

Of all the reactions Hazel had had in this dizzying dialogue, he hadn't felt any distrust. Until this moment. "Do you mean ou want me to leave my portfolio with you?" she asked, slowly itting erect again.

"Well, yes," Mr. Snow answered, puzzled by the question.

Before she spoke, Hazel thought for a moment, carefully choosing er words. "Mr. Snow," she said, holding her hands still in her lap, what guarantee do I have that if my designs are produced, I will et the credit?"

"Ah." The agent's hands lifted in a gesture of understanding. "I ee your apprehension. And find it perfectly reasonable." He rubbed is chin between his thumb and forefinger while he considered the ilemma.

Finally he said, "I'm willing to give you a receipt listing each esign that you're leaving. Also a letter stating that if any of the esigns are produced without prior contract, you will be entitled o a commission. Will that be satisfactory?"

For the first time since this interview began, Hazel felt relaxed. "Yes, it will," she said, sitting back in her chair again and smiling.

For several minutes there was only the sound of a pen scratchi
as Mr. Snow worked up the list and the letter. Then he blotted ther
folded them, and handed them to Hazel. "Any other questions
concerns?" he asked.

"Yes," she said. "When can I expect a response?"

"Friday morning," Mr. Snow answered promptly. "If it's co
venient for you, why not come again at ten?"

Hazel stood. "Ten o'clock on Friday morning," she confirme
holding out her hand. "Thank you, Mr. Snow. I'll see you then

"I look forward to it," Mr. Snow replied, shaking her pro
fered hand.

She was halfway to the door before she suddenly turned. "O
more thing, Mr. Snow."

"Yes?" Misgiving flashed across the agent's face.

"In your letter you said that we might be able to help ea
other. It's obvious how you are helping me, but how will I he
you?"

Mr. Snow's face cleared. "Simple," he answered, smiling. "M
tenure at the West Atlantic Mill will be determined by its succe
or failure. As I told you before, I feel that its fortune is tied to th
excellence of its designs. I would sleep more soundly if I kne
you were in charge of that department."

Extremely lightheaded, Hazel turned again and left.

If the previous weekend had seemed interminable, the days unt
Friday were worse. Time crawled by as Hazel awaited the fatef
decision. During the day she wandered aimlessly around the hous
unable to concentrate on any activity. At night she tossed restless
in her bed. What little sleep she did manage was disturbed by da
and ominous images.

From a haze of cigar smoke, the board of directors appeare
Scowling men in somber suits with gold watch chains stretche
across protruding bellies. Fingers wagging, they advanced on he
demanding that she tell the truth about being married. They cam
closer and closer until, terrified, Hazel confessed. She turned
take her husband's arm, but standing there was Frederick, n
Marco. As she stared in horror, a gunshot rang out, and Haz
sat bolt upright sobbing.

"Wake up! Wake up!" a voice insisted. "It's only *un incubo*.

Hazel opened her eyes and saw Agata leaning over her bed, h
freckled brow furrowed in worry. With a gasp of relief, Hazel fe

ack on the pillow. "Thank heaven it's you," she said fervently.
I was having the most awful dream."

"*Un incubo*," Agata agreed.

"Yes, a nightmare." Hazel massaged her temples with shaky
ands. "And then I heard a gun."

Agata sat down on the edge of the bed. "No guns," she said.
Firecrackers. Remember? Today is the Fourth of July."

"Of course. That's what it was." Her relief was even greater.

"Get up," Agata urged, tugging Hazel's arm. "I'll make us a
ood American breakfast with pancakes and bacon and coffee,
hen we'll go see the parade."

Giving a little laugh, Hazel allowed herself to be pulled up.
The parade will be a welcome diversion," she acknowledged,
but if you don't mind, I'll forego the pancakes and bacon. My
tomach is a touch nervous."

"Mine, too," Agata confessed. "I'll make tea and toast instead."

The parade did distract her for a while. As did the events that took
place in the Common afterward. Drinking lemonade and watching
he sprints and dashes and three-legged races helped Wednesday
go by. Somehow she got through Thursday.

Friday morning at exactly ten o'clock, Hazel again arrived at
he West Atlantic Mill. Though still elegant and composed, there
vere faint shadows underneath her eyes. They gave her a slightly
ragic air. She was shown into Mr. Snow's office immediately.

"Good morning, Miss Merriwether," the agent greeted her as
e came around his desk to hold out her chair.

"Good morning, Mr. Snow," she responded, sinking gracefully
nto the seat.

"I trust you had an enjoyable holiday?" he asked, returning to
is own chair.

Hazel thought about her endless days and tortured nights. "Quite
njoyable, thank you," she replied. "I hope yours was, too."

"Indeed." Mr. Snow folded his hands on the blotter in front of
im. "Well," he said. "Shall we get directly to business?"

The first time Hazel tried to answer him, her words got lost in
er throat. The second time she managed to say, "Yes, please."
Then she held her breath.

"The board of directors has empowered me to offer you a con-
ract."

Her breath came out in a rush. For a moment Hazel felt as though
he were going to faint. Her head was banging and her vision

danced and it seemed as if Mr. Snow were miles away. When eventually, her mind began to clear, one thought kept drumming loudly. I did it.

Getting no response to his statement, Mr. Snow leaned forward. "I hope you haven't changed your mind, Miss Merriwether," he said anxiously. "In reflecting on the project these past few days, did you, perhaps, decide it didn't interest you?"

That forced Hazel to draw herself together. "Oh, no, Mr. Snow," she reassured him. "I'm still very interested in the project." Then she made her pulse stop pounding and instructed herself to concentrate. More calmly she added, "Shall we discuss the terms of the contract?"

Over the next two hours they discussed not only the contract but every other detail of the arrangement as well. It was to be Hazel's responsibility to provide a collection of designs, ranging in suitability from sheer to heavy woolens. Seven of her present designs would serve as the base. Each design was to be presented in three or more combinations of colors, to be repeated throughout the collection.

It was also her responsibility to supervise the transfer of her designs to weaving drafts and layouts, making sure her artistic intent survived the technical translation. She was to confer with the wool buyer, specifying the type and grade of each fiber required. Most important, she was to work with the head dyer to achieve exactly the color she envisioned.

In return for all this, Hazel was to receive ten dollars for each design she delivered. As soon as production started in September she would, in addition, receive three percent of every yard sold. When she finally left the mill at noon, her head was in the clouds. And in the purse that dangled from her wrist lay a check for two hundred and fifty dollars. Mr. Snow called it a good faith bonus. Hazel called it proof that she'd taken control of her fate.

"Quick, Agata!" she cried, dashing into the house twenty minutes later. "Change your clothes. We have to catch the one-fifteen to Boston."

In the midst of kneading mounds of bread dough to ease the jitters of waiting, Agata jumped when Hazel burst through the kitchen door. "What?" she asked, startled by Hazel's sudden appearance and confused by her urgent orders. "My clothes?" she looked at her flour-smudged skirt. "Boston?" She looked back at Hazel's face. It was radiant.

"What?" she said again, this time demanding. "What happened? What did they say? Why are we going to Boston? Tell me."

"We are going to Boston," Hazel replied, "to purchase paints and paper and brushes." She pulled the check out of her reticule and held it up. "The finest that money can buy," she added grandly. Then she started laughing.

"*Ce l'hai fatto!*" Agata shouted, hurrying around the table to catch Hazel in an exultant embrace.

Still laughing, Hazel returned the hug. "Yes," she agreed. "I did it."

By three o'clock they left the art supply store, laden down with packages. Not yet ready to go back to Lawrence, they went to Jordan Marsh, where Hazel bought each of them a summer bonnet. Then she took the increasingly awed Agata on a carriage tour of Boston, driving past the Congress Street Grounds, the temporary home of the Beaneaters, and past the house on Marlborough Street where she and Cornelius used to live. Surprisingly, Hazel felt hardly a twinge.

They ended the tour in front of Baily's and went in to have sundaes. Hazel ordered hot fudge with coffee ice cream and had to admit that Marco was right once again. It was delicious. For the first time since she left the mill, Hazel felt a shadow creep across her good mood. Seeing her old house hadn't caused her a bit of sorrow, but thinking about Marco did. They caught the six o'clock train home.

The next morning Hazel started drawing. And continued drawing and painting all summer. Occasionally she went to the mill to meet with Mr. Snow or with the wool buyer or the draftsmen. Several times she talked to the dyer, bringing him samples of colors so he could start blending his powders.

She spent hours every day in her chair at the kitchen table, creating designs for luxurious woolens. Sometimes it was hard to think about winter fabrics when her sleeves were rolled up against the summer heat. Then she would sit back in her chair and listen to Agata singing Italian love songs as she stuffed manicotti with cheese or ironed her husband's uniforms.

When he wasn't playing in other cities, Cornelius came home every evening. Unless the game went into extra innings and he missed the last train. Just as the sky was fading, they would sit down to dinner, laughing and talking, recounting the day's events.

Cornelius always had a good story or two, and Agata always ha
something delicious to eat. No longer feeling like the third stockin
in a pair, Hazel basked in the family warmth.

In fact, she hadn't been so happy in a long, long time. But unlik
the complacent contentment that used to cocoon her, this sense ha
its base in the satisfaction and self-esteem she'd discovered since
There was no more talk of moving to Boston. Now they had t
consider Hazel's career. They vaguely discussed finding a bette
house, and maybe, come winter, they would. For the moment
though, life seemed fine as it was. Cornelius's dream had com
true, Agata's had been exceeded, and Hazel had not only realize
she was entitled to one of her own, she'd built it from scratch an
was fulfilling it.

There was an empty space, though, an ache in the bottom of he
heart, and Hazel knew very well what it was. Life without love
wasn't enough. Every day that passed, every design she drew
brought memories of Marco flooding into her mind. She had onl
to close her eyes to see him standing in a fresco-filled room in Mantu
or striding through the Highland heather with Roger running circle
around him. Each time she made herself open her eyes, hoping tha
soon those images, and the ache, would diminish.

# CHAPTER

## 22

Hazel, may I ask something for you?" Agata paused in the middle of sweeping the kitchen.

"Of me," Hazel corrected automatically, studying the sketch pad before her. This was to be the last design of the collection, but she was having trouble getting it right. Maybe it needed more contrast. Or maybe the spacing was wrong. She scratched her head with the end of her pencil and wondered if she ought to just tear this one up and start anew. Suddenly remembering Agata, she looked up guiltily and saw her leaning on her broom, quietly waiting her turn.

"I'm sorry, Agata," she apologized. She put down her pencil and pushed the sketch pad away. "I got distracted. Of course you may ask something of me. Ask me anything."

At first Agata hesitated, and then she plunged ahead. "May we go to the baseball game this afternoon?" she asked quickly.

"Today?" The question startled Hazel. She didn't know what she'd been expecting, but it wasn't that. "In Boston?"

"I know you are very busy making the designs," Agata acknowledged, "but today is the last day Cornelius will pitch in Boston. On Thursday night the team goes away for three weeks. Then the season is over." Looking down, she swept the toes of her shoes. "I would like very much to see him play," she added softly.

Even more startled, Hazel exclaimed, "The season can't be over! It's just begun."

Agata shrugged. "It's September," was all she said.

319

"It is, isn't it?" Hazel responded, mentally tracking down th
month. "Of course. It must be. The Labor Day parade was ye:
terday." After another moment's thought, she flipped closed th
cover on her unfinished design and stood up. "In that case," sh
said, "we'd better have an early lunch and catch the one-fifteei
We don't want to be late for the game."

Agata's round face lit up. "Oh, good," she said happily, resumin
her sweeping with vigor. "In a minute I'm through with this, the
I'll make some sandwiches."

"Go slowly," Hazel advised. "You're stirring up more dust tha
you're catching. I can make the sandwiches. That's one thing
know how to cook."

While Agata slowed to an appropriate pace, Hazel went ov
to their new icebox and took out a plate of leftover chicken. Li
certainly was easier now that they had a little money. "You know
she mused as she gathered together the bread, the mustard, an
a ripe tomato, "I've never seen a baseball game before. I'm n
even sure I'll understand what's happening."

"*I* understand," Agata assured her, pausing again. "I will te
you everything."

A few hours later, in the newly built grandstand at the South En
Grounds, Hazel had her first lesson. Where to sit. It wasn't ver
crowded, but the spectators in attendance were bunched togeth
on the benches behind home plate. "That's where we want to b
too," Agata informed Hazel.

Hazel eyed the congregation of men uneasily, suddenly havir
second thoughts about the wisdom of this adventure. "There a
so many empty places," she protested. "Why don't we sit off b
ourselves?" She turned to head for the seats along the third bas
line, but Agata pulled her back.

"We have to see the ball come over the plate," she insiste
"Then we know if the umpire makes a good call."

"Oh," Hazel conceded reluctantly. She doubted she would kno
a good call from a bad one wherever she sat.

As they approached the chosen area, the laughter and talkin
suddenly ceased. The men turned to stare. Ladies, especially on
as elegant as Hazel, did not appear at baseball games unescorte
And not at all on a Tuesday afternoon when only the hard core c
faithful supporters showed up.

It was an awkward moment. While the men craned their neck
to gape, Hazel and Agata stood in the aisle, searching, in vai

r a place to sit down. Hazel was more than ready to admit defeat
d retreat to the third base line, when the Bostons took the field to
arm up. "Oh, look," Agata said, pointing, her attention diverted.
There's Cornelius." The same instant Cornelius turned around,
d she waved.

An expression of utter astonishment came across Cornelius's
ce. Then he started to laugh. As he trotted over to the grandstand,
azel and Agata went down to the rail. "What are you doing here?"
e asked, obviously delighted.

"We came to see you pitch," Agata answered. "You must promise
win."

"I'll do my best," he said, laughing again. "Where're you sit-
ng?"

Hazel looked longingly at the empty section to her left. "Perhaps
e ought to try over there," she suggested.

"No," Cornelius disagreed. "You can't see the pitches come
ver the plate. You should sit right here. Say, fellows," he said,
ddressing the open-mouthed occupants of the first row, "how
bout sliding over so my wife and sister can have a seat?"

The men nearly tripped over themselves to comply with Cor-
elius's request, vacating twice as much space as Agata and Hazel
eeded. Almost gingerly Hazel took her seat. She still had her
oubts about the soundness of this idea. But Agata was thrilled
be there, and after a while the buzz of talk began to rebuild
round them until it reached its normal level. They were accepted,
nd soon the game began.

The first pitch that Cornelius threw was a called strike on the
nside corner. The next one was a twister that just missed. Ball
ne. The third pitch was a hellacious fast ball that the Louisville
atter popped up behind second and into Bobby Lowe's glove. An
asy out. An explosion of applause, cheers, and whistles rocked
he grandstand and made Hazel jump.

After the second out, though, a weak grounder to Tommy Tucker
t first base, she was ready for the roar. By the third out, a foul
hat Charlie Ganzel caught at the plate, she joined in. While the
ides changed, she bought a five-cent bag of peanuts, beginning
o enjoy herself immensely.

"We should have done this all summer," she said, passing the
ag to Agata. "This is fun."

"Next season we'll come more times," Agata agreed. She took
handful of peanuts and passed the bag back.

"What excellent seats," someone said. "Have you saved th
one for me?"

Shocked, Hazel turned toward the familiar voice just as Marc
sat down beside her. Her heart leaped at the sight of him. Ever
time she saw him it was a fresh and stunning surprise, no matte
if he'd been away from her for three minutes or three months. An
it was never until that breath-catching moment that she realize
just how much she'd missed him. His immense vitality defie
containment as a memory in her mind.

But however glad she was to see him, she was also very war)
After all, the last time she'd seen him, he'd expressed no intere
in calling on her in Lawrence. Not to mention the fact that Luc
Whitaker had been on his arm. In lieu of a greeting, therefore
she demanded, "What are you doing here?"

Although her words were identical to the ones her brother ha
uttered only a little while before, her tone wasn't delighted as h
had been, but distrustful. Marco, however, seemed unoffende
"I've come to watch Cornelius pitch," he replied in almost exa
repetition of Agata's answer. He helped himself to a peanut fro
the bag held limply in Hazel's hand. "I often do," he added. "He
remarkably good." Then he leaned forward to look at Agata, sittin
on her other side, saying, "*Buona sera. Come va?*"

Glancing uncertainly at Hazel, Agata answered, "*Bene*. Ver
well, thank you."

"Good." Marco leaned back, cracked open his peanut, an
extracted the two tasty morsels. Popping them into his mouth
he said to Hazel, "I trust you have also been well?"

"Yes, yes. Fine," she answered, impatiently dismissing that deta
and returning to the more urgent issue. "How do you know he'
good?" she asked. "What do you know about baseball? I'm quit
sure you never played it in Venice. Nor even at school in Englan
And I didn't notice any baseball diamonds in the Highlands."

"True enough," Marco cheerfully confessed, scooping sever.
more peanuts out of the bag. "Baseball is distinctly American. Lik
maple syrup." While he paused to crack open the shells, Haz
turned pink, remembering the raw December day he'd broug}
her a jug of maple syrup. And what had happened afterward.

"Actually," he went on, emptying the peanuts into his paln
"it was the fire last May that piqued my interest." He offered he
the nuts. Hazel eyed them dubiously and shook her head. "D
you remember the day I saw you? En route to view the ember

d ashes?" He leaned around her again to offer the shelled nuts
Agata. Shrugging, she accepted them.

Marco didn't seem to expect an answer to his question, and
azel didn't give one. Being reminded of his excursion with Lucy
aused a pain to seize her heart. When he reached to get a few
ore peanuts, she thrust the bag into his hands. "Here," she said
oughly. "Take them."

Only a flicker of a glance showed that Marco registered her
istress. Setting the bag on his knee, he continued smoothly. "I
ought I'd find the usual tragic destruction. Which, to be sure, I
id. But I was amazed to see the playing field virtually untouched.
here was something about its simple, green symmetry in the middle
f a charred and wasted ruin that really struck me."

For a moment he paused again and looked beyond the railing,
s if seeing the field as it had been on that day. Then shaking
way the image and looking back at Hazel, he concluded, "In
ny event, it was enough to start me reading the baseball notes
a the evening paper. When I saw Cornelius's name, I came at
nce, and as with maple syrup, it was instant infatuation."

A burst of cheering quickly brought their attention back to the
ame at hand. Herman Long was standing on first and Tommy Tuck-
r was in the batsman's box. "*Cos' ha successo?*" Marco demanded,
eaning forward to look at Agata.

"The wheelman hung an inshoot and Germany drilled it up the
niddle," she answered matter-of-factly. This was one subject that
idn't translate into Italian.

"He's having the best season of his career," Marco commented.
Ie cracked open a few more peanuts and offered them to Hazel.

Still not sure how to react to his presence in the ballpark, she
gain shook her head and focused on the playing. On a three-two
ount, Tucker hit a high fly ball that was caught in deep left field.
Aore cheers greeted this play. "Why is everyone applauding?"
Iazel asked, looking from Marco to Agata. "I thought he was
ut if the ball is caught before it touches the ground."

"He is out," Marco explained. "But see?" He pointed at the
econd base bag where Herman Long was now standing. "After
he ball was caught, Germany retagged first base and was able
o advance to second before the ball was thrown there."

"Sacrifice fly," Agata added.

"I see," Hazel said, absently picking a peanut out of the bag
nd cracking it open. "Now why is everybody applauding? The

batsman hasn't done anything yet."

"That's Hugh Duffy," Agata said almost reverently.

Laughing at Hazel's puzzlement, Marco enlightened he
"Duffy's a phenomenal hitter. He's batting four thirty-eig
this year, which I'm convinced will be a record for years
come. In addition, he has the most home runs and the most ru
batted in of any player in the National League. All he has to
is pick up his bat for the crowd to start cheering."

"I see," Hazel said again. Chewing her peanuts, she watche
the stocky ballist more expectantly. He didn't disappoint. He too
an oh and three fast ball and sent it sailing over the right-fie
fence. The Beaneaters were ahead two to nothing. Hazel was o
her feet with the rest of the spectators, yelling and clapping a
Duffy loped around the bases, victorious.

"I think I understand what you mean about instant infatuation
she said to Marco as she took her seat, her trepidations abo
him temporarily forgotten. "It's very easy to get swept up in th
excitement, isn't it?"

"It is," Marco agreed, smiling. He handed her the half-emp
bag of peanuts and said, "Pass these to Agata. I'll get some mo
for us."

Fortified with peanuts, they cheered as Bobby Lowe walke
then groaned as Tommy McCarthy hit into a double play. "Is th
it?" Hazel asked. "Doesn't Cornelius get a chance to hit?"

"He'll be up in the next inning," Agata told her.

Not until the lull in the action, when the teams changed place
did Hazel remember her apprehension. She snuck a glance
Marco. With his magnificent nose and wild mass of curls, h
seemed almost bigger than life. She looked forward quickly.
wasn't only baseball that easily swept her into its thrall. A fe
minutes before she'd kept her figurative distance. Now she wa
literally eating out of Marco's hand. Edging closer to Agat
she sought to reverse that situation. It was too dangerous to d
otherwise. She had already forfeited her place in his life.

Elbows on his knees and chin in his hand, Marco watche
Cornelius take his warm-up tosses. "He's improved a great de
since the beginning of the season," he commented, not taking h
eyes from the lanky figure on the mound. "Earlier on, he wa
lacking in confidence and control. I'm inclined to feel that th
one is dependent on the other, though. Wouldn't you agree?"

"Possibly," Hazel replied noncommittally. "I've no knowledg

with which to judge. This is the first game I've ever attended."

"You'll pick it up," Marco assured her, still watching Cornelius. "I had only a superficial awareness of the sport when I came to my first game in June. How many strikes for an out. Who the best ballists were. That sort of thing. But now I feel quite well-informed."

Hazel heard more in his statement than a reference to baseball, and it hurt. "It would seem, then, that you've spent the summer in America," she said. She meant to keep her voice level, but when she thought about him being here for months and not coming to see her, it quavered.

Startled by her abrupt change of tone, Marco turned from studying her brother's movements to studying Hazel's face. Her lovely features were composed and still. Only a faint flush of color on her clear cheeks and a slight tightness around her steady gray eyes betrayed any agitation.

"Yes, I have," he answered, sitting up slowly, as if he were stalling for time until he discovered a clue to her behavior. "As I'm sure you know, the Wilson tariff became law on the twenty-seventh of August. The business opportunities it created are every bit as intriguing as I hoped they would be. As a consequence, I've been spending more hours with solicitors—lawyers, you call them here—than I care to think about."

It was Hazel's turn to keep her eyes on Cornelius, though she barely saw him begin to pitch. "I'm sure it's been very tedious," she sympathized tonelessly.

Although she didn't see it, Marco broke out in a grin. "Mind you," he said, "I haven't had my nose to the grindstone absolutely every minute. For a few weeks in August I managed to escape the heat of the city, and what a joy it was.

"Hazel, I found the most extraordinary island off the coast of Cape Cod. It's called Nantucket. Do you know it? Is it another one of your American secrets?"

"I've heard of it." She kept watching Cornelius. The player he'd been pitching to was walking away. Agata and everyone else in the grandstand was cheering. She no longer felt like joining in.

"What's that?" Marco interrupted himself, looking out to the field. "A strike-out. Good for him." He turned back to Hazel while Cornelius was sizing up the next batsman.

"As I was saying, Nantucket is a perfect jewel in the middle of the Atlantic Ocean. The town itself is terribly stately, an example

of New England architecture at its most impressive. But beyond
the town it's gloriously wild, except for a few scattered hamlets
and a handful of sheep. The moors just roll on and on until they
end at spectacular beaches." He shook his head in awe just thinking of the beauty. "I've never experienced such sublime sea bath-
ing."

As he talked, Hazel couldn't help but be drawn in. In part it was
his enthusiasm for the island, but in part it was also the endearingly
familiar pattern of his travelogue. She found herself waiting for
him to start describing the savory foods he'd sampled, and when
he did, she could scarcely keep from smiling.

"You can't believe how sweet and succulent the clams and mus-
sels are," he told her. "And the oysters. Ah." He threw up his
hands in surrender. "There aren't words to express their delicacy.
To stand hip deep in the sea and slide a perfectly chilled oyster
down one's throat is like a taste of heaven."

Another round of applause greeted a ground ball to second
and Marco again interrupted himself to inspect the field. He
nodded in satisfaction. "Cornelius is going great guns today,"
he pronounced. "Now. Where was I?"

Despite her best efforts, the smile emerged. "The oysters,"
Hazel reminded him.

"Right." He nodded again. "Just incredible. I'm told the bay
scallops are an unforgettable treat, too. I must make a point of
returning when they're in season. It's not that much of a journey,
even though Nantucket is thirty miles at sea. Actually," he added,
"I can't understand how you've missed going all these years."

"We always spent our summers in Marblehead," Hazel explained, feeling easier. Her eyes were on the game again, but it was
to watch the play rather than to avoid looking at Marco. "It's also
quite lovely, and Papa could go back and forth to Boston quickly.
Oh, dear," she said, pointing. "That batsman got a hit."

"Cornelius got the pitch too far inside," Agata fretted.

Silent then, they watched as Cornelius started the next batsman
off with two balls. The catcher called for a time out and trotted out
to the mound for a conference. Cracking open a few more peanuts,
Marco idled away the wait. "Marblehead," he said speculatively.
"I considered going there for precisely the same reason. It was
convenient to Boston and I could keep an eye on business."

He gave some of the nuts to Hazel and tossed the rest in his
mouth, then dug into the bag for some more. "I was afraid if

I went there, though, I'd run into various Whitakers, and that put me off the North Shore completely. I'd rather plant a fist in Frederick's face than shake his hand. As for Lucy. Well. I tell you, Hazel, a single chance encounter with that one is more than enough."

Hazel's head turned sharply before she could stop it. "Chance encounter?" she blurted out.

"Yes." He held out some more nuts, and she automatically opened her hand. When he dropped them in her palm, though, she left them laying there uneaten. She couldn't swallow. Her heart was in her throat.

"It was that day at Baily's. Do you remember?"

How could she forget? It had been interfering with her happiness ever since. But all she said was "Yes."

"Like you, I'd been pulled through the door by an irresistible urge for some ice cream, though, God knows, not for that sickly sweet sundae you had in front of you." He upended the bag into his cupped hand, and the three remaining peanuts fell out.

"And there she was when I entered, fresh from a tiff with her brother because he had disapproved her plans for some sailing party. She snared me immediately." Snatching a handful of air with his free hand, he demonstrated how Lucy had trapped him.

"How better to take her revenge on Frederick than by being seen in the company of a man he heartily disliked? So there you have it. She clung to me like glue for the rest of the afternoon, manipulating me into taking her for a drive." He started to pass Hazel the last shelled nuts when he saw that she still had some in her hand. "Aren't you going to eat those?" he asked.

She burst out laughing in relief.

Marco's eyebrows raised. "Is that funny?"

"No, no," she answered, obligingly dropping the nuts into her mouth. "I was just having difficulty imagining you being manipulated." She was practically floating. Even if Marco no longer loved her, at least she hadn't lost him to Lucy Whitaker. It didn't seem as if that ought to make any difference, but it did. She had suffered enough at the hands of that family.

Any reply that Marco might have made got cut off by the crack of the bat on a ball. The crowd went completely quiet as it watched the horsehide shoot into the sky. It went back and back. Then, at the edge of the field, Jimmy Bannon caught it. Everyone was on their feet yelling. Out on the mound Cornelius looked thankful.

As they waited for the sides to change again, Marco casually asked her, "And your summer? Were you busy with work as you anticipated?"

For a moment Hazel hesitated, trying to decide if he were teasing her or being serious. In the interim Agata spoke up.

"*Lavora sempre,*" she told Marco. "*Passa tutti giorni facendo dei desegni bellissimi.*"

"*Da vero?*" Marco's eyebrows raised again and he looked at Hazel for confirmation. "You've been working every day? I take it, then, you've had luck selling your designs?"

This time Hazel answered before Agata could do so for her. "Yes, I have," she said hastily, giving Agata a warning frown. "I've done quite well."

Unintimidated, Agata added loyally, "She has a contract for three years. They want many more designs."

"Agata!" Hazel exclaimed, simultaneously moved and embarrassed by such devotion.

"Hazel, you have to say so," Agata replied in objection to the censure. "You have to say that you made a big success."

"She's right," Marco agreed. "This sounds like very good news. You ought to share it. Who are 'they' and what is the contract for?"

With another reproachful glance at Agata, Hazel answered his question. "It's a small mill in Lawrence," she explained. "A new corporation has taken over from one that went bankrupt. They've contracted with me to supply the designs for all the goods." That summed it up succinctly.

"Woolens?" Marco probed. He folded his arms across his chest and regarded her intently.

"Yes," Hazel answered, hesitating again. Then it all spilled out. It wasn't enough to sum it up, to sketch out the basic elements. It suddenly seemed very important to make him understand just how much it meant to her. To share it with him, as he'd suggested, but not simply the fact of her success or failure. She wanted him to feel both her satisfaction of the accomplishment and her delight in the designs. After all, it was he she saw over her shoulder when she sat down to draw every day.

"They're all fancy goods," she told him eagerly. "The corporation bought the mill for the purpose of competing with European imports. Only the finest fibers to create the most luxurious product. They want the very best. No sensible serges or pedestrian worsteds. The emphasis is on elegance." She gulped for breath and rushed on.

"You see, it's their theory that the free list will make the fancy fibers more accessible and less expensive. That will enable them to manufacture goods that compare favorably with the English and French fabrics in both price and quality." She paused again to look at him anxiously. "Do you think that's true?" she asked.

Marco considered it for a moment, then nodded his head. "It sounds logical to me," he decided.

Another whoosh of relief swept through her, and she hurried to tell him the best part. "They also feel that the entire fate of the venture lies in having the proper designs. Ones that glorify the fine fibers and make a unique and beautiful cloth. And Marco," she concluded, pride swelling her voice, "they chose mine."

"Excellent taste!" he applauded, literally clapping his hands. "They're obviously men of superior sensibilities."

Though Hazel laughed, a thrill ran down her spine. "You haven't seen the designs," she protested. "How do you know?"

"Because I know you," Marco replied softly. He refolded his arms on his chest and stared into her eyes.

Hazel felt her face flame and her heart start to pound. Looking down abruptly, she studied her hands, suddenly tongue-tied. It had been a long time since she'd heard that tone, as tender as a caress. If only she hadn't sent him away. If only he hadn't stayed banished.

"Tell me something, Hazel," Marco said, his tone once again conversational. "I'm quite curious. How did you ever come up with the idea of making designs for woolens?"

She shrugged as her heart began to beat more normally. Peeking up, she said, "If I tell you, will you promise not to laugh?"

"Laugh?" Marco's eyebrows shot up in surprise. "Certainly not."

Raising her head a little, Hazel cautiously confided, "We made a list."

"A what?" He sounded even more astounded.

"You promised not to laugh," Hazel reminded him.

He held up his hands and shook his head in denial. "I'm not laughing," he insisted. "I'd just like to know what was on that list."

Feeling more than slightly uneasy as she remembered the inci-

dent that had precipitated the list's creation, Hazel looked down
again. If it hadn't been for their stupendous fight, those fat block
letters never would have filled the pages of Agata's exercise book.
"It was a list of all the things I knew and was good at," she murmured.

"Do you mean like geography and mathematics?" Marco
prompted. "Like subjects you learned in school?"

Still not looking up, Hazel shook her head. "No," she said.
"It was more encompassing than that. Drawing and painting
topped the list, but it also included everything from lovely dresses
to flower arranging to my lessons at the University of Sheep. When
we boiled it down, it became evident that I had an artistic talent, an
eye for clothes, and some knowledge of wool. My trips to Europe
and appreciation of art became sources of inspiration. And voilà.
Or *ecco*, as Agata would say. I started making designs."

There was a pause when she finished, which the crowd filled
with a roar, but neither of them looked at the field to see what
caused it. Finally Marco said simply, "That's remarkable."

When Hazel lifted her head, she saw an expression of frank
admiration on his face. She drew a quick breath and smiled.
Actually, she glowed.

"*Attenzione!*" Agata commanded, nervously flapping both her
hands. "Cornelius is at bat."

"What's happened?" Marco asked quickly, turning back to the
game. He squinted at the bases. "Charlie Ganzel's on second,"
he observed. "What did Billy Nash do?"

"Sacrifice bunt to move the runner over," Agata said, without
taking her eyes from her husband. "*O Dio!*" she wailed as he
took a big swing and missed.

Cornelius stepped out of the batsman's box, ostensibly to rub
his hands in the dirt, but he took the time to look up at Agata and
glare. She clapped her hand over her mouth, horrified to think she
was distracting him. The brackets around his grin were beginning
to appear when he turned and resumed his stance. Another ball
came whizzing past him, and he took another slice. "Strike two!"
the umpire yelled. Cornelius connected on the third pitch, but it
was a line drive into the shortstop's glove. He was out.

In the fourth inning he got a base hit, which drove home a run.
He led off the sixth by walking, but was thrown out at second
when Germany Long blooped a hit into center field. In the eighth
Cornelius popped up to first. What was more important, though,

he pitched a fine game, striking out six batsmen and allowing only two runs. Boston won nine to two.

All in all, it was a wonderful afternoon, and Hazel hated to see it end. From the second inning on, they'd focused on baseball, without any more personal discussions, but her glow refused to fade. It felt so good to have Marco beside her, filling the entire grandstand with his presence, his faint scent of sandalwood soap mingling with the smell of peanuts. It felt natural. Comfortable. As if he were a part of her life.

But he wasn't. As the satisfied spectators started to stroll away, Hazel felt a painful wave of regret. It would be hard to watch Marco disappear while she returned to live her life alone. On the pretext of waiting until the crowd had dispersed, she remained in her seat, delaying the inevitable. Finally the stadium was empty and she was forced to rise.

"I'll take you to the ballists' entrance," Marco offered as they made their way to the top of the aisle. "You can meet Cornelius there as soon as he changes his clothes. Here," he said, leading the way between two rows of seats. "Let's cut across. It'll be quicker."

"I suppose I shouldn't be surprised that you know every inch of the grounds," Hazel commented, following his lead without question. "You do have a knack for making yourself at home wherever you are. Still, the ballists' entrance seems like a rather particular point of interest."

Laughing, Marco glanced over his shoulder. "I believe that's what's known as a left-handed compliment," he said. "At the risk of ruining my reputation, however, I must confess I only know its location because occasionally I meet Cornelius there myself."

This time Hazel definitely was surprised. "You do?" she asked, staring in amazement at the back of his head. "He's never mentioned it."

"Hasn't he?" Marco's tone was mild as he gave another glance over his shoulder. "Once or twice, when the game ended early, we've gone for a cold ale before his train. No doubt he'd forgotten all about it by the time he reached home." He signaled the insignificance of those meetings with a deprecating wave. "I know I would," he added. "Especially if I were coming home to a charming wife who makes pepper biscuits and pasta. And to a sister who has far more important news of the designs she's creating for the West Atlantic Mill."

Although Hazel chewed her lip, perplexed by her brother's uncharacteristic behavior, she didn't press the matter any further. She could bring it up with Cornelius later. Threading through the rows of seats, her thoughts turned instead to the left-handed compliment with which Marco had repaid her. Apparently he was impressed with the success of her designs for the mill. The idea pleased her. He probably . . .

Hazel stopped so suddenly, Agata nearly trod on her heels. About to say something, she caught a glimpse of the frozen look on Hazel's face, of the intense stare she was fixing on Marco. Changing her mind, Agata quietly pivoted and retreated. Hazel didn't hear her go.

"I never told you the name of the mill that's buying my designs," she said, her voice deadly level. "How did you know?"

Unaware that she had halted, Marco was almost to the far aisle when her question reached him. He turned and looked at her, his eyebrows lifting, before he walked back down the row to meet her. "I don't know," he replied with a nonchalant shrug. "More than likely Cornelius mentioned it in some conversation."

Hazel wasn't as easily dissuaded by his vague answer this time. There was too much that didn't add up. Folding her arms in front of her, she said, "You seem to know so much about my affairs, while I know so little about yours." Her voice was calm and still. "For example, I don't believe I heard you say exactly which business opportunities you found so intriguing. Or what legal transactions kept you closeted in lawyers' offices all summer."

Though she hadn't asked any questions, it was obvious she expected some answers. Sighing, Marco put a foot up on a seat and leaned an arm against his knee. "No, I didn't go into specifics," he agreed. His voice matched hers in evenness, but where her tone was cold, his was resigned. "I've contracted with a broker to buy my wool," he told her. "George William Bond and Company, if you must know."

When she didn't respond, but just stood there waiting, he sighed again. "And I've bought a mill," he added.

"Where?" The single word was like the shot from a gun.

"In Lawrence," he admitted.

There was silence for a moment as Hazel drew a long, slow breath. "The name?" she asked tightly.

After another silence Marco answered. "The West Atlantic Mill."

Hazel let her breath out. She opened her mouth as if to make remark, but on second thought clamped it shut. She felt monstrously betrayed, the satisfaction of her success turned to ashes and dust. Consumed by a fury more terrible than anything she'd ever felt, she spun around to plunge away.

"Wait, Hazel," Marco said, stepping off the bench and grabbing her arm. "Just listen—"

"Get your hands off me!" she shouted, her wrath exploding. Spinning back toward him, she beat his arm with her fist until he let her go. Released, she stumbled a bit, then caught herself and straightened up. "I'm not interested in listening to anything you have to say, ever again," she told him, her voice shaking with rage. "For once, though, you'd better listen to me. *I will not be bought!*" She yelled each word distinctly.

All it took was one angry word for Marco's own temper to be triggered. "Don't be ridiculous," he snapped. "I'm not trying to buy you, for God's sake, I'm trying to help you. Can't you understand that?" He threw his hand in the air.

"You're the one who can't understand," Hazel retorted, her fists clenched in front of her and her rigid body slanted forward. "I didn't ask for your help. In fact, I told you more than once that I didn't want it. Why couldn't you respect my wishes? Why couldn't you leave me alone?"

"Because I couldn't stand by and watch you starve while you played the melodramatic martyr," he answered, leaning forward, too, until their flushed faces were separated by only a furious bit of space. "How anyone ever got the idea that you're frail and helpless is beyond me. You're as strong *and* as stubborn as a mule."

With an outraged gasp Hazel pulled back. "If you really believe that unflattering analogy," she cried, "what made you think I couldn't survive without your assistance? Why didn't you just turn me out to pasture and let me fend for myself? Why did you have to interfere, Marco? Why?" With each question, she pounded her palm with her fist. "Why did you have to treat me like a . . . " She flung her fist out. "Like a *pet?*"

"I'm not treating you like a pet," he thundered in return. "You're confusing me with Frederick again. A comparison *I* find unflattering. Frederick would never have treated you as I am. He would have—and did—abandon you to twist in the wind. Instead, I'm treating you as what you are: a talented designer caught in the

middle of a depression. You had a brilliant product, Hazel, an
no place to sell it. I simply supplied the market."

She was beside herself, stamping her feet and churning back an
forth. "As if I were a charity case?" she demanded, slamming he
hand against her chest. "Some sort of orphan in need of milk?"

"The West Atlantic Mill is hardly a charity," Marco roared
"It's a legitimate business from which I fully expect to realize
profit. I wouldn't have started it otherwise. I would have sent yo
anonymous envelopes full of money instead. God knows, it woul
have been easier. Given that fact," he went on, jabbing his finge
in front of her face, "I can't comprehend why you should fin
it less objectionable to sell your designs to some cigar-chompin
stranger than to me."

Hazel swatted his finger away. "At least with a stranger I coul
be sure he was buying my designs because he liked them," sh
hissed. "Not because he was Santa Claus in disguise."

Marco greeted that statement with a disdainful snort. "Now
you're acting like a child," he informed her. "You're being naive
This hypothetical buyer isn't motivated by personal taste. He'
motivated solely by the desire to make a profit. He's not intereste
in beauty, Hazel, unless he can turn it into cash.

"Besides," he added, his temper cooling, "when did you eve
know me to buy something I didn't like? Those lavender tweeds
for example. I told Horace I thought they were too pallid and cold
He had you do them over, didn't he?"

"Oh, yes, Mr. Snow," Hazel said, taking her cue from Marc
and lowering her voice. Her tone, however, remained bitter. "How
could you?" she asked. "How could you force Mr. Snow to li
like that? All that nonsense about the board of directors and thei
objection to my being a woman. What pressure did you have t
apply to make him perform that embarrassing act?" She grimace
in disgust. "Have you no sense of decency? You even convince
my own brother to plot behind my back. I can just see the two o
you, convivially sipping beers while you meted out my fate."

"You're wrong about that, too," Marco said, shaking his head
in exasperation. "No one is plotting against you or planning your
life. Contrary to your conviction, that performance was Horace
Snow's idea, not mine. There were no guns held to his head."
His finger wagged in denial. "He was a very willing participant.
And he was because he admires you, Hazel. Both your work and
your spirit. He only wanted to see you succeed."

Seeing that she was at least listening to him now, his irritation bated. "As for Cornelius," he continued, crossing his arms over is chest and standing with his legs braced apart. "Will it ease our mind if I tell you he is unaware of my connection to the ill? Your brother believes only that I'm an old friend who is oncerned about your well-being. Which, I might add, is true."

Unmoved by his latter remark, Hazel pounced on the former. f Cornelius thinks your presence is so innocent, why did he eep it hidden?" she demanded. "Why didn't he tell me he'd seen ou?" Plumping her hands on her hips and narrowing her eyes, he warned, "And don't tell me some story about his memory eing overcome by Agata's cooking."

For the first time since their battle commenced, a shadow of umor crossed Marco's face. "I wouldn't dare to tell you a story," e said, with mock meekness. "The truth is, Cornelius didn't men- ion seeing me because I asked him not to. He believes it's because f the fight we had the day of Edgar's funeral, but really, I was fraid you'd get suspicious and fit the pieces together. You might emember telling me, for example, about Mr. Snow's interest in our designs.

"In any event"—he waved his hand—"I had the feeling your eaction to such a discovery might be, um, shall we say, reluc- ant? To be honest, I was afraid you would disown the project. Then, not only would you be out of work, but I would be out a onsiderable investment. I'd be left owning a big brick building ull of expensive machinery and wools and workers, and no means f making money."

"There are other designers," Hazel scoffed. "There must be a core or more in Lawrence alone who would jump at the oppor- unity for a job."

"No doubt," Marco agreed with surprising equanimity. "All xceedingly skilled at designing . . . what did you call them? Sensible serges and pedestrian worsteds.' Which are a drogue n the market just now. Horace Snow wasn't inventing tales when e told you the fate of the West Atlantic Mill is inextricably tied o unique and beautiful designs. *Your* designs."

Despite her still simmering anger and her adamant rejection of his appeals, his words caused a warm ripple to stir her heart. Even so, she crossed her arms on her chest and tapped her foot impa- iently. "Very prettily put," she said flatly, "but party to deceit nonetheless. Just how long were you planning to keep your vil-

lainous role in this fraud from me? Or was it to remain a secr
indefinitely?"

Marco shook his head again, wearily this time. "No, it wasn't
he answered. "I had every intention of telling you the whole stor
this fall. After production had started and the goods were on th
market. I thought that if you had the woolens in your hand an
the commission checks in the bank, you'd be more inclined
accept the fact that I wasn't just jollying you, but backing a seriou
artist."

He unfolded his arms and leaned forward then, his voice gettin
a great deal softer. "I wish you'd believe me, Hazel," he said
almost imploring. "I'm not trying to interfere with your decision
or ambitions. I'm simply trying to help you implement them.

"Don't you understand?" He held out both his hands as if h
could physically hold out his thoughts. "I admire and respect yo
tremendously," he told her. "You've done something very rare
Something I'm not sure I would have had the courage or wits t
do. You've pulled yourself up by your bootstraps, extracted you
life from ruins. Hazel, you've taken control of your fate."

Though Hazel didn't say a word, her eyes grew wide and th
tight twist of her arms grew slack.

Marco nodded and took a step in her direction. "You wante
to be in charge of your destiny, and that's exactly what you are
And you did it with the most startling and graceful simplicity. B
making a list."

He shrugged his shoulders and lifted his hands in wonder. "Yo
listed your talents and examined your life and found out precisel
who you are. Then you acted on it. Even more remarkable, yo
did this in the midst of disaster. You didn't just lie there, kickin
your feet, like a turtle on its back. In an incredible exhibitio
of strength, you righted yourself and started moving toward you
goal."

He took another step closer until he was only inches away, unt
Hazel could practically feel him breathe. Her own breath cam
harder. "But, Hazel," he said, even more softly, "you can't ge
there alone. No one can. No one's life is lived in isolation. W
can't pull inside our shells. There's no single destiny, no solitar
fate. Everyone's is intertwined with someone else's."

Stretching out his hand again, he ever so carefully touched hi
fingers to her cheek. "That's what I've been trying to do," h
said. "I've been trying to be the someone else in your life. Not t

interfere, but to intertwine. I don't want to tell you how to live, I just want to help you do it. I want to share your life, Hazel. And I want you to share mine." Slowly leaning over, he brushed his lips across her mouth.

"I love you," he told her.

Hazel sat down abruptly, his kiss burning on her lips. Hot and cold by turns, she didn't know what to think. He had an answer to her every charge, and he made them all seem logical. Maybe even gallant. His praise and admiration were like a balm on her wounded soul, and she knew, all too well, that what he said about being alone was true. To say nothing of his declaration of love. That left her breathless. But the fact remained, he'd still deceived her. Hadn't he?

Shoving her hands between her knees and studying an empty peanut shell on the ground, she said, "The least you could have done was ask me first." Her voice was very small. "You didn't have to hatch schemes behind my back."

Marco clasped his hands together and shook them in frustration. "I did ask you, Hazel. I did," he protested. "How many times? I can't count. I even came racing back from Scotland once. When you rejected my proposals of marriage, I volunteered help of any nature that you could name. But you refused those offers, too. I did ask you," he repeated reproachfully.

She pushed the peanut shell back and forth with her toe, absorbing what he said in silence. He was right about that as well. He had asked her. And she'd turned him down because she was afraid of having her life wrested out of her control. Because she'd been determined to never again put herself in the position of being left vulnerable.

Sitting there, she considered the result of that decision. To be sure, there'd been the euphoria of creating the designs. The satisfaction and pride that could never be erased. But then there'd been the horrible rounds as she tried to sell them. She remembered the humiliating waits on hard benches only to be brusquely dismissed or, worse, to feel a clammy hand creeping up her skirt. She remembered the pinch of poverty, the specter of living on the street. Mostly, though, she remembered the omnipresent ache. The cold, hollow ache of being alone. Just she and her fate. The third person of a couple.

Inhaling sharply, Hazel made another decision. She again took her destiny under control. Raising her head, she looked at Marco with eyes that were misty and large. Her voice was hoarse and not completely steady. "Ask me again," she said.

Marco sank down on the bench beside her and pulled her into his huge embrace. He set soft, sweet kisses on her forehead and smoothed her silky hair. Settling her into the crook of his arm, he studied her lovely face intently. With a gentle finger, he slowly traced its shape.

Then his head bent closer and her eyes fluttered closed. His lips touched lightly on hers. They touched again. This time they lingered. It was a long, deep kiss that sent shivers of pleasure rippling through her body and radiating through her soul. It thawed the cold ache in her heart and filled the hollow void. The bleak and terrible loneliness melted away, forgotten in a distant time.

"I love you, Hazel," he told her again, whispering in her ear. He pressed his moist lips against its tender lobe, then trailed them across the lustrous skin of her cheeks. They found the delicate spot under her chin and the tiny dot above her mouth. "Will you marry me?" he asked.

Hazel drew in a shuddery breath and slid her hands around his neck. Losing her fingers in his mass of curls, she met his mouth in another kiss. As wonderful feelings infused her heart, wonderful memories flooded her mind.

She remembered the glorious afternoon in Venice, when Marco had first unlocked her passion. And the magical day on his Scottish island when he'd made it come alive. She remembered how much she'd looked forward to his visits in Lawrence, how he'd brightened her life with presents and stories. How he'd comforted her in her moments of grief and anguish, supporting her with his great strength. She remembered that, after all, it was he who had made her determined to be in charge of her life, goading her, prodding her, insisting that she be aware and informed.

And then she remembered how she'd felt only a little while before. How happy and comfortable she had been while they watched the ball game together. How natural and right it was to be near him, as if he were part of her life.

Slipping back, she opened her eyes and looked directly at him. "Yes, Marco, I will," she accepted gladly. "I love you, too."

His kiss this time wasn't slow and sensual, but hard and fast and joyous. "Dearest Hazel," he exulted. "I've been waiting for this moment for nearly a year and a half. I've tried every trick and tactic I could think of to coax those words from you. I've pleaded with you, argued with you, wheedled, and cajoled. I've tried deluging you with gifts, and when that didn't work, I've tried ignoring you. You can't know how elated I am to hear you say them at last."

At the end of this speech Hazel looked thrilled, until suddenly she began to laugh.

"Now what?" Marco asked, holding her off in astonishment. "What's so amusing about that?"

She shook her head, still engulfed in giggles. It was a moment before she could speak. "I'm sorry," she finally managed to gasp. "It isn't your persistence that struck me so funny, but the means you employed to achieve your end. I've heard of giving romantic gifts, such as flowers or chocolates or jewels. But, honestly, Marco," she said as another giggle escaped. "A mill?" Falling back against his chest, she said, "How like you to do something so enormous."

Marco laughed, too, and pulled her closer, laying his cheek on her head. "You know," he mused, in a more serious tone, "that mill was intended to be just for you, but it's turned out to be a gift for me, too."

"Yes, I know," Hazel assured him, running her finger along the top of his collar. Her mirth had subsided and a warm swell of happiness had taken its place. "Don't worry. You don't have to keep persuading me that your investment in the mill is sound. I believe you when you say you think you can make a profit."

"I'm glad we've finally settled that issue," Marco replied, with a hug. "Though it wasn't exactly what I had in mind."

"Did you mean satisfaction, then?" Hazel asked easily. Her eyes drifted closed, though there was nothing sleepy about the way she felt. Inside she was wide awake, her happiness bordering on bliss. "I remember you once told me it would be an interesting experiment to run a mill with decent wages and working conditions. Does it please you to think your experiment might be successful?"

"It always pleases me to see my theories vindicated," Marco admitted, rubbing his hand down the length of her back. "But in this case, my satisfaction goes even deeper than that. It could almost be said that owning this mill grants a wish I've been making for years."

"Oh?" Hazel's eyes opened and she leaned back again, her expression puzzled.

Marco smiled and brushed a strand of hair from her face. "I've
spent most of my life pursuing the exquisite," he explained. "I've
sought out anything and everything that is rare or beautiful wheth
er it be a painting or a delicious meal or an inspiring thought.
can find it and I can buy it. Or taste it or ponder it. I can store
it in my mind. I can build houses and museums to display it in
But the one thing I can't do is create it. You can."

He outlined her lips with the edge of his thumb. "For as long as
I can remember, I've wanted to share in the creation of something
beautiful. The West Atlantic Mill is the answer. In my own way
and with my own resources, I can finally be a cog in the creative
wheel. So you see," he concluded, "by letting me help you, you're
actually helping me."

Hazel thought about that for a moment, then her chin swept up
to recapture her perfect poise. "In that case," she said calmly
"we'd better discuss the absurdly low rates you are paying me."

Marco threw back his big head and laughed until his rosy cheeks
shone. "Very well," he agreed, still chuckling. "We'll renegotiate
the contract. Let's see. I'm prepared to offer you an equal partner-
ship in the mill, as well as an equal place in my life. Will that be
acceptable?"

"Thank you," Hazel answered politely. "Yes."

# EPILOGUE

Lucy marched into the breakfast room and thrust the morning *Globe* in front of Frederick. He took one look at the pique distorting his sister's pretty features and set aside his soft-boiled eggs. Mottled color jumped into his own pale face as he read the simple announcement.

> Miss Hazel Merriwether and Mr. Marco MacGregor were married yesterday in Lawrence. Miss Merriwether is the daughter of the late Edgar and Lydia Merriwether, formerly of Boston.
>
> Mr. MacGregor is the son and heir of Malcolm MacGregor, Baron Strathdorna of London, England, and Scotland, and of the Contessa Serafina Menini of Venice, Italy.
>
> Miss Merriwether was given in marriage by her brother, Mr. Cornelius Merriwether, pitcher for the Boston baseball team. She was attended by her sister-in-law, Mrs. Agata Merriwether.
>
> Following a wedding trip to Nantucket Island, Mr. and Mrs. MacGregor will pursue their businesses in the wool and woolens industry from their homes at Strathdorna Manor, Palazzo Menini, and in Boston.

Frederick handed the newspaper back to Lucy without a comment though his expression was harsh as he returned to his breakfast. The eggs had gotten hard, but it didn't matter. He couldn't taste them anyway.